I0523164

THERE ARE DARKER THINGS ON THE CHICAGO STREETS THAN JUST GANGS…

"Stop!" I screamed, but I'd already begun pulling the trigger by then. I don't know how many shots I fired—I just kept squeezing them off, one after another. The first shot hit him square in the chest and stopped his advance for a moment, but most of them, he just dodged. Even at this distance, he *dodged* them. I let my emptied gun drop to my side.

"What *are* you?" I asked.

"Someone who likes to play with my food…"

Also by Kevin Wright

The Danse Trilogy:

THE KNIGHT OF CUPS

THE QUEEN OF PENTACLES

THE KING OF SWORDS

THE KNIGHT OF CUPS

— The Danse, Book One —

Kevin Wright

© 2015 by Kevin Wright. All rights reserved.

Note: All other works used in this book have been cited to give their authors credit, and are presumed to be in the public domain. If any are not, please contact the author so that fair use may be protected.

This is a work of fiction. Names, characters, places, and incidents either are the product of the author's imagination or are being used fictitiously, and any resemblance to actual persons, living or dead, business establishments, events, or locales is entirely coincidental.

Dedicated to

Wendy, Megan, and Alex, for their encouragement, support, and love

and to

Dad, Mom, Lindsay, Craig, and my whole family, for their inspiration

and to

Mrs. Oretta Smith, because I always keep my promises

Table of Contents

Preface

Preface

I want to tell you about the time that I killed my first vampire.

No, that's a horrible way to start a book—it takes all the suspense and fun out of it. I'm not really much of a writer, but I guess two out of every three cops want to write a book about their jobs at some point (it's just that nine out of ten of us really don't have that much new to say). Personally, I didn't really have anything particularly exciting to write about my own life until six months ago.

I mean, don't get me wrong—I think that every day on the job is pretty important stuff. But I'm just not your typically unrealistic, "movie cop" kind of detective. I can take care of myself pretty well, but I'm far from the best cop on the force (I'm not even the best one in my *district)*. My marriage isn't perfect, but it's not like I'm burned out and on the verge of divorce or anything. I actually *like* my lieutenant, and I haven't even been in a real car chase in my eleven years on the force. Up until six months ago, I was just your average "serve and protect" kind of detective, with no great stories to tell anyone (though, if you'd gotten me in just the right mood, after just the right number of drinks, I might have told you about that time that Tony de Tullio and I got in the middle of a throw-down between some Gangster Disciples and the Mickey Cobras down on Division—yes, we took them down, but I was in the hospital for over a week and Tony lost two of his fingers).

But six months ago, everything changed. Because six months ago, I started investigating the murder of Hector Flórez. And six months ago, I felt forced to kill Pieter Durant. And nothing will ever be the same again.

Before I go on, I should probably confess that the only reason that I'm writing this at all is that the guy who *should* be writing this totally refuses to do it, and that I recognize that no one's going to believe what I'm writing here. Five will get you ten that, if this ever even sees print, it'll be in the fiction aisles, even though I've been doing a lot of research over the last six months, and I've tried to include relevant historical documents that I've found since then to help explain things. But I just think that people really ought to know what's going on all around them, even if they don't want to know.

That'll all just have to make sense to you as you go along, I guess.

Chapter 1
The Body in the Alleyway

Let's be honest—no one is a Cubs fan based on silly things like whether or not they actually *win*. That sort of record-keeping is for the petty fans of lesser teams. No, Cubs fans are Cubs fans because they're Cubs fans, and it's that simple. You love your team, even though you don't actually expect them to, y'know, get to the World Series or anything.

So we had tickets, and we were all ready to go to a Cubs game that night. We'd blocked out the time, and everyone in the family was looking forward to it. But then the weather started turning sour in the early afternoon, and the rain came down so heavy that we just knew that the game was going to be rained out. Joanna was disappointed, but she wasn't mad. Not yet, at least.

Of course, the twins were still young enough that they barely knew where they were half the time, so they didn't care. And Chelsea is at that age when having a cop for a dad is kind of like having a superhero for a dad, so finding out that we'd be able to spend the whole night at home together as a family for a change struck her like a "win-win" scenario, and she was giddy.

It was a little while after dinner that I got the call, and that's really when things officially went south for the evening. I know that I'd said that I'd be home all evening, but that's the job, isn't it? Scratch that— I'd *promised* that I'd be home all evening.

"Tom, you *promised* us!" Joanna yelled at me, rubbing that word in my face like it would somehow make a difference. She'd been quiet as we'd gone all the way downstairs into the laundry room for me to grab those pants that I'd just thrown down there earlier in the day, and then quiet all the way back up as I searched for the single shoe that Chelsea had hidden, trying to see how good a detective I really was (hint: she almost always hid it in the pantry), and then quiet all the way to the couch, where I sat down to tie my shoes after I'd collected them both. When I thought about it later on, of course, I realized that it was the deafening quiet coming from her that should've tipped me off to the firestorm that would come once the quiet had ended.

"You promised *me!*" she emphasized. "You haven't been home with us for a whole evening in over a month!" and so on…

Now, to be fair, that wasn't entirely accurate, since I'd been home for a whole evening just a little over a week earlier, but that was a hair that I didn't see a need to split right then and there, and it wouldn't have helped my case. But as I clipped my badge to my belt, I tried to help her to understand that the problem wasn't really that I was leaving—or even that I was breaking my promise. The real problem was that a smart cop never makes a promise like that in the first place.

"It's not like I get to decide when stuff happens, or when things get investigated…" and before she could jump in with her next argument (and believe me, she was winding up for it), I added, "or who has to lead the investigation. This is why I get paid the big bucks." I smiled when I said that last part, hoping to break the tension. It didn't even dent the tension.

Now, don't misunderstand me—Joanna's always been great about all of this. I mean, she knew that she was getting a cop when she married me, and she knew the sorts of problems that come with being on the job. She knew all of that, and yet she'd always been patient and supportive of what I did. I think that it was just one of those moments when the stars all line up—*wrong*—and that one, last, particular bit of crap is just too hard to take. I can't really blame her. Life just stinks sometimes.

Joanna didn't respond to what I said. She just stood there, red color rising in her cheeks and tears beginning to well up in her eyes, wavering between biting my head off and breaking down into a good, deep cry. But she never got to make that decision.

"Da-DEE!" Chelsea's voice broke the tension between us. I turned to see my daughter in her little cloud pajamas, standing between me and the front door, holding her little pink umbrella in her hands. "You gotta take a 'brella or you're gonna get wet!"

There's something about a four-year-old's voice that can change your entire emotional disposition in the blink of an eye. If they're whining, it can drive an otherwise sane adult crazy, but if they're happy, it can make even the worst moment seem not only bearable, but downright heartwarming. Though nothing had changed between Joanna and me as a couple, we both found ourselves transfixed, watching our four-year-old beam with pride as she held out a plastic pink umbrella with a kitten on it to help protect her daddy.

"You take good care of Daddy, don't you?" Joanna asked, sniffling just a bit.

"That's my *job*, Mommy!" Chelsea pouted, still holding the umbrella out to me, impatiently waiting for me to take it from her. I smiled, took the umbrella, and thanked her. Her face just glowed, and she wrapped her little arms around my legs in as big a hug as she could muster. "Go get 'em, Daddy!" she commanded with a giggle, and then she ran off into the other room to play with her little brothers, her world a simple place with no burdens worth worrying about to weigh her down.

I turned back to Joanna and sighed. To my astonishment, she just walked right past me, opened the front closet, pulled out my own black umbrella, and handed it to me.

"Go get 'em, Tom," she said, with a faint little smile on her lips. "It's *my* job, too."

I took the umbrella and hugged her tightly. "I love you so much, Jo..." In response, she just silently pecked me on the cheek, stepped back, and opened the door for me. I couldn't imagine asking for more than that, so I just stepped out into the rain carrying *both* umbrellas, and hopped into the car.

*   *   *

On the drive over to the crime scene, I went over the details in my head again. Hector Flórez had been found dead earlier that evening in an alleyway on a little street just off of Armitage. Apparently, a deli owner was throwing out some garbage into the dumpster behind his business. It had gotten dark early that night because of the storm, but the alley was apparently well-lit—or at least it had enough light to see that much. I knew that I'd need to talk with him myself a little later, but from what I understood, the man swore up and down that the body hadn't been there that afternoon when he'd gone out a few hours earlier. If that were true, it would give us a time of death somewhere between 4:00 and 6:30.

I pulled up to the curb and opened the car door just as the rain started picking up. For a second, I almost reflexively reached for the pink umbrella that Chelsea had handed me, but then I thought better of it. In fact, I thought better of even taking the one that Joanna had given me. I was going to be standing out in the rain for a while, and I knew that I wasn't going to want to be holding an umbrella the whole time. Besides, there was no way that my partner, Tony de Tullio, was going to be carrying an umbrella with him, and there was no way that I was going to give him any ammunition for another one of his "I'm tougher than you are" monologues tonight. So I left them both sitting side-by-side on the seat, warm little reminders that my two favorite girls were looking out for me and supporting me, even when neither one had really wanted me to leave home in the first place. I smiled to myself as I just turned up the collar of my overcoat and braced myself for the cold.

As it happened, Tony was actually walking up to the scene at the same moment that I arrived, shuffling his over-stuffed body across the sidewalk toward me. He was wearing a windbreaker that, at one time, presumably, had fit him, but now was impossible to even stretch across his broad belly, much less snap closed. I caught a little glint in his eye as I approached.

"Have to break any plans for this tonight, Tony?" I asked.

"Not with them Cubs rained out, I didn't," he growled back, smiling. "Lucky fer us we got a stiff." I'd known Tony for almost seven years, but I was still trying to wrap my head around his sense of humor. He seemed to laugh at things that made other people uncomfortable, and bark at things that other people found funny. It's like somewhere along the line in his childhood, "up" became "down" for him and "right" became "left"—like he was speaking another language from everyone else around him, and it was all the rest of us could do just to keep up with the translation effort.

We found Officer George Quesada on the scene, standing over the body with his long raincoat drizzling rivers of rainwater onto the corpse. I'd worked with Quesada before, and he was a good beat cop, but he wasn't the brightest bulb on the force, and I'd never want to see him even try to make detective. I waved to him to move him away from the crime scene so that he couldn't contaminate it any more than he already had, and he turned the beam of his flashlight onto us as we walked up.

"Detectives Chapel and de Tullio," I said perfunctorily as we flashed him our badges. "What do we have here, Quesada? And where's forensics?"

Quesada cleared his throat before speaking, like he was intimidated by talking with detectives and wanted to make a good impression. For me, that never makes a good impression. I figure that the best impression that you can make on someone is to demonstrate that you're confident enough not to really feel the need to make a good first impression. But Quesada didn't come across as overly confident, even when he tried. *Especially* when he tried.

"Um, forensics isn't here yet," he said, which we'd obviously already figured out. "But as for what's going on, we got one Hector Flórez here, age 19, with his throat slit."

I walked over to the body while Tony took a shuffling stroll around the alley to get a lay of the place. Hector was laying face-down near a pile of empty cardboard boxes and a bunch of old newspapers.

"How do you know his name, Officer?" I asked. "Did you go through his pockets for an ID?"

"No, sir. Of course not," Quesada said defensively, and then his voice went more quiet. "I know his family. We both go to St. Peter's, down on Madison." I stopped myself from asking any more questions for a minute, reminding myself that a beat cop is a different animal than a detective. As much as I like to think of my job as a step up from the street level, I always have to remind myself that the meat and potatoes of our "serve and protect" work happens on a daily basis on the curbs and corners. Guys like me can too often just see crimes as kind of like puzzles to sort out—guys like Quesada help to *prevent* those crimes in the first place by being half policeman, half parish priest. So this sort of thing was more than just a crime to be solved for him—it was like someone killed one of his extended family members. For the time being, I let him just share what he knew at whatever pace he was comfortable with while I looked over the scene.

According to Quesada, the deli owner said in his statement that he had apparently seen Hector's leg sticking out from under the boxes, and had moved them to get a better look at the body. God preserve us from the help of amateurs. I noticed that Hector was wearing the black and green colors of the Insane Deuces, with a green flannel shirt tied around his waist by the sleeves and a bandanna covering the top of his head. I also noticed that he was only wearing one shoe.

"Where's the other shoe?" I asked.

"Oh, we found that over there," Quesada answered, pointing toward another alley across the street between a dry cleaners and an abandoned building. I nodded and kept looking at the body while I put on my gloves. At first glance, I didn't think that the throat had been cut with a knife—the wound was too large and irregular for that. It was more like a gash than a slice, like someone had gone at him with a hacksaw or a hatchet. But the strange part was that the wound itself was remarkably clean. In fact, without moving him, there seemed to me to be little to no blood anywhere, except on his t-shirt and around the gash on his neck. I stepped back and started looking under the boxes.

"Did you clean up the blood, Officer? Or did the deli owner?"

"No way!" he yelped. And then he calmed down and composed himself. "No, sir. I guess the rain just washed all the blood away, right?"

"Nope," I corrected, dropping to one knee next to look at the body a little closer. "A big tough guy like Hector here probably had about 14 or 15 pints of blood in him when he was still walking around. That's almost two gallons of blood, Quesada. Do you really think that a little light rain is going to completely wash away two gallons of blood without a trace here?" I lifted Hector's head from the flattened cardboard box that it was resting on. He had an eagle tattooed on the side of his face, with its wings stretching above his left ear. "Besides, if he'd bled out here in this alleyway, this box would've been soaked in blood—rain or no rain." Instead, the cardboard showed only a couple of small, reddish-brown blotches from a few drops of blood, and there was no blood that I could see on any of the other boxes. By this time, Tony had made his way back toward the body and stood next to me. "Flórez was obviously killed and drained practically dry somewhere else, and then had his body dumped here in this alleyway." I laid the head back down and stepped back to look down the alley toward the street. Tony squatted down next to the body and started poking around in Hector's clothes.

"Why would anyone wanna do that?" Quesada asked.

"It's a gang thing..." Tony muttered without looking up, continuing to go through pockets.

"It's a *Latin Kings* sort of thing," I added. "I remember in Stateville back in '83, a couple of LK's chopped up a guy named Robles—"

"Like, two days before he's gonna be released," Tony interjected without looking up.

"Right," I continued. "Like, two days before he was going to be released from prison. He'd disrespected a high-ranking LK, so they killed him in the basement, drained out all of his blood, chopped his body up, and then had some Gangster Disciple buddy in the prison kitchen grind him up and put him into that night's meatloaf."

Quesada was turning pale, and he was looking at Hector's body in a whole new way. "So..." he caught some bile in his throat. "Madre de Dios... You're saying that they *ate* him?"

"Naw," Tony chuckled, finally looking up to see Quesada's face. "All them LK's an' GD's was clued in not to eat the meatloaf that night. A sudden an' unexpected case o' vegetarianism..." He stepped back from the body and walked under the fire escape to get out of the worst of the rain, pulling out a cigarette. "Ya woulda thought that mighta seemed suspicious to someone, but no..." He grinned as he lit up, the extra two fingers on his left glove flapping in the night air. "Knowing Stateville, I'd think a lil' cannibalism woulda been more normal t' expect than vegetarianism."

Quesada looked like he was going to be sick, and Tony was starting to laugh, so I started looking across the street again. My problem is that, once I start thinking about something, it's hard to get it out of my head until I've thought my way all the way through it. A murder investigation is like a subway tunnel, with lots of cross-tunnels and side-tunnels, all leading off in different directions. I mean, there are no limits to where you can let it lead you, but you know that only one of those tunnels is actually going to lead to the right conclusion. Once I get started, it's hard to turn it off until I've figured out where it's leading—or, more to the point, where it's going to end up. Part of that process is figuring out which tunnels *not* to take.

For instance, even though I knew that the Latin Kings and the Insane Deuces were warming up their on-again, off-again gang war, something still wasn't adding up in my mind, and the more I thought about it, the more my head hurt. There were pieces that just didn't make sense. My mind drifted back to looking for my shoe in the pantry, and I couldn't stop wondering why Hector wasn't wearing his.

"Hey, Quesada," I called back. "Where did you say that second shoe was found?"

Quesada seemed more than relieved to have a reason to leave the crime scene (and, for that matter, Tony). He came up to me and together, we walked out of the alleyway and onto the sidewalk. "We found it over there," he said, pointing to the other alleyway across the street. "Just on the other side of that chain link fence. Do you really think that they were going to eat him?"

"That's not what we were saying, Quesada," I corrected. "But I'm trying not to make any kind of conclusions until I've got all the details." Like why the shoe was across the street.

I realized that the CSI guys really needed to get there to the crime scene soon, because the rain was starting to come down even harder, and it was going to screw everything up for them. So I left Tony to do whatever he could before they showed, and Quesada and I crossed the street to look at the other alley. "How much blood did you find around the other shoe?" I asked as we walked.

"None," Quesada responded. "But I just figured that because of the rain..." He stopped in mid-sentence with a sheepish look on his face. "But it doesn't work like that, does it?"

"No, it doesn't," I answered. "But don't feel too bad. Most people would've thought the same thing." I patted him on the back as we entered the alleyway. "At least you get points for learning."

This alley was in worse condition than the one we'd just come from. The ground was cluttered with garbage, and the concrete was broken and greasy, and the rain's puddles had an oily film on them that made rainbows under the orange light coming from the nearby streetlamp. We walked down the alley and up to the fence. It was a rusty old fence that stood about six feet tall, and connected from one building to the next, completely closing off the end of the alleyway. As I shined my flashlight through the fence, Quesada pointed out where they'd found the shoe on the other side.

It just didn't make sense. There was no gap or gate in the fence for the LK's to have taken the body through, and they wouldn't have dragged the body around the block by hand, so they would have had to have dumped it out of a van or a car or something. But then why would they have taken Hector's body from one alley and thrown it into another one? And for that matter, if he wasn't even killed in *this* alleyway, then why was his shoe here? Why kill him in one place, drop a shoe here, and then dump his body across the street? The subway tunnels in my mind just weren't connecting right.

I shined the light toward a dumpster on one side of the alley, and then to a door on the other side that looked like it hadn't been opened since the Daley administration. Then I shined it onto the fence to look a little more carefully, and that's when I saw something that opened up a whole new subway system for me.

Caught in one of the rusty twists at the top selvage of the fence was a tuft of green flannel—the same green flannel that Hector Flórez was wearing across the street. And it had dark reddish-brown stains on it. I made a note in my notebook and left it where it was for the CSI guys to collect, and I told Quesada to look around for more bits like this, but not to touch anything. I ran back down the alley and across the street to Tony, who was still making his examination of the body and crime scene.

"Let me see something, Tony," I said. "Can I roll him over a bit?"

"No prob," Tony replied. "I'm pretty much done here 'til CSI gets here. Just be careful not to mess anything up."

"Says the guy smoking too close to a crime scene..."

I pulled the body up slightly and looked at the flannel shirt around the waist. Sure enough, it was torn where it draped over his left leg, and there were the tell-tale reddish-brown stains of blood on it. In fact, the tear corresponded to a tear in his jeans, on the front of his left leg. There was a sizable gash there, and it had bled a bit into the denim. Ironically, it was the most blood that we'd seen yet at the crime scene, even though Hector's neck was half sliced through. I looked down the left leg to Hector's sock. It was black and greasy on the bottom, like he'd stepped in something—the same grease that I found on the bottom of the right shoe. And, though I'd need the CSI guys to confirm it when they got there, it looked like there was a smear of rust between the toes of the sock.

"Tony, we've got a problem," I sighed.

"Whussat?" Tony asked.

"I'm thinking that Hector died in this alleyway after all."

"Oh, c'mon, Tom," he growled. "We been through all that with Quesada over there. Ain't no way he bled out here in this alley without there bein', y'know, like *blood* all over the place!"

I nodded, but I kept putting the pieces together in my mind. A shoe on one side of the fence, the flannel caught in the twist, the grease on the sole of the foot, and the rust on the toes. Maybe the CSI guys would find grease on the sole of Hector's right foot when they took off his remaining shoe, or maybe that wasn't rust at all on his toes. Maybe I was all wrong.

But it sure looked to me like Hector Flórez went over that fence, and I couldn't figure out how a blood-drained corpse could have bled into his jeans from a cut like that, or stepped into a greasy puddle afterwards. It sure looked to me like he had to have been *alive* when he went over the fence. It sure looked to me like Hector had run through that other alleyway, dropping his shoe in the process, but moving so fast and so furious that he decided that he'd rather keep running through a dirty alley than to stop and put his shoe back on. It sure looked to me like he had climbed over the rusty fence, tearing his leg and his shirt in the process. It sure looked to me like he'd run across the street in the rain and made it only as far as this next alley before whoever was chasing him stopped him, slit his throat, and drained his blood, with only a few drops splattering enough to stain the cardboard beneath his head.

Maybe I was all wrong, because that last part didn't make any sense to me at all. Maybe I was totally, thoroughly, completely wrong. But I knew that I wasn't. And I knew that these tunnels in my mind were going to get a lot more complicated before I found the end.

Background
**From *Posthumously Collected Letters and Journals of General
Richard Phillips, Esqe.* (1752, Richard Phillips, British Governor of
Nova Scotia)**

17 November 1720...

... As for the damnable red Indians of the Passamaquoddi and Malécite tribes, they have again made a nuisance of themselves, this time by attacking our night patrols. The savages nonetheless blame their ridiculous Apotamkin men for the crime but I should think that any energetic investigation into this matter would yield the more reasonable answer. I am thus ordering an increase in both strength and number of our patrols as well as a thoroughgoing punitive expedition against the Malécite encampment nearest our position...

22 November 1720...

Captain Lloyd reported this morning two more men found slaughtered in the woods by the savages. One wonders how they can imagine such horrors much less perpetrate them. Though the bloody Malécites maintain their innocence it is quite obvious that they are attempting to persuade His Majesty's forces to abandon our position here through tactics of intimidation and terror, but we shall not be moved. Major Lethbridge-Stewart is taking his men out tonight to run the devils to ground and to punish the Indian savages responsible. Given his background with these people I am certain that there is no man alive more capable and more determined to accomplish this task, for they fear him almost as much as they do their imaginary Apotamkin monsters...

23 November 1720...

Major Lethbridge-Stewart and his entire command were wiped out last night save one young Scotch imbecile who while in hospital suffering from his wounds, mumbles all but incoherently that they were attacked by some bogey-man whom he described as "a large fanged buggbear which set upon us with such great ferocity that we were overcome," according to Surgeon Guilford. I am convinced that the boy is either feverish or an idiot as the attack was certainly not that of a wild animal, since they were neither ripped apart nor devoured but rather splayed and mutilated in a manner which is more indicative of a diabolically clever savage than an animal; neither was it the attack of a sole individual, as every musket had been fired in defense against a great multitude and yet no trace of the attacker or any injury thereof has been found. In point of fact there was relatively little to no blood to be found at the site at all, even including that of Lethbridge-Stewart's men. One can only assume that the Malécites bled the men and took their blood with them back to their encampment for some sort of unholy ritual of their pagan religion, though repeated expeditions into their squalid little community have found nothing…

26 November 1720…

The Malécite chieftain whose name is something like Tomach or Tomash or somesuch babbling contrived to meet with me today, explaining that he had discerned how one of his braves was actually the Apotamkin whom they charge with the guilt of the attacks on our men. They had killed the young man by some means of a torturous fashion and then remanded the mutilated corpse into our custody in order that we might cease our raids on their village. I went along with this farce only since it is obvious that this is the savage man's means of expressing his intention to stop their attacks. Only time will tell if they shall keep their end of this ridiculous charade…

Chapter 2
Roscoe Village

Karen Gage in the coroner's office told me that they determined that Hector Flórez had died from exsanguination a little after 6:00 in the evening. His obituary in the *Tribune* would say that he was survived by his mother, four brothers, and two sisters, and that his funeral Mass would be held on that Thursday at St. Peter's in the Loop. And on paper, that's about all that most people would ever know about the life of young Hector Flórez.

Most people wouldn't know about the years that he spent in juvie for the assortment of petty thefts and assaults that he'd perpetrated in his early years. Or about the time when he was 13 when his father breezed back into town and they ended up in a knife fight in the kitchen, while his baby sister sat in the corner and cried. Or about his love for painting, and how that was the one thing that he missed about high school when he dropped out. Or about the time last year when he and his "brothers" in the Insane Deuces beat a homeless guy half to death just because it was a Saturday night and they were bored (even though we could never pin it on them). Or about how he was trying to use his strength, fighting skills, and increasingly vicious disposition to rise through the ranks of the ID's as an enforcer.

At least eight Insane Deuces have been given life sentences that I know of—most of them under the age of 25—and the ID's are trying to build themselves up as a power on the streets. Part of Hector's job in the gang was to recruit and train "shorties"—children whom they could use as runners and low-end muscle, and eventually fold in as troops themselves. Chelsea's face popped into my mind for a moment, but I pushed it back out again to try to stay objective. Hector himself was a suspect in six shootings, one of which he'd apparently used one of his 10-year-old shorties to help pull off, but investigations hadn't been able to nail anything to him yet. Of course, all of that was now moot, so far as Hector Flórez was concerned.

I have to admit, the more I investigated this case, the less I liked Hector. But again, that's the difference between my job and a beat cop—I have no relationship with the people whose deaths or crimes I'm investigating. The more I care about them personally, the less effective

I'm going to be as a detective. It's all a series of tunnels in my mind, a series of switches to be turned off or on in the investigation. Whether the victim was a gang enforcer or an elderly nun, it didn't make any difference. At least, that's what I was supposed to keep telling myself the whole time.

I popped down to Karen's office to get more information, and she met me at the door as she was walking out. She's one of those people that you can't quite tell if they're pleasantly plain or subtly attractive. She had wavy brown hair and bright green eyes behind light, pretty glasses. But the glasses were a relatively cheap knock-off of a far more fashionable style, her hair was coiffed in a way that would've worked better if it were slightly longer, and her face and form were both a bit soft and plump. But then again, she was soft and plump in all the right places, so it didn't sit on her form as particularly unattractive. So half the men in her office tepidly flirted with her out of habit, while the other half barely noticed her at all. Personally, I try to notice everyone and everything, and I've made Karen my contact in the coroner's office primarily because she's intelligent and resourceful, and secondarily because I never really got along with her boss, Bill Saunders.

"Tom…" she said, stepping out into the hallway and pushing her glasses up out of habit, even though they weren't sliding down her nose. "I didn't realize that you were coming over."

"I just had a couple of questions about the Hector Flórez case, Karen," I replied. "Can we step inside for a second?"

She darted a glance back at the door, pulled it shut, and said, "Why don't we just take a seat here in the hall?" and stepped toward one of the benches nearby, pulling me with her.

"What's going on, Karen?" I asked. It wasn't like her to be so nervous.

She sat down on the bench and set a file down next to her. "Please sit down, Tom."

I sat down and looked at the file. It read, "Flórez, Hector J."

"I was actually coming to see you, Tom," she said. "Things are getting strange here." And she looked around furtively, making sure that no one was around to hear her.

"Talk to me, Karen," I said. "What's up?"

She glanced around again before she responded. "I did the autopsy and I recorded and filed the results, just like normal, and then everything hit the fan. Saunders came in and took the file out of the drawer, and he told everyone in the office that this was getting 'bumped upstairs,' whatever that means. People are saying that this has some sort of international connections, and I've been officially told not to share any of my findings with anyone." She looked genuinely frightened. "I never told anyone about this copy of the file—I've kept it locked in my desk drawer with my purse."

"Did you tell anyone that you'd already spoken with me?" I asked.

"No, not yet."

"Good—I don't want you getting into trouble on my account," I said. "But I hate to say it, that makes your report all that more important for me to see." I put my hand on the file. "Can I take a look at this?"

She took a deep breath and smiled bravely. "That's why I was bringing it to you."

I smiled back and opened up the file. I was expecting to see something jump out at me, something that might justify all of the cloak and dagger response, but it looked fairly normal—pretty much what I'd expected, given what we'd found in the alley off of Armitage. Hector Flórez died from exsanguination early in the evening. He was otherwise as strong as an ox, apart from the gash on his leg, some scarring from past wounds, and the beginnings of lung damage due to a lifetime of smoking, albeit a short lifetime. There was some bruising on his wrists, and he'd suffered two cracked ribs in the process of whatever struggle had killed him. There were also defensive wounds on his hands, and some dermal tissue under his fingernails (probably from his assailant) that they were analyzing, but that was to be expected, given the circumstances. About the only strange thing was that there was also a residue of saliva on part of the neck wound—which could mean just about anything, from his murderer licking the wound afterwards to Hector making out with someone before the attack. But it appeared, at least from their preliminary tests, that the tissue under the fingernails was from the same person as the saliva was, so both were probably from his murderer. And they couldn't tell as of yet what weapon made the actual laceration across the throat, but it did appear to be jagged and irregular—so it wasn't a knife or a hatchet. Maybe it was a jagged chunk of metal. Maybe it was a junkyard dog's claws. Maybe Hector's crazy grandmother ripped his throat out with her fingernails. It was maddeningly vague, but it wasn't particularly suspicious—nothing in the file suggested anything that would make all of this melodrama make any sense.

"This is it?" I asked, confused.

"This is it," she replied, stiffening. "What have you gotten into, Tom?"

I sat for a minute, wondering that myself. There was nothing about Hector Flórez himself, and nothing about the crime scene, and nothing about the file in my hands that would point to anything bigger than just a murder of a gang banger. It didn't make sense. Then I looked over at Karen and saw worry on her face—particularly, worry for me.

"Actually, I'm going to blame Tony," I chuckled, trying to ease the tension. "He probably said the wrong thing to the wrong person at the wrong time once too often, and I'm going to end up with an official reprimand on my file. They'll probably even take back that gold star sticker they put on it last week."

She half smiled, nervously.

"Seriously, Karen, it's probably nothing. Maybe we just stumbled onto some larger DEA operation going on or something, and we'll never find out any more than we know right now, and this will be the end of it. Just go back to work, focus on the other cases, and don't worry about this one." She nodded, but didn't respond. "But, for both of our sakes, do you mind if I keep this file?"

"Absolutely," she answered quickly. "Take it. Maybe you should burn it."

I chuckled and thanked her, but she still looked nervous. I got up to leave, but she grabbed my hand.

"Tom, I've seen jurisdictional disputes with the Feds before, and it wasn't like this. This is different. Somebody important is scared. Please be careful."

"I will," I promised her. "Just go back to work, okay? And I owe you another gelato for this." She smiled weakly again, and moved back toward the door.

"Be careful," she whispered again.

I nodded, and I walked away, tossing up a little prayer that she'd be okay and that what I said to reassure her was even remotely true. Why would Saunders take the file? And did anyone know that Karen had made this copy in my hands?

I chewed on it more and more as I walked back to my office, and those subway tunnels in my mind still weren't connecting. There were too many elements that just didn't make sense, and I knew that I wasn't going to be able to lay this down until I could see where everything was leading. In fact, I made it a point to make sure that I didn't run into Lieutenant Chacon, just in case he was ready to clamp down on my investigation like Saunders did on Karen's file. I wanted some answers.

As I was walking, at least one thing did stick out to me about the file—in fact, it struck me so strongly that I stopped and re-read the file in its entirety. There was only physical evidence of one assailant, and no evidence of any blunt trauma to the skull or ligature marks or the use of a sedative. Hector wasn't tied up or knocked out, so far as we could tell, so it seemed for all the world that one lone assailant chased him down, physically overpowered him, broke his ribs, and ripped out his throat. Hector Flórez wasn't a very good man, but he was a very tough one— and one who was well-acquainted with fighting in life-and-death situations. So who was it that could intimidate and overpower a guy like Hector Flórez so completely?

*   *   *

Tony and I decided to hit the area near Hamlin Park known as Roscoe Village (which required a courtesy phone call to the Area 3 detectives over on Belmont). I know that it was a couple of blocks north of the murder scene, and I knew that Tony wanted to go crash the Insane Orquestra Albany at Logan Square or the Imperial Gangstas down on Fullerton to "shake the bushes" for a lead from the nearest gangs, but I wanted to talk to the Insane Deuces first and get some background—and that meant Roscoe Village. What was Hector doing that close to Insane Orquestra Albany territory? Why was an enforcer like him with his own personal posse out there alone? And what kind of action would scare a tough guy like Hector Flórez into running for his life instead of standing and fighting?

It was just about dusk when Tony and I crossed under the metra tracks into Roscoe Village. They say that the Meskwaki Indians settled this area after the Fox Wars in the early 1700s, when there were only 500 of them left on the whole planet, and that the ghosts of all of those dead Meskwaki braves still haunt Roscoe Village. Personally, I don't believe in ghosts, and it's hard to picture the ghost of a 300-year-old Indian haunting Mario & Gino's Ice Cream Shop. Still, there's a weird feeling you get when you pass under those tracks, especially at dusk—the feeling that this isn't really Chicago anymore, that it's really some isolated, insulated village that Chicago just happens to be built around. I always have the strangest sensation of having to go underground to get there, like the whole place is actually in a cavern, but you just can't see the roof. It's a silly thought—Roscoe Village is a great neighborhood, it really is. Just something seems… *different* about it…

We drove around for a little while, trying to figure out where was the best place to find some ID's, when we got lucky. We saw two of them, dressed in their black and green, walking down the sidewalk on Roscoe Street, just outside Robey Pizza Company. We pulled over to the side of the street and Tony leaned out of the window toward them, flashing his badge. I watched the immediate "flight" reflex kick in, but they were smart enough not to bolt without knowing what we wanted to talk with them about. Besides, I knew both of them, and they couldn't help but recognize Tony.

I parked the car, and Tony and I got out. Tony did his best cop swagger, making sure that his badge flapped conspicuously, and that his sidearm was clearly visible. The Deuces rolled their eyes and sighed, accepting what I'm sure they saw as harassment. All in all, it was kind of like watching a primitive greeting ritual—everyone knowing the steps they're supposed to make so that they can get through the preliminaries and yet still look cool in the process. It was all posturing and posing, and it always made me think of those old, racist safari movies where the bwana has to make some entreaty to a native tribe, and goes through all these motions to open up negotiations. Everyone has a "face-saving" technique that they have to perform to feel in control, beads are exchanged, yadda, yadda…

"Y'know what we got here?" Tony asked, lighting his cigarette and taking a long drag. "We got us the whitest white boy an' the blackest black kid I ever seen." He blew out his cigarette smoke in their general direction. "That's like two-thirds of a Oreo cookie, I'm lookin' at here…" I always considered Tony to be a walking defamation lawsuit, just waiting to happen. I wonder sometimes if that's the reason Chacon assigned us together in the first place.

"Bite me!" grumbled the big one—Montrell "Mojo" Cade, one of the tougher young Insane Deuces, a teenaged thug with a rap sheet as long as his thick, heavily-muscled arm. Basically, he was a gorilla… and not a particularly *bright* gorilla at that.

But the other one—Billy "The Kid" Rivers—laid his hand on Mojo's shoulder and whispered, "Chill…" I'd known Billy for about a year now, and he always struck me as better educated than your average ID—like he was some rich white kid from the 'burbs who was doing "the gangsta thing" on a lark, either to relieve his boredom or to annoy a set of parents who'd probably really wanted him to go to Northwestern and study English lit.

"Enough, Tony…" I said, coming around the car and trying to dial down the testosterone. "We just had a couple of questions, and then you can head on out—"

"To yer next convenience store robbery…" Tony interjected. Now it was my turn to sigh.

"We've just got some questions," I finished off.

"Why you gotta mess with a brutha?" Mojo growled. He angrily pointed at Tony and barked, "Why you gotta stand with this—" but he suddenly shot a look at Billy and softened his tone, turning his gaze down toward the sidewalk. "Why you gotta hassle me, man?"

"First off," I responded, "don't even start with the 'brother' thing— this has nothing to do with that." Tony snorted, but I didn't even pause between sentences. "Secondly, we're not hassling anyone. I just want to talk to you about Hector Flórez."

"What *about* Hector?" Billy asked. "We've been here all day—ask anyone."

Tony was about to jump in, so I answered quickly. "This isn't about anything today. This is about last night." I flipped open my notebook and jotted down their names and the time. "When was the last time that either of you saw Hector Flórez?"

Mojo looked at Billy, and Billy frowned for a second. "Golly, officer, I couldn't say," he replied sarcastically, and Mojo chuckled.

"Screw this!" Tony huffed. "This ain't gettin' us nowhere!" He spitefully swatted away a ladybug and started to walk back to the car. I couldn't tell if he was playing more of "bad cop" game or if he was really intending to drop this line of investigation and go back down to Logan Square.

"Hector Flórez was murdered last night," I added, testing the waters. They both looked genuinely surprised at that, and Billy glanced at Mojo.

"Who done him?" Mojo asked, with a mixture of grief and rage.

"That's what we're trying to figure out, Mojo," I said. "That's why we need to know what Hector was doing down on Armitage alone last night."

"Armitage?" Billy asked. "Are you thinking it was the Orquestra Albany down in Darwin City?" Mojo's hands turned to fists, and he spat out an unintelligible curse under his breath.

"I'm not coming to any conclusions yet, Billy," I replied. "I'm just looking for some facts. Do you know why Hector was on Armitage last night?"

"No, I don't," Billy said, his brows furrowing again, "but I'm going to find out." Mojo nodded in angry agreement. "And there will be hell to pay."

"Don't do anything stupid, guys," I warned, seeing where this was going and how fast is was getting there. "We don't need the Deuces and the Orquestra Albany going to war over this—we don't even know if they're involved or not."

"Oh, they gonna pay, bro…" Mojo growled, a sick little grin curling his mouth into a snarl. "They gonna pay…"

"This was such a good idea, Tom," Tony laughed, turning toward the car again.

"Seriously," I repeated, "we're on this, and we'll find out what happened to Hector. If you want to help, then *help*." I specifically looked at Billy and tried to catch his eyes. "Don't muddy this up with a gang war. Just find out why Hector was down there and give me a call."

I pulled out my card and handed it to Billy—who surprised me by actually taking it.

"We really do want to find out who killed Hector, Billy," I reiterated. "If you want to find out, too, then help us do some legwork here."

Billy looked down at the card, then up at me, then over to Tony, then back to me. "If you mean that," he said eventually, "then you've got it—for *now*." He looked over to Mojo, who was grinding his teeth and digging at the sidewalk with his toe. "But you've got to realize that this is going to explode into something very big, very quickly." This time, Billy made it a point to make eye contact with me. "Find a killer for us soon, or you're going to have a lot more killings to handle."

I wasn't sure if that was a manipulative threat or a motivational warning. Either way, I knew that he was right, and that this was going to get ugly. I just had no idea how *bizarrely* ugly it was going to get, or what form that ugliness was going to take.

For that, I'd have to meet Pieter Durant.

Background
From *De Graecorum Hodie Quorundam Opinationibus* (Leone Allacci, 1645, trans. M. Summers)

The vrykolakas[1] is the body of a man of wicked and debauched life, very often of one who has been excommunicated by his bishop. Such bodies do not like other corpses suffer decomposition after burial nor fall to dust, but having, so it seems, a skin of extreme toughness, becomes swollen and distended all over, so that the joints can scarcely be bent; the skin becomes stretched like the parchment of a drum, and when struck gives out the same sound…

It is impossible that a dead man should become a vrykolakas, unless it be by the power of the Devil, who, wishing to mock and delude some that they may incur the wrath of Heaven, causes these dark wonders, and so very often at night he casts a glamour whereby men imagine that the dead man whom they knew formerly, appears and holds converse with them, and in their dreams too they see strange visions. At other times they may behold him in the road, yes, even in the highway walking to and fro or standing still, and what is more than this he is even said to have strangled men and to have slain them…

Immediately there is sad trouble, and the whole village is in a riot and a racket, so that they hasten to the grave and they unbury the body of the man… and the dead man—one who has long been dead and buried— appears to them to have flesh and blood… so they collect together a mighty pile of dry wood and set fire to this and lay the body upon it so that they burn it and they destroy it altogether…

It is the height of folly to attempt to deny that such bodies are not infrequently found in their graves incorrupt and that by use of them the Devil, if God permits him, devises most horrible complots and schemes to the hurt and harm of mankind.

---

[1]   *Derived from the Slavic words, "vâlk" (meaning "wolf") and "dlaka" (meaning "fur"), "vrykolakas" originally carried more of a sense of a werewolf than a vampire. Over time, however, the two creatures became functionally synonymous in many of the legends (though, to Romanians, the "vârcolac" is still primarily a wolf demon).*

Chapter 3
Pieter Durant

This was the day that would change my life forever, though it didn't seem like it at the time. It was another rainy, sleepy morning, so I hit the snooze button and lay with Joanna a little longer than usual. Just watching her sleeping next to me—totally vulnerable, and yet totally peaceful—and listening to the rain lightly pelting the window… it's like all of the ugliness and pain on the streets that I deal with on a daily basis can just melt away, if only for another nine minutes.

Chelsea was almost certainly up already (being the only "morning person" in our family), though the twins probably wouldn't start waking up until I got into the shower. I could picture Chelsea sitting cross-legged on the floor, playing with her Legos or her dolls or maybe having a tea party with her favorite bears, and I tried to remember—tried to *imagine*—what it was like to live in a world that *simple* again. What was it like to find total, absolute comfort sitting in your room, playing with your toys, and letting everything else fall by the wayside while you poured imaginary tea for Mr. Bear? No bills to pay, no monsters in alleyways, no alarm clocks to remind you that you *have* to get up in the morning. Instead, for her, the morning is a time of wonder, a time of sunshine and quiet playtime and excitement about a day that holds nothing but surprise and promise.

There had to have been a time like that for me when I was a child—I remember having an overall fun childhood—but I couldn't remember the actual *feeling* of it. I couldn't remember what it felt like to have no cares, no concerns, no responsibilities weighing down on me. I suppose what I'm saying is that I couldn't remember what it was like to have that level of absolute innocence about the rest of the world. Maybe I never really will again. I couldn't help but sigh a little and grieve a little, looking forward to the day that lay ahead of me. I thought of Tony de Tullio and Hector Flórez and the Insane Deuces, and about how they all seemed to inhabit an entirely different planet than the one I was laying in at that moment. Had there been a time when Hector Flórez had just sat cross-legged on his floor and played with cars, oblivious to everything else, peaceful to his core? I couldn't picture it. Or had his life always been one layer of horror laid over another? Had there been a time when Tony de Tullio had ever just beamed in innocent rapture, gazing at a stuffed bear?

I have to admit, that thought made me smile again.

I looked over at Joanna's face on her pillow, and I was reminded that some responsibilities, I wouldn't trade for all the world. She wouldn't have to get up for at least another hour yet, but no matter how stealthily I'd try to climb out of bed, she'd always wake up and shamble out of the room to help me. In seven years of marriage, she'd never complained about it, either.

Oh, she'd complained about me having to miss that anniversary two years ago because of the job—she'd complained a *lot* about that one, and for a long, long time. And she'd understandably complained about a few evenings, right after the twins were born, when she had to take care of three young children (and figure out how to feed two babies) without my help because I was out looking at a murder scene or filing a last-minute report. But she'd never complained about *helping* me do the job. Sometimes, when I'm frustrated, I can let myself wrongly think that she hates me being a cop, that she resents the job, but in my more lucid moments, I know that's not really the truth. She knows why I do it, and she supports me in it. She just doesn't want to be left alone.

I leaned over, kissed her forehead, and whispered, "I love you."

She didn't move a muscle or change position. Her mouth was slightly open, and I figured that at any second, a drizzle of drool would trickle out onto the pillow. But I confess that at that moment, I don't think she's ever looked more beautiful to me. I may work in a world of murderers and monsters and rapists and fiends, but I *live* in a world that's populated with stuffed bears and tea parties, children who always cheer for me when I walk through the door, and this wonderful woman who supports me, even though I've put her through so much over the years.

I smiled, turned off the alarm before the snooze went off again, and slid as quietly as I could out of the bed to get ready for work. Joanna shifted her body and slowly began to wake herself up.

*   *   *

Sitting at my desk, I must have read and re-read Karen's file on Hector Flórez a dozen times. No matter how many times I read it, and how many times I looked over my own notes from the crime scene, I came up with the same conclusions.

Hector Flórez was chased down an alleyway, losing a shoe and gashing his leg as he jumped over a fence, but didn't slow down in either case. His murderer or murderers caught up with him, and he fought back, punching them and scratching them with his nails. Why would a big guy like Hector—a seasoned hand-to-hand combatant—finally resort to scratching at someone like a teenage girl in a catfight in a high school hallway? His assailant or assailants grabbed him by the wrists so hard that they caused bruising, and held his torso with such force that they cracked two ribs. They ripped his throat open with some sort of sharp, jagged object, drained his blood (into what, a bag? a bucket?), and then someone, what, kissed him? licked him? spit on him?

Why?

And how did whoever did it—who must have been covered in the blood that Hector *wasn't* covered in—get out of that alleyway without being seen? They hadn't been in a car, since they'd been chasing him down that alley. Did they have an accomplice who joined them after the fact and picked them up in front of the deli? Or did he pick them up at the end of the alleyway, next to the dance studio?

But we'd had officers questioning shop owners up and down the block. This hadn't been at 2:00 in the morning—it had been around dinner time. Yes, it had been raining, so walk-in business had been down, but surely somebody, somewhere would have seen something. There were people coming in and out of the deli the whole time that the murder was going on, but no one saw a car pick up a rain-soaked, blood-soaked murderer. The dance studio at the end of the alley has a huge window on the front that wraps around to the side, and there had been a dance class going on that evening, almost certainly at the same time as the murder. Fifteen girls couldn't *all* have missed seeing a bloody set of murderers jumping into a car right in front of their studio, and yet, none of them said they saw anything. It's like whoever killed Hector Flórez just vanished afterwards.

Of course, there was the other possibility that they had just gone back the way they'd come—back over the fence and down the alleyway toward the old apartment buildings. I told Tony to have our guys bang on some doors in that neighborhood to see if anyone saw anything going back that direction. But why would you carry off a bucket of blood? Voodoo ritual?

I needed more information, and I decided that maybe Tony was right that we should go talk with the Insane Orquesta Albany at Logan Square, even as I resisted the idea. I'd had nothing but very bad experiences with the OA's, and their current alpha dog over at Logan Square was a very bad guy whom they called *"el Buitre"*—the *Vulture*—though I never had heard his real name. More than anything else, Buitre was famous for two things—his bald head, covered in so many dark tattoos that it almost looked painted black from a distance, and his penchant for very sudden, very brutal violence. Now, under other circumstances, I would've jumped for Buitre as a suspect in a crime like this (I mean, ripping a guy's throat out would've been right up his alley—pardon the pun), except that he always made sure that the OA's somehow got credit for their terror. He was smart enough to keep his crew from getting arrested too often, but they always made sure to leave their OA graffiti at the scene so that everyone knew who ruled those streets.

They just weren't afraid of prison time—in fact, most of them felt like a little jail time improved their street cred immensely—and they *wanted* people to be afraid of them. They wanted people to be more afraid of them than they are of the cops, or the Deuces, or the Latin Kings, or the bogeyman. So for a killing like this to go on this close to Logan Square, and yet Buitre and his posse to stay this quiet about it…? It just didn't fit his way of doing things. If Buitre had done this, then *everyone* would know it—and yet we probably still wouldn't be able to prove it.

Nonetheless, I had to admit that we'd probably have to sit down with Buitre and the Orquestra Albany at some point. Even if they weren't behind it, they'd probably know something, at least, that we could go on. But it's funny how I had so much more trepidation about going to the OA's than I had had about going to the ID's the day before.

I looked over, and Tony was drinking his last cup of coffee for the day. Right around noon, Tony switched to Coca-Cola, and he'd nurse three or four cans over the course of the rest of the day. He had some sort of unwritten rule about coffee being a *morning* drink, and Coke *not* being a morning drink, but I'm not sure that I ever really caught the subtle distinctions that he made. One time, I caught him trying a sip of Diet Coke, but he denied it so strongly that you'd have thought I was accusing him of being a Cardinals fan. Tony was a connoisseur of fine junk food.

I was about to suggest to him that we should contact Sweet Jimmy and ask for an audience over at Logan's Square with Buitre, when Tony looked up and saw Lieutenant Chacon coming over to us. "Straighten up, Tom. Here comes trouble." I never really understood Tony's aversion to Chacon. Was it that Tony hated pretty much everyone who wasn't Italian? Or maybe Tony had just seen too many cop movies and had just *assumed* that he shouldn't like his lieutenant. I don't know. But, ironically, this time, Tony accidentally turned out to be right. Trouble was entering my life at that moment on a level I would have— *could* have—never imagined. Because this was the moment that I would meet Pieter Durant.

"Gentlemen," Chacon greeted us as he walked up, his gentle baritone voice commanding both calm and obedience at the same time. "I would like you to meet Inspector Durant, from Interpol." He waved his hand back toward the man behind him, and Durant stepped forward.

I remember every detail of that moment—it's now etched in my brain, just as surely as the day Chelsea was born.

Everything about Durant was deliberate, and everything was gray. He moved with an absolute muscular control and a graceful efficiency that somehow seemed unnatural, even unsettling. His charcoal-colored hair and beard were perfectly trimmed and styled, with streaks of silver at the temples and on either side of his chin. His long, gray Belstaff overcoat had obviously been tailored to fit his tall form, and it lightly brushed the floor when he walked. He wore a blue-gray Armani suit, with a gray vest that perfectly offset the overcoat, and a pale blue silk Hugo Boss tie—perfectly tied in its Windsor knot, perfectly dimpled, perfectly matching his perfectly arranged pocket handkerchief. At a glance, you'd almost have taken him for a fashion designer, or a high-powered, Fortune 500 type. But looking at him closer, I developed a quite different opinion.

Durant was a predator.

Every deliberate motion that he made, every step that he took, it was like watching a tiger moving in the tall grass. He was tall and slender, but you could see thick shoulders moving under the overcoat, and his hands were hard and calloused and knotted with muscles. And his *eyes*... Pieter Durant's eyes were a piercing clear gray, hooded under dark, thick, charcoal brows, and they never seemed to miss a thing. Even as I shook his disconcertingly strong hand, I saw him take in not only me, but Tony, our desks, Officer Jenkins filing reports in the cabinets behind me... *everything*...

"Inspector Durant has come all the way from France to work with you on this Flórez thing," Chacon continued, "because Interpol apparently suspects some sort of terrorist connection. So you will extend to him every courtesy—and *that* means," he nodded toward Tony for emphasis, "that you will include him in on all information, you will show him complete respect, and you will defer to his lead in any area in which he might want to direct this investigation... Do you understand?"

Tony snorted something out that I didn't quite catch as he shook Durant's hand, and sat back down, but I could tell that he found Durant disconcerting as well. I think it must have been something like, "Gee, we'll try not to get in your way," or very similar, because of Durant's response.

"No, no, Detective de Tullio," he responded, with a strange accent and a cavernous voice that sounded like he'd gargled ground glass that morning. "I shall simply be a fly on the wall of your investigation. An advisor, if you will."

"You don't sound French, Inspector," I interjected, my detective instincts kicking in for reasons that I didn't yet fully realize. "Where are you from, originally?" Durant shifted his gaze from Tony to me in a manner which could have indicated that he was intrigued by my question or mildly angered by my question, but I couldn't tell which yet.

"Originally?" he replied, cocking his head. "England, actually."

"First time in the Windy City, huh?" Tony asked.

"Not even remotely, no," he responded.

"But you don't sound English, entirely," I continued, watching for more of a reaction from him. Somehow, it sounded almost German. Maybe South African? No, that wasn't it, either.

"You have a good ear, Detective Chapel," he said. And that's *all* that he said. And just like that, it was clear that our little conversation was over.

"So everyone play nice," Chacon said at last, breaking the uncomfortable silence. Tony snorted again. "Inspector Durant and I have a few more procedural things to discuss, and then I'll let you all get more acquainted later." Durant nodded at me again, and I noticed that he hadn't blinked during that entire interaction. I noticed, because I realized that I hadn't blinked, either, and that my eyes were starting to hurt. Durant pivoted perfectly and Chacon led him back toward his office. As he passed by, almost everyone looked up from their desks or their work, and more than one seemed to shiver. I knew the feeling.

"Now that Frog is some piece o' work..." Tony growled. "Who's he think he is, takin' over our investigation, huh?"

I just watched Chacon's closed door for a moment, trying to let it all sink in. How could a guy like Hector Flórez be involved with anything that could involve a guy like Pieter Durant? And a "fly on the wall" wouldn't pull Hector's file like that and put a lid on the investigation like this. Had Buitre gotten the OA's involved in something so big that its scope had crossed an ocean?

Just who was a predator like Durant hunting, here in Chicago?

"Well, first of all," I finally answered, breaking the frustrated silence, "he's English, not French—and no one calls them 'Frogs' any more but you." Tony chortled, and mumbled something about soccer and bad food as he slurped from his can. "Secondly," I continued, "he's a bigger fish than either you or I will ever be, so maybe we better just keep our mouths shut for right now."

That's when Matt Yee hung up the phone behind me and threw a pencil at my head.

"Hey, Tom," he said. "It's your lucky day!"

"How so?" I asked.

"Because there's been another murder, same M.O.," he responded with a grin, "just down the street from your other one, in Logan Square. You can take your new creepazoid buddy on your first date..."

Tony belched as he swore.

"Another Deuce, or one of the OA's?" I asked Yee.

"Neither," he responded, finishing the note he was scribbling for me. "Vic was a little old lady in her apartment."

I grabbed the note from him as I walked toward Chacon's office to pick up our new "advisor" on the way out to Logan Square…

Background
From *The Descent of Ishtar to the Underworld* (Assyrian myth, c. 1600 B.C., trans. M. Jastrow)

To the land of no return, the land of darkness,
Ishtar,[1] the daughter of Sin directed her thought,
Directed her thought, Ishtar, the daughter of Sin,
To the house of shadows, the dwelling, of Irkalla,
To the house without exit for him who enters therein,
To the road, whence there is no turning,
To the house without light for him who enters therein,
The place where dust is their nourishment, clay their food.
They have no light, in darkness they dwell.
Clothed like birds, with wings as garments,
Over door and bolt, dust has gathered.
Ishtar on arriving at the gate of the land of no return,
To the gatekeeper thus addressed herself:
"Gatekeeper, ho, open thy gate!
Open thy gate that I may enter!
If thou openest not the gate to let me enter,
I will break the door, I will wrench the lock,
I will smash the door-posts, I will force the doors.
I will bring up the dead to eat the living.
And the dead will outnumber the living."

---

[1]   *Ishtar was the Assyrian goddess of sexual love, fertility, and warfare. In this myth, she desires to descend into the Underworld (Irkallu) in order to restore life to her deceased lover, Tammuz.*

Chapter 4
A Dark Kind of Love

On our way over to Logan Square, I talked on the phone with the officer on the scene. He said that the building's superintendent found the body of one Amanda Raffey, age 73, in her apartment that morning. There were some details that didn't make sense as he shared them, so I made a note to talk with the super when we got there. But it was clear to the officer that she had been brutally murdered, and in a manner similar to the way Hector Flórez died. The CSI guys were uncharacteristically already on-scene, so I was also looking forward to talking with them a bit.

As we drove, I watched Durant in the rearview mirror. His eyes were watching everyone on the rain-slick streets, as if he were looking for someone or something in particular. I made another phone call back to the office to have Jenkins dig up some background on Amanda Raffey, and the whole time, Durant's eyes never stopped scouring the sidewalks. I noticed a couple of OA's huddled here and there as we entered the Darwin City area—mostly Latinos, wearing their brown and gold colors. Their graffiti was everywhere in the alleyways—the diamond, the "O" with an overlapping "A" sticking out the bottom, assorted other Folks Nation crap. What I found interesting was that there were more crosses painted on the walls than I'd remembered seeing before—that wasn't usually an OA sort of thing, and I wondered if some other gang was trying to muscle into Buitre's turf. Maybe Hector had stumbled onto something bigger than we could see yet.

The OA's certainly have no shortage of enemies, of course. Since their start in 1971, La Orquestra Albany have gone to war with just about everyone. The Gaylords, the Simon City Royals, the Yates Boys, the Latin Eagles, the Imperial Gangsters, the Latin Kings—the list is endless. It seems like they're always at it with someone, and yet always growing in number.

But that's the whole idea of a gang. They exist to fight, and fighting justifies their existence—it's an endless loop. For instance, the Latin Kings will tell you that they started out as a strictly Latino gang, trying to protect other Latinos from discrimination, but they quickly used their power base to terrorize everyone else. And within the first couple of years, they started adding other ethnicities to their ranks—anything to build up their numbers. We're talking about a gang with 25-30,000 members in Chicago alone, a gang that all but runs the drug trade in the city, a gang who are responsible for at least half of the violence in Illinois prisons. The nature of a gang isn't to prevent violence and horror—it's to perpetrate them. You build an army to fight a war, and the next block over has to build *their* army to fight the war, and strangely enough, that erupts into a war.

It's kind of like watching nations in microcosm. *We* build missiles so *they* build missiles to defend against *our* missiles. The Latin Kings build an army so the Imperial Gangsters build an army to defend against their army, so the Insane Deuces build an army to defend against those other two armies, so the Orquestra Albany builds an army to defend themselves against all of those other armies being built up everywhere around them. You can pretend that it's all in defense, but if they weren't all building their own private armies, they wouldn't have needed armies to defend themselves to begin with. The real nature of a gang is to be a gang, not to be a protective force. They make a pretense of being a "family" for these kids, and yet they destroy the families and neighborhoods that the kids come from. They exist for terror, and so they thrive on terror. The more violence, horror, and bloodshed there is in the neighborhood, the more the gang sees a need and a justification to arm itself and prepare itself for violence, horror, and bloodshed— disregarding the fact that the existence of the gangs themselves is what's creating all of the violence, horror, and bloodshed in the first place. It's a cycle that perpetuates itself, and the more it grows, the more it's *going* to grow.

There was a growing sense of horror on the streets of Logan Square, and I could feel it, even before we got out of the car. For the first time, Buitre and his army were feeling fear instead of dishing it out. The OA's were out in force, patrolling their own personal war zone. If we didn't get a handle on what was going on here soon, this place was going to explode. And it would take Roscoe Village, and Humboldt Park, and West Town, and the Motherland with it.

*   *   *

Amanda Raffey's apartment building was falling apart. It was a ramshackle, two-story, concrete box, with graffiti in the halls, and a staircase that creaked so much when Tony walked on it that I was afraid he'd fall straight through it to the floor below. As he and Durant went upstairs to the apartment, I knocked on the superintendent's door to get a few questions answered.

The super was a man named Carmine Wisniewski. He was in his mid-forties, heavyset, and unwashed. His thick moustache hung over his upper lip, he reeked of cheap cigar smoke, and his beard stubble looked rough enough that he could use his chin to sand a board. He didn't appear happy to be talking with yet another policeman, and he didn't invite me in. So we stood in the hallway with his door ajar, some loud and shrill sit-com blaring from the television in his garishly-decorated living room behind him.

"So you found the body today, Mr. Wisniewski?" I asked, opening my notebook.

"Yeah, I covered dis wid de guys upstairs," he snarled, with a Chicagoan accent so thick that it made my uncle from the South Side sound like a Texan. "I got stuff ta do…" And the laugh-track from his sit-com peaked in volume from behind.

"Well, you're covering it again," I responded, without looking up. "What made you go into her apartment in the first place?"

"Well, dere was dese guys who was up dere de odder night," he said. "An' I didn't like de look of 'em." And then he leaned in closer and added more quietly, "Gangbangers…"

"This was Monday night?"

"Yup." The night of Hector's murder.

"And how did you know that they were 'gangbangers,' Mr. Wisniewski?"

"Dey got dat look, ya know?" he said, scratching himself. "An' dem colors an' all."

"Brown and gold?"

"Naw," he answered. "Green an' black…"

I stopped writing and looked up at him. He was still scratching, but it was obvious that he was certain of his information. Green and black. Insane Deuces.

"What did these 'gangbangers' look like, Mr. Wisniewski? Other than what they were wearing?"

"Well, I only seen de one, o' course," he said. "But he was a big fella. Like a Chicano guy or somethin'. A real greaser, ya know?"

"Was he wearing a white tank, with a green flannel shirt tied around his waist, and a bandanna across his forehead?" I asked, thinking of Hector Flórez in the alleyway.

"Yeah," he said. "Dat's right."

"Any distinguishing marks?"

"What?"

"Like a scar or a tattoo, Mr. Wisniewski."

He thought for a second, and then answered, "Well, I din't see it so good, but he had somethin' on his face."

"Something?"

"Yeah, like a tattoo of a cross or a bird or somethin'..."

"Which side of his face?"

He frowned for a second, trying to remember, touching one side of his own face, and then the other. "De left, I guess."

Hector Flórez. He'd been here the night of his murder.

"Now, how is it that you saw only one of these 'gangbangers,' Mr. Wisniewski? Where was the other one?"

"Well, I heard one o' dem goin' up de stairs one time, an' den de odder one goin' up about a half hour later, but den I heard dis fracas in her apartment—"

"A 'fracas,' Mr. Wisniewski?"

"Yeah, dere was all dis crashin' and yellin' upstairs, an' I comed out to yell at 'em, but dis greaser kid comes runnin' down de stairs past me. Dat's when I seen 'im. He didn't say nothin'—he just runned right past me."

"Anything in his hands?"

"What?"

"Was he carrying a gun, a knife, a weapon of any kind?"

"Naw," he said, scratching himself again. "He was jus' runnin'..."

"And how soon did you hear this 'fracas' after the second person went up the stairs?"

"Like, right den."

"The second person went up the stairs, and that's when the crashing and the yelling started? Immediately?"

"Yup." I made some more notes.

"How did he look?"

"Huh?"

"The Latino youth who came down the stairs. How did he look?"

"Whaddya mean?"

"Did he look anxious, or angry, or guilty, or neutral, or what? In your opinion, what was his emotional state as he ran past you?"

"In my opinion?" he said. "Dat boy looked scared as a cat bein' chased by a pitbull!"

"And the other one?"

"I guess he was still upstairs, I guess. I didn't see 'im."

"Then how do you know that the other one was a 'gangbanger,' too, Mr. Wisniewski?"

"'Cuz dey *all* is dese days," he grunted, and he snorted in his nose.

I made notes of all of this in my notebook, and then I asked another clarification question. "So that's when you checked on Mrs. Raffey?"

"Well, no," he answered, a little sheepishly.

"Why not?"

"Well, 'cuz dey stopped bangin' around den," he said. "Dat kid had runned off an' everything."

"But you suspected that there was at least one more 'gangbanger' upstairs with an elderly tenant, correct? And that there'd been a violent episode?"

"Well, I figgered dat dere *could'a* been…"

"Mm hmm…"

"But, ya know, it wasn't really my—ya know—my place to make a big deal or nothin'…" He was becoming more uncomfortable the more we talked.

"Mr. Wisniewski," I asked, "Just one more question. If you didn't check on Mrs. Raffey that evening, then why did you check on her today?"

"Well…" he started, fumbling with his doorknob, obviously wanting to get back to his television and away from this conversation, "I mean, de rent was due dis morning, ya know…?"

I had no desire to keep talking with this man.

*   *   *

So Hector Flórez had been in that building on the night of his murder with Amanda Raffey. But he hadn't been alone. He'd come in by himself, and he'd run off by himself, but he hadn't been alone in there.   Someone else had joined them that night, and something happened in there that had terrified a gang enforcer who thrived on terror. When I walked inside that apartment, I could understand how.

In all the years I've been on the job, I don't think that I've ever seen so much blood splattered around a crime scene. Amanda Raffey's body lay in the middle of the room, but her blood was everywhere. It painted the walls, it pooled on the floor, it splattered the ceiling. This isn't the sort of thing that could happen just as the result of a violent crime—her killer had consciously done this for a reason. But what reason, and for whose benefit?

The blood made for some timeline issues that I couldn't resolve yet—if this murder was, itself, indeed the 'fracas' that Carmine Wisniewski heard, and if Hector Flórez ran off immediately afterwards, and if the murderer left close enough behind Flórez that he could catch up with him in the alleyway a few blocks away, then how did he have the time to splatter all of this blood everywhere? Why was Hector there in the first place? I had multiple pieces of the puzzle, but no idea how they all went together yet.

The CSI guys were there, of course, taking samples, and Durant was talking with them with his usual intensity. Tony was going through some of the items on a nearby day desk, and there was a smell in the air that reminded me of something, but I couldn't quite put my finger on it. As I was trying to think, I was surprised to find that Karen Gage was in the apartment as well.

"Karen," I asked, walking up to her as I put on my gloves, "what are you doing here? You don't do field work."

Her eyes darted around nervously to see who heard me. "Tom…" she said, standing up and moving me away from the body.

"What's going on, Karen?"

She pulled me near a side table full of photographs. "Tom, they're going to take this one, too."

"What are you talking about?"

She took a deep breath. "They came in and took the Flórez body this morning. I don't know where to, but Saunders looked like he was scared out of his gourd. And now they're talking about taking this Raffey body, too."

"*Who* is?"

"That guy over there," she answered, pointing to Durant. "He had them take Flórez away, and everyone was talking about them doing the same here, and I wanted to see the body before they did."

Sure enough, Durant seemed to be directing them to do precisely that, and the CSI guys were arguing with him.

"You shouldn't be here, Karen," I said. "Go back to the office…"

"But Tom, it's almost the same M.O. as the Flórez murder," she said. "And what does an old woman have to do with international terrorists?"

Durant was becoming insistent, and Tony started to walk over to the body to get into the conversation. That couldn't be good.

"Wait a minute, Karen," I said, and I went over to where everyone was arguing.

"Must I contact your precinct and demand your cooperation through official reprimand?" Durant was saying to Tony. "I shouldn't think that you would want that, Detective de Tullio."

"Yeah," growled Tony, "I'll tell ya what ya should think…"

"Tony!" I interjected. "Let's all just take a deep breath and calm down here." I turned toward Durant. "Actually, Inspector, in Chicago, we don't have precincts—we have districts. Would you like to tell me what's going on here?"

"This guy wants to take the body out of here!" interrupted one of the CSI guys. "We're not even done yet!"

"You have done everything required of you," replied Durant, with a sharpness that made the guy shrink back toward the body. "This conversation is ended." He turned and looked at me, locking those gray eyes on mine with smoldering intensity. "Isn't it, Detective Chapel?"

I stood there for a long moment, trying to decide just how far to push this. Chacon's words echoed in my mind, as did Durant's insistence that he would just be a "fly on the wall."

He's a pretty big, ugly, stinking fly.

I crouched down and looked at the body. Amanda Raffey's throat was sliced open, just like had been done to Hector Flórez. But in this case, her head had been almost completely severed. To my eyes, it looked as though her throat had been torn like Hector's, and then ripped through the rest of the way. I wasn't sure what that indicated, but I'd hoped that Karen could tell me more later on. For a fleeting moment, I was glad that she'd broken protocol to be there.

On Amanda's left hand was a ring—an engagement ring. It was obviously quite old, and it hadn't been cleaned in some time, but it was still attractive and probably still worth quite a bit. I looked up toward the desk where Tony had been ruffling through things, and saw her undisturbed purse sitting there amongst the papers. Neither Hector Flórez nor the other man who'd been there had touched it. I could see her bedroom through an open door in the corner of the room, and it looked eerily serene, compared to the living room. I had little doubt that we would find a jewelry box in there on a night stand or a dressing table, filled with the detritus of a life's accumulation of gold and silver memories.

This wasn't a robbery. And Pieter Durant already knew what it *really* was. The only way that I was going to find out was through *him*, not through the CSI guys.

I stood back up and looked at the guy who'd spoken up earlier. "What's your name?" I asked.

"Me?" he asked, surprised. "Roecker. Dan Roecker."

I met Durant's eyes again. "I guess we're done here, Dan." Tony threw his hands up in disgust. "But double-check with Lieutenant Chacon, just to make sure," I said to Roecker. Durant's expression didn't change. "Is that all right with you, Inspector?"

"It is... satisfactory, Detective," he replied. He crouched down beside the body himself, and examined the wound one final time. As he moved, his jacket opened, and I saw a strange leather pouch on his left hip, roughly the size of a small purse. It seemed terribly incongruous, given his chic wardrobe, to have an ancient brown satchel like that with him. It had obviously been carefully repaired many times over the years, and though the leather itself looked worn, it had also been regularly oiled and taken care of. Tony noticed it, too, and chuckled.

"So, ya got yerself a man-purse, huh?" he asked, trying to get a rise out of him. Durant didn't respond. "Or do ya call that a 'European shoulder bag?' or somethin'?"

"It's my *got uechan*, actually," Durant replied, brushing a stray hair across Amanda Raffey's face with an almost... tenderness... that surprised me.

"An' what's that?" Tony continued.

Durant stood up, drew his jacket back over the bag, and stood face-to-face with Tony. I was reminded of how tall and angular his body was by comparison. "It's a *got uechan...*" he said. Tony met his glare for a time, his chest puffed out in defiance. But then, after a moment, he glanced toward me. I shrugged, but Durant didn't move, his gaze transfixed on the body. After another moment, Tony shrunk back away from Durant and started shuffling through the papers on her desk again—obviously looking for nothing, but grumbling quietly to himself. Only then did Durant move. He pulled out and glanced at an expensive-looking pocket watch, and then said to the group, "I expect this body out of here within the hour, gentlemen." With that, he strode purposefully out of the room and into the hall.

Karen had wisely stayed out of the whole interaction, and was still standing by the side table. I walked back over to her. "Tom, do you want me to test any of this blood against Hector Flórez? Maybe this is where he was killed?"

"Go ahead and test it," I replied. "But none of it is going to be Hector's. I'm convinced he made it out of here without a scratch, and then died in that alley a couple of blocks away. I don't know what happened to his blood, but that's where it happened." I was going to ask her again to leave, before any of this blew back onto her, but then something that she'd said bounced back into my mind.

"Wait, you said, 'almost...'"

"What?" she asked as she was gathering her things.

"You said that this murder *almost* fit the M.O. of the Flórez killing. Aside from all of the blood here at this crime scene, what else would you say is different?"

Her eyes darted around again, and she pushed her glasses up again nervously. "I don't think that there's any saliva at the wound site this time," she said. "I mean, I won't know for sure until I get back to the lab to run some tests, but it doesn't look like it." She slipped a couple of sample vials into her purse as we talked. "But I am sure that the murder weapon was the same thing both times." She cleared her throat. "And I'm pretty sure that I know what it was, now that I've seen it twice."

She paused and stared at me, as if she wasn't sure that she really wanted to tell me.

"And that would be...?" I asked.

"It was a nail. A human fingernail," she said. "I actually even found a little fragment in the wound this time." She quietly flashed me a little evidence baggie with something in it, before slipping that into her purse as well.

"Karen," I said, more than just a little incredulous, "you should know even better than I do that any nails long enough to do this kind of damage would be too brittle to do this kind of damage. Besides, the kind of strength you'd have to put behind ripping through someone's—"

"I'm not telling you *how* it was someone's nail, Tom," she interrupted. "I'm just telling you *that* it was someone's nail." She was breathing heavily now, and her eyes moistened just barely. "What's going on here, Tom?"

"I don't know, Karen..." I replied, and I looked at the photographs on the table. Now that I looked more carefully, I realized that none of them were photos—they were all little paintings, personal portraits. Suddenly, I recognized the scent I'd smelled earlier. Oil paints and thinners. My aunt had been a painter, and I remembered being in her house as a kid and smelling those smells a dozen times. I realized that I'd been so focused on the blood and the body that I'd neglected the apartment itself. I looked more carefully around the room, and, sure enough, there was an easel in the corner, and a box that undoubtedly contained painting supplies. A few old brushes were sitting on the windowsill nearby.

I looked back at the table with the pictures—all of them painted by the same artist, and all of them signed with a little red "A. Raffey" in the corner—and I noticed that above the table, the wall was slightly discolored. There was a large, oval patch on the wall that was slightly lighter in color than the rest of the wall around it—an oval patch with a bare nail near the top of it. And, more to the point, an oval patch that had no blood splattered within it.

"What is it, Tom?" Karen asked.

I looked down at the table again, and I saw that there was a disturbance in the dust, and a gap between two of the picture frames.

"Tony!" I yelled across the room. "See if there's a photo album somewhere."

"A what?" he asked.

"An album, a photo album," I said. "And look for any personal letters—love letters, stuff like that." Tony shook his head, but went into the bedroom to look around.

"What are you looking for, Tom?" Karen asked again.

"There was a portrait hanging here before her murder," I said. "And it was an important one. All of the others are scattered around this table, but this one was special to her—and obviously, to the murderer."

"Maybe Hector Flórez took it when he left?" she suggested.

"No, Carmine would've mentioned that," I said. "Plus, the murderer also took another portrait off of the table—probably a picture of the same person that was in that oval one on the wall."

"So why did you want to know about some love letters?" she asked.

"Because you don't paint a portrait of an acquaintance and put it on the wall above all of your other portraits in a place of distinction," I replied, jotting all of this down in my notebook, and making a special note to have Jenkins do a more thorough background check on Amanda Raffey. "This was someone she cared about…" I turned and looked at her body one more time, as Roecker and the CSI guys were starting to prepare her for transport.

"She had an engagement ring on, but no wedding ring to go with it," I said. "And it was an old ring that she never took off…" They carefully put her body into a bag, making sure not to finish pulling the head off in the process. The last thing that they placed into the bag was her left hand and that old, expensive ring. "Tony?" I called into the other room. "Look for *old* letters, *old* photos. We're looking for someone she knew a long time ago…"

Karen cocked her head to the side. "Are you suggesting that an old lover killed her?" she asked. "What does that have to do with Hector Flórez or international terrorists?"

"I don't know who killed her," I replied honestly, "though I doubt an 80-year-old man chased Hector Flórez down an alley and killed him, too. But I never try to assume anything—I just want to check everything." I looked back at the table with the paintings. "But whoever did this, it sure seems like he didn't want us to see who was in those two portraits."

Just then, Tony popped back into the room with a devilish grin of victory on his face. He was carrying an old shoebox in one hand, and an old, well-worn envelope in the other. "There's at least two dozen o' these in the box, Tom," he said. "Ain't none o' them from this century…"

Karen looked at the oval on the wall behind her and shuddered.

"How could love turn so dark?" she asked.

I didn't have the heart to tell her that not every love is bright to begin with…

Background
**From *La Corruption Fin-de-Siècle* (Léo Taxil, 1891, trans. H.N.
Fitch)**

There is one singular, sadistic passion which is the most frightening
of those most deranged among us who desired to call themselves by the
name of "vampire." These lunatics desire to violate corpses. "The
depravity of this sexual deviancy," said Dr. Paul Moreau de Tours, "is a
most extreme deviation from a healthy form of sexuality…"

It is a common practice in many houses of ill repute to make
available in a "burial crypt" of sorts for their patrons when asked,
complete with black curtains and a deathbed;—in short, a whole gloomy
apparel. But in the most prominent brothels of Paris, these special
chambers are a permanent fixture for their customers who desire to
experience vampirism for themselves.

The walls of the room are draped with black satin, studded with
silver teardrops. In the middle of the chamber is a catafalque, an
exquisitely-adorned raised bier, upon which a woman, apparently
lifeless, lies in an open coffin, her head resting on a velvet cushion. All
around her are long candles, planted in large silver candlesticks. At the
four corners of the room, funerary urns and caskets, burning with
perfume and incense;—a mixture of alcohol and cooking salt;—with
pale flames that illuminate the catafalque, give the flesh of the pseudo-
dead the coloring of a corpse.

The mad deviant, who paid perhaps ten pounds for this meeting, is
ushered into the room. There is a small bench upon which he may kneel
before her body, as if in unholy prayer. An harmonium, situated in a
hidden cabinet, plays the *Dies Irae* or the *De Profundis* to set the somber
mood. As the music of the funeral service builds to its inevitable climax,
the vampire rushes in ecstasy toward the girl, who is simulating the
deceased;—and who has orders not to move, whatever happens…

Chapter 5
William Raffey and Other Fables

Everyone who knew her had always just called her "Mrs. Raffey." The people in her building reported that she was a sweet old woman, and that she liked to teach the children in the building how to paint—years ago, she even volunteered at schools as the "art lady" for the kids. She planted flowers in a window box, and apparently liked chocolate, given the contents of her cupboards. All in all, talking with her neighbors, she sounded like a sweet, old woman. Not at all the type of person you'd expect to be involved with international terrorism or a local street gang.

Aside from an apparent aversion to dusting, she kept up her home fairly well. She had the usual assortment of pill bottles and ointments in her bathroom, old perfumes and clumpy make-up at her changing table in the bedroom, well-worn clothes in her closet, and a cracked, highlighted, and obviously beloved Bible on her nightstand. Nothing out of the ordinary in any of that.

Back in the office, we read through 27 ancient love letters to a young Amanda from "Your beloved William"—who had written in such a florid, old-fashioned style of treacle that I felt like I needed to brush my teeth afterwards ("I know that I should never find a love so sweet as ours, should I search to the world's end and seek for all time..." etc.)— and all from a six-month period from 1960 to 1961. None of them had actually been mailed, so they must have been hand-delivered to her. As we talked with the people in her building, we pieced together that this "William" had to have been William Raffey, her late husband from several decades before. No one could agree about whether he died or just ran off, but certainly no one had ever met the man personally.

Funny thing was, when we looked into her background, we couldn't find that she'd ever actually *been* married. In fact, her name wasn't even *Raffey*—it was really Amanda *Cairns*. She'd never even bothered to have it changed legally, so half of her mail, all of her credit cards, and her driver's license were actually for Amanda Cairns. Instead, she just more or less called herself by that name, and everyone else just followed suit over the years.

Just as strange, as we looked at her old photo albums, it appeared that she'd been a very attractive young woman back in the late '50s and early '60s—and yet, there were no pictures of her with William or any other young man. Oh, there were lots of pictures of her with friends—especially during her teenaged years in the 1950s—but none that appeared to be of her with an obvious young lover. So she'd been a happy, sociable, pretty young woman who'd liked her friends and liked to take pictures… and then, suddenly, she just wasn't anymore. We only found one album with any photos later than 1961, and there were only a handful of pictures in that one, scattered across several decades, and almost none of those were of her. They seemed mostly to be of places rather than people, with a few of a cat that seemed like they'd been taken in the 1980s. And that was it.

Things got even more colorful when we actually tried to dig up some background information about William Raffey. We found roughly a hundred "William Raffeys" across the United States who would be about the right age to have been the guy who'd written those love letters, including two who still lived in the Chicagoland area. Chacon sent Rodriguez and Taylor to check those two out. But Jenkins had done his own detective work and had uncovered another "William Raffey" who'd lived on Dewitt in Chicago in 1961, and who had then apparently dropped off the face of the planet. I was betting that *this* "William Raffey" was the guy we were looking for—on all sorts of levels.

This "William Raffey" was under investigation by the Chicago PD, though they never got around to making an actual arrest. He'd disappeared before they could find him. But the man had no background, no past priors, no *anything* that they could find when they'd done a background check on him back then. But he was apparently a very, very bad boy.

According to what we could piece together, the vice squad had been investigating some reports from a series of prostitutes who had complained about a "john" who'd been abusing them in particularly nasty ways. He didn't even seem to be interested in sex, as much as in inflicting unease, pain, and humiliation on women. More than one of the women reported that he had tied them to the bedposts and—among several other truly repellant things—had made multiple tiny cuts on their bodies, licking up the blood like a dog, grunting and chuckling while he did so. One of them said that she'd screamed for help, but he'd shoved a sock so deeply into her mouth that she'd gagged on it, vomiting. Apparently, this "john" had paid the women and their pimps well enough that most of them had simply chalked it up to a bad experience and pocketed the money, vowing to be more careful the next time in choosing their customers.

But then, on Friday evening, April 28, 1961—three days after the last letter that we'd read from William Raffey to Amanda Cairns, and a week before the scheduled wedding that never occurred—this "john" had gone too far. He had gone to the Edgewater Beach Hotel up on Sheridan, and had picked up a prostitute named Connie Dillard, taking her up to her room. There, whether because things just went too far, or because he couldn't hold back any longer, or whatever, the paraphiliac torture slid into murder. It seemed to investigators that the evening had begun much like all of the others, with the same sorts of cruelties inflicted upon Connie's body as had been perpetrated on the other women up to that point. But somewhere along the line, things became more heated, and the tortures had become more intense. Connie had a golf ball thrust into her mouth, with a gag tied around her to keep her quiet, and the gashes on her body were longer and deeper than the others on the women before. But then, at the end, the "john" had finally slit her throat with some sort of jagged instrument and bled her dry. What struck me, reading the reports, was that, for the 34 separate lacerations on her body, including the rip across her throat, there was actually very little blood on the bed itself. I couldn't help but picture Hector Flórez in that alleyway.

He'd gotten away with far less in the past, but this time, the "john" had made two crucial mistakes, both of which ultimately stemmed from picking Connie Dillard up in such a public manner. First was that, though the perp had apparently been careful not to prowl the same areas twice, for fear of being recognized, one of the other prostitutes at the hotel—one Sheila Benson—had just started working the Edgewater and had immediately recognized him as the same man who'd brutalized her two months earlier when she'd worked the streets farther south. So when Connie's body was found the next morning, Sheila finally broke her silence and went to police with her story, which had then led the homicide detectives to compare notes with the vice cops, and the pattern began to emerge.

The other mistake he'd made was his driver's license. It seems that this same "john" had picked up another prostitute named Kelly "Kiki" Sorenson a few months prior to meeting Sheila Benson, and that she'd taken the opportunity while he was otherwise occupied to rummage through his wallet to see what kind of cash he'd had on him. She'd seen his driver's license, belonging to one "William Raffey," residing on Dewitt. She probably would have never remembered his name, had it not been for the night of torture she'd later endured at his hands—and she certainly never would have approached the police with his name, had it not been for the investigation launched because of Sheila Benson coming forward after the death of Connie Dillard. One domino falling had led to the next, and to the next, and suddenly, William Raffey was the prime suspect for the murder of Connie Dillard.

But that's when the trail had run cold. I have no idea how he'd gotten the driver's license, but William Raffey had never existed in the system prior to August of 1960, and he completely vanished after the murder of Connie Dillard in April of 1961. When the police checked his apartment, he'd cleaned it out completely, as if he'd never been there at all. The manager of the building had never even seen him come in since that night, much less move out all of the furniture and belongings.

The detectives continued the investigation for a little while, of course, but the murder of a prostitute wasn't going to be high on their priority list in 1961. I don't know how many hundreds of people were murdered in the city of Chicago that year, but the hard truth is that a hooker like Connie Dillard wasn't going to be missed. Hey, this was the same year that William "Action" Jackson—a juice loan operator for the Chicago Outfit—was tortured for three days and murdered in a meat plant by "Mad Sam" DeStefano, and it took years to finally pin it on that psychopath. Connie's murder investigation didn't make it past June before it was dropped in the cold case file and forgotten.

Of course, that doesn't mean that her death wasn't important. It was important to Sheila Benson, and it was important to everyone who'd known Connie and cared about her. In fact, you could make an argument that Raffey's little spree, though not well-known to the general public, was also one of the subtle, background factors that led to prostitution finally being declared illegal in the city of Chicago with the passing of the Criminal Code of 1961.

But it was also important to a young woman named Amanda Cairns, who was about to be married the next weekend. She never saw her fiancé again, and I don't even know if she ever even found out *why*, since none of this ever hit the papers. I would have expected that the police would have questioned her about Raffey, but her name wasn't in any of the files—there may have been nothing from his end to connect his life back to hers, and that may very well quietly be the saddest part of the whole affair. It appears that all Amanda knew was that the beautiful young man she'd loved had suddenly just disappeared. As the years passed, she took his name anyway, withdrawing from her friends and family into her own little world. She painted portraits of people, probably because a portrait is a deeply personal thing, and it's got a sense of concreteness and permanence that a snapshot of a cat just can't match—so maybe Amanda felt like painting people meant that they couldn't leave her, like William had. We'll never really know.

But I was left with one particularly unsettling problem that I didn't know what to do with. It looked like Karen might've been right after all—that the man in the portraits may very well have been the same William Raffey who'd murdered Connie Dillard half a century ago, and that he may also have killed Amanda Cairns and Hector Flórez as well. And that's hard to imagine in a septuagenarian...

*   *   *

When I got back to the office from lunch, Pieter Durant was sitting at my desk, tapping away at my computer. God only knows how he got the password to get into the system.

"That's my desk, you know," I said, taking off my jacket and laying it across the chair in from of the desk.

"Mmm..." he muttered without looking up.

"It's my computer, too."

"I am aware of that, Detective Chapel," he replied. "Thank you for extending the courtesy..."

No Armani today, I noticed. Today, Durant was wearing a black Vivienne Westwood—impeccably tailored, of course. And he'd made it a point to pull the jacket forward on his left side as he'd sat down in the chair, but I could still see the telltale bulge of that odd little bag of his that he was trying so hard to hide. He was self-conscious enough about it that he didn't want it to be seen again, but he still wore it nonetheless. It was obviously important, somehow.

I plopped down into the chair in front of my own desk and waited. Durant didn't look at me. I cleared my throat, and Durant didn't respond. Finally, I'd had enough.

"You know," I ventured, "we could probably help you more if you'd share what you know about all of this. I mean, particularly what a gangbanger and an old woman have to do with international terrorism."

"You know all that you are currently required to know, Detective Chapel," he responded, clicking away at the keyboard intently.

"Well, can you at least tell me what you're looking up on my computer?"

"Elements regarding the case."

I sighed. "This is getting old, Inspector," I said. "If you leave us out in the cold, then we can't help you in your investigation, and you're just obstructing ours."

With that, Durant pivoted in the chair to face me. His eyes burned under those bushy brows with an intensity that was almost physically painful.

"Are you officially accusing me of obstruction of justice, Detective?" he growled.

"No," I replied, suddenly realizing the hornet's nest I'd stepped into. "What I'm saying is that—"

"Then I would think that you should choose your words more carefully," he snapped, turning back toward the computer screen. The conversation was over, from his end, and I debated the wisdom of continuing it. Should I press the issue, now that he'd specifically warned me not to? Or should I just drop it—as he obviously wanted me to—and back off yet again? I chose a third option.

"We've got a lead on a possible suspect," I offered, hoping to stir the pot a bit. "We've got to run down some other possibilities, and Tony is checking with a guy called Sweet Jimmy about—"

"Follow whatever leads seem best to you, Detective," he replied. "Simply keep me apprised of any progress that you make."

"That's precisely what I'm *trying* to *do*," I growled back. "But you seem more interested in whatever it is you're doing on my computer than in learning about our investigation." That comment made him turn from the computer screen again and face me. "I'm left to wonder what it is that you're really trying to accomplish here..." He sat and looked at me for what seemed like roughly an hour, and I watched his glare shift from anger to resignation to... something else. Amusement, maybe?

"Presuppositions are the bane of critical thought, Detective," he finally countered. "In 1474, those idiots in Basel, Switzerland, burned a rooster at the stake for witchcraft, since it had lain an egg of so bright a color that they had considered it *unnatural...*"

"But roosters don't even lay eggs," I replied.

"My point exactly, sir," he said, the edge of his mouth turning upward ever so slightly. I didn't even know he was capable of coming that close to merriment. He leaned back in his chair and examined me more carefully, as if sizing me up for something. He pulled out and checked his pocket watch, nodded, and then asked me, "What exactly are *you* trying to accomplish here, Detective?"

"I want to get to the truth," I answered.

"Do you want the truth, or do you want the murderer?" he asked.

"I'm not sure that I understand the distinction," I replied. "Why can't we get both?" His eyes narrowed as he continued staring at me.

"But what if you cannot have both?" he asked again. "What if I could assure you—*guarantee* to you—that the murders would cease, that the killer would be stopped, but you were nonetheless ultimately forced to choose between arresting the culprit and uncovering the truth? Which would you choose? Be honest."

The question caught me off guard, as you could imagine. But something in his eyes suggested to me that he was actually being serious, that he was asking in earnest. His gaze made me want to take the question seriously as well. Which *would* I actually choose?

My first thought, of course, was that we'd want to get the murderer off the streets and behind bars. That's what every good cop is supposed to want, right? But really, the more I thought about it, the more I realized that reason I wanted to make sure that he was off the streets and behind bars was so that he never murdered another innocent person again, that justice was served. If, hypothetically, we guarantee that he would face justice and never murder again, what would my personal priority actually be? If I had to choose between actually putting away the murderer—but never understanding what actually happened that night—and stopping him but *not* putting him away—but actually knowing the truth—which would I really choose?

"I—I'm not sure," I said at last.

"I asked you to be honest," he responded. "Is that your honest answer?"

"It's not a fair question," I countered. "There's no way to guarantee that you'll stop the murderer without either arresting him or killing him."

"But what if there were…?" he asked again. "What if there were a way? Would you be willing to forego an arrest, to leave the case officially unsolved, if it meant that you could unofficially know the truth about what happened to Hector Flórez and Amanda Raffey and stop their killer?"

"Cairns," I corrected.

"Excuse me?"

"Her real name was Cairns, it turns out…"

"Interesting," he muttered, more to himself than to me. "But you appear to be avoiding the question."

"Why do you care?" I asked. And yes, I recognized that I was still avoiding the question.

He leaned forward and pointed to my pistol in its holster on my hip, "I see that you carry a SIG SP2022."

"Yes," I answered, a little confused.

"Chambered for 9x19mm or .40 Smith & Wesson cartridges?"

".40 Smith & Wesson, but I don't see why—"

"Most of your peers carry a Glock these days. The Glock is lighter and can hold three more rounds in its magazine than the SIG Sauer you carry."

"Okay, yes," I replied again, beginning to get a little defensive. "But the action and workmanship on the SIG are just better. I like the feel of it, and I think it's a more accurate piece."

"Detective—"

"And the Navy SEALs carry the SIG," I continued, interrupting *him* for a change, "so that's a pretty good commercial for it, too."

"Detective," he said again, waving his hands in front of him. "I am not attempting to challenge your choice—I'm attempting to *applaud* it. You demonstrate that you are not bound by the pressure of your peers, nor are you particularly swayed by their preferences. I find that most interesting."

Was that a compliment? Did the scary ice man just compliment me?

"You appear to be a man who desires first and foremost to do the right thing, and that is to be admired," he continued. "You make your own decisions, and you do so intelligently. And you are not afraid to endanger your own career to do the right thing, though you do not act recklessly."

Now, I wasn't so sure that I liked where these compliments were going.

"So I ask you again, Detective—do you want an arrest, or do you want the truth?"

I met his gaze as I thought about the question, and I knew that I already knew the answer.

"I won't stop until I know the truth, Inspector," I said. "Though I'd also *like* an arrest..."

He nodded, then turned back to the computer to continue typing. I really couldn't tell whether I'd passed his test or flunked it royally. But I couldn't resist asking a question of my own.

"So... What about that *got uechan* of yours?" I asked. "What kind of sidearm do *you* carry, Inspector Durant?"

"Interpol agents do not carry firearms, Detective," he replied without missing a beat or looking back at me. "But then, certainly, you know that already." And that was the end of his willingness to converse with me.

Luckily, that's also when Tony de Tullio poked his head in the door with a sneaky grin on his face. "Hey, Tom," he said. "Come 'ere fer a sec, will ya?" Durant was obviously done with me, and Tony wasn't coming into the office, so I got up from the chair and walked over to the door.

"What's up, Tony?"

"I figured ya didn't want the creep in on this," he nodded toward Durant, "but Sweet Jimmy got us a meet with el Buitre."

"That's great, Tony. Maybe we can prep by—"

"It's *now*, Tom," he interrupted. "It's *right now*..."

Background
From *Personal Papers* (Inspector Franz Dürrenmatt, trans. [1938] K. Gunnar)

14th April, 1924, Coblenz;—Finally, a lead in the murders, after the deaths of seven children have yielded nothing but frustration. A witness saw a glimpse of the murderer as he exited the school where young Grethe Volkmann was slain last evening, and described a stocky man with large, piercing eyes, dressed in a dark coat, who seemed to melt into the night-time fog of the damp street. The witness also said that he'd heard a faint musical sound, but could not make it out from where he was standing.

It is not much to go on, but no investigation is simple. It's all in the reports in the office.

15th April, 1924, Coblenz;—Conflicting reports from witnesses about the large-eyed man in the neighborhood near the Kindergarten where Grethe Volkmann was murdered. Some who saw a man near the Schulstraße on 13th April fitting that description said that he was small-ish and slightly hunched, while others described him as of medium height and build. One elderly man said he stopped and spoke with the man, and reports that his accent sounded English or American, while a young couple who spoke with what appears to be the same man swear that his accent was Bavarian.

The coroner has verified that Grethe was bled dry by the same means as the other children, and that she died within minutes. It is a cold comfort to know that she did not suffer. But this matter has now reached the Parlewuhs, and they have put a lid on any news being printed that might cast their occupation in a negative light, so at least we have little to fear about meddling from the press.

17th April, 1924, Coblenz;—As I suspected, our French masters have begun to muddle this with their interference. I was visited at my office today by one Hptm. B———[1], of their Deuxième Bureau. I have heard

---

[1] *In the original German copy of these records, the name "Benoît" is*

tell that, during the War, he had been attached to the AEF, but why an intelligence operative has any purpose in a murder investigation is beyond me.

The man himself seems pleasant and competent enough, of course, but it is his very presence which offends me most. The mandate that we must work with this Franzmann is a constant reminder that we are a conquered people in our own land, and I have already found myself second-guessing my instincts in order to placate this man, and this is never helpful in an investigation.

Still, B——— brings some resources to the case which would not otherwise be available to us. I can now access city records that have been closed to me since the occupation began, and he has offered to help with any information uncovered during the War which might shed light on the investigation. We will see.

18th April, 1924, Coblenz;—Yet another murder last night. A little boy called Hermann Fischer. This time, the child was killed in his own bed, while his parents slept soundly in the room next door to him. God in Heaven, please give us something tangible to work with to stop this monster.

19th April, 1924, Coblenz;—Fingerprints found on the window of Hermann Fischer have matched those of a war profiteer known to the Deuxième Bureau. Though the name "Harold Kalk" was almost certainly an alias, it nonetheless gives us something to work with, as the French had compiled several records regarding this man during the War. It appears that Herr "Kalk" had posed as a doctor, and had used the War and the subsequent shortages to purvey illegal pharmaceuticals to both sides of the conflict. Nothing is known of him since 17th November, 1919, when he somehow miraculously escaped from a trap laid for him by police in nearby Rüdesheim. Some accounts, however, suggest that Herr "Kalk" may have escaped to the Americas, which I believe may help to explain the discrepancies in witness accounts regarding his accent.

Hptm. B——— is tracking down a photograph of Herr "Kalk" which we might use to help run him to ground, and he has promised to bring me the dossier which the Deuxième Bureau had compiled so that I might better study his habits and behaviours.

21st April, 1924, Coblenz;—Back in the office today, after visiting

---

handwritten over the typed "B———" but it is impossible to verify this name one way or the other, since the relevant records of both the Deuxième Bureau de l'État-major general and the modern Service de Documentation Extérieure et de Contre-Espionnage remain sealed.

Hedda's family in Darmstadt yesterday afternoon. They complained about us not bringing their grandchildren with us, but I am quite used to their complaints by now, and I stood unfazed. I was, however, the victim of quite a tongue-lashing from Hedda on the drive home last night, and am happy to be in the office instead of at home.

Hptm. B——— had both a photograph of our suspect, "Harold Kalk," and his dossier on my desk when I arrived. I find myself beginning to appreciate B——— and his professionalism. If he weren't a Parlewuh, I may actually have liked the man.

"Kalk" had dark hair, a full face, and large, hooded eyes that burrowed into me when I looked at the photograph. There was a note, however, that due to an accident of some sort, "Kalk" no longer looked the same, though no specific differences were noted. Typical Parlewuh incompetence there. But apparently, sometime in the autumn of 1919, this "Kalk" was involved in some sort of attack on his person while traveling in Hanover (apparently at the hands of the murderer Fritz Haarmann) which had changed both the man and his habits. He became reclusive, and never ventured forth, even to carry out his business activities, during daylight hours. The French conjectured that he was terrified to be seen, self-conscious due to unspecified scars brought about by the attack, but I suspect that narrowly escaping from the hands of a maniac such as Haarmann creates its own scars of an inward variety.

Apparently, the police at Köln were seeking Herr "Kalk" for his illegal activities, and had some difficulty finding him, much less apprehending him, in their own district, and were able to discern somehow that he was heading in our direction. I do vaguely remember the bulletin five years ago, telling us to be on the look-out for this man, but there were so many fugitives from the law in those early post-war days that they all begin to blur in the mind. He apparently passed through Coblenz at some point and was in hiding in Rüdesheim. Apparently, according to the French records, the house he was in had been surrounded by officers, they had visual confirmation that he was inside of the house, and the only exits were the front and rear doors. And yet, somehow, he had been able to walk straight through their siege and escape. The officer in charge, Lt. de F———, reported that, once the light had dimmed at dusk, he had simply vanished; but there was also a handwritten, anonymous report in the dossier that Herr "Kalk" had merely walked out of the back door, and, somehow, just *talked* the officers at the rear into letting him past. As one of the officers was quoted as saying, "Il était logique de compléter à la fois pour lui permettre de passé, bien que j'ai maintenant ne sais pas pourquoi…"[2]

---

[2]   *"It made total sense at the time to allow him past us, though I don't know why now."*

I have ordered that copies of the photograph be posted around the city, and we have also sent for Herr Dr. Erich M———, an alienist who teaches psychology at the University of Frankfurt, to ask if he could try to help us to understand the motivations behind a man who hunts and murders children. Though, I confess, I am not at all certain that I truly wish to understand the mind of such a man.

22nd April, 1924, Coblenz;—Another murder last night. We have no way to know when or where this fiend will strike next, and the whole city appears to be his hunting grounds. The lifeless, bloodless body of young Kurt Staudinger was found just outside of his home on the Kurfürstenstraße. I feel impotent to help, and I fear for my own little Friedrich, though Giesl should be old enough to be outside of the range of his depredations. I have asked both of my children to stay indoors once the sun goes down, and I have taken to checking the lock on their window each evening when they retire, and sitting in the doorway of their room all night with my pistol in my lap. This cannot continue.

I was made all the more uncomfortable today by the interaction which Hptm. B——— and I had with Herr Dr. M———, who finally attended our invitation and joined us just as I was about to leave the office to come home. He is a strange man with a commanding presence, and I found it frustrating how many persons in our office deferred to him, as if he were the chief of police or the Lord Mayor. Even I confess that I shared more of the information of the case with him than I had originally intended, such was his ability to persuade. He has the voice of a lecturer.

When we shared with him why we had sent for him, he admitted that he had not heard of the case before, which I found strange. He teaches in Frankfurt, not Munich;—I should think that our horror would be quite well-known in Frankfurt by now. Nonetheless, I am unfamiliar with the eccentricities of academics, and we were obliged to inform him of the facts in their entirety. He seemed particularly moved by the photographs of the crime scenes, saying, "Such beautiful children, brought down so long before their prime..."

Dr. M——— believes this murderer to be a psychopath, a man who kills without logical reason or discernible motive. To the psychopath, there needs be no motive for a given murder beyond a personal gratification received from the act itself;—thus, the psychopath does not need to murder out of a perceived need for personal revenge, or to cover a robbery, or any of the other common motives which help us stop them. Thus, we have little way of finding this creature before he strikes again.

Dr. M——— specifically addressed "Kalk's" probable mental state when he commits these crimes. "To Kalk," he said, "people are playthings, non-persons. He does not see them as being peers or individuals, but rather as objects to be used for his own purposes, as he sees fit." He then cited the illegal pharmaceutical trade that "Kalk" had engaged in during the War, and the people who died because of his substandard or tainted drugs, as an obvious indication of a lack of moral conscience when it comes to others. "It may be," he said, "that he feels no morality whatsoever, that he is a moral and emotional void inside, and these murders are a means of forcing himself to approximate the ability to feel anything at all."

We asked Herr Doktor why the murderer targeted children. "It could simply be the obvious, that they are the softest, most defenseless, and thus the easiest to kill," he said. "But more likely, there is something about their beauty, their innocence, which compels him to slaughter them. Perhaps his own innocence was lost at an early age, and he wishes to punish these children for enjoying what he himself cannot. Or perhaps he simply abhors the very concept of innocence and vitality which these children represent. One cannot know the mind of such a fiend without meeting him personally."

I confess that our all-too-brief meeting with Dr. M———, though somewhat informative, provided no insight which I can see that could help our investigation. Perhaps "Kalk" does hate children because of what they represent. Perhaps his own father beat him once too often as a child and now his brain is scrambled within his skull. Perhaps a fairy mouse comes to him each night, inciting him to murder. But how does any of that actually help us in finding the monster, or in preventing his next murder?

Dr. M——— made a telephone call to a colleague of his at the Berlin Psychoanalytic Institute, hoping that he might also be able to come out to consult with us within the week, but it seems that the earliest we might be able to expect him to come to Coblenz would be perhaps next Monday, the 28th. Until then, we are at the mercy of a phantom who strikes at will, and then disappears. No grocer has seen him, no passers-by during the day, no neighbors, no one but those who have seen him near a murder scene.

As he left my office, Dr. M——— made a disturbing comment. He said, "I doubt that you shall ever capture this man, Herr Inspector. Such criminals are often beyond the abilities of local constabulary." At first, I thought that my discomfort was due to my own pride, and my frustration at being told that my office was too incompetent to bring the creature to justice. But as I've thought about it more at length at home this evening, I believe that it was more due to his manner when saying it. It almost seemed as if he were being more than just condescending;—it was as if he were being prideful, as if he resonated more with the criminal than with the police. It could simply be his extensive experience as an alienist and his work to understand the unhealthy minds of the mentally disturbed, or it could be that I am simply too tired and I am taking things overly personally, but one wonders about his own upbringing and allegiances.

23rd April, 1924, Coblenz;—This Dr. M——— made me so uncomfortable at the end of his visit that I investigated his background a bit this morning. He has been teaching classes at the University of Frankfurt for only the past eighteen months, and has been instrumental in helping them develop their Institute for Social Research, alongside Herr Dr. Kurt G———, who subsequently died suddenly under strange circumstances. On a hunch, I took his fingerprints from the telephone receiver, and I am having them checked against any known criminals. I also asked Hptm. B——— to check his prints against their files at the Deuxième Bureau, to see if he had been involved in any activities during the War. B——— was happy to help in this, as he sees the Institute as a harbinger of socialism and fascism, and thus a dangerous influence. I believe that B——— is an alarmist, but in his position, I suppose that is to be expected.

23rd April, 1924, Coblenz;—My God, Dr. M——— *is* Harold Kalk. He is much changed from his photograph, unrecognizably changed, though he still maintains those large, hard, dark eyes. The monster stood in my office just this Tuesday, discussing the case with absolute detachment. I have seen murderers and miscreants in my years, but I have never beheld such cold and unadulterated evil as this man. His comment about the beauty of the children now chills me to my bones.

Hptm. B——— and I have agreed upon a course of action. Dr. M——— does not know that we are aware of his true identity, nor that we now know that he is the murderer whom we seek. We have therefore invited him back to the office for one more consultation on the case. With luck and prayer, he will walk back to us of his own accord, and we will make an end of this. We must make an end of this. He was standing in my own office, damn his soul!

25th April, 1924, Coblenz;—I have tendered my resignation from the police, and I will continue this on my own. Hedda does not understand, nor do I expect her to. But this must end.

Hptm. B——— and I carried out our plans perfectly, and Herr Dr. M——— strolled into my office this evening as if he had not a care in the world. I had three of my officers discreetly block the exits from the office, while B——— and I began speaking to Dr. M——— at my desk. Everything appeared to be working out, even better than I could have expected. But then, when I pulled my pistol out and accused Dr. M——— of being "Harold Kalk";—and, therefore, our murderer;—he simply smiled. B——— was as unsettled by this as I was.

"This will never do, Herr Inspector," he said. "I will never be taken into a jail cell, not even for one evening." I disregarded this as vain rantings, and B——— proceeded to bring out a pair of handcuffs to restrain him. "Hptm. B———," he continued, "how important is Adolf Hitler to you?"

B——— froze as if a statue. "Qu'avez-vous dit?"[3] he asked. Dr. M——— smiled all the more, yet I was confused. Everyone has heard of Hitler, of course, after that mess in Munich and the ridiculous trial that followed. What had Hitler to do with any of this? The man is rotting in prison in Bavaria, and will be for the next five years. His little band of political extremists has broken up, even with all of the publicity that the trial churned up. I could not see the connection.

"We at the Institute for Social Research have a great deal of information about both Hitler and his movement," Dr. M——— continued, casually eating an indigestion tablet, "and about the inevitable rise of national socialism in the German Empire. How important would that information be to you?"

I realized that B——— had not moved forward, and so I urged him to continue with the arrest. He responded, "C'est plus compliqué que vous le comprenez, Dürrenmatt,"[4] and stepped back from Dr. M———, setting the handcuffs on my desk.

"No, it isn't!" I cried. "No, it isn't! This monster is a murderer!"

Dr. M——— continued smiling, and his rich voice seemed to fill the room with his presence. I noticed that the officers had left their posts at the exits to listen;—but, God help me, I do not know why that seemed completely appropriate to me at the time. But I believe that something about his voice made all of us want to listen to him, just as those officers at Rüdesheim had done five years ago and let this creature escape from them then.

"In exchange for immunity and for a new life elsewhere," Dr. M——— offered, "I shall tell you everything that I know about Herr Hitler and his people, and what I know shall happen next."

"Don't do this, B———," I begged. "Hitler is an idiot, and he's in prison at Landsberg. He's no threat to anyone, political or otherwise."

But B——— insisted that Hitler "n'est pas un imbécile mais un très adroit demagogue,"[5] likening him to Mussolini, but far more dangerous and less ridiculous. I have no idea if B——— truly believes this, or if is the horrific strength of Dr. M———'s powers of persuasion that have convinced him, but either way, B——— has officially released Dr. M——— into the custody of the Deuxième Bureau. The fiend is free to kill

---

[3]   *"What did you say?"*

[4]   *"This is more complicated than you understand, Dürrenmatt."*

[5]   Hitler *"is not an idiot, but rather a very cunning demagogue."*

again, and I just stood there and allowed him to walk away to freedom. It was as though I were in a fog, and all of this seemed like a dream from which I could not wake myself. How could I let him walk out of there? What have I done?

As he left my office with B——, Dr. M—— smiled fully, and, God in Heaven, I believe that I saw fangs glint in the light. He is a monster who must be stopped. What have I done?

<u>*3rd August, 1924, Solingen*</u>[6];—Almost caught up to the creature in Düsseldorf, but he slipped through my fingers yet again. I had forgotten to bathe this week, and the authorities were alerted to my presence by a shopkeeper who complained that I was a vagrant. I was taken to the edge of town, even though I explained that I had been a former inspector of police in Coblenz, and that I was hunting a vampyr who was being sheltered by the government. They are fools. I must remember to contact Hedda and the children, as I have not spoken to them since June. But so long as I stay in pursuit of the fiend and keep him in front of me, I know that they remain safe at home. I am also convinced now that the creature had hunted in Berlin in 1921 as well, going by the alias of "Karl Großmann" at the time, though I have no access to his fingerprints, and the photographs do not match. But I also know that this monster is a master of obfuscation, and that he can apparently distort his features so as to deceive even the most discerning eye. It makes it all the more difficult to follow his trail, but I pray that God will keep my path clear. One wonders which of the people on this very street he may be.

<u>*20th September, 1924, Dortmund*</u>;—Lost him lost him lost him lost him again. Again! Must remember to sleep every day so that I stay alert. Everyone seems to be helping him. Are they all under his control now? Am I the only sane man left in Germany? Why won't anyone believe me?

<u>*17th October, 1924, Braunschweig*</u>;—I have not stopped my pursuit of this fiend, nor will I ever stop. I can no longer afford hotel rooms, but I have been staying in my automobile at night, and that is sufficient until the weather truly fouls. I telephoned Hedda yesterday from the local post office to ask about the children, but she continues to call me "obsessed," as if the problem were somehow with me, and she refuses to answer any of my questions. I understand that she has finalized the divorce proceedings, and that she has no desire to see me again, but that cannot undermine my efforts to locate and destroy this creature.

---

[6]   *This section is handwritten, as were almost all of the entries written after April of 1924.*

According to an old friend of mine now with the Freikorps, the monster has been relocated to Berlin ("so as to avoid friction with the political extremist groups of the outerlying German states, and unnecessary interactions with criminal elements with whom he had been previously associated"), and has been given yet another alias;—"Hans Beckert." The authorities will never stop this thing. No one but I can stop his assault on our children. No one else seems to even care. Why are they letting him do this? Why? I am traveling to Berlin tomorrow to finish this. God help me and God help us all.[7]

---

[7] *This section is the final entry in Dürrenmatt's papers. The former inspector was never seen in Berlin nor heard from again.*

Chapter 6
The Vulture Is a Scavenger

"fnd anther lead w/saliva n nail," Karen texted me while Tony drove us to the meet with Buitre. "im on th L. chk w/u whn i get home." I texted her back that we'd probably still be a little busy, but that I'd call her later. "gd," she responded. "i dont like L anymr. kids kp bthrng me." I laughed and told Tony what she'd written.

"Yep," he replied. "I never did get why you an' Joanna made so many…"

"Well, your *own* kids are great," I answered as I texted her to tell their mothers to shut them up. "It's everyone *else's* kids that are monsters…"

"lol," she texted back. "not ltl kds. teens kp bmpng me n laffng. ltl scry."

I replied that it was probably nothing, but that she should stay in well-populated areas, and, if she felt like they were threatening her at all, she should look for a cop on the platform when she got off. Most importantly—don't go anywhere alone.

"nprob," she texted back as we pulled up to a stop light. "stil wish u were here ☺"

I smiled, and I noticed that Tony was reading that last text while we waited for the light to turn green. "Ask you a question?"

"Sure, Tony. What?"

Tony cleared his throat before he spoke again. "How comfortable'd you be showin' Joanna a cute lil' exchange like that?" The light turned green, but he still sat there, looking at me.

"I'm not sure what you mean," I lied.

"Yeah," he said with a sigh. "An' yer the detective, right?"

"Listen," I snapped back. "She's just a nice girl, and she's scared. She's a friend, that's all."

He pulled out into the intersection. "Hey, I ain't sayin' she ain't pretty an' all," and before I could interrupt to respond, he added, "an' I ain't sayin' that you're sleepin' with her or nothin'—I'm just sayin' that there's *all kinds* o' cheatin', buddy, an' ain't all of it physical, ya know?"

"I've never cheated on Joanna," I growled quietly. "Not ever. Not even when we were dating. And I'm not about to start now."

"An' I never did cheat on Nita"—Juanita, his ex-wife—"until I finally did. An' by then, I realized that I'd been kinda cheatin' on her fer a while, at least 'tween my ears…"

"Then what gives you the right to lecture me on anything, huh?"

Tony swerved over to the side of the road and squealed on the brakes. He turned to me and pointed his three-fingered hand at me, glaring.

"I'm the guy what loves you an' Joanna and yer stupid kids!" he shouted. "An' I'm the guy what's done way too much stupid crap that I don' wanna see *you* start doin'!"

I sat there, looking at him, and knowing—at least a part of me knew, though I wouldn't admit it—that he might just have a point. No, I wasn't having an affair with Karen Gage. No, I didn't *want* to have an affair with her. But suddenly, I had to admit that it felt awfully attractive to be someone's knight in shining armor again, to see that gleam in her eyes when you walk into the room. I hadn't consciously recognized it, but I think I'd been enjoying it anyway. To be honest, I'd never really thought about any of it before Tony brought it up, but the moment that he did, I'd felt an immediate pang of guilt, like I'd been unconsciously leading her on because it'd made me feel *good* to lead her on.

I remember a pastor when I was a kid saying that there are really only two reactions to being shown your guilt by someone else— repentance, or spite. I'd automatically jumped for spite. But, while we're being honest, I'll tell you that I think that most people usually do. It's a hard thing to own up to something you're ashamed to admit to, to even *think* about being guilty of. I couldn't tell him that he was right, but I couldn't tell him that he was wrong. So I just sat there, boiling in my own spite.

And he just sat there, glaring at me.

We waited in silence for what was probably just a minute, but felt like maybe a week, until I finally broke the tension.

"El Buitre's waiting," I muttered. Tony sighed and pulled back into traffic.

*   *   *

Tony and Sweet Jimmy had set up a meet with Buitre at lunchtime in a public place where we'd both feel safe. Within reason, of course. We drove through Logan Square to Bucktown, following the Blue Line to a little Latino/Korean fusion restaurant in the shadow of the tracks. I mean, really—where else are you going to find an all-beef Chicago hot dog topped with kimchi salsa and egg noodles?

Bucktown itself is kind of a fusion joint, when you think about it. It started off with European immigrants—Polish and Germans who never did learn to speak English. Then, about a generation ago, there was a big influx of low-income African Americans and Latinos, mostly Puerto Ricans, because the property values had fallen low enough that they could afford to live there. That changed everything. Forget the gangs— the *neighbors* had turf wars. Within a few years, the whole place had become a war zone, and after the gangs moved in, the area was a zoo.

But that's not all. Because of the affordability and the "local color," the new Bohemians started moving in over the past decade. Cheap bistros and goofy, trendy shops took over the gritty neighborhoods, and these days, you'll be just as likely to see a 20-something computer programmer with a knit hat in the summertime on the sidewalk as you would be to see an elderly German or a middle-aged Puerto Rican... and far *less* likely, at the moment, as you would be to see one of the Orquestra Albany. They seemed to be just about everywhere we looked.

We pulled up to the restaurant, and three OA's were standing outside, looking about as casual as a West Point review. They knew exactly who we were—they'd started coming up to the car, with their hands already reaching under their jackets, undoubtedly fingering automatic weapons, before we'd even opened the doors. Their job was to keep noncombatants out of the restaurant during the meeting... and to keep an eye on Tony and me.

That's why it surprised me when a tall redhead came out of the restaurant while we were getting ready to go in. Tony and I were each standing there, with our arms raised up while the OA's frisked us for weapons, when she'd walked past us. I have to admit that I was stunned—she was one of the most strikingly beautiful women I'd ever seen, even with her eyes hidden behind her mirrored Yves Saint Laurent sunglasses and her long legs hidden under her green Trussardi jacket. Maybe it was just her fashion sense, but somehow, she reminded me of Durant. On so many levels, this was not the kind of woman you'd expect to find walking out of the Belly Shack in Bucktown. And not today, of all days.

She smiled seductively as she glided past us, and here's the weirdest part—she smiled at *Tony*. Now, I'm not saying that I'm all that easy on the eyes, necessarily, but *Tony?* Coke-swigging, chain-smoking, belly-bouncing Tony de Tullio with the perpetually stained shirts? That's just unnatural. And don't think that Tony didn't notice it, too. He grinned from ear to ear, which just made her smile all the more, though she never even slowed down as she continued past us and down the street.

"Y'see that, Tom?" he asked, beaming.

"I saw it, Tony..."

"She wanted me!"

"She wanted to *laugh* at you," I responded.

"Oh, no," Tony came back quickly. "She was totally into me." And I had to admit that, almost unimaginably, it sure had seemed like that at the time. But our conversation about Tony's potential love life was cut short by the gangstas who'd finished frisking us.

"Inside!" they ordered, and inside we went.

The place was cleared out, except for several OA's and a few very nervous-looking employees behind the counter. El Buitre himself was sitting at a stool at one of the tables in a corner, scooping up his barbequed beef with some flatbread. At his side stood two of his lieutenants—an ape with crossed arms whom I didn't know, and a slender Puerto Rican whom I knew only too well. His name was Raphael Camacho, but everyone called him "The Angel"—and not because of his disposition. Rumor had it that he picked up the name because every time someone saw an angel in the Bible, their first inclination was naturally to be afraid of them, and it was no different with Camacho. He was about average height, and his lean physique made you underestimate how physically tough he was. But what made the Angel so dangerous was what lay beneath those dreadlocks—a cold, calculating, utterly amoral mind. He'd been a numbers runner for the OA's back a few years ago, but had made his way up the ranks over time to be second only to Buitre by being ruthlessly smart. I'd run into him two years earlier, after he'd been part of an assault on a family down on Lyndale. Apparently, a Logan Square grocer had refused to pay his protection money, and the Angel had taken it out on his family instead of on his store ("You want a egg, you don' strangle the goose," he'd been quoted as saying, "you jus' crack a freakin' egg…"). One son was hospitalized, one daughter was ultimately institutionalized, and the mother was forced to watch the whole thing, along with the other children. We began our investigation, but the grocer suddenly dropped all charges against the OA's, saying that he'd been confused, that the Angel and the gang were not the ones who'd brutalized his family, that none of his family could remember anything more about the crime, and that he refused to help us out in any way. His wife ended up divorcing him and moved away with their kids fairly soon after that. A little over a week later, the store was closed, denying the Angel his "goose" after all—so the next morning, it was looted and burned to the ground. Within a day, someone had spray-painted yellow OA symbols all over the charred remains.

The Angel smiled as we walked toward the table, and I have to admit it—my first inclination was to be a little scared. I couldn't help but think of Joanna and the kids.

And then there was el Buitre himself. His head was huge, and yet his neck was thicker than his head. He looked like a linebacker for the Bears, only tougher. He was dark-skinned, though not as dark as the

Angel standing next to him, and his bald head was covered in black tattoos. Packs of dragons and tigers all wrapped around the letters IOAN on one side and 30C on the other, their tails curling onto his cheekbones and down into his black beard—and then past his beard, down his neck, disappearing into his shirt. But most prominent of all his tattoos was the vulture whose wings spread over the top of his head, and whose neck and head dominated his forehead, ending at the bridge of his nose. The tattoos kind of reminded me of those tā moko tattoos that you see on Maori tribesmen, but talk on the street was that he was originally Chilean, though he was obviously a bit of a fusion himself—surrounded by all of that darkness covering his face and head, Buitre's bright, blue eyes shone out like pale sapphires. He finished his beef and then licked his fingers clean, one by one.

"You wan' talk wif me, eh?" he broke the silence, finally. The Angel cocked his head and smiled again, waiting for my reply.

"I know that you probably know more about these murders than we do, Buitre," I answered. "And I know that you're as concerned about them as we are."

"Wha' murders, ese?" he replied. "Wha' you talkin' about, eh?" The Angel and the ape both laughed with Buitre. I hate these kinds of territorial games, but when you're dealing with a tribal mentality, they're just part of the process.

"Lissen," Tony growled. "You guys got a situation here—"

"Shut you face, cracker!" the Angel interrupted. "You let the *men* talk, no?" The ape uncrossed his arms and took one step toward Tony, but Buitre motioned him to stay where he was.

"Hector Flórez and Amanda Raffey," I answered. "Both of them in your territory." El Buitre just sat there, looking at me. "Both of them bled like a slaughtered pig." Still no response. "Any of this sound familiar at all?"

"You sayin' something, Chapel?" the Angel asked at last, and it concerned me more than just a little bit that he knew me by name.

"It could be the Latin Kings," I responded, trying to move the implication of guilt away from the OA's. "And maybe you think so, too, with so many of your soldiers out on the streets these days."

"They respec' they *jefe*, you know?" Buitre said. "They out there, showin' they respec'…"

"I know that they respect you, Buitre," I replied. "But I know that they're also showing they're more than just a little scared."

"You don' know nothin', ese!" Buitre growled, and his voice grew louder. "You belong to me! Que podría comer su corazón y beber su sangre, si yo quería! I *own* you, Paco!" He started to stand, but the Angel put his hand on his shoulder and leaned down to whisper something into his ear. Buitre nodded and visibly relaxed. "No me empuje..." he grumbled as his body eased back onto the stool.

"I'm not trying to push you, Buitre," I replied. "I just know that you know something—and you're preparing for it."

"No se puede preparar suficiente para este, ese..." he said with a sigh. "They no way to prepare for this—you don' know, man..."

"Then enlighten me," I said. "Tell me what's going on. Who are you preparing for war against? Tell me what you know about these killings."

El Buitre looked over at the Angel, who shrugged in response. Tony was about to say something stupid—I could see it on his face—but I reached over and put a hand on his wrist to stop him, shaking my head.

"Why I should tell you, ese?" he asked, building up his frustration again. "Maybe we jus' gonna pick up the pieces when this all is over, you know? Maybe we wan' everyone good an' miedo, eh?" But I could tell that *he* was scared—and that he was already well on his way to convincing himself to tell me what he knew. "Soy bien chingón ..."

"I know that you're pretty tough, Buitre," I replied. "But I still think that you'll tell me what we need to know—because if you're that tough, and you've still got that many soldiers out on the street about all of this, I don't think that you'd mind having some soldiers in blue out there, too."

Buitre closed his eyes and muttered something under his breath that I couldn't make out. After a moment, he opened his eyes again and nodded at the Angel, who then leaned over and whispered something to the ape. The big man barked at everyone else in the room, "Todos ustedes—lárgate de aquí!" The place cleared out immediately, including the employees who were back in the kitchen. Within a few seconds, only the five of us were left within earshot.

"You gonna lissen, eh?" Buitre asked me, leaning over on his stool.

"Of course I am," I assured him.

Buitre dipped a handful of his spiced fries into the last bit of curry mayo, and then stuffed them into his mouth. "I know who killin' all these people, *ese*, but you no' gonna like it..." he said, chewing with his mouth open.

"Try me," I replied. Buitre finished gulping down his mouthful of fries, glanced one more time toward the Angel, and then cleared his throat.

"Es un *vampiro*, man..."

*   *   *

"That may've been the single dumbest waste o' time I ever took part in," Tony grumbled at me as we got back into the car.

"Probably," I responded. "But, for the record, it was your idea to begin with."

"Yer a butt-wipe," Tony snarled, glowering at me.

"Classy…" I chuckled. But then, I sat back and thought more about it. "You know, though, it may not have been such a big waste after all."

"What, you mean we should bust out the garlic an' holy water?"

"No," I replied. "But I really think el Buitre actually believed what he was saying. I think that he really thinks that it's a vampire we're looking for."

"Then he's a idiot."

"Arguably so, but the Angel isn't," I countered. "I don't think that it was the OA's that killed Flórez and Cairns, and there's some reason why they don't think this it was the Latin Kings, either. In and of itself, that's some progress."

"So we're lookin' fer Bela Lugosi?"

"No," I said, "but it sounds like we may not be looking for a gang. Maybe he's a lone killer with a vampire fetish or something?"

"Naw," Tony said. "No one guy coulda done all that—and sure not to a guy like Hector Flórez…"

Both of us would have kept chewing on the problem, but that's when my cell phone rang. I was shocked by who was on the other end of the line. It was none other than Billy "the Kid" Rivers, calling from up in Roscoe Village. I know that I'd given him my card, but I never really seriously thought that he'd actually make the effort get back to me.

"Billy," I answered, catching Tony's attention—who mouthed the words "the Kid?" in total surprise as I nodded. "What's up, Billy?"

"I think I've got something for you, Chapel," he said, "if you're still interested."

"Absolutely," I replied. "What did you find out?"

"Well, it seems that our little friend, Hector—"

And that's when my cell phone battery died.

Background
From *De Dødes Bog* (Peer van Draeck, 1642, trans. K. Nooteboom)

Any primer on vampires, I should think, must begin with an exposition of the nature of evil, since vampires are, ultimately, simply that—walking evil. We have watched the conception of evil shift and change dramatically over the centuries, and perhaps we have forgotten much of the nature of that which we fear… or, perhaps more accurately, of that which we now far too often do *not* fear.

Today, people fear what they do not know (whether that unknown is evil or not) and they fear that which causes them pain (whether that pain is ultimately for their own good or not). Thus, we have seemed to have forgotten to truly fear evil—we simply fear those unseen things in the dark which may cause us discomfort, and we call *those* things "evil."

But what is unknown to us—*since* it is unknown to us—could just as easily bring good fortune to us as ill fortune. And even what we often consider ill fortune could, in the long run, actually be for our benefit or the benefit of others. We abhor pain and discomfort, even though they are integral parts of maturation, parts of childbirth, parts of many of the elements of life which we otherwise cherish. We would flee from pain and discomfort, even when to do so would stunt our maturation, undermine the glory of giving birth, or in some other way remove us from the truly wonderful gifts in life which the Lord has bestowed upon us. In short, we often remove ourselves from the good, simply because of the uncertainty or potential discomforts which that good may bring into our lives as well—and, in doing so, we often wrongly equate those uncertainties or discomforts with evil.

But when it comes to *true* evil, we are far too often oblivious. We see some immorality as familiar, and since it *is* familiar and predictable, we dismiss it as "just the way things are," and we defer from seeing it as actually evil. Or we see some immorality as pleasurable, and since it *is* pleasurable and brings us at least a temporary enjoyment, we diminish it as "just a little bit of naughty fun," and we defend our right to participate in it—and not only to participate in it, but to do so without having to face the unpleasant accusation that one is doing something "evil" by doing it.

But evil is, by definition, *selfish*. It is not at its core sexually enticing, or exciting, or empowering. At its core, evil simply wants its own way, its own passions, its own pleasures, its own pride, and it will approximate sensuality, or excitement, or empowerment in order to achieve its own satisfaction. But it is a hollow satisfaction at best, and one which always leaves the participant feeling hollow in its wake, because its supposed "benefits" are always mere shadows, deviant echoes of real objects of joy which God has created—it does not yield a genuine fulfillment of a long-lasting love, but only the temporary sating of a selfish lust (whether that lust be for sexual fulfillment, personal power, monetary gain, or any other phantom that would seem to be a satisfying joy at its outset).

Vampires are simply the clearest physical example of this sinful perspective. They have no life themselves, but only a tainted approximation of it. The sating of their hunger only leaves them all the more ravenous the next night. And—romanticized fallacies aside—they do not care for anyone or anything but themselves (though they are certainly not beyond a pretense of affection in order to suit their purposes). They are the purest expressions of Satan's "quod vis fac,"[1] and the farthest antithesis from Christ's "non mea voluntas sed tua fiat."[2] Where our Lord was willing to give His blood to provide eternal life for others, the vampire sustains itself by stealing the blood of others to perpetuate its own temporary, shadowy un-life. As I shall endeavor to explain in the following examples, this is only one of the many ways in which the vampire is an intentional corruption of Christ.

---

[1] *"Do whatever you will."*

[2] *"Not my will but yours be done." Jesus Christ's prayer in the Garden of Gethsemane in the* Gospel of St. Luke, *xxii, 42.*

Chapter 7
For Want of a Rye

When I was in college, I had a biology professor who called himself a "Luddite" because he preferred to use an overhead projector rather than using PowerPoint. I had no idea what he was talking about, so I looked it up in the library the next time I was in there.

Apparently, there was a group of workers in the early Industrial Revolution who opposed the use of modern machinery—which they believed would put them out of work. They named themselves after a worker named Ned Ludd, an early saboteur (who may or may not have even ever existed). Anyway, they destroyed the mechanical looms that they thought were taking their jobs all throughout England. My economics teacher a year later said it doesn't even work that way—that the Industrial Revolution actually helped *more* people become employed, since businesses could make more products for the same cost if they used both machines *and* a full cache of employees, but apparently Luddites never take economics classes. Over the centuries since, the label "Luddite" has been attached to anyone who hates or fears technology.

I say all of that to explain why I think that Tony de Tullio is a Luddite. No, he hasn't broken any mechanical looms with a sledgehammer, but he seems to want to stay away from technology as much as possible. I remember how loudly he protested when they took most of the typewriters out of the squad room and replaced them with computers. "I ain't never had no piece o' paper *crash* on me an' lose all o' my work before!" he argued. I guess that he had a point, and he may be the reason why we still have a couple of typewriters banging around here and there—that, and the occasional form that still needs to be typed out.

So when my cell phone died, I knew that I couldn't charge it in Tony's car, or even borrow his own cell phone. Oh, I know that he's *got* one—it's policy that he *has* to have one—but I knew that odds are, it was sitting on his desk, uncharged, where he always "forgets" it every day. I swear, there are some days when I think that the only machines that Tony trusts are his car and the soda machine down the hallway (scratch that—Tony hates his car). Besides, I had no idea what number Billy the Kid was even calling me from, since the number was stored *on my phone*, which was now basically just a glorified paperweight.

So we just started driving up to Roscoe Village, in the hopes that we'd be able to find him by nosing around a bit. I knew that it was a bit of a longshot, but we were right there—Roscoe Village was, at most, only a ten-minute drive away. We were already on Western Avenue, so we just took it on up to Roscoe Street to begin looking for ID's to tag.

"So you think that wasn't a waste, huh?" Tony asked me on the drive. I could tell that he was still frustrated that we weren't "bustin' more heads," as he likes to put it.

"Wasn't a *total* waste, no."

"So should we be puttin' together a vampire huntin' kit?" he chuckled. "If you got a couple o' stakes, I can get th' garlic an' th' crucifix pretty easy." He pointed to the rosary hanging from his rearview mirror, and I could still smell the remains of the garlic bread still haunting the backseat from some past meal.

"And the holy water," I joined in. "Don't forget that."

"I'll talk with th' padre at Mass about that…"

"Seriously, Tony, I know that the perp's not a real vampire, but it does help us to know that the OA's are running scared, and that they're not the ones who did the killings."

"We don' know that, Tom," he corrected. "They only *said* they wasn't th' ones."

"No, I believe them. Buitre is scared—for that matter, the *Angel* is scared, and he doesn't scare that easily. Remember the time last year when the Imperial Gangsters made a move on the OA's from Devil Side? Who was that guy with the airbrushed Pink Panther on his shirt?"

"Ya mean Emilio?"

"That's right—Emilio García. Kid must've been, like, ten feet tall. Emilio comes in to the pool hall where the Angel was shooting pool, and he's got how many, five or six IG's with him?"

"Story is ten."

"Right, so five or six Gangsters backing him up, and he's the size of a house. He comes up to the Angel and starts talking smack about something, just to start a fight."

"Story is, he said somethin' like, 'I did yer girlfriend *an'* her momma las' night,'" Tony said.

"Classy. Anyway, the Angel just keeps shooting pool, like Emilio's not even there. Not a drop of sweat on his brow under all those dreads. He's alone—"

"Nope," Tony interrupted. "Sal Vargas was there with 'im."

"That's right. Okay, so the two of them are there alone, facing this walking mountain and half a dozen Gangsters, and the Angel doesn't even bat an eyelash about it. He just finishes his game, even though the IG's are goading him and pushing him. Didn't Sal try to move for a door or a phone or something?"

"I heard he tried for th' back door, but one o' them pink ladies broke a pool cue over his head."

Again, Tony's cultural sensitivity showed through. "You realize that if any of the Imperial Gangsters ever heard you call them that, we'd be in a world of hurt, right?"

"Hey, what kinda street gang wears pink? I'm jus' sayin' is all…"

"Anyway, so Sal is down, and it's just the Angel and the IG's. And so he says, something like, 'I don't want any trouble,' and reaches for a stuffed animal on a table nearby, right?"

"It was a blue bunny rabbit."

I started laughing. "That's right, it was a blue bunny rabbit. He grabs the rabbit, like he's leaving and taking it home to his kid or something, and that's when Emilio pulls a knife on him. And, again, without breaking a sweat or raising his voice, the Angel just holds the rabbit in his arms."

"An' shoots Emilio right in th' face with the 10 mil he's got stashed in the bunny!"

"Yep. Took out all six of them, if the story is true—by himself, without so much as a stutter-step of hesitation or emotion."

"What's yer point?"

"My point is that the same Angel who had no problems standing his ground alone against a pool hall full of enemy Gangsters is now scared enough that he's encouraging el Buitre to ask for our help in stopping what he genuinely believes is a vampire. I can't help but see that as significant."

Tony drove for another block in silence until we got to Roscoe Street.

"So I'm keepin' th' rosary handy," he said finally.

*   *   *

We turned onto Roscoe, and drove for a couple of short blocks. As we crossed Seeley, I had an idea, so I asked Tony to pull over.

"Let me out here, Tony," I said. "I want to walk back a block or two and check on some things. Why don't you go down to Hamlin Park and look around there? Come swing by and catch me at Riverview Plaza in an hour, okay?"

"Yer th' boss…" he said, and dropped me off at the gas station on the corner, then peeled off down Damen toward Hamlin Park. I keep expecting some cop to pull him over one of these days for his driving habits, but so far, I consider Tony the luckiest bad driver in the world.

Before I turned back west, I decided to cross Damen and poke my head into Robey's to see if any ID's were hanging out there, but no luck. In fact, when I talked with one of the waitresses about Billy the Kid, she said she'd never seen him or Mojo there—and she'd worked there for months. No one there had any idea where I might find them, either.

I poked my head into the Riverview Tavern, and Mulligan's pub, but no one had seen him recently. I did get a bit of luck at the vintage record store down the way—the girl with more piercings than face told me that he had been there about an hour earlier, looking through the vinyl for some old Grant Green albums. I had no idea that he was into jazz—I knew that there was something about that boy that I liked. Apparently, the girl liked him, too, since when she talked about him, she smiled really wide, her cheeks flushed, her pupils dilated, and she started breathing just a little heavier. She said that he came by fairly often, so I gave her my card and asked her to have him call me again.

As I kept on walking westward, I couldn't help but chew on the elements of the case. Who would want to steal an old woman's painting? Why would he have no problem splattering her blood everywhere around her apartment, but then care enough to take the time to siphon off Hector's blood just a few minutes later on? What had Karen found out about the saliva and the nail fragment?

I realized that I was doing it again—that I hadn't really thought about Hector Flórez or Amanda Cairns for some time now, that I was spending more time thinking about their killer than about the two people he'd killed. That's what you have to do, of course. You have to focus on the perp, get into their head, try not to think of the victims as *people*, but rather as elements of the crime. That's what you have to do. I'm just always more than a little uncomfortable with how easily and how quickly I slip into that way of thinking.

As I walked past a little Thai restaurant, with its little golden Buddha statues and plastic cherry blossoms in the window, I thought of William Raffey. Was he even still alive? And if he was, had he hired someone to kill Amanda Cairns so that he could steal his portrait back from her? And if so, why did he wait half a century to do it? What happened to make our perp suddenly decide to kill an elderly woman in order to steal an old portrait? And why was Hector Flórez even there in the first place? None of it made sense. I really needed to talk with Billy to find out what he'd uncovered.

As I made my way toward Village Tap, I passed by Rudy's Bakery, and I remembered that it was Friday. See, Friday is the day—the *only* day—when Rudy's bakes their rye bread, and Joanna is absolutely certain that it's the best rye bread in Chicago. More to the point, no offense to the Starbuck's down the street, but I personally think that Rudy's serves the best cup of coffee I've ever had. I knew that Tony would kill me if I told him I got a cup of their coffee while he was dragging his bulk all around Hamlin Park, but I couldn't just walk past a fresh rye and a good cup of coffee and do nothing. Besides, Rudy's was one of those places who quietly stood up in the 1990s against the growing gang presence in the neighborhood, even making their shop one of the "kid safe" businesses that schoolkids could duck into if they were getting hassled by gang members on the street, so I like to throw them my business whenever I can.

Now, I didn't know how I'd get the rye home without Tony figuring out that there had probably been a coffee purchased at the same time, but I figured I'd cross that bridge when I came to it later. Of course, by the time I was walking out of Rudy's Bakery a few minutes later, all of that suddenly became moot. As I stepped out of the door, I saw some figures move around quickly in the condo lobby across the street, and my instinctive reaction was that it meant violence. I set the rye and the coffee on a bench on the sidewalk next to a dangerously greedy-looking red squirrel, and then, with my hand on my holster, I glanced to see if I could cross the street.

While I was waiting for the lines of oncoming cars to provide an opening, I looked across the street more carefully, to see what I was getting myself into.

To my shock, I saw Pieter Durant, throwing some guy in a suit up against a wall in the lobby. He looked like he was playing "bad cop" with no "good cop" in sight, but what surprised me more than anything else was the speed and the strength with which he did it. I mean, the guy was more or less average size, but Durant was flinging him around like a rag doll. In fact, as he leaned in to snarl something in the guy's face, I realized that he had him suspended about a foot off the floor, held up with only his left hand. I knew that I sure couldn't hold someone up that high for that long with only one hand. How is it that Durant could do it so easily?

I watched the last car speed on by, and I saw my opening. I turned back toward the condo lobby, and Durant was gone. I don't mean "he was leaving," but that he was *gone*. The whole front of the lobby is windows, and I only glanced away for a second—no way he could've moved that fast. In fact, I actually saw the guy slumping back to the floor as I looked in. Somehow, within a split second of letting go of the guy, Durant was out of the building.

I raced across the street and into the lobby. The guy was still on the floor, badly shaken when I came through the door.

"What did he want?" I demanded. "And where did he go?"

"Wh-what?" the guy stammered.

"Don't worry, sir. I'm a police officer," I said. "The man who was just here—the tall guy in the coat. What was he asking you about?"

"I-I am not sure," he replied. I heard the remnants of an accent, but I couldn't place it at first. "He asked about the neighborhood, and then he asked if I knew of anyone new with a name like 'Raffey' around town." The more he talked, the more it sounded Eastern European.

"An elderly man?" I asked.

"What?" he looked surprised. "N-no, he was asking about a young man, or perhaps a middle-age man. He nodded and almost smiled when I told him that I know nothing of this."

"But he specifically used the name 'Raffey,' right?"

"Yes," he said, finally starting to stand up. I helped him to his feet, and he brushed himself off before speaking again. "Who was this man?"

"You mean he didn't identify himself?" I asked, surprised.

"No," he replied. "He just came in and began asking me the questions."

"Why did he throw you against the wall?"

"I-I don't know," he answered, obviously holding something back. "He was just an animal."

"You didn't say anything or do anything to provoke him?"

"Nothing," he said—but his eyes told me that he was lying. I decided that I could better get to the bottom of this from Durant's end of things.

"Where did he go just now?" I asked him.

"I did not even *see* him go, officer" he said—and this time, he was telling the truth. I gave the man my card and I asked him for his contact information. His name was Frank Sydor—shortened from František Yevhen Sydor back in the old country—and he worked as the desk man at the condo. I told him to call me if he could think of anything else, or if Durant ever came back, though I decided to refrain from telling him that I knew Durant already. Durant was obviously over the line, but I didn't completely trust this Sydor, either, so I thought it best to play things close to the vest for now. I didn't want to muddle up my own investigation by having to put Durant up on charges as well—at least, not yet.

I went back across the street, only to find that my coffee and rye were gone. No surprise there, I thought. Welcome to Chicago. But I did go back inside to ask if I could use their phone to call in to the station. The woman working behind the counter smiled and said that she was happy to help a policeman—especially one who liked a good rye bread.

When I got through, I asked for Jenkins. The moment he answered, I said, "Jenkins, it's me—Chapel. I want you to do two things for me." Jenkins seemed to want to say something, but I was in a hurry. "First, I want you to do a little background check on Pieter Durant, our visiting psycho from Interpol, but you'll have to do it quietly, or it's both our butts in a sling. Second, I want you to see if an Insane Deuce by the name of Billy Rivers has left any messages for me there somewhere."

"Sure thing, Detective," he said. And then, after a pause, he added, "Are you okay?"

Was I *okay?* What kind of a question was that?

"Of course I'm okay, Jenkins," I replied. "What's going on? Why do you ask?" There was another uncomfortable pause on the other end of the line.

"So you haven't heard?" he asked.

"Haven't heard what, Jenkins?"

"I'm really sorry, sir," he said, obviously not wanting to continue. "Someone really should have called you."

"Called me about what, Jenkins?" I asked, starting to get a little frustrated with him. "My phone's dead, so I'm calling you from a bakery." The woman behind the counter smiled warmly at me and pointed to another rye on a cooling tray. I was in the process of debating about whether I should try getting another one for Joanna to make up for the one I'd lost when Jenkins finally decided to spit it out.

"Karen Gage is dead, sir."

Background
From *Nagareboshi wa Sora no Namida* (Ishida Hideyori, 1698, trans. Oda Mitsunari)

Selections from *Hitotsubatago ga Saku Toki*

The Fourth Son of Heaven[1] sat in the ruined castle,[2]
    and the ears of the Kirishitan,[3] were open to his words.
        He spoke to them of the cherry blossoms and of the wind,
           and of the grass in the fields.
"All that we know will pass away,
    and all that we have will find its path on the wind,
        but all that we are will be remembered forever
           in the songs of our children and the heart of our Lord."
"Though we are only a few and our enemy is legion,
    we will stand, for we walk on the Way,
        we will stand, for we speak for the Truth,
           we will stand, for we have our being in the Life."
"Therefore, though we may die today
    or though we may watch our families die tomorrow,
        we cannot turn from what our souls speak to us,
           or turn our backs to the Lord who gave us life."

The snow flower bloomed early that year,
    with its sea shine petals gleaming white in the daylight
        and its beauty catching the moonlight in the night.
           And his people knew that it would be their final bloom.

---

[1] *Masuda Shirō Tokisada (also known as Amakusa Shirō), the leader of the Shimabara Rebellion and the supposed saviour of Japan's persecuted Christians (the Kirishitan, whose faith had been officially outlawed in 1614 under the Tokugawa shōgunate). He was the son of Masuda Jinbei—himself a retainer of the former Christian daimyō Konishi Yukinaga, who was publicly executed following the Battle of Sekigahara in 1600.*

[2] *Hara Castle, which the Christians of Shimabara fled to and re-fortified in 1637.*

[3] *Japanese Christians.*

Two-score samurai stood with the Kirishitan,
    but a thousand times that stood with the bakufu at the gates.
        Yet in the face of this swarm of locusts of Shimabara,
            the children still sang with joy in the pathways of Hara.
For Drake-san[4] also stood with the Kirishitan, and he knew no equal.
    Even the Tokugawa samurai trembled with fear to face him in battle,
        for his blade never faltered, and his blood never spilled,
            and he moved with the whispers of the night breezes.
Amakusa Shirō-sama and Drake-san prepared for the siege,
    and the big ikokujin[5] brought forth his gleaming blade,
        straight and long and sharp, and touched by God.
            The ikokujin and the Fourth Son of Heaven stood together.
Drake-san wished to fight alongside his brother Kirishitan,
    but the yosuzume[6] sang at night, and the okuri-inu[7] howled,
        and Drake-san followed them to a dark path in his quest
            for the demon who had first drawn him to the Island of
                Dragonflies.
He set out to hunt the kyūketsuki[8] on the mountain of Inasa,
    but the wandering ghosts had deceived him—
        —for the demon was closer at hand than he knew,
            and its black heart sought to douse the light of God.
The Fourth Son of Heaven stood alone with his people,
    his samurai with their readied blades,
        his people with their prayers,
            his castle with its heavy stones.
The walls of Hara stood against the winds,
    and against the arrows of Tokugawa Iemitsu,[9]
        and against the blade of Niten Dōraku,[10]

---

[4]   *Most modern scholars believe "Drake-san" refers to naturalist/mercenary Peer van Draeck, whose widespread travels would have placed him in southern Japan at this time. Little is known about the historical van Draeck beyond folktales about his exploits around the world, and his own well-known book on supernatural creatures,* De Dødes Bog *(1642).*

[5]   *A foreigner.*

[6]   *A mythical bird whose call was a harbinger of evil.*

[7]   *A dark, phantom hound.*

[8]   *An undead creature of the night, said to gorge itself on the blood of the living, much like a vampire. It may, in fact, actually be a vampire, but many of the legends are obscure.*

[9]   *The third Tokugawa shōgun. Famous for his* Sakoku-rei *of 1635 which effectively closed Japan off to all foreign commerce, except with the Dutch. This edict stood for more than two centuries, until the signing of the* Nichibei Shūkō Tsūshō Jōyaku *("Treaty of Amity and Commerce") with the United States in 1858.*

[10]   *This is almost certainly referring to the famous swordsman, Miyamoto*

and against the unkind night of Matsukura Katsuie.[11]
Amakusa Shirō-sama faced the onslaught of his foes,
> but he did not fear them, nor fear his own death,
> > for he had known the Son of God
> > > and he had seen the snow flower in bloom.

*   *   *

Selections from *Namida o Shishi no Tategami ni*

Matsukura Katsuie found the people of Hara bitter opponents
> for though they had but few samurai,
> > they did have the guns which his father, Matsukura Shigemasa,
> > > had taught them to use so well.
They fought with the hearts of tigers.
> For months, they had withstood the onslaught of Katsuie's samurai
> > and the soldiers of the Tokugawa shōgun.
> > > Against all, the walls of Hara stood, immoveable.
In desperation, Itakura Shigemasa sent for the Dutch barbarians,
> and they sent their ship of guns to fight the people.
> > For two weeks, their guns fired from a safe distance,
> > > but their cowardly fire could not harm true men.
Then Amakusa Shirō-sama sent Itakura Shigemasa a message—
> "Is there no courage left in Nihon to fight us?
> > Is there no shame in calling for the help of ikokujin
> > > to make war against our small band?"
The heart of Itakura Shigemasa was struck down by the message,
> and he sent the ikokujin back to Hirado,
> > to build their storehouses of stone
> > > and disgrace their own agreement with the Tokugawa
> > > shōgun.

...

When Itakura Shigemasa died, the Tokugawa shōgun acted.
> He brought in Matsudaira Nobutsuna, the wise daimyō from
> > Kawagoe,

Musashi, who was an advisor at the siege of Hara Castle under daimyōs Itakura Shigemasa and Matsudaira Nobutsuna.

[11] *Daimyō in Shimabara, and son of Matsukura Shigemasa—who was infamous even amongst his peers for his persecution of the Kirishitan, torturing them in various ways, and often boiling them alive at his hot springs at Unzen. Katsuie inherited a great deal of debt from his father's rule, and levied burdensome taxes in order to pay it off. Like Shigemasa, he was also known for his cruelty, including lighting his own peasants on fire in the evenings for his amusement.*

who watched the castle in the winter,
    and who camped outside, planning its downfall.
Itakura Shigemasa had sent in ninja to deceive the Kirishitan,
    But Izu no Kami[12] knew that ninja are cowards,
        and they surrendered to the Kirishitan when they were captured
            swimming in the moat, halfway across.
Matsudaira Nobutsuna waited and watched in the winter.
    He paid Yamada Uemonsaku to spy out his brother Kirishitan,
        and, as a traitor, he painted the portrait of a people starving,
            and still Matsudaira Nobutsuna waited and watched.
A month before the fall of Hara, the Kirishitan attacked outside the walls
    and killed a hundred score of the soldiers from Hizen.
        Hizen's Kuroda-shi pledged the deaths of Amakusa Shirō-sama
            and all of the people whom he loved.
The Kirishitan took heart, and yet foragers from the castle
    attacked the camp of Matsudaira Nobutsuna, looking for food.
        He had them killed, and their stomachs contained only grass
            and leaves.
        Izu no Kami knew that their end was near, and he acted.
The forces of the Tokugawa shōgun attacked in force as a storm.
    Their arrows were like black clouds over the sun,
        their cannons were like thunderclaps against the walls,
            and their blades were like sharpened hailstones across the
                flesh.
Kuroda Tadayuki and his Hizen samurai broke through the wall
    and there was no defense against them.
        Children screamed and women wept as their blades swept
                through
            and all of Hara lay before them, naked to the sword.
And with that, Amakusa Shirō-sama drew his sword and faced his
                enemy.
    He spoke to the wind and exclaimed to the rising sun,
        "Now, those who are with me under siege in this castle
            will be my companions in the next world."[13]

---

12   *"Izu the Wise"—Matsudaira Nobutsuna's name at court.*
13   *On April 12, 1638, the Tokugawa shōgun's 125,000 men broke through the
    defenses of Hara Castle and killed Masuda Shirō Tokisada, slaughtering the
    more than 27,000 Christians under his protection—most of whom were
    noncombatant women and children. Shirō himself was beheaded, and his
    head was placed on a pike and carried to Nagasaki to be put on public
    display. The remaining Christians in Japan were executed or deported... but
    the faith continued for centuries afterward as an underground movement
    known as the Kakure Kirishitan ("hidden Christians").*

*   *   *

Selections from *Tada Ariake no Tsuki zo Nokoreru*

The shōgun Tokugawa Iemitsu would not be stilled,
   and he punished all those who had allowed this rebellion
      with the ruthlessness of the black bear
        and the wisdom of the ancient fox.
The Mōri-shi were decimated in their homes.
    The Amagasaki-han and the Akashi-han felt his wrath.
      And the whole of the Great Country of Eight Islands
        trembled at his terrible anger.
Chief among those whom the shōgun hated
   was the evil Matsukura Katsuie—the daimyō of Shimabara,
     the night monster, the child-eater,
       and the most cursed among all daimyōs.
For on one autumn evening, lost hunting in the deep woods,
   Katsuie had stumbled without respect into the Hyakki Yakō,[14]
     and the yōkai[15] had placed upon him a terrible spell.
      His own dark heart was blackened.
From that day forward, Matsukura Katsuie became kyūketsuki—
   —and he feasted upon his own people.
     Upon their blood, and upon the blood of children,
      Katsuie fed his unholy appetites.
But so powerful and so evil was his father, Shigemasa,
   and so complete was their control of Shimabara,
     that Katsuie's transformation was hidden from the people.
      No one knew of his horror, of his curse, of his hunger.
Even Drake-san, who hunted the kyūketsuki in the mountains,
   who knew the invisible footsteps of Yuki-onna,[16]
     who grappled with the jibakurei[17] of Fukuoka,
      even Drake-san did not recognize that Katsuie had been his
      quarry.
And so it was a blessing both to Katsuie and to the Shimabara-han
   when the shōgun ordered the death of the evil daimyō.
     the fiend who burned his own children at night
      was allowed to commit seppuku[18] in his home.

---

[14] *"The Night Parade of One Hundred Demons"—an assembly of supernatural creatures, usually in October.*

[15] *Supernatural creatures or spirits.*

[16] *A "snow woman" mountain spirit who appears to mortals primarily during violent blizzards.*

[17] *An "earthbound spirit" who remains tied to the area of its death.*

[18] *Ritual suicide, performed to preserve one's honor.*

He plunged Chi no Yokubō[19] into himself, but no blood flowed.
    He dragged the blade across himself, but no blood flowed.
        He pulled the blade up, but no blood flowed.
            And then his kaishakunin[20] took his head.
Katsuie's face smiled and laughed, even as his head fell.
    He muttered curses into the dust, and the okuri-inu bellowed
        on the hills outside his castle walls.
            The women wailed, and the men drew their breaths.
Again and again, they hacked at his body, to no avail.
    Only when they had burned the body of him
        who had burned so many of his fellows in life
            did that semblance of life leave it.
Drake-san wept at the dawn when he heard about this,
    for with Katsuie's fall, his own path was broken.
        His premature departure from Hara was shown to be
            unnecessary.
        He had left his brothers to die alone in vain.
A thousand score and more Kirishitan had bled
    because he had left Hara to hunt the demon,
        only to find that the true demon was there in their midst,
            hunting his brothers and sisters, whom he had abandoned.
The lonely ikokujin faced the new morning in tears,
    and he called out to to the rustling winds,
        "I came to find the end to my quest, but
            the only thing I found was the moon of early dawn..."[21]

---

[19] *Matsukura Katsuie's personal katana, rumoured to have been made by
master swordsmith Muramasa Sengo himself a century earlier. It was not
uncommon for important swords to be given names that reflect the
dispositions either of their makers or their owners (for example, "Chi no
Yokubō" means "Bloodlust"). It was, however, quite uncommon to make use
of a katana to commit seppuku—usually, the tantō (long knife) was used
instead, for obvious logistical reasons. However, in Katsuie's jisei (death
poem) the daimyō expressed that he considered this particular sword the
only blade in the world worthy of taking his life from him.*
[20] *The traditional "second" in the ritual of seppuku, whose job it was to
perform the coup d'grâce at the end.*
[21] *Here, Drake-san (or van Draeck) quotes from a poem in Fujiwara no Teika's
Ogura Hyakunin Isshu ("One Hundred Poems by One Hundred Poets—The
Ogura Collection," c. 1200).*

Chapter 8
Play Foul

We hadn't officially been called in to investigate Karen's death, since it wasn't demonstrably part of the same case as Hector Flórez and Amanda Cairns. Kingery was handling this one with Schroeder, but they weren't necessarily considering it a homicide.

Tony and I made it over to Karen's apartment building within an hour after I got the news anyway. He suggested that it might be a conflict of interest for me to be involved, but that argument didn't end up going anywhere pretty. I wasn't going to stomp on Kingery's investigation—I just had to see for myself what happened. The last thing that Karen had told me was that she was onto something new, and then she died "of natural causes" within, what, 30 minutes? I wasn't going to buy that theory easily.

Problem was, when we got there, Schroeder met us at the door and gave us more of the details. Karen had gotten into the building and was checking her mail while talking with two of her neighbors when she collapsed. Both witnesses verified that no one had touched her. They said that she was complaining of flu-like symptoms, and one of the neighbors—Mrs. Kelly—suggested that she drink some warm tea with honey in it and lay down for a nap. They talked for another minute or so, when Karen suddenly became faint and crumpled to the ground. She never regained consciousness.

Now, several obvious things come to mind when you hear something like that. A horrible disease is usually the first probability, but it would've had to have come on fast—even the Ebola virus or bird flu or that cholera epidemic back in Haiti don't move that fast. Even so, the CDC guys were on their way, and everyone she'd come in contact with had been quarantined. I couldn't help but think about all those people that she'd been bumping up against on the train.

But realistically, with symptoms coming on this quickly, it suggests some sort of poisoning instead, and Schroeder assured us that they were already going to be checking for that in the autopsy. I thought of Bill Saunders and I hoped that they'd have someone more competent working on her case when the time came.

I asked if we could see the body, and Schroeder reluctantly agreed. I mean, he couldn't reasonably *refuse* us—unless he wanted to play the CDC card and tell us that we had to wait for them to say the situation was clean—but it really wasn't our case, and there was no reason for us to be there, other than that this was Karen. We put on masks and gloves and entered the lobby of the apartment building.

Karen was laying there on the tiled floor, near the mailboxes. Her skirt had ridden up when she fell, and I fought the urge to reach down and pull it down for her. I've never had that reaction at a crime scene before, and it was quietly the most disturbing part of the whole thing for me. I wanted to fix her glasses, because they were twisted on her face, and I wanted to pull her hair back behind her ears, the way she liked to wear it. This isn't the way Karen would want to be seen.

But I had to remind myself that this wasn't Karen—this was her corpse. Until the CDC guys told me otherwise, I was sure that this was a crime scene, and that meant that I should treat it like one. Look for clues, examine the context, distance my emotions from the subject, learn from the victim what had happened to them. "Mortui vivos docent," the detective who trained me used to say—"the dead teach the living."

Karen's face looked gaunt, sunken-in. It was a huge departure from her usual round-faced softness. It's not like she'd lost weight, although the visual impression you'd walk away with was very similar to that, as if she'd lost way too much weight way too quickly—that haunted, shadowed look that you see on photos of Auschwitz victims and Hollywood starlets. But moreover, it was like she had suffered a prolonged illness and it had taken a lot out of her… which, of course, hadn't happened. She had dark circles under her eyes, and her face and lips were pale—much moreso than you'd expect to see this soon after death, since postmortem lividity hadn't really kicked in yet. It was like the life had just been sucked out of her, like in the horror movies.

And yes—though I feel fairly silly now even admitting it—given my conversations with Tony earlier, I reflexively glanced at her neck for bite marks. I mean, I knew at the time that it was stupid, that el Buitre and the Angel were just running scared, that there's no such thing as vampires. I *knew* all of that. But, when you subconsciously find yourself admitting that all of the pieces do line up that way, and that it would certainly answer a lot of questions, and it's bouncing around in the back of your head, and you're looking at her face, looking like that— well, all I can say is that it's a reflex action. Her neck was clean and soft and unmarred, and I dismissed the idea as ridiculous and moved on.

The floor was a little dusty, with some dirt and road salt and such tracked in here and there, but in general, the lobby was clean and well-kept. The mailboxes were shiny and the nameplates were printed carefully by hand on each one, under the numbers. It seemed like a nice enough building, and Schroeder said that the neighbors all seemed to get along with one another, especially with Karen. There was no sign of foul play on that end. So if she'd been poisoned, who did it? Why poison her at all? And when had it happened? If it really *was* a crime, we were short on means, motive, opportunity, and suspects.

I saw Nate Kingery over in the corner, talking with a couple of people, including a photographer. I asked Tony to have him come over while I looked a little more carefully at Karen's body. Her mail was scattered out across the floor near her, but her purse was undisturbed, still dangling from her shoulder. I wondered if inside, she still had the samples that she'd stuffed away in there. She'd almost *have* to still have had them in there, since she was taking them home, and she'd never gotten into her apartment. I was tempted to look inside, but that's when Kingery walked up.

I stood up to talk with him, and that's when I noticed that one of the people in the corner was none other than Pieter Durant. I have no idea how I missed him before, but his eyes caught mine, and he nodded slightly in acknowledgment. Why was our least favorite Interpol agent here at Karen's apartment building? If her death had nothing to do with our Hector Flórez case, then why was he even interested? More than ever, I was certain that this was now a crime scene. It was another murder.

But if Karen had been killed by the same people who killed Flórez and Amanda Cairns, then why change their M.O.? And *how* did they do it? *Why* would anyone do it?

A sudden, sinking thought popped into my head. For whatever reason, Durant was keeping a tight lid on this case, commandeering the bodies even before we had a good chance to go over them at the lab, sticking his nose into the crime scenes, muscling Bill Saunders and even Lieutenant Chacon into jumping when he snapped his fingers. If he'd found out somehow that Karen had been concealing some evidence so that we could examine it ourselves…

I wondered just how long ago Durant had arrived at Karen's apartment building. And, given what I'd seen with him and Sydor over in Roscoe Village, I wondered just how ruthless he was willing to be in order to control this investigation. More than ever, I wanted that background that Jenkins was digging up on Pieter Durant.

Kingery and I moved over into a relatively unoccupied corner of the lobby. I couldn't help but notice that as we stepped away from Karen's body, Durant stepped up and hunched down next to her.

"What are you guys doing here, Tom?" he asked me. I couldn't tell from his voice whether he was a little frustrated with me overstepping my bounds, or if he was a little concerned on a more personal level.

"She was a friend, Nate," I answered. He looked at me for a few seconds, and then he sighed.

"I know that, Tom. She was a great gal, and we'll find out what happened to her. I *promise*." Over Kingery's shoulder, I noticed Durant stroking her hair out of her face and off of her neck, much like he'd done with Amanda Cairns. For some reason, I found myself getting angry about that. He leaned in closer, and it looked like he was playing with the dirt on the floor, near her purse.

"—don't think so," Kingery was saying, and I realized that I had stopped listening somewhere a while back. "But we're not going to rule anything out until we've done a complete investigation." I focused back on Kingery's face, and re-engaged in the conversation.

"I don't think that she was sick," I said. "She was fine an hour ago. I think that she was poisoned or something. Make sure to check for toxins in her bloodstream."

Kingery frowned. "I just said that, Tom," he replied, looking more worried than anything else. "Are you okay?"

"I'm fine, Nate," I answered. "I'm sorry. I'm just—" *What?* I honestly didn't know how to finish that sentence. I preoccupied? I'm emotionally involved? I'm watching that Interpol agent over there and wondering if he should be our chief suspect? What do I say?

"We'll handle it, Tom," Kingery said, helping me save face. "Just go on home or go work on your own cases or go grab a cup of coffee." He smiled warmly, but then he added, "But you really probably ought to just go, okay?"

Out of the corner of my eye, I noticed Durant pull back from her body and surreptitiously slip something small into that strange little pouch of his. It took a second for it to even register, since I was re-focused on Kingery, but the more I thought about it, the more it concerned me.

"Okay, Nate," I replied. "But when you finish up here, just let me know what you find."

"Sure thing, Tom," he said, scribbling something on his iPad as he turned away.

"Nate," I said sharply, getting his attention. He looked up from his note-taking. "I mean it. This one is important to me. Let me know *anything* you find."

"I promise, Tom," he said, and he put his hand on my shoulder. "We all liked her, too. We'll do it right, and I'll let you know." He smiled again, nodded, and then walked back over to the photographer in the corner of the room.

Now, here's where things got interesting. I mean, how should I approach this thing with Durant? I *thought* I just saw an Interpol inspector—to whom I had been ordered to "extend every courtesy, *yadda, yadda*"—take evidence away from a crime scene and hide it in his pocket. If I flat-out accused Durant of evidence tampering, would I get reprimanded? Would I get fired? Would there be an international incident? I didn't trust this guy as far as I could throw Tony de Tullio, and I was already investigating him regarding that Sydor business, but this? This was crossing a line both legally and personally, and I couldn't just let it go.

I walked over to Karen's body as casually as I could and asked, "So, have you found anything interesting, Inspector?" Durant didn't even look up, but continued what I recognized to be aimless poking around at the body—he was only *pretending* to investigate at this point. Whatever he'd put in his pocket had ended the investigation for him already, and now he was trying to pad the time to cover it up. "I'm not even sure why you're here in the first place, but it kind of looked like you found something," I repeated, pressing the issue... or, at the very least, pressing for a response. I stood over him, waiting for an answer. I stood there for quite a while, actually, waiting for an answer.

"Not really," he finally responded, coldly, pretending to examine her mail. "I believe that I am finished here."

"Let me put this another way," I said, allowing a little more of an edge to my voice. "I watched you put something in your little purse thing." He stopped poking around in her mail. "What might that have been, Inspector?" For a moment, it seemed like time stood still. I didn't breathe, it didn't look like Durant breathed, and my entire potential future career flashed before my eyes—crashing and burning.

Finally, Durant sighed and stood up from Karen's body. His gray eyes burned coldly at me under those dark brows, and he answered, with a quiet forcefulness that seemed to suck the air out of the room, "My *pen*."

Now, I knew that Durant hadn't been carrying a pen, and Durant knew that he hadn't been carrying a pen, and Durant knew that I knew that he hadn't been carrying a pen, and we both knew that we both knew all of those things, so this had suddenly become very serious. No more vague feelings of uneasiness, no more subtle evasions, no more uncomfortable silences. He was drawing a line in the sand and challenging me to step across it or to shut up and stop pressing. His eyes continued to smolder as he waited for my response—would I call him on it and directly accuse him of lying? Or would I back down and prove to both of us that I'd let him get away with it? For a moment, I didn't know myself what I would do.

"Your pen..." I repeated, finally deciding where to go with that. Durant's expression didn't change, and he waited. "Great," I said, pulling out my notebook from my own jacket pocket. "Mine just died. Would you mind if I borrowed it for a second?" I reached my hand out to him, now waiting for *his* response. His eyes narrowed and his brow furrowed just the tiniest bit, and then he did the one thing that I didn't expect—he *smiled*.

And then he walked away.

*   *   *

I can't abide a dirty cop under any circumstances, much less when it comes to the death of a friend. I didn't know what Durant's angle was, but there was no way that I was going to let him get away with tampering with evidence—especially not with evidence at the scene of Karen's death.

She deserved better than that.

We clear, what, a third of the murders that cross our desks here in Chicago? I didn't want Karen's death to be one of those two-thirds that get thrown into the cold case files—certainly not because of some freak of an Interpol agent who might or might not have been involved in it.

I touched base back at the office, where Durant was in Chacon's office with Chacon and the Area Commander, and Jenkins was still trying to muster up the courage to start digging into Durant's past. I assured him that no one would know but me, but he didn't seem very convinced. Only when I told him that it might help in the investigation into Karen's murder did he seem willing to try it. I crossed my fingers and hoped that he'd find something important.

As if that wasn't bad enough, I decided to go one more step off the reservation. After I'd charged up my phone, I saw that the number he'd called me from was a payphone down at DePaul University—as it turns out, there was no way I'd have been able to find him by running around Roscoe Village that afternoon. So I asked Tony to see if he could sniff around DePaul and see if he could chase down Billy the Kid to find out more info. I knew that it was pointless—I knew that if there was any real chance that he'd find Billy still floating around there, I should really be with him to make the connection myself. Honestly, what I was actually doing was just getting Tony out of the way so that I could tail Pieter Durant.

Tony would have loved to have helped me with that, but that's why I had to get rid of him. I couldn't let him know what I was doing, or else he'd be dumb enough to do exactly what I was planning to do and torque off Chacon's visiting golden boy. I knew that there was a good chance that I'd lose my job over this—but more than that, having seen Durant with Sydor and beginning to suspect him in Karen's murder, I figured that it might actually be a lot more dangerous than just that. I couldn't ask Tony to stick his neck out for this.

Funny thing was, for all of his "Mr. Mysterious" act up until that point, he turned out to be pretty easy to follow. I mean, he'd always just seemed to show up places, and then disappear to God knows where, and then reappear at my computer in the office. I'd never even seen the guy so much as stop and get a sandwich anywhere. He was like a ghost or something, and I really didn't think that I'd be able to keep up with him.

But, contrary to what he'd ever done up until then, he was actually very public about when he left the office. He stopped to talk to the desk sergeant, which I don't think he'd ever done before. In the lobby of the station, he even stopped to look at one of the decorations in the lobby, and then checked that pocket watch of his. It was as if he were consciously taking his time to leave the building.

He must have called ahead, because when he went outside, there was a cab waiting for him near the bus stop there on Grand. Maybe that's why he had been moving so slowly—because he knew that he'd have to wait for the cab. But Durant didn't seem the type of guy who would dawdle on his way to get the cab. Somehow, he'd find a way to use that time to do, well, *something*. Luckily, he talked with the cabbie long enough for me to jump into my car and begin to follow at a discrete distance. Then again, maybe it wasn't luck at all. I couldn't help shake the feeling that he knew that he was being watched—that he was leading me somewhere on purpose. Even so, if it *was* a trap, that's just all the more reason to follow Durant into it to expose him.

I wasn't really surprised when the cab took him back to Roscoe Village. They went straight down to the Hungry Brain on Belmont, and Durant went inside the bar. The cab stayed out on the street, and I didn't see Durant pay his fare yet, so I assumed that he wouldn't be long, and that the cabbie was waiting for him. On a Friday night like that, keeping a cab on tab was usually a pretty good idea, since they were few and hard to come by otherwise. Sure enough, within five minutes, Durant was back out in the cab and they were off again.

This time, they only went a few blocks, to a warehouse on Clybourn, south of Diversey. By now, it was well past business hours, so I was suspicious when Durant paid the cabbie and moved toward the building. The cab drove off and I pulled my car onto the side of the street, with a good view of the area. Durant went up to the nearest door and turned the knob, but it seemed to be locked. He turned it again a bit harder, and it opened right up, so I assumed that the door had just been jammed.

He was obviously going to be a while, so I nestled in, poured myself a cup of coffee from my thermos, and waited.

*   *   *

When you're on a stake-out at midnight, things can start messing with your head. That's reason #287 why you shouldn't do what I was doing and sit in your car for hours by yourself. The amber streetlamps flickered and gave the illusion of movement in the bushes nearby. The light hit different surfaces funny and made it look like a malevolent yellow face was looking at you from behind a dumpster in the alley, or like the mirrored walls in the hair salon across the street were on fire. A dog barking in the distance sounded menacing, when it was probably just some kid's cute little Cocker Spaniel or something that would've been adorable under other circumstances. All of a sudden, it's like you're four years old again, laying awake in your bed and wishing that you'd had either the presence of mind to close your closet door before you'd turned out the lights or the intestinal fortitude to get up and do it now. That shirt hanging over the chair casts a shadow in the nightlight's dim glow that looked an awful lot like a monster, even though you knew that it was still just the shirt you'd tossed there ten minutes before. It didn't help when you started yawning and you knew that your eyes and brain were getting more tired than your heart was. That's why God invented coffee. I wasn't going to let Durant get past me just because I was too sleepy to notice him leaving the building.

Oh, have I mentioned that Pieter Durant didn't exist? It's true. Around 9:00, I'd connected with Jenkins and asked what he'd found out. Now, like I said, at first, he'd been hesitant to do much, since digging around to investigate Interpol agents who intimidate your Lieutenant is a good way to get yourself kicked off the force. But no decent cop is going to ignore a chance to help solve a cop killing, and the more he dug up on Durant, the more interested he got in digging.

Jenkins ended up pulling out all the stops and spending most of the late afternoon and evening doing deep searches and hacking databases and doing far more than he ever really should have tried doing. But he said that prior to 1996, when he joined Interpol, there *was* no Pieter Durant—no record that the man I'm looking for was ever born, no records from an education, no previous addresses, no next of kin, nothing. In fact, he has no place of residence even now on file, and what scant data Jenkins could find on Durant were obviously forgeries. For instance, according to Interpol's records, he'd supposedly graduated from Eton College in 1970, but Jenkins did some digging and found out that Eton had no record of a Pieter Durant attending there at all in the 1960s or 1970s. Besides, that would've made Durant roughly a decade shy of Amanda Cairns' age by now, and that was obviously not the case.

Now, either Interpol did a lousy job of screening their agents in the 1990s, or Pieter Durant wasn't all that he seemed. I was wondering if he was actually some sort of spy or international assassin or something like that—or, if he was maybe part of the same cartel that he claimed to be investigating. That would certainly explain why he was working so hard to hamper our own efforts—even why he would then have killed

Karen—but not why he'd killed Flórez or Amanda Cairns in the first place, or why he had such clout in Interpol.

The weather was getting cold outside, I'd been sitting there in the dark for hours, and I was now out of coffee. That streetlight kept flickering, those bushes kept deceptively moving, that false yellow face kept staring at me, that hair salon was still fictitiously on fire, that dog kept barking, and I was beginning to get lost in the monotonous drone of all the pointless details. Maybe I'd lost Durant altogether. Maybe he'd made me follow him on purpose, then ducked into the warehouse, only to come out another door on the far side, with the cab waiting for him there. Maybe I should poke my head into the warehouse myself to see if he was still there. Maybe, maybe, maybe... This is when it would be really good to have a partner around to back you up and to offer some suggestions.

I rubbed my eyes, half to get the sleepiness out of them and half to try to press back the headache that I'd been building over the past couple of hours. I wondered how Joanna and the kids were doing, and I wondered why I was still sitting here in my car, staking out a possibly empty warehouse when there was a murder investigation that I was supposed to be working on.

I looked back up and suddenly, I was wide awake. In fact, the chill that I was feeling at that point was now coming from the inside, not from the weather. See, the streetlight was still flickering like it was before, the dog was still barking, the hair salon was still aglow...

...but the yellow face was now gone.

Background
From *Histoire Des Vampires et Des Sciences Occultes* (Pierre de Ruhr, 1952, trans. P. Durant)

Perhaps, in discussing the vampyri themselves, I should begin with the corrective clarification that they are not human beings infected with some sort of virus—in point of fact, they are not even the humans whom they appear to be. They are in actuality demons who have infested the dead human form like spiritual parasites, moving its limbs and mimicking its voice and personality from life in order to better hunt amongst their prey—the living. But this is the modern form of the vampyri. Such was not always the case.

Ancient Sumer was the birthplace of the *original* proto-vampyri, the Lilitu,[1] created for Satan by the demon-goddess, Ishtar. The Lilitu were night haunts who rode the winds and storms, or took the form of prowling dogs in the streets, in order to close in and prey upon the blood of pregnant women and infants to sate their foul hungers. In fact, their depredations gave rise to the later myths of "Lillith," the first wife of Adam in the Garden, who was supposedly excommunicated from Eden in part because of her thirst for blood.[2] Though this Lillith was a myth, the Lilitu themselves were fact, and an horrific fact at that. The most powerful and evil of Ishtar's Lilitu was golden Lamashtu, who led her sister proto-vampyri in a plague of hunting newborns across Sumer, leaving death and pain and loss in their wake, until they were finally eradicated in a massive hunt led by the king, Ubartutu (though one could also argue that, since Ubartutu was the last king prior to the Great Flood, it was the sudden lack of food sources or dry ground to rest upon during the day that truly destroyed the Lilitu). Powerful though the Lilitu were, they were also relatively fragile—their physical forms were not, even in the remotest sense, "alive," but rather fleshy homunculi which even the simplest weapons or smallest deprivations could destroy.

---

[1] *A name derived from the Semitic root of L-Y-L (meaning "night")—as in the Hebrew* לַיִל.

[2] *In the Jewish Kabbalah (see Zohar 23b, 55a), this "Lillith" was later to become the consort of the demon Samael (aka Asmodeus). See also Schwartz (1988) for more information.*

As history and humanity continued, so did Satan's attempts to create the perfect creature of anti-life. He could not create life—only Jehovah can do that—but he could twist and corrupt it to his own ends, when given the chance. Thus, the Egyptians had their Sutekh-Apopheratu,[3] the Mayans their legends of Camazotz,[4] and the Chinese their Jiāng Shī[5]—all of which stood as bizarre corruptions or amalgamations of humans and beasts, which Satan had cobbled together to suit his vile purposes. But even the most grotesque and powerful of these were only the demonic prototypes of the *true* vampyri—the creatures known as Vrykolakas[6] or Katakhanades[7] or Upir[8]—that were yet to come.

(Perhaps a note here, before I continue. I realize that, in modern popular vernacular, the word, Nosferatu, is often used to speak of the vampyri. This term is often said to be of Romanian origin, but it was actually invented by British author Emily Gerard for her 1888 book, *The Land Beyond the Forest: Facts, Figures, and Fancies from Transylvania,* and then made popular by its use in Bram Stoker's 1897 book, *Dracula.* Having said that, since the word actually derives from the Greek word, nosophoros—meaning "disease-bearing"—it is perhaps more apropos than people suspect, even if not particularly authentic, since vampirism in point of practice shares much in common with the spread of communicative diseases.)

Though the spiritual infection of the undead has spread to the Indian

---

3   *A vampyr-like creature from ancient Egypt which periodically needed the blood of the living to reverse its decrepitude, its name is derived from the Egyptian god of darkness and the open desert.*

4   *Derived from the Qatzijob'al words, "kame" (meaning "death") and "sotz'" (meaning "bat").*

5   *Which translates roughly to "stiff corpse"—undead who traditionally moved around by hopping, due to their stiffness.*

6   *Derived from the Slavic words, "vâlk" (meaning "wolf") and "dlaka" (meaning "fur"), "vrykolakas" originally carried more of a sense of a werewolf than a vampyr. Over time, however, the two creatures became functionally synonymous in many of the legends (though, to Romanians, the "vârcolac" is still primarily a wolf demon).*

7   *Uncertain derivation from a combination of the Greek "kata" ("toward") and "chanō" ("to lose")—thus, presumably, either those who have lost their lives, and yet still live, or those who bring about loss.*

8   *The Czech "upír," Russian "upyr'," or Polish "upiór" (and the Magyar "vampyr") are all often said to be slavic words for "leech" (or "blood-sucker"). This is problematic, however, since, for instance, the common Polish word for a leech is "pijawka," the common Russian word is "piyavka," the Czech word is "pijavice" (or, sometimes, "felčar"), etc. Even the compound word, "blood-sucker," would be "krovopiĭtsa" in Russian. These terms are more likely carryovers from "ubyr," the Tatar word for "witch," brought to the Slavic states through interaction with the pre-Ottoman Turks.*

Vetala, the Romanian Strigoi,[9] and beyond, the first *true* vampyr—the unholy amalgamation of demon and human corpse—was actually born in the little village of Gitta, in Samaria, and *re*-birthed as the Unholy Father of the undead (ironically enough) in Rome. Satan had long been experimenting with the creation of this perfected warrior of death, and had come to the realization that the strongest version of this creature would be a possessed human. But in life, that demon could always be exorcised, and it usually manifested itself in bizarre fashion (such as the periodically aging Sutekh-Apopheratu or the bat-like Camazotz). What Satan realized that he needed was a way for a demon not only to find camouflage by occupying a human body, but also to occupy an otherwise *unoccupied* human body... and he found that way finally through a Samaritan sorcerer named Simon.

---

[9]   *A Romanian word derived from the same root as the Italian word for witches, "strega," much like the Czech "upír" is derived from the Tatar" ubyr."*

Chapter 9
Cat and Mouse

I remember when I was a little kid, I was about to climb into bed when I saw a centipede on the wall above the covers. At the time, my four-year-old brain decided that it was roughly twelve feet long, but in retrospect now, I figure that it was probably only about three feet or four. Anyway, I called for my mom or dad to come kill the monster so that I could safely sleep in my bed that night.

Unfortunately, my older brother beat them to it. He came in, reading his *Sports Illustrated*, and asked what the commotion was all about. When I pointed to the centipede, he rolled up his magazine and walked over to the bed. I thought he was going to smack the thing, but he ended up just lightly brushing it off the wall. The last thing I remembered seeing was the centipede rolling itself up into a protective ball and falling onto the brown crocheted afghan on my bed, blending in perfectly. The thing was now *on my bed*, camouflaged, and probably angry.

That was the longest night of my young life. I was terrified for hours—not so much because of the centipede itself, but because I knew that it was out there, but *I had no idea where.*

I tell you this because at that moment, sitting in my car outside the warehouse, I suddenly felt four years old again. A part of me desperately wanted to turn the key, slam the car out of there, and go straight home— but another part of me, a stronger part of me, needed to know to whom—to *what*—that face belonged. Something had been sitting there, unmoving, for hours, staking me out just as certainly as I was staking out the warehouse. I wracked my brain to remember exactly what the face looked like, in every detail. It couldn't have belonged to Durant— *couldn't* have—because it was too gaunt, and it had no beard. In fact, I say "some*thing*" because it hadn't looked entirely human, which was in part why I'd never really suspected up to this point that it had been anything other than an optical illusion. It had looked more like a yellow, hairless, anthropomorphized rat face, but with squinty eyes. But maybe that distortion was, itself a trick of the light. But what kind of psychopath can sit so absolutely motionless for so long, and then move so suddenly, so quickly. The only other thing I'd seen move that quickly recently was Durant himself. But it couldn't have been Durant.

I looked around the car in every direction, from every angle. I didn't want this guy jumping at me from behind. But I couldn't see anything but that flickering streetlight and the rustling bushes—though I spent a good, long time examining those bushes from the front seat of my car. Nothing.

I took a deep breath and got out of the car, drawing my pistol in the same move. Instinctively, I reminded myself that the SEALs carry the SIG Sauer, and that it's a really good piece. I had a sudden, anxious flash of myself stretched out on Bill Saunders' morgue table, next to Karen's body, with Tony shaking his head and sniffling, "If only he'd carried a Glock…"

I did a double-take to look behind me again, then started moving toward the alleyway where I'd seen the face. This is, of course, another point at which I really should have called for backup from Tony. I knew that, and I wasn't ordinarily the reckless kind, but what was I going to say? Would I explain to him that I'd been staking out our own Interpol guy, by myself, and then gotten scared by a yellow rat face? I backed up against the wall, glanced behind me again, and then ducked my head around the corner and back. Nothing.

I pointed my pistol in front of me and turned the corner into the alleyway. It was empty, except for the dumpster and some torn-up cardboard boxes, and it was a blind alley, closed off by an inner wall that connected the near section of the building with the farther one. Nothing on the fire escapes, no open windows. Nothing. There was no way that he could've moved fast enough to have gotten out of my line of sight coming *out* of the alley before I'd looked back up—nothing moves that fast. That meant that he had made it through one of the doors and into the warehouse.

There were two doors in the alley—one on the inside wall, and one on the wall I had my back to. I hugged the wall as I went to that first door, constantly glancing backwards, upwards, toward those torn boxes, toward the dumpster. Could he have gotten into the dumpster? No, he'd have to have opened it, climbed inside, and then closed it again before I'd looked up. Impossible. He had to be inside one of these doors.

Another deep breath. I reached for the knob of the first door. Impossible to tell if it had been opened recently. I glanced behind me again, then back. This works so much better with backup. I turned the knob. Nothing. It was locked. He could've locked it from the inside once he'd gone through, but it was unlikely. The other door, then.

I cut across the alleyway toward the inner wall, and I glanced behind me again as I did. No way he could've gotten up the fire escapes and then drawn up the ladders again before I could've seen him. He had to be in the building. Behind this door.

Another deep breath. I reached for the door knob, when suddenly, I heard a crash behind me. A big, fast, black form, silhouetted from the streetlight, burst from the dumpster and lunged toward me. Instinctively, I spun and fired three rounds into it, and it was gone. Sometime in-between the eyeblinks of my firing, it was *gone*. My gunshots echoed in the alley, along with the faint ripples of what sounded like… laughter? Not any kind of laughter I'd ever heard before.

I realized that I was breathing hard—nearly hyperventilating. I tried to calm down.

It had gone into the dumpster. *How* could it have gone into the dumpster? How can anything in the world move that fast? I shot it three times—I had to have hit it at least *once*. I *had* to have. And yet, it was gone.

"Es un *vampiro*, man…" I remembered el Buitre's words in my head.

Ridiculous, I thought. There's no such thing as a vampire outside of old horror movies or modern pseudo-romance novels. Guys with black capes and tuxedos, or pale-looking, Goth-wannabe, twenty-something underwear models. They aren't real. The echo of the laughter began to fade, and the lid to the dumpster clanged shut. That fast. Nothing in this world is that fast…

I had to know. I was terrified, but I *had* to know. I moved forward, with my pistol pointed straight out in front of me, and I prayed that an innocent vagrant didn't happen to wander across the opening to the alleyway at just that moment. "Can a pistol even kill a vampire?" I thought, then shook myself back to reality. No such thing as a vampire. They don't exist. I don't know what this guy is, but he's not a vampire. Maybe he's just a really quick guy who doesn't even realize that he's been shot because he's so high on PCP or something that… that…

Nothing in this world is *that* fast…

I got to the end of the alleyway, and I could see the front end of my car. This is the angle he'd been watching me at all night. I was about to pass by the dumpster, when I realized that—fast as he was—it was conceivably possible that he'd gotten back in before the lid had fallen shut. No way I was going to put my back to that dumpster now. I took another deep breath, cracked my neck a couple of times, pointed my pistol, and whipped open the dumpster lid.

Nothing. Nothing but garbage. I let the lid slam shut again, and as I did, I heard that faint laugh again… from *behind* me.

I spun around and pointed the pistol, but I couldn't see anything. One door, the next door, nothing. But then I saw it, in an upper-story window. That same face, now pale instead of yellow, since it wasn't under the streetlight any more. It was looking at me through the broken window on the third floor, shaking its head. And laughing. It slowly stepped back, away from the window, until it disappeared into the blackness of the building.

A sensible man would leave at this point. A good cop would leave at this point. You'd have to be a teenager in one of those dumb slasher movies to follow a thing like that into a dark, empty building. People in the real world know better than to do that sort of thing, right?

The sad thing is, in my experience as a cop, I've found that an amazing number of people do precisely that sort of thing in the real world. Children trust strangers with ice cream. Women trust that nice young man with his arm in a cast who needs help loading his groceries into his van. Truck drivers stop by the side of the road at 3:00 in the morning to help that woman whose car has appeared to have broken down. Beat cops run alone into deserted crack houses to chase down a purse-snatcher. We do what we do because it makes sense at the time, or because it seems harmless at the time, or because we just need to know what's going on. I could leave now, and all of this would be for nothing. I'd never know what this guy had to do—if *anything*—with Pieter Durant.

Could I live with that? Decision time.

Since I was at the edge of the alley anyway, I ran out into the street past a sleepy old red cat and over to the door that Durant had opened earlier. I saw that the deadbolt had been ripped through the door jam so hard that not only had it splintered the wood of the frame, but it had bent the bolt itself. I remembered how I'd thought that the door had simply been jammed when Durant had first tried it, and how easily it opened when he'd tried it again. Had it looked like this *before* then...?

I whipped open the door and burst inside, spinning in every direction with my pistol. It was fairly dark inside, and I jumped back against the wall and slid into the corner until my eyes adjusted to the darkness. There was nothing particularly frightening about the place— this part was just a front office, with dirty desks and old computers, and remainder filing cabinets lining the walls. But I could still feel my heartbeat in my throat, thumping away as fast as it ever had in my life.

I heard the laughter again, coming from a distant room, so I ran across the room to the inner door and ripped it open. The laughter echoed throughout the large warehouse area in which I now found myself, its rippling sound dying slowly out in the darkness. The thing wasn't close to me, I knew, but, like that centipede, I had no idea just *where* it was now.

Why was it playing with me? It obviously could have gotten to me at any time. Had it even been trying to kill me when it burst out of the dumpster? If not, why not? And if so, had I, what, *impressed* it with my reflexes?

I was in the middle of trying to decide which direction to try first, when I heard a crash from the far right. I sprinted in that direction, barely avoiding a heavy, black machine that suddenly jutted into the walkway in the dark. I slowed only a little, but watched my step more, until I found myself at a junction of machinery and boxes. Right, left, or straight?

Another crash, straight ahead, and a scream. Or a yelp? Hard to say. I ran straight for it, and saw another office door, with frosted glass. Something was painted on the glass, but I couldn't read it in the dark like this. But an orange light shone through the glass and under the door, and I realized that this office must face out toward the streetlight. Had I gotten that turned around? I realized that I no longer knew which way I'd come in, or which way to go to get back out. Through the frosted glass, I saw movement in the office—a fast blur here, a crash there, flickering orange light. Something slammed up against the wall on the right side of the office with a great thud, and there was another horrific screech of pain and anguish.

I ran to the door and kicked it in, pointing my pistol and yelling "Freeze!" to whatever I might find there. What I saw was... shocking, at best.

I saw two men grappling against the side of the office, one holding the wrists of another and pinning him to the wall. I didn't recognize the man who was being held there—his face was largely obscured by a spray of blood coming from the side of his head where his left ear used to be. But the man holding him there was Pieter Durant.

He turned toward me, and he spat the human ear onto the floor, his own face a mass of blood and rage. "Detective!" he growled.

The man against the wall wailed in pain and fear. "God!" he screamed. "If you're a cop, *help* me for God's sake!"

I pointed the pistol at Durant. "Let him go, Durant!" I demanded.

"Get out of here, Detective!" he bellowed. "Go now!"

"Sweet God, help me!" the man screamed, wriggling in Durant's grasp.

"Drop him, Durant!" I yelled again.

"Go!" Durant yelled back.

"I'll shoot!"

Durant turned toward me, and I fired. I killed Pieter Durant. I shot him four times, straight in the chest. His blood splattered everywhere, and he stumbled back, releasing his victim and finally crumpling behind the desk.

I killed him. My heart pounded in my ears. I'd killed Pieter Durant. My pistol. Ballistics would match the slugs to my gun. Durant wasn't even armed. How could I even explain what I'd been doing there? I'd killed Pieter Durant, and my life would never be the same again.

I looked back up at the man he'd been fighting, who was standing there, looking down at Durant's body and holding the bloody gash where his ear had been with his hands.

"Are-are you okay?" I stammered out, a little shell-shocked myself. The guy just stood there, looking at Durant, as if he were in shock. "Buddy," I asked again. "I said, are you okay?"

The man turned back toward me and coughed. "Yes," he said... and then smiled. "Yes, I'm just fine now." I saw his face, and I watched it go gaunt again as his eyes squinted into a smile. It was the same face that I'd been chasing—the face in the alleyway. "Protect and serve, Mr. Detective," he hissed at me, beginning that low, quiet laughter again. He started to walk toward me, slowly.

"S-Stop where you are!" I demanded, but he kept walking.

"Or what?" he hissed. "Will you shoot me... *again*?" and the laughter grew louder.

"Stop!" I screamed, but I'd already begun pulling the trigger by then. I don't know how many shots I fired—I just kept squeezing them off, one after another. The first shot hit him square in the chest and stopped his advance for a moment, but most of them, he just dodged. Even at this distance, he *dodged* them. I let my emptied gun drop to my side.

"What *are* you?" I asked.

"Someone who likes to play with my food," he chuckled with that hideous laugh, and with that, he was on top of me. His face was pale and gaunt, his hands were gnarled and bony, and his fingernails were long and sharp, with splits and chunks broken out, caked with dirt and gore underneath. His breath smelled like rotten meat, and his eyes smoldered with pale irises set against a bloodshot background. He smiled, and his rotted teeth looked splintered and sharpened. I'd expected fangs.

"But now you die, Mr. Detective Boy," the thing hissed one last time as he reached for me with those grotesque hands. I knew that there was no way that I could outrun him to escape. "Enjoy hell when you get there..."

"You first, devil!" I heard someone say, and a long blade burst through the thing's chest from behind, then sliced him in half with a silver blur. But before the two sections could each fall to the ground, the silver blur had whirled again, lopping the head off from the neck while they were still in mid-air. The three portions of the thing's body all fell to the floor with a loud, wet, thump.

I gasped when I looked up and saw Pieter Durant standing in front of me, his torn shirt covered in his own blood, and holding a bloodied medieval broadsword in his hand.

Background
From *Libro Verborum Dierum Viventium et Mortuorum* (Gildas Sapiens, 542, trans. R. Beresford)

During the early days of the Church, as both Scripture and secular history teach us, persecution broke out against the Christians. Long before the Romans were throwing them to the lions, the Jews were actively hunting them down and dragging them before their religious courts. As St. Luke tells us in his *Acts of the Apostles*, a young Christian leader named Stephen was executed by stoning while a young Pharisee and vitriolic Christian-hunter named Saul of Tarsus held the coats for his murderers.[1] As the persecution blossomed, the Church spread out, away from their birthplace, and into other countries—including Samaria.

When the deacon Philip arrived in Samaria, he found a local sorcerer who held vast numbers of people in his sway, calling himself "The Great Power of God." This Simon the Magus claimed that he could perform miracles, raise the dead, tell fortunes, and otherwise exhibit the power of his pretended divinity amongst the people. But when he saw the power—the *true* power of God—which Philip demonstrated every day on every street of Samaria, he recognized his shortcomings, and joined in the confession of faith in Jesus Christ. However, as our Lord said, "Multi dicent mihi in illa die Domine Domine nonne in nomine tuo prophetavimus et in tuo nomine daemonia eiecimus et in tuo nomine virtutes multas fecimus et tunc confitebor illis quia numquam novi vos discedite a me qui operamini iniquitatem..."[2] and we must not attribute more faith to Simon than we should, particularly given how the character of his life unfolded as time went on. Not everyone who professes to know God is necessarily truly one of His children—in fact, it is far more common than the Church desires to admit that those who most vocally fling God's name into their

---

[1] *in the* Acts of the Apostles, *vii, 54-60.*

[2] *"Many will say to me on that day, 'Lord, Lord, did we not prophesy in your name, and in your name drive out demons and perform many miracles?' Then I will tell them plainly, 'I never knew you. Away from me, you evildoers!'" Jesus Christ speaking to the crowds in the* Gospel of St. Matthew, *vii, 22-23.*

conversations least understand what it means to make Him their Lord. His name thus becomes little more than a verbal fetish—which not only breaks His commandment never to use His Name in vain, but also places one in terrible jeopardy when the *genuine* use of the Name becomes of paramount importance, as the seven sons of Sceva found out to their chagrin when they attempted to use it in Ephesus as an incantation instead of as a sincere invocation.[3]

Just because Simon followed the Christians with great curiosity doesn't mean that he ever truly followed Christ, for when the Apostles Peter and John came to Samaria, and the Samaritans received the gift of the Holy Spirit, Simon—ever the professional Magus, ever eager to increase his own profit and power—offered them money so that he could add this "trick" to his stage performance. Even when presented with the power and presence of the Holy Spirit, Simon was nonetheless still a slave to his own greed, and stood as an example of what I expressed earlier—namely, that evil is attracted primarily to mere shadows of the substance of good things. Thus, Simon found himself drawn to the more spectacular elements of the Holy Spirit, and missed the genuine power of Him entirely, much like a moth being drawn to the light of the flame.

St. Luke tells us that the Apostle Peter recognized that Simon's heart was not with God, but rather with his ravenous quest for personal power. "In felle enim amaritudinis et obligatione iniquitatis video te esse,"[4] Peter said, rebuking him. And indeed, Simon was entirely captivated by evil, in every aspect of his being. But, alas, though his portion of the Bible's account concludes at this point, his personal story does not, and our world is a far darker place as a result.

Rather than praying in repentance for his sins, Simon took it upon himself to co-opt and "improve" upon Peter's Christianity. He decided that, if he could not *purchase* the power of our Lord, he would simply *counterfeit* it. And with that, the first true Christian heretic began his infernal ministry. Epiphanius[5] tells us that he began to preach that he himself was, in fact, the only true God, and that he was a greater, more powerful Messiah than Jesus had ever been. He found a prostitute in Tyre named Helen, and presented her in his services as the Holy Spirit. In fact, he claimed that, through sexual union with her, he had himself originally created the angels of Heaven and all things that exist in the universe. As part of this perversion of the Trinity—that he, in his pre-incarnate self, was the Creator Father; that Helen was the Holy Spirit; and that their sexual union had re-created Simon again as their incarnate Son—he would conclude his worship service by publicly having sexual

---

[3]   *in the* Acts of the Apostles, *xix, 13-17.*

[4]   *"For I see that you are full of bitterness and captive to sin." St. Peter in the* Acts of the Apostles, *viii, 23.*

[5]   *in* Contra Hæreses *(c. 370, Epiphanes).*

relations with Helen on the altar, and then allowing the rest of his "congregation" to join in. This was entirely natural for them to do, Simon taught his followers, since it was out of carnal lust for Helen that the angels had warred and fallen from Heaven to begin with. May God in His grace forgive those who found themselves lost in his vile teachings.

For as Hippolytus wrote,[6] Simon taught that those who would desire to truly know the *Logos* of God must understand the mystery behind the teachings of the Patriarch Moses. *Genesis*, Simon taught, was intended to introduce us to the vision of Creation, but *Exodus* was intended to enable us to understand that vision. Just as the Israelites were called to walk through the Red Sea—that is, according to Simon, to drink a sea of blood—we also are called to drink the bitter blood that will be changed within us, through the deeper, mysterious understanding of the Word, to become a sweet and cleansing water, just as the wine of the Eucharist is changed within us, through the mysterious work of the Word made flesh, to become a sweet and cleansing blood. "Mare Rubrum est a semita futurus ingredior, ut plumbum nos ut a scientia huic vita nostri laboriosus quod acerbus sors,"[7] he taught—and thus, it is only through drinking the blood that we can truly understand the horrors of this life, and how to surmount them.

Whether or not Simon and his followers truly drank blood as part of their rituals is a matter of some scholarly debate. But the basis of what was to follow was surely built upon those foundational teachings, as a corruption of Christ's gift of the Eucharist to us all. And, perhaps, it also stands as the original reason behind St. James' wise prohibition against the drinking of blood which St. Luke records in the *Acts of the Apostles*.[8]

Simon quickly became a favorite court magician of the mad Emperor Nero, through his powerful demonstrations of his supernatural abilities. For instance, Tyrannius Rufinus[9] tells us of an episode when, during a battle with rival sorcerer, Dositheus, Simon made his body become smoke to let Dositheus' staff pass through him. Aquila and Nicetas spoke of seeing Simon pass through solid walls and locked doors, animate common objects such as dishes or sickles, and cast illusions to blind the eyes of men. In his *Homiliæ*, Tyrannius Rufus also describes how Simon was able to mystically create a simulacrum of a man to do his nefarious bidding:

First of all the spirit of the man having been turned into the nature of

---

[6]   *in* Refutatio Omnium Hæresium *(c. 220, Hippolytus)*
[7]   *"The Red Sea [of blood] is a path to be trodden, that leads us to a knowledge in this life of our toilsome and bitter lot."*
[8]   *in the* Acts of the Apostles, *xv, 20.*
[9]   *in* Homiliæ *(c. 405, Tyrannius Rufinus)*

heat draws in and absorbs, like a cupping-glass, the surrounding air; next he turns the air which comes within the envelope of spirit into water. And the air in it not being able to escape owing to the confining force of the spirit, he changed it into the nature of blood, and the blood solidifying made flesh; and so when the flesh is solidified he exhibited a man made of air and not of earth. And thus having persuaded himself of his ability to make a new man of air, he reversed the transmutations, he said, and returned him to the air. When the converts thought that this was the soul of the person, Simon laughed and said, that in the phenomena it was not the soul, "but some daemon who *pretended* to be the soul that took possession of people..."

Thus, Simon came to the attention of the Emperor Nero, who appointed him to his court and provided him ample public opportunities to display his powers to the people. Justin Martyr even wrote (in his *First Apology*) that there was, at least in his time, an inscription to Simon on a statue in Rome itself, reading, "Simoni Deo Sancto."[10]

In fact, the beginning of the end of the beginning for Simon came during an attempt to impress Nero at the Campus Martius—an action which might also more accurately be seen as an attempt to overshadow the ministries of Peter and Paul in Rome. Simon and Peter had crossed paths several times over the years since they had first met in Samaria, most notably when the prefect Agrippa had asked them each to demonstrate their power by raising the dead. Where the Apostle Peter could—through the power of our Lord Jesus—actually raise the dead, Simon's powers could only *approximate* bringing life to the corpse, allowing it to shamble and open its eyes, but not to truly live again.

Thus, to stop the preaching of the Gospel by Peter and Paul once and for all, we're told[11] that Simon used his popularity with Nero to convince the Emperor to give him the opportunity to prove his superiority. Nero had a large wooden tower built to honor Mars, and compelled all the greatest people in Rome to come to witness the power of Simon's magicks. Peter and Paul were also brought to the field to bear witness and to be thus humbled.

Simon declared that he was the Son of God, come down from the Heavens, and that back to the Heavens he would ascend—and that, doing so, he would then send his angels to Nero to bring him up into the Heavens as well. Dressed in the finest garments and adorned with laurels, Simon climbed atop the tall tower, stretched forth his hands, and began to fly. The crowd gasped in amazement, and many applauded.

---

[10]   *"To Simon, the Holy God."*

[11]   *in the* Acts of Peter and Paul

Nero himself chided Peter and Paul for persisting in their belief in Jesus Christ as the Son of God in the face of such clear power and authority.

Paul wept at the display of ignorance, and Peter prayed against the demonic angels who were carrying Simon in their invisible hands. Peter declared out loud, in the hearing of all the people of Rome, "Adjuro vos, angeli Satanae, qui eum fertis in aere ad decipienda hominum infidelium corda, per Deum creatorem omnium, et per Dominum nostrum Jesum Christum Filium ejus quem tertia die suscitavit a mortuis, ut eum ex hac hora jam non feratis sed dimittatis!"[12] Immediately, Simon plummeted from the air and was dashed against the Via Sacra, his body broken badly. Though Simon's hold on the empire and his cult of followers were broken as well that day, this episode also ultimately led to the deaths of both Peter and Paul, and thus, many sins can be laid upon Simon's head, and may he be damned for all eternity for them.

Though the *Acts of Peter and Paul* mistakenly records that Simon died that day after his fall, Hippolytus tells us in his *Refutatio Omnium Hæresium* how the life of Simon Magus actually came to an end. As with many cult figures, there comes a time when the leader and presumptuous false Messiah must take the final step toward proving his authority, or lose it all. That is to say that, after the cult leader has driven his deluded flock to follow him for a period of time with ever-increasing claims of his own divinity, he inevitably arrives at a point where he must invest himself fully in his claims. It is no longer feasible to simply continue the sham—he must bring it to its logical conclusion, even if that conclusion necessitates the functional end of his cultic reign. Whether that takes the form of the death of the prophetic founder, or the mass suicide of the entire cult, there comes a point when the leader cannot remain merely an earthly, human leader any longer—the continued deception simply can no longer continue. Such was the case with Simon and his cultists.

Hippolytus wrote that, with both his life and his hold on his followers in jeopardy due to his grave injuries from his fall in the Campus Martius, Simon declared to all the ultimate sacrilege, the most extreme expression of his attempt to create a fraudulent Christianity with himself at its crux. Simon declared that, if they were to bury him alive, even in his current state of brokenness, he would nonetheless rise again on the third day, just as our Lord Himself had done decades before. In this manner, he would prove to all the world that he was, in fact, Simon Deus Sanctus. Nero himself believed that he would succeed, and cast both Peter and Paul in irons until the three days were up.

---

[12] *"I adjure you, you angels of Satan, who are carrying him into the air to deceive the hearts of the unbelievers, by the God that created all things, and by Jesus Christ, whom on the third day He raised from the dead, no longer from this hour to keep him up, but to let him go!"*

Simon's followers placed his broken body into a carved pine coffin, and Helen placed a final lascivious kiss on his bloodied lips, and Simon, one final time, declared that he would rise again and bring the reign of Jesus Christ to an end. Closing the lid of the coffin, his followers lowered it into the ground, covered the pit up with dirt, and waited. But this pride became his own undoing, for, as Hippolytus writes so eloquently,[13] "He bade that a tomb should be dug by his disciples and that he should be buried in it. Now they did what they were ordered, but he remained there until now: for he was not the Christ."

---

[13] *again, in* Refutatio Omnium Hæresium *(c. 220, Hippolytus)*

Chapter 10
The Cheese

The sheer tonnage of confusing images hurt my head. What was that thing in pieces on the floor? How was Durant standing here, alive, when I'd shot him repeatedly in the chest? What's with the sword? Where did it even come from? I was in shock.

"Wh—?" was all that I could get out. Durant scowled at me, his sword pointed vaguely toward my body. With my pistol empty, if he chose to come at me with that thing… But then, I remembered his speed and I remembered what little my bullets seemed to do to him the *last* time I shot him. If he chose to come at me with that thing, it wouldn't matter if I'd had a full magazine or not.

"I—I *shot* you!" I finally stammered out.

"Indeed…" was his only answer. Those cold, gray eyes stayed locked onto mine. I just stood there, watching him watching me. He wasn't even breathing heavy. Blood all over his beard and chest, shirt torn open from my bullet holes, that sword in his hands with what looked like an ivory and gold cross-guard and a jewel-encrusted pommel. I'd never seen a sword built quite like it—but I confess that I wasn't really thinking too much about that right at that moment.

"What—" I said finally, breaking the tension. "What are you going to do?"

He glared at me for a moment more, then sighed.

"I am going to clean off my sword," he replied. And with that, he hunched down to the body at his feet, and began wiping the blood off of the blade with the relatively clean sleeve of the corpse's shirt. I took this as a good sign, since I didn't think he'd clean off his blade if he'd intended to get *my* blood on it within the next few minutes as well.

"Why aren't you dead?" I asked, immediately sorry that it came out quite that way.

"That is a far more interesting question than you know, Detective," he replied, working to get a particularly sticky bit of gore off of the blade.

"Seriously, I *shot* you," I continued. "And who was—*what* was that thing that attacked me? And what's with the sword?" My frustration was beginning to overwhelm my shock. "What's going on here, anyway?"

Durant finished his cleaning and stood back up. "Yes, you shot me. This was a vampire. And this is my sword, since Interpol agents do not carry firearms." I got the distinct impression that that last bit was intended to be mildly humorous, but neither he nor I were smiling. "As to what is going on here tonight, I was forced to flush the creature into the open in order to obtain some very vital information from it, so I brought you into the equation for a little game of 'cat and mouse'..."

"With me as the mouse!"

"Not at all, Detective," he replied. "You were the *cheese*..."

"Either way, you used me as bait!"

"Just as you say. A gambit which would never have worked, by the way, had you not chosen to illicitly follow me in the first place, Detective."

"You *used* me as *bait*!"

"I shouldn't think that you would have been in any danger, had you not chosen to *shoot* me in the *chest*..." he growled. I threw my hands up in disgust. This was obviously not getting us anywhere. I re-holstered my pistol, and when I looked up, the sword was gone as well.

"Where's the sword?" I asked.

"*What* sword?" he answered, looking as innocent as Chelsea when she's eaten a cookie before dinnertime.

"Oh, come on!" I barked. "Where did you even get that sword in the first place?"

"Originally?" he asked. "I found it on a ship, actually..."

"No," I growled, getting frustrated. "I mean, where did it come from tonight? It doesn't look like you've got it under your coat there."

"Not properly, no," he answered, cocking his head to the side. "But surely my sword is not truly what you are most concerned about this evening, is it?"

Of course not. But where do you start? I mean, something—a vampire?—that moves like lightning, attacks me, I see them grappling in the office, Durant biting his ear off...

"You bit his ear off."

"I bit *its* ear off, Detective. I refuse to think of a vampire as a human being anymore."

That's the part of the sentence he focuses on?

"So, wait—are you telling me that it really *was* a vampire that we just killed?"

"We?"

"Fine—that *you* just killed?" I corrected myself. "That's an actual *vampire* on the floor?"

Durant leaned back against the desk and crossed his arms, resigning himself to this conversation. From what I'd seen, he could've been out of that room in a blur before I'd even seen him start to move, or he could've smashed me into a fine, red mist before I could have even raised my arm to try to block the blow. The fact that he was willing to talk about this was significant, I could tell. I just didn't realize at the time *how* significant it was.

"Have you ever hunted a *human* culprit that strong and that fast in your years of experience on the police force, Detective?" he asked.

"Yeah, no—" I responded. "But, a *vampire*?"

"'There are more things in Heaven and Earth than are dreamt of in your philosophy,' Detective," he said.

So maybe Tony wasn't too off-base to suggest the vampire-killer kit. What's next? Werewolves? Mummies? Frankenstein's monster? It was all too ridiculous to believe. But then, I thought of all of those clues— all of those tunnels, leading up to this point. I thought of el Buitre and the Angel, and how convinced they were that it was a vampire. I thought of how strong Hector Flórez had been, and how Amanda Cairns' body had been flung around so easily. I thought about why there was almost no blood at the scene of Hector's death. As a rational, grown-up, professional detective, I was almost ashamed to admit how well the ridiculous conclusion actually fit the facts.

"So this is the guy?" I asked at last. "Why didn't he drink Amanda Cairns' blood, then?"

"No, this was not our culprit, Detective," Durant replied. "This was a mere errand boy, though I should have expected the fiend to make use of a revenant for this sort of thing, rather than another vampire..." Durant looked genuinely concerned about that fact. I should've asked him why.

"Wait a minute!" I interjected. "How do you know? What makes you so sure that this isn't the guy we've been after all along?"

He sighed again. "Because *this* is merely the vampire whom I've been hunting to draw out the big game of the *true* Vampire Lord," he answered, as if what he was saying explained everything. "This is only a low-level thug of a vampire. This one would not employ a vrăjitorul of its own, nor would it have left the breadcrumbs that our *true* quarry has left for us to draw us into this trap."

"I thought it was *your* trap," I said.

"Indeed it was," he responded. "But our quarry had originally planned it as *its* trap for *us*. You would be surprised how often this is the case..."

"But everything points to this being our man—our *thing*," I said, unwilling to let it go. "I bet the saliva matches up. And the fingernail fragments."

"Doubtful," he replied. "But feel free to check them. That would make Miss Gage's death feel far less meaningless for you at this point, would it not?"

That's when I realized that I'd been clenching my fists. I hadn't realized how emotional I'd been getting about all of this. That's the worst thing you can do in an investigation. If you don't care about the victims at all, then you have no motivation to find their killers—but if you care too much, you'll jump to conclusions, you'll miss things, and you'll screw it up. I didn't want to screw this up.

"How do I know that *you're* not the killer?" I asked at last.

"You *don't*," he replied, shifting his weight on the desk and re-crossing his arms. "And that is *precisely* the level of open-mindedness which I would expect, coming from you." He half-smiled at that, and I could see the blood still caking his white teeth. "That is also the sort of thinking which might just keep you alive through all of this, Detective."

Alive is good. I'd like to remain alive. "So what's a 'revenant'?" I said, trying to change the subject and turn this back to my real concerns about Durant.

"Hmm?" he responded, as if unused to being questioned like this. "Oh, it's a foul creature inhabited by a lesser imp, with all of the weaknesses of a true vampire, but only some of its strengths. In many ways, a bit like a zombie…" He continued babbling on about revenants for a moment, as if what he was saying could somehow casually be confused for a normal conversation topic.

"But *you* bit *his* ear—*its* ear—off. I mean, *it* wasn't trying to eat *you*…" I interjected.

"What?" He looked confused for a moment, and then suddenly became frustrated. "Oh, *zombies*… Your understanding is obscured by your Hollywood-infused upbringing. Absolute bunk. Zombies are not resurrected corpses, shambling through the streets and biting people whom they happen to run into. That's utterly ridiculous. How could one possibly be frightened of a monster which could so easily be thwarted by the use of a *doorknob*?" He rolled his eyes at the concept. "No, *real* zombies—actually called *nzambis*—are simply people who have been brought back from a deathly torpor induced by a human *bokor* through the combination of a neurotoxin such as tetrodotoxin and a psychoactive tropane alkaloid such as those found in drugs like datura. The victim is left in a highly suggestible state, and is thus usually used as slave labor. Neither supernatural nor infectious in any way. But as these powerful drugs often reduce the victim's mind to something of a tabula rasa, vampire bokors tend to make use of supernatural revenants rather than drugged zombies for situations such as this. Though serving many of the same functions as a zombie, a revenant is in fact created by—"

"*You. Bit. His. Ear. Off…*"

"Yes." He seemed utterly unaware that this action was anything other than commonplace.

"You don't think that was, maybe… excessive?"

"Just because the creature was no longer truly alive, that doesn't mean that it could no longer feel pain, Detective Chapel." He reached into his jacket pocket, withdrew a handkerchief, and began to wipe the blood from his lips and teeth. The handkerchief was monogrammed "P.d'R." and it was a fine—if slightly faded—white silk. "One does what one must in the hunt. As I said earlier, I was attempting to obtain information from the creature when you stumbled upon the scene and ruined—"

"When I 'stumbled on the scene'…?" I interrupted. "I was the *cheese*, remember?"

"Quite right," he responded.

"Listen," I said. "I want some answers right now. You can kill me if you want to, but I need to know what's going on. What *are* you?"

Durant stopped wiping his mouth and looked at me carefully. It was obvious that he was trying to decide something about me, but I couldn't be sure at the time what that might be. I honestly couldn't tell if he was going to respond or not, so I added, "And if you say, 'I'm just an Interpol agent,' I'm gonna hit you so hard that even *you* might feel it."

With that, Durant nodded. I apparently passed another test in his mind.

"Are you a vampire, too?" I asked again, almost afraid to hear the answer.

"You think me one of the undead?" Durant responded with something that chilled me to the bone—he leaned back and laughed a deep, cold, dark laugh. "Detective Chapel, I am quite assuredly the *least* undead person who has ever lived."

"Listen, Durant," I pressed. "I've seen things tonight that—well, that I can't hardly believe. I mean, I just *shot* you, for crying out loud!"

"First of all, in doing so, you ruined a perfectly good suit," he replied with a sigh, picking at the bloody tatters of his fine clothes. "Why, the Burberry shirt and Aspinal tie alone were together worth well over £200. Secondly, my name is *not* Pieter Durant." With that, he began to remove his tie, looking far more distraught over his wardrobe than over any of the horror of the past few minutes.

"So what *is* it then?" I asked.

"Well, I suppose it *is* Pieter Durant, but that has been my name only *recently*…" he replied, examining his overcoat for additional traces of blood.

"How recently?" I prodded.

"Roughly half a century."

"And that strikes you as *recent*?"

"Detective Chapel," he said finally, with one last, heavy sigh of exasperation, "I was born in Caer Ebrauc—in York—in 504 AD." He paused for a moment to let that sink in, though I confess that, at the time, it didn't. "Though some have called me 'Perceval' over the centuries, my given name is actually 'Peredur, son of Efrawg'..." He turned to lock his gaze onto mine, his gray eyes burning cold under those bushy brows. "I am the keeper of God's Holy Grail, and I am immortal..."

Background
**From *Rey Arturo y los Caballeros de la Mesa Redonda* (Jorge
Cortázar, 1963, trans. K. Denning)**

from *Capítulo 9: La Canción de Sir Peredyr el Bravo*

Sir Peredyr[1] has always been and continues to remain a paradox within the Arthurian mythos. Second only to Lancelot in knightly capability, second only to Gawain in valour, and second only to Galahad in purity, Peredyr is at once both a second-tier knight and the most well-rounded knight in sheer power and competence. He is a simple naïf, but also the conqueror of kingdoms. Even his ancestry yields both peasantry and nobility—an outsider, and yet, like Arthur, one who was touched by magicks and greatness, even at an early age. And unlike several of Arthur's knights, Peredyr has a traditional mythos of his own—and one which is, at many stages, arguably richer than the Arthurian mythos which has co-opted his story. Perhaps more than any other of Arthur's chivalric heroes, Peredyr merits our attention as we examine the literature surrounding King Arthur himself.

One should not easily believe the myths and legends which one has heard over the years—and yet, one should not readily discount them, either. Before we might be tempted to understate the merits of Peredyr as a mere supporting character, we must remember that this was one of the most respected knights in the court of the greatest king that this world has ever known—a knight who beheld the Lady of the Lake; who quested for, found, and protected the Holy Cup of Christ; who wielded the bleeding spear of Longinus; who had drawn *l'épée aux estranges renges*[2] from its ancient scabbard and had set himself in the Siege

---

[1] *Also "Peredur" or "Peretur" from the original Old Welsh. After the popularity of romances by Chrétien de Troyes* (Perceval, le Conte du Graal, 1181) *and Thomas Malory* (Le Morte d'Arthur, 1485), *the Francized "Perceval" or "Percival" or even "Percyvale" became the more accepted form of the knight's name, which itself was later Germanized as "Parzival" (i.e.; by Wolfram von Eschenbach in his famous* Parzival, 13th century) *or "Parsifal" (i.e.; by Richard Wagner in* Parsifal, 1882).*

[2] *Cortázar does not attempt to translate the French here (which would*

Perilous[3] and had lived to speak of both. All these things are true, and yet none of them is truly quite as the romantics have written.

In the centuries after the death and resurrection of Christ, Rome folded slowly under its own weight. And as it did so, Rome pulled its legions from their posts in foreign countries to defend its own shrinking empire. Britain was left to defend itself, and Hadrian's Wall[4]—once a strong bastion against the Picts from the north and their brutality—had deteriorated into a crumbling ruin, not much more than a series of frontier outposts on the northern border of what used to be Roman Britannia.

The world of Peredyr, then, was not that of shining armour and pageantry. It was a world of cold mud and blackened blood, of hardened leather armour and Roman standard-bearers, of foreign conscripts and half-breed Roman warlords.[5] England was a land fragmented between shrinking fiefdoms, growing tribes of maddened, headhunting savages, and the last, struggling vestiges of Roman occupation and finery.

Peredyr himself was the son of Evrawc, a Yorkish Earl who "maintained himself not so much by his own possessions as by attending tournaments, and wars, and combats,"[6] and who, through his constant addiction to combat, lost six of his seven sons in battle. Because of this, Peredyr was raised by his mother and tutored by a wandering, black-maned monk who called himself Merlinus,[7] a Nestorian priest and *grúagach*[8] who would be there one day and gone the next, just like the

---

translate properly to "espada con vínculos extraños," or "the sword with strange ties"), but rather leaves it in the original as a title for the sword—as if this were the sword's proper name. The sword itself is first mentioned in Perceval, le Conte du Graal *(Chrétien de Troyes, 1181), but its origin is explained in more detail in the 13th century work,* Queste del Saint Graal.

[3]   *Literally, "the dangerous seat"—a chair at the Round Table reserved only for the knight who had successfully completed the Quest for the Grail. It meant certain death for anyone else to presumptively sit in it (thus, the peril).*

[4]   *A stone wall dotted with fortresses, built across the border between England and Scotland under the Emperor Hadrian in the 2nd century AD.*

[5]   *Such as Aurelius Ambrosius, a 5th century Romano-British leader who may be the historical basis for King Arthur.*

[6]   *From* The Mabinogion—*a 14th century collection of early Welsh sagas. Cortázar thus distinguishes this Peredyr from the son of Eleuthur and brother of Gwrgi, though it is also possible that he conflates the two legendary figures together.*

[7]   *The same "Merlin" from the Arthurian mythos who helped to raise young Arthur in much the same way. Other traditions connect this man with the historical Myrddin Wyllt, a mad priest who lived in the 6th century Caledonian Forest of Scotland.*

[8]   *A hairy, laughing prophet from Celtic traditions*

blackbird whose name he bore.[9] It was Merlinus who taught him languages and Holy Scripture, as well as how to wield the great axe which the monk himself bore into battle. Ironically, though quite sheltered in his youth, Peredyr was also therefore unusually well-educated for his time.

Thus it is that when Peredyr first encountered knights of the round table, he was told by his mother that they were angels rather than men, and he was naïve enough to believe her—but still well-trained enough to think it possible to join their ranks. Unfortunately, in Camelot, he was constantly accosted by Sir Kès,[10] who dismissed Peredyr as a simple country bumpkin. In fact, it was precisely Peredyr's youthful naïvete that allowed him to take seriously Kès' malicious suggestion that he should ride out against the dangerous Vermilion Knight,[11] defeat him, and take his armor. When one of Queen Guinevere's ladies in waiting laughed and said that any man as brave as Peredyr must someday become a great knight, Kès actually slapped her for her suggestion, as well as kicking a court jester who had concurred. Tellingly, none save Peredyr came to the lady's (or, for that matter, Peredyr's) honor.

In this manner, according to Chrétien de Troyes,[12] Peredyr attained his famous blood-red armor and proved his warrior's mettle. In reality, it was undoubtedly the leather covering of his armor which had been dyed red, instead of an anachronistic painting of plate mail (as in romantic paintings), or even a dyed jupon[13] (as in later 19th century illustrations)—which would have been far more commonplace in the 12th century than the 6th. But the core of the mythos is the important detail here—that Peredyr's innocence walked hand-in-hand with his bravery, and thus, with his conquests.

---

9   *The name, "Merlinus," literally means, "blackbird," and is almost certainly an epithet in reference to his thick, black hair, rather than his actual, given name—real names were often considered to be worth hiding from others, since to learn someone's real name was to be granted power over them (as in the Lohengrin cycle later in the Peredyr mythos). Other legends have claimed that Merlin's real name was actually "John," and that when he left the court of King Arthur, he ventured eastward to found his own Christian kingdom in India, which he then ruled for five centuries. Selkirk (1941) has persuasively argued that this was undoubtedly a fiction intended to encourage medieval crusaders.*

10   *Sir Kay—or Cei—the foster brother of young King Arthur.*

11   *Cortázar specifically refers to Sir Ither as the "caballero bermellón," rather than identifying him with the more common "caballero rojo," in an attempt to emphasize the classic color of his impenetrable armor—according to Parzival (13th century), Peredyr ended up having to slay Sir Ither by thrusting his hunting javelin through the visor of the helmet.*

12   *In his 12th century compilation,* Perceval, le Conte du Graal.

13   *Or surcoat.*

It was also an expression of Peredyr's naïvete that, when he joined the round table, he innocently and ignorantly sat down in the Siege Perilous—so named by Merlinus himself because sitting in the chair meant instant death except for "he who would surpass all other knights" by finding the Holy Grail[14]—a seat which had already claimed the lives of six other great knights. His continued existence proved to all of the other knights that Peredyr was destined for greatness.

Peredyr also demonstrated his innocence in terms of his relationships with women. Training under Lord Gornemant of Gohort, he fell in love with Gornemant's niece, the Lady Blanchefleur,[15] and after he completed his portion of the Grail Quest, they consummated their love in marriage.[16] However, even then, he was at various points innocently deceived by a demoness who made herself appear to him as Blanchefleur,[17] as well as being later—again, innocently—seduced by the witch Rigantona into a short and tragic marriage.[18] Though he learned to become wise, it was certainly a long and slow process, with many slips and slides along the way.[19]

After joining the round table, Peredyr joined the other knights in their ongoing battle to unite Britain, from as far south as the English Channel to as far north as Gryme's dyke.[20] And again, in the process, Peredyr's story is interwoven and confused with many of the other knights' tales. Is it Peredyr or Galahad who discovers and takes as his own *l'épée aux estranges renges*[21] aboard the ship of Solomon? Is it

---

[14] *As quoted from Thomas Malory's 15th century work,* Le Morte d'Arthur.

[15] *"White Flower"—or "Gwynblodau" in the original Welsh.*

[16] *At least in some versions of the story. In several iterations of the Peredyr mythos, the hero never consummates his love with Blanchefleur at all, and instead, lives out his days as a hermit in the forest.*

[17] *In Manessier's fourth continuation of Chrétien de Troyes'* Perceval, le Conte du Graal.

[18] *Also called "Rhiannon" in* The Mabinogion *(though this tradition may conflate Peredyr's story with that of Pwyll).*

[19] *Note in particular his innocently ignorant interactions with the Fisher King in* The Mabinogion, *where his slavish adherence to the maxim, "He who talks too much commits a sin," prevents his early attainment of the Grail, and undermines his vengeance on the nine hags of Gloucester.*

[20] *Almost certainly a reference to the Antonine Wall—a wall of turf and stone erected in Scotland in the mid-2nd century AD under the Emperor Antoninus Pius, 160 km north of Hadrian's Wall.*

[21] *This sword is elsewhere referred to as the Sword of David or the Sword of Solomon. According to tradition, it was also the sword used by Judas Maccabeus in his reconquest of Israel, the sword used by King Varlan of Wales to kill King Lambor of Listenois (dying himself in the process), and perhaps even the sword later used by Charlemagne (which he named "Gioisa," or "Joyeuse"). Its scabbard was said to have been made from wood from the Tree of Life in Eden, and its hilt was said to have been carved*

Peredyr or Bedwyr[22] who is asked to throw the sword, Excalibur, into the lake by a dying Arthur after the tragic battle against the bastard Mordred at Camlann? Is it ultimately Gawain or Galahad or Peredyr—or, in some traditions, even Bors—who finally completes the Grail Quest and takes over the charge of the Grail at the mystical castle of Corbenic in Listenois?

From the earliest traditions, we see a Peredyr who is a mass of contradictory elements—a hero with healthy pride but little ego, with wide-eyed naïvete but worldly cunning, with noble blood but country simplicity, with strength and power but also a gentleness of heart and spirit that far outstrips any of the other knights in Arthur's retinue. His legend is worth examining in its own right, even outside of its Arthurian context, and we will do so at length here.

---

from the ribs of a mythical serpent called the Papagustes and a fish called the Ertanax. Peredyr's virginal sister wove her own hair into a baldric for the scabbard—thus, giving the sword its epithet, the "sword with strange ties." Other traditions connect the sword with Caladbolg, the sword of the Celtic hero, Nuada of the Silver Hand, since both swords carry the same blessing and curse—namely, that its rightful wielder could never be beaten in combat, but that touching it would scald the hands of anyone who attempted to wield the sword unworthily.

[22]　*Also known as Sir Bedivere.*

Background
From *Knights of King Arthur's Court* (Jessie Laidlay Weston, 1896)

SIR PERCEVAL—

> "I ride adown the forest aisles
>   From morn till evening shade,
> Beneath the stars of heaven my head,
>   At fall of night, is laid.
> No comrade wendeth at my side,
>   No voice bids me God-speed,
> Alone by hill and vale I ride,
>   Alone by wood and mead.
> "For somewhere, near, or far away,
>   One waiteth long mine aid,
> I may not rest, by night or day,
>   Until his grief be stayed.
> For many a year, with prayer and tear,
>   I've sought to find the way,
> But rough or smooth, the path I choose
>   Still leadeth me astray.
> "I may not rest from off my quest,
>   I may not stay my hand,
> Tho' Life and Love be waiting me,
>   Far in a distant land.
> I may not see my wife's fair face,
>   I may not faint nor fail,
> Till I have won Anforta's grace,
>   And found the Holy Grail."

> Sir Gawayne hath sought the isles of light
>   Beyond the shores of day,
> Where morn never waneth to shades of night,
>   And the silver fountains play;
> There he holdeth high court as the Maidens' Knight,
>   In the Maidens' Isle, for aye.

And Tristan sleeps by his lady's side,
  To the dirge of the sounding sea;
And the foaming wave and the flowing tide
  Hide the twain, that no man may see
Where they take their rest, and their fate abide,
  Till the dawn of Eternity.

But Lancelot wrought a penance hard
  To win from his sin release,
And his face was by fast and vigil marred
  Or ever his pain might cease.
Now his body lieth in Joyous Gard,
  And his soul hath gotten peace.

And Perceval, doth he wake or sleep?
  Ah, no man shall tell that tale—
Perchance he lieth in slumber deep
  With the Eastern sands for veil;
Or perchance, in a distant land, doth keep
  Watch and ward o'er the Holy Grail.

Chapter 11
A Certain Open-Mindedness

"You have got to be kidding me," I said.

"Of course I am," Durant replied, still glowering at me. "I am renowned for my jocularity."

Yeah, right. Durant was as "jocular" as Tony de Tullio was slim.

"Uh-huh… So how on earth are you 1500 years old?"

"The Grail sustains and heals me," he replied. "So I have 550 years on Methuselah, Detective. Truthfully, is that really the hardest thing to accept that you have run across in the past few days?"

A vampire on the streets of Chicago—no, apparently *two* vampires—killing at will, an Interpol agent who moves faster than I can see and bites the ears off of suspects who wanted to drink my blood, Karen being… gone… No, Durant's age wasn't the hardest thing to accept, under the circumstances.

"All of this, all at once—it's just hard to wrap my head around," I confessed.

Durant nodded, and then reached down into a caddie on the desk to pull out a pair of scissors. Opening them up, he dragged the sharpened edge of the blade across the back of his left hand, wincing reflexively. A deep gash opened up, and blood poured out of it as he held it in front of me. But then, within a few seconds, the gash closed itself up left-to-right, as if being stitched by an invisible surgeon.

"Did that hurt?" I asked.

"Of course it did," he replied, wiping his hand with his handkerchief. There wasn't even a scratch left under the blood—not a mark that he'd cut himself at all.

"Good," I said. "Do it again."

"Why not just shoot me again?" he asked, the frustration evident in his voice.

"I would, but I'm out of bullets in this magazine."

He put his handkerchief back into his jacket pocket and sighed again. "You don't care very much for me, do you, Detective?"

"Can you think of any reason why I should?"

"Well, I *did* save your life just now," he offered.

"My life didn't *need* saving until you used me as bait."

"You could not have *been* bait if you had not followed me as if I were a common thief."

And so we're back to that little dance.

"So how do I know that you're not just another vampire?" I asked, taking a different tangent.

"Hold a cross out to me," he replied.

"Does that really work?"

"It does if you have faith," he answered.

"So it only works if you *think* it's going to work?" I asked.

"Not faith in the cross as a fetish," he corrected. "Faith in the one to whom the cross points us. If you have no faith in the Christ, then his cross is just bits of wood to you… and thus, to the vampire as well. The cross, holy water, blessed communion wafers, the Bible, what have you—these only have power in that they are *emblems* of the *true* power."

It was then that I saw what I *should* have seen several minutes before, if I'd been paying attention to the details instead of just reacting to the situation. Under Durant's ripped shirt, dangling on a little silver chain, was a small silver crucifix. It was very simple, and actually somewhat… feminine.

"You mean, like that?" I asked, pointing to the necklace. Durant looked down, and suddenly became uncomfortable, self-conscious. He pulled his shirt together to cover it and cleared his throat.

"Yes…" he said quietly. "Like that…" And that was obviously the end of that conversation.

"Okay," I said, moving on. "If all of this is true—and the jury's still out on that—then why are you telling me this now? I mean, if you think that anyone would buy any of this, then why not get Chacon and the whole CPD in on it? And if you think that it's all flat-out unbelievable, then you're right—so why tell me at all?"

"In answer to your first question," he said, "I have found the Chicago Police Department… less than helpful in the past, except in the most basic investigatory functions that I have made use of you and your partner to accomplish. Even the special unit of yours that deals with supernatural creatures has traditionally refused to—"

"Wait a minute!" I interrupted. "*What* special unit?"

Durant looked up and almost smiled at me. I think that he's actually at his creepiest when he's close to smiling. "You would not have heard of it, of course. They control information rather closely, I am led to believe."

"You're saying that we have a 'monster squad' on the job? That's crazy!"

"No," he continued. "What's 'crazy' is that, for no discernable reason, though they regularly dispatch the veritable flood of fantastical monstrosities that seems drawn to this city on a regular basis, they nonetheless consider the vampyri to be complete and total fiction. Unfathomable to me…"

A special unit of the Chicago Police Department, just to deal with things like the vampire lying in pieces at my feet? That seemed a bit too far-fetched for me.

"I dunno…" I said.

"I would investigate the Golden Eagle Dry Cleaners on State Street, were I you," Durant said, cryptically. "Unless they have moved their headquarters once again…"

"A dry cleaners?"

"A dry cleaners in Chicago, an antique store in Brooklyn, an exporter in London—a common shopfront is often the best place to hide something of great importance in plain sight…"

"Fine, fine," I said. "So you don't want to work with the Department."

"No, I received more help in Chicago from a *private* detective whose acquaintance I made prior to the war against Hitler," he said. "Of course, that brings us to your second question."

"How so?"

"I confess that, in the past, it has been… helpful… to make use of the investigative skills of others," he said. "Too many times, we rely on what we *think* that we know, instead of what is more subtly true, and that can make all of the difference."

"So you're saying that you need a detective?"

"I am saying that it can be quite helpful," he said. "Ali Lakshmi was far more of a detective than I, and his talents enabled Lakota Rainflower and me to successfully hunt Rakshasas in New York back in 1974. Léo Saint-Clair's detective skills were of immeasurable assistance when we fought the Alouh T'Ho in Lyon together in 1933. Even that arrogant windbag, de Grandin, had his uses, though I could never understand what a decent man like Trowbridge saw in him…"

It was like someone was pouring out a bottle of information, and Durant was losing me in all of the details, so I tried to focus him. "What does all of that actually have to do with me?" I asked.

"In my line of work," he said, "I have had periodically need of someone with not only exceptional investigative abilities, but also a certain… open-mindedness… to the unusual."

"That's kind of putting it mildly, isn't it?"

"Fair enough," he agreed. "I have needed someone whose courage and commitment to the truth were more important than his commitment to maintaining the mundane status quo."

Things started clicking into place in my own mind now, and I began to see his line of reasoning.

"Is this why we had that little chat about pistols and arrests back in the office?" I asked.

"Just so," he replied. "So I ask you again, Detective—if you had to choose between the two, would you want an arrest to close your files, or would you demand to know the truth?"

I looked down at the body on the floor. I saw the teeth, the fingernails, and I thought of its speed and strength. According to Durant, this wasn't even the nastiest version of this kind of thing out there. Would I want a clean arrest record that wouldn't make everyone think that I was nuts, or would I want to make sure that things like this didn't exist in the same town that I was raising three kids in?

"I see your point," I said. "I'm in—*if* you can verify that you are who you say you are."

"I can and will verify nothing," he replied. "Shall I produce a birth certificate from the sixth century? Would that prove my identity to you, if it had ever even existed?"

"No, but—"

"I served King Arthur all his days," he interrupted, "and I have served his memory thereafter. Galahad and Bors and I found the Grail, and I have been its custodian for well over a millennium, sustained by the power of the blood of the crucified Christ which had touched it, doing God's will throughout the world as his servant. Believe me or do not believe me."

"You ask a lot," I said.

"No, I *demand* it," he countered. "Your city is under a shadow of evil, Detective. Whether or not it can be saved from that shadow is completely dependent upon whether or not those involved have the faith to believe what their mundane existences have repeatedly taught them to find ridiculous." His eyes smoldered again under those dark and heavy brows. "Have I invested myself in the right man, Detective Chapel, or have I made a grievous error that may doom this place?"

"This can't be all on me," I responded. "That's not fair..."

"I have lived for more than 1500 years, Detective," he said, his voice softening just a bit, "and I have never known life to have been in the least bit 'fair' by our reckoning. Fairness is a concept for eternity and the Divine to decide, not for our finite minds, bounded within this broken place."

I kept thinking about Joanna and the kids. As hard as it was to believe what I was coming to believe was true, could I really afford *not* to? If Durant was right—about *any* of this—didn't I more or less *have* to commit myself to following through with it to the end, no matter where it took me? The only reason that I wasn't dead was that Durant wasn't even remotely normal. Should I turn my back on him now, in the hopes that the problem didn't really exist, or that it would just magically disappear on its own, or that the Chicago Police Department could handle it? Apparently, the guys who handled this on a regular basis weren't even going to be able to handle it.

"So you need a detective…" I said.

"Indeed I do," he said. "That realization was cemented in my mind a little more than a century ago when I hunted a great Thing in London which had been foolishly brought aboard the *Matilda Briggs* from Sumatra."

"A *Thing*? What kind of Thing?"

"A giant rat—as well as its insidious Master…"

"A *giant rat*?" I laughed. "Okay, now you're pulling my leg."

"Would that I were," Durant snapped quickly, his voice and face becoming suddenly far more harsh and hard. "I tracked the Thing through the sewers of London, desperately seeking its lair and the lair of its Master, the terrible Vampire Lord who had taken control of the Tong of the Black Scorpion, only to find that somehow, the fiend had used it to create several… *copies* of it. I've no idea how many young women they had murdered before we finally stopped them, but if it were not for the serendipitous intervention of a detective not entirely unlike yourself and a bizarre, curly-haired doctor, I may never have been able to bring the creature and the villain who had created it to ground."

Seeing Durant's intensity, I suddenly felt bad about laughing before. A vampire sounds ridiculous, but a giant rat? I'd grown up in Chicago— I'd seen plenty of rats in my time. But somehow, this one sounded fundamentally different. I mean, if it rattled a guy like Durant this much…

"Well, tell me more about this rat thing," I said.

Durant shook his head and stiffened. "The Doctor killed one rat in the sewers, and I destroyed the rest, including the Great Thing which had spawned them—but the detective and I agreed that we would never share that story, nor any details of the horrors which we found in its Master's lair in Limehouse. Even the Doctor promised to… *change* certain details of his end of the affair… But I have undoubtedly spoken too much of it already." His eyes glazed a bit as he stared past me at nothing—or at something, or maybe someone, long dead and gone for over a century. "Let us speak no more of history…" he said, his brow crinkling in some quiet, distant pain. "I find at times that dwelling too much on too long a life can be… fatiguing. Far more fatiguing than you could possibly imagine…"

And again, just that quickly, the cork was back in the bottle, and the conversation was over.

*   *   *

I was exhausted—and, in his own way, I think Durant was, too—so I asked if we could talk more about this at my place the next evening, after I'd had some time to sleep on things and to chase down the lead I had with Billy the Kid. I was about to tell him my address, when he interrupted me.

"I already know where you live, Detective," he said, and, with a blur, he vanished. I noticed that the corpse was no longer at my feet, either—all that was left was blood and property damage. In no way was any of that comforting to me in the least.

I don't remember actually walking all the way back out of the warehouse and getting into my car—I guess I did so in a daze, because the next thing I recall, I was making my way down Diversey, heading toward home. There's something more than just a little unsettling about realizing that you've been driving and making turns without really thinking about it. The last time I remember doing that was on long trips coming home from college.

All the way home, I thought about what Durant was telling me. If it wasn't true, then what was *really* going on? And would it be any easier to believe than what I'd just heard? Oh, Tony would probably happily suggest that it was somehow connected to the government—that the creature in the alleyway was an escaped experiment gone horribly wrong, and that Durant was some sort of rogue super-agent who was part of some sort of huge conspiracy or something. But then, Tony watches a lot of really bad sci-fi on late-night cable, so he's not the best source of possible conclusions.

Obviously, Durant wasn't what I'd normally consider to be "human" any more—and neither was the thing that he'd killed in the warehouse. Is it really that much easier to accept a science fiction movie plot than a horror movie plot? And that thing about King Arthur—what was up with that? But then again, it would help to explain the bizarre sword and the funky Interpol records. I refused to come to conclusions about any of this without more facts to back them up. I resolved to maintain "a certain open-mindedness" about the whole thing.

It was almost 5:00 in the morning when I walked into my home. It all seemed fairly surreal by that point. I mean, there was my front door, and the rug in the front hall, and the little blanket that Chelsea had carelessly left on the living room floor when she'd gone to bed nine hours earlier—everything was normal at home, as if the world had just kept turning the way that it normally did. When I'd left home earlier, the world had made sense, even if in a brutal, unpleasant kind of way. There were bad guys and good guys, and I tried to be one of the good guys. But now, there were actual vampires biting people, and King Arthur was a real guy, and one of his knights was still alive and working for Interpol because apparently the Holy Grail was real, too—and yet, nothing had changed here at home.

I walked into the nursery and looked over into the twins' crib. There they were, sleeping as if they didn't have a care in the world. The innocence on their faces was breathtaking. Not a worry line, not a wrinkle. I felt the weight of the planet on my shoulders, and all they felt was warm and safe. How could we exist in the same world? How could the same planet that they felt so comfortable on now seem so unfamiliar and terrifying to me?

Chelsea was already starting to wriggle around in her bed, so I stepped past her quickly and quietly, making my way into my own bedroom. Joanna was lying there, wrapped up in all of the covers, leaving my side of the bed bare. I set my pistol and holster gently onto the dresser, and then sat down on the chair and slid my shoes off, thinking that she was probably happy to have the bed to herself, so that I didn't make her share the covers with me, and then I saw her face. Even as she slept, her brows were crinkled into a worried frown, and she was grinding her teeth in her sleep. She didn't even know what she was worried about—just that I wasn't there, and that that meant that there was probably something to worry about. I slipped into bed and turned toward her, brushing a clump of hair off of her face so that I could see her better. She wrinkled her nose and turned away from me... pulling the covers over with her.

I sighed and got up to grab the afghan that lay over the back of the chair, when I heard a creak in the hallway. In a flash, before I even realized that I'd grabbed it, my gun was in my hand, and I whipped open the door. There was Chelsea, rubbing the sleep out of her eyes. And there was I, pointing my gun at my daughter.

"G'mornin', Daddy..." she mumbled, clutching her teddy bear in her free arm, not even noticing the gun. I dropped my hands to my side.

"G'mornin', baby girl," I replied, leaning down to kiss her on the top of the head. "I love you so much..." I almost felt like crying as I cradled her head in my left arm... and hid the gun behind my right leg.

Chelsea smiled and hugged my left leg. She felt totally safe, and I'd almost shot her. I could feel my heart beating fast, and my hands were shaking with adrenaline. I'd never, *ever* reacted like that at home— never come that close to hurting someone I love.

I knew that I had to finish this. No matter what. I vowed that none of this darkness would ever touch my family. Whatever needed to be done, I was going to finish this.

Background
From *Kitab al-Azif* or *Necronomicon* (Abd-al-Hazred, 730, trans. [Latin] O. Wormius, trans. [English] J. Thode)

And it happened that a sorcerer who was buried alive in the mouldering earth near the sea did succumb to the madness of the inky dark. He scratched frantically at the lid of the box he was buried in until his fingernails cracked and broke and bled, and still he scratched fruitlessly. He screamed and cried out and spoke words which came from the Outer Dark and which had not been spoken upon the Earth for thousands of millennia—and never by human tongues.

And from the Outer Dark, from the vapors outside the veil of time and space, came an

Answer. Yog-Sothoth, the Lurker in the Threshold, whispered to his fevered mind of the Twisted Ones Who Were to Come. It whispered in something deeper and more horrific than words, and its Answer brought an icy damnation to the Magus in his tomb, a wretched resignation that sealed his part to play in the cosmic dance that was coming upon the world of Man.

He felt the Lurker drawing close to him, its tentacled mass wet, slurping, oozing in hideous malevolence. It was slipping in and out of the tomb with him, it was slithering *within* him, it was whispering its horrors into his very soul with nameless, wordless, terrifying images that pushed his mind beyond all natural boundaries. The limitless emptiness of all space, and the Tchagal Things which dwell *between* the emptinesses, all conspired to drive him to a new level of sensation, to a new depth of horror—and his eyes burned at what his mind could now see.

And it was within that darkness within his mind, in stark terror of what he had seen coming, that the Magus surrendered himself to the Elder Gods, and promised them that he would serve them for all time. He promised them his soul and his body and the still-beating hearts of infants and the rivers of blood of all of the living if he could but step out of that tomb again to breathe the air of the living world. He promised them all of this, and in the depths, frothy Things gurgled with an unholy delight...

Background
From *Cultes des Goules* (François-Honore Balfour, Comte d'Erlette, 1702, trans. E. Geraud)

It is said in church traditions that Simonius[1] was buried in Rome before his death, and we must at least conjecture that this may well be the very sorcerer of whom the Mad Arab wrote as having been "buried alive... by the sea."[2] Thus it was in this crypt that Simonius sold his soul to the powers of darkness in order to regain even a semblance of his life. And yet only a semblance was precisely what he was given in return.

For Simonius wanted power and worship for himself, the power of a god to stand as a dark messiah in the place of the Nazarene, supplanting the Other's glory. But what he was given by the Black Prince was a mere puppetry. He gave his body and soul to Hell, and then he was shackled inside of them, just as surely as he had been buried alive in his grave. It was a dæmon who now rode his form, who now controlled his steps and words, and Simonius was reduced to a prisoner within his own corpse. Infelix ego homo! Quis me liberabit de corpore mortis huius?[3]—a fittingly ironic punishment for him indeed.

And thus, it was this *faux* "Simonius" which dug himself out of Simonius' grave three days later. There is some controversy amongst occultists why the vampire did not make use of Simonius's original plan and present himself as a risen Christ figure to Simonius's awaiting followers. It is possible that none were still actually waiting by that point, but that is debatable. It is also possible that the dæmon had not yet realized Simonius's full plans, but that is highly unlikely, since he had access to all of Simonius's thoughts. But the most likely answer is, unfortunately, also the most pedestrian—Prinn's argument that the dæmon simply chose not to out of an expediency.

When Simonius's corpse was to be disinterred, it was bright

---

[1]   *The Comte d'Erlette refers here to Simon the Magus, a sorcerer from the* Acts of the Apostles, *viii.*

[2]   *In Abd-al-Hazred's* Necronomicon *(730).*

[3]   *"O wretched man that I am! Who shall deliver me from the body of this death?" (from the* Letter *to the Romans, vii, 24).*

noonday, and, though a "mature" vampire can withstand the sunlight well enough—though it nonetheless robs them of many of their dark abilities—a *nascent* one most certainly cannot. The rays of its pure light are an anathema to the undead, and for the first few weeks of its existence, no vampire may withstand them. This, combined perhaps with a perplexity at the novelty of its situation, convinced the dæmon to make its own exeunt from its tomb on that dreadful eve of the disinterment.[4]

No doubt unused to walking on human legs, the Thing crept through the dark like a fiendish vermin, searching for a morsel to sate its ravenous needs. We're told that the first victim of the first true vampire was one of the Deity's most innocent ones. Like the ancient Babylonian vampires named in Scripture the *"Ithaï"* and held in forced servitude to King David,[5] Simonius's first murder was to feast upon an infant ripped from its mother's womb, gulping down its tender blood even as the mother watched on in horror, only to die moments later herself at his unholy hands. Thus, with the blood of an unborn child, was the vampire baptized into this world of Man…

Another question that has created no little amount of discussion is that of the infectiousness of the vampire. If vampirism is, in fact, a demonic disease, then why is the world not overrun by its plague? The answer to that is one of self-preservation on the part of the fiends. One should note that the vampire's bite is infectious only so far as the victim dies by the bite itself. Thus, the monster can decide whether or not to create its hideous progeny by killing its prey before feeding or, as it appears to be preferred, to feed as close to the pale of death as possible, withdraw its fangs, and then snap the victim's neck. Thus is the population controlled by the population itself.

As Simonius surmised, an uncontrolled population of vampires yields two undesired results—first, that they would draw direct attention to themselves as a group (and the vampire, though a powerful predator, prefers to hunt in the shadows), and second, that they would become their own primary competitors within their hunting grounds (and the vampire is, at its core, consumed by what van Draeck called an

---

[4]   *For an extended discussion of this argument, see* De Vermis Mysteriis *(1503, Ludwig Prinn).*

[5]   *The Comte d'Erlette appears to have confused the proto-vampires of ancient Sumer known as the* "Lilitu" *with* "l'Ithaï"—*a French translation of the name* "אִתַּי" *(*"Ittai" *from Gibeah, who was one of King David's Thirty Men described in* II Samuel *xv and xviii), and then has misattributed the creatures to later Babylonian lore instead of the earlier Sumerian from which they came. As Bertin (1976) has noted,* Cultes des Goules *is often "rather disappointing because its author had possessed more fantasy than knowledge about the hideous things he was writing about."*

"egoïstische verlangen").[6] In short, for the vampire to maintain its safe place of hiding within the realms of folklore, and to protect itself from the predations of its own cannibalistic kind, Simonius soon instituted what Abdul Alhazred called the *"Dabkeh"* or *"Danse."*[7]

According to legend, after several years of its new existence, Simonius called together the vampiric offspring whom he had created, and pronounced the six-fold *Pacte de le Danse* to them all—

> Only one vampire Seigneur[8] may hold sway over a given territory—the one proved *strongest*.
>
> All other vampires in that territory shall give obeisance to their Seigneur.
>
> No vampires may turn new vampires without the consent of their Seigneur.
>
> No vampires may kill other vampires without the consent of their Seigneur.
>
> No vampires may hunt in packs—each must fight his own battles and earn his own kills.
>
> No vampires may draw attention to the existence of vampires—it is a *secret* Danse.

With this Pacte in place, Simonius created an order and organization to his "Family" of the undead, with himself installed as its eternal Father and ultimate Seigneur. In an unholy ceremony on the darkest night of the year, deep in the bowels of the catacombs of Rome, Simonius initiated the first coven of vampires into the Danse. Onto an altar which he had built for this purpose, he opened a burlap bag filled with squealing infants, each crying more loudly and pathetically than the last. He took the plumpest one and wrung off its head with his hands, pouring its lifeblood into his gaping mouth, and allowing the rest to splatter across his face and neck. He then licked his hideous lips and spoke to his congregation a conscious mockery of the words of the Nazarene, "Ecce hic est calix novum pactum in sanguine suo quod pro vobis funditur sanguis enim eorum pro anima est. Qui et bibit hunc sanguinem habet vitam aeternam et ego resuscitabo eum in novissimo die."[9] At this,

---

6   *"a selfish lust," as quoted from* De Dødes Bog *(1642, Peer van Draeck).*

7   *"*دبكة*"—again, from the* Necronomicon, *though this is almost certainly not the context in which al-Hazred originally intended it. Note: the Comte d'Erlette repeatedly and inaccurately writes Abd-al-Hazred's name as "Abdul Alhazred," and may in fact be the original source of that common modern error.*

8   *That is, "Lord."*

9   *"Behold, this cup is the new covenant in their blood which is poured out for you, for the blood is the life. He who drinks this blood has eternal life, and I*

the whole congregation of monsters descended upon the altar and fed greedily on the mewling babes.

Thus was formed the *Pactum Mortuorum*—the "Pact of the Dead" or the "Covenant of the Dead." It is known in various lands as *le Pacte, il Patto, der Vertrag, el Pacto* (or *el Convenio*), but the Pacte itself is unchanged and unchangeable—the rules are unbreakable by any vampires, and they hold their semi-regular "worship" services together as sacrosanct. Any vampires who break the Pacte are summarily hunted down and destroyed by the one or another of the coven, as ordered by their Seigneur.

Thus is it that Simonius maintains his order from his stronghold in the underbelly of Rome herself, though none who lives knows from precisely where. It is rumoured that upon each sunset, three beautiful vampire brides attend to Simonius by opening his crypt and crying, "Exsurge, Domine!"[10] Other reports say that it is three beautiful *living* maidens from his cult of blood-crazed Simonians—a *different* trio each evening—who offer themselves willingly to sate his hunger. Still others say that he feeds on the ichor of other vampires who have broken the Pacte. Who can say? For the Vampire Seigneur who rules over all the darkened corners of this world is one whom no living man has ever seen and lived to speak of. For who could hope to stand against such horrific forces and live? When even the golden queen of the *Ithaï*[11] quaked in fear of the Undead King, who among us could dare to hope in the face of such bleak hopelessness?

We are all doomed—cattle to be fattened and fed upon when the vampires so choose. To sleep with any other thoughts in our heads is but the delusion of an ignorant madness…

---

will raise him up on the last day."

[10]   *"Arise, O Lord!"*

[11]   *It is uncertain to whom the Comte d'Erlette refers here, but he is most likely anachronistically nodding to the ancient Sumerian night monster, Lamashtu, the strongest of the Lilitu—though the two creatures would never have been contemporaries.*

Chapter 12
Flying All Around Town

When Chelsea was a toddler, she was afraid of grass. I'm not kidding. I sat and watched "Jaws" with her on my lap, and she never batted an eye—in fact, she cheered for the "fishie" whenever she saw the shark. But grass terrified her. I don't know if it was that her feet were overly sensitive, or if it tickled or what—maybe when she's thirty, some therapist will show her how it was due to some trauma she experienced in the womb. But whatever the reason, she hated the grass.

On the plus side, that meant that we could take her to the park, plop her on a blanket, and never have to worry about her wandering off when we turned our heads. She'd stand on the edge of the blanket, looking out at the field of green grass as if she were shipwrecked on a desert island, waiting for a ship to appear on the horizon to take her home.

The funniest part was when she'd actually be stuck out in the grass for some reason or another. She'd whimper slightly, lifting one foot and then the other, as if trying to figure out how to lift *both* feet at the same time and thus avoid having to step on the grass at all. Oddly, that never worked for her.

Aside from giving me a good chuckle, her reaction taught me a good lesson that I never forgot: there are some things that you can't just step out of when you're scared. The more she tried, the more she found herself right back in that same situation—lots of effort for no return on the investment. The trick isn't just to try to sidestep the thing that you're scared of—the trick is to either change the situation, or to overcome your fear... or preferably, to do both. Either way, to *deal* with it.

On the job, I've seen countless people get themselves into trouble by trying to skirt around actually dealing with other troubles. They don't want a fight about the fact that they'd been at a bar all night, so they lie about it—and then get into a worse fight because of their lying. They don't want to deal with their problems at work, so they start snorting coke to escape their situation—and then lose their job because they're high all the time. It never ends well.

So I can honestly say that, as I sat there in my bedroom thinking about all of this, it never entered my mind to just bury my head back in the mundane world and pretend that none of it was going on. You can't stand there and lift both feet and expect keep off the grass—you've got to deal with your situation for what it really is. I could quit my job, pack up my family, and move to Indiana, but that won't change the fact that people are dying here in Chicago—and it won't change the fact that suddenly, my world now includes things like vampires. I don't know if they'd have vampires in Indiana, but I'd know that they still exist out there somewhere, and I wouldn't be able to sleep at night, knowing that I did nothing to stop them.

Which brings us back to Pieter Durant. Was he a hero, putting himself out there to try to stop the vampires? Was he a lunatic who was totally delusional? Was he lying to me about the whole thing? I just didn't know. I mean, I've heard enough stories about the Holy Grail to know the basics—that it was the cup that Jesus drank from at the Last Supper, and the cup that someone caught some of his blood in at the cross, and that it was supposed to heal wounds and grant eternal life or whatever. But just because a delusion lines up with a popular myth, that doesn't make it believable. I could think that I was a Bigfoot and start letting my hair grow out and living in the forest, but that wouldn't make any of it true. I made a mental note to have Jenkins do some more background work for me about Durant. Maybe there was something out there that corroborated his story—or that totally disproved it.

But right then, I was utterly exhausted. I don't think I'd ever felt as tired as I did right at that moment—tired physically, mentally, and emotionally. So I decided to try to catch at least a couple of hours of sleep before jumping back into all of this. I texted Tony that I'd be coming in around noon—and yes, I knew that he'd probably never see the message, but at least I could prove to him later on that I'd sent it, so any ignorance on his part would be totally due to ignorance on his part, and then I turned off my phone, wrapped myself up in the afghan, and flopped onto the bed. I was asleep in seconds.

*   *   *

I had a dream while I slept. I dreamt that I was flying across the city, far above the tops of the buildings. The river was a bright blue, and I could see across the entirety of Lake Michigan, filled with sailboats and people smiling in the sun. Every building seemed to gleam, to shine as if it had just been cleaned and polished. I didn't see any cars anywhere, but the streets were filled with people walking to work, to lunch, to the store, to church, to wherever. Everyone seemed to be happy and everything was right in the world.

Then I saw Joanna by the lakeshore with the kids. She looked radiant—as beautiful as that first day I saw her in college. They were skipping stones across the water, and everyone was laughing. I wanted to join them, but I couldn't seem to lose any altitude—every time I tried to dive down to them, I found that I ended up banking to the right or the left instead.

I noticed that the clouds were rolling in, and I wanted to be able to spend at least a little time with them before the rain made everyone have to go inside. I tried calling to her to stay where she was and wait for me, but no sound came out of my mouth. I couldn't even whistle.

As the lakeshore got darker and darker, I noticed also that the people around them weren't smiling any more. At first, I thought it was just that everyone was sad that the sunshine was gone, but then I looked closer. Their faces were becoming harsher, sharper. Their eyes were darkening, and everyone seemed to become more menacing—it was like all the colors were bleeding out, except for my family. I tried to shout to Joanna to look around her, but I couldn't make a sound. She and the kids just kept smiling and skipping stones—they didn't even seem to notice that the sun was gone.

Slowly, the people around them—the people in the streets and out on the lake, *everyone*—began moving toward them. I saw their fingernails split and their teeth yellow and sharpen, and I realized that everyone in Chicago was a vampire. I tried to fly down to them to help, but I couldn't seem to get any closer, no matter how hard I strained. I screamed silently, but Joanna and the kids were happily oblivious to what was going on around them. Even my tears seemed to hang in the air with me—nothing I could do could reach them in any way.

I watched in horror as one leering, drooling thing that used to be human reached out for Joanna's neck and grabbed at her. There was nothing that I could do to stop it. She screamed, and I saw the horror flash across her face as she suddenly realized what was happening.

And that's when I woke up, drenched in sweat.

*   *   *

I didn't tell Joanna anything about any of this—how could I? I just told her that I'd been on a stake-out all night, and that I was tired. I also told her that Pieter Durant would be coming over sometime in the evening.

"Am I supposed to feed him?" she asked.

"I—I don't think so," I said. What would he eat? *Did* he even eat anything any more? "He's not coming over for dinner, hon. We've just got to talk about some things regarding the Hector Flórez case this evening."

"Why are you doing that here?" she asked. "You usually do that sort of thing in the office, don't you?"

"Well, normally, yes," I said. "But this is kind of complicated. I just wanted to do it outside of everything going on down there."

She looked at me uncomfortably, as if she didn't entirely trust what I was saying. I didn't know if she would let it drop, or if she would try to chase it down. It all depended on the day.

"Thomas Chapel," she said—and that's when I knew that I was in trouble, since she used my full name—"what is going on with you? What aren't you telling me?"

"Honey—" I began, trying to reassure her.

"Don't 'Honey' me, Thomas Chapel!" she interrupted—full name, twice in a row. "Something isn't right here. It hasn't been right for a couple of days, and I want to know what's going on."

I felt like I was flying overhead, like the words couldn't come, even if I'd wanted them to. All I knew was that I couldn't tell her anything until I knew more about what was going on myself. But I also realized that every second I spent trying to decide what—if anything—to tell her was another second that proved to her that something was wrong. It's a nasty cycle to get into. That's when I actually thought about Chelsea and the grass—and whether or not I should keep trying to lift another foot to try to get off of it. Like I said, that never ends well.

"You're right, hon," I finally admitted. "We're dealing with some very weird stuff right now, and I don't know how it's going to come out." I watched her face get pale listening to me, and I could see the worry setting in. "But I'm going to ask you to trust me. I can't explain it to you right now, but I'm going to work on this with Durant, and we're going to make things right. I promise."

"But you don't even like this guy," she said, almost in a whisper. That scared her all the more.

"No, I don't," I agreed. "But I *trust* him." The words came tumbling out of my mouth before I'd even really thought about them, and I confess that it surprised me even more than it surprised Joanna. Was that *true*? *Did* I trust him? He was a crazy guy with a bad attitude and a sword who thought he was an immortal knight, for crying out loud! He obviously wasn't a normal human, and he kept hiding things from me. Did I really trust him?

He could've killed me—*easily*—but instead, he saved me. And he saved me from a thing so horrible that I couldn't afford to deny that it existed in the world. And, seeing how they both moved, seeing the sheer power at play, I realized that Durant may be the only guy on the planet that I could picture actually being able to take one of those things down. I couldn't deny any of that, either.

Did I trust Durant? The truth is, I realized that yeah, I was beginning to. He wasn't a nice guy—he may not even be a *decent* guy— but I was thinking that he might just be a *good* one.

"We will make this right, Joanna," I said, and she nodded. Without a word, she moved in slowly and buried her face in my shoulder, hugging me very softly, as if she was afraid that I'd break or something if she hugged too hard. I wanted to squeeze back and kiss her, but then I realized that it wasn't *me* she was worried about with her hug—I think she felt like if she hugged too hard that *she* would break. So I just put my arms around her as gently as I could, and I held her for as long as she needed me to. It turned out to be a really long hug.

*   *   *

Joanna promised to clean up the place and the kids for Durant's visit, but made me promise to call her as soon as I found out what time he'd be over. I promised, but for the record, I need to honestly say that I never did call her—I never even saw Durant during that day, but I confess that by the time I would have, I had utterly forgotten about calling home.

I got into the office to find Tony de Tullio chewing the walls.

"Where you been?!?" he growled. "This's so not the day ta be sleepin' in, Tom..."

Rodriguez had apparently been following up on an angle on the case that had involved the disappearance of several homeless people down off of Armitage, and they'd fished the body of one of the missing persons out of the sewers this morning. The rats had gotten to him pretty badly already, but it was still clear to Bill Saunders and his team that the body had been totally drained of blood before it had found its way down there. Somebody had murdered the guy, then shoved his body into an unused branch of the line, hoping that it'd be long-chewed before any medical examiner got a chance to look at it. But we'd lucked out and a water engineer had been down there first thing that morning, checking for leaks into the groundwater in the older sections, and she'd literally stumbled over the body.

Suddenly, our investigation had officially changed from investigating two possibly-related killings to investigating a potential serial killer. Chacon was on the phone with the FBI's regional office, Rodriguez and Taylor were off to the sewers to look for more information—and, possibly, more bodies—and Tony had spent the last hour compiling all of our notes and trying to get a hold of me. That's when I reached down and turned my cell phone back on, by the way.

"Tom, about Karen..." Tony started.

"Yeah," I interrupted. "What did the coroner's report say? The CDC was all over that."

He just stood there and looked at me, dumbfounded—and maybe just a little bit hurt.

"That's not what I was gonna to talk about, Tom," he said.

"But that's what I need to know right now, Tony. What did Kingery say?"

Tony stiffened up and gritted his teeth a little. "Heart failure," was all he said. That's the classic "catch-all" of forensics—if you don't know anything else, then at least you could say that the victim died because their heart stopped pumping blood.

"Nothing else? No cause for the heart failure? Nothing that explains the way she looked? No indications of disease found? Nothing?"

"Heart failure," he repeated. "That's what ya needed to know, right?"

Now it was my turn to tense up. "Actually, yes," I said. "That's what I needed to know."

"Yer remindin' me o' Durant…" he said with a grunt, turning back to his desk. Maybe that's why Durant was such a jerk—because it's hard to interact with people when you know you're keeping things from them, when you know that you're keeping them at arm's length. When you do that, you almost have to start treating people like dirt, just to justify it in your own mind. That's not what you *should* do, of course, but it's what you do anyway. Wrongness breeds more wrongness.

Tony let me know that he had actually gotten a line on Billy the Kid since I'd last spoken with him. Apparently, Billy often hung out at a house just off the DePaul campus with a couple of other Insane Deuces and their girls. Tony said that there was a decent chance that he was there right at that moment, but all of this stuff with the homeless guy had come up before he could get over there that morning. I got the address from him and started to run back out the door.

"No, you don't!" Tony bellowed at me. "You ain't gonna leave me with all o' this to go through all by myself!"

"Tony, I've got to connect with this guy!"

"Where was you yesterday when I was lookin' for him?" he asked. "An' last night—you just up an' disappeared on me. I don' like the way yer handlin' all o' this, Tom."

"Tony," I said, "I've got to get going, or I'll miss him again. But if you do this for me, I'll make sure that there's a Giordano's pizza in it for you."

Instinctively, Tony licked his lips. It was like ringing a bell for Pavlov's dogs.

"Awright," he said. "But we're talkin' a meat-lovers here—an' none of that thin crust crap."

"Deep dish," I promised, heading out the door.

"It *better* be!" he yelled after me. But I knew that it was going to take more than a pizza to placate Tony on this. He was rough around the edges, but he was too good a detective and too old a friend to miss that I was consciously keeping him out of the loop on something, and it was all starting to gnaw on him. But I was counting on the fact that he also knew me well enough to know that if I was doing that, it was for a good reason—a reason that it was better for him not to know just yet. Once I got my bearings on this case, I'd try to figure out how to let him in on everything, but the last thing that I needed right now was Tony de Tullio either running afoul of Pieter Durant or accidentally sticking his nose into a nest of vampires. To be honest, I wasn't even sure which of those would end up being worse.

I saw Jenkins in the hallway as I was leaving, so I pulled him over to the side.

"Did that information I gave you last night help, Detective Chapel?" he asked.

"Absolutely," I said. "You did great. In fact, I'd really appreciate it if you'd dig a little deeper."

"Deeper?" he asked, a little concerned.

"Yeah. Dig around and see if you can find any connection between Pieter Durant and the initials 'P.d'R.' anywhere. Family, a girlfriend, a former alias, etc. "

"Alias?" Jenkins said, sounding worried. "I know that we couldn't find much on the guy before, but are we considering him a suspect or something?"

"No, no," I assured him. "Nothing like that. I just want to find out who Durant was before he started with Interpol. Maybe he attended Eton under a different name."

"He'd still be too young to have gone to Eton in the 60s or 70s…"

"Let me worry about that part," I said. "Just see what you can do. Thanks." I patted him on the shoulder and walked off—not because I wanted to be rude, but because I didn't want to give him the chance to say "no" to me. I knew that I was asking a lot of the guy, but I also knew that he'd come through for me before, and that he'd even taken it a few more steps than I'd asked him to take the night before. I figured that I could at least get one more chunk of research out of him before his cold feet made him too uncomfortable to keep going—at least, that's what I was counting on.

*   *   *

The house near DePaul was a run-down mess—not quite "crack house" level, but several rungs down the ladder from "frat house" level. I knocked once, but when no one answered, I stepped inside. There was ID graffiti all over the place—a spade with a stylized "2" inside of it, the words "Insane 2 Deuces" written in fancy script, etc. A Roman numeral

"II" was painted on a door that opened into the basement, and a stack of beer cans was piled into a pyramid shape on the stairs that led up to the second floor. In fact, the remains of probably *several* parties were littering the floor.

"Billy?" I shouted. I didn't want anyone to run off, but I also sure didn't want anyone to think that I was trying to get the drop on them. I really didn't need an itchy-fingered ID getting surprised as I walked into a room and shooting me as a reflex action.

"Billy?" I called out again. "This is Detective Chapel. You wanted to talk with me?" I heard some movement upstairs, and some movement in a back room on the first level. I would have to either stay where I was, or turn my back to one sound to get closer to the other. I started kicking myself for not bringing Tony in, at least on this part of the investigation. I was doing this all wrong, and one of these times, I was going to get killed doing it all wrong.

"I'm not here for anything or anyone else," I said again, standing in the middle of the living room. "I'm just here to talk with Billy the Kid. He called me." More skittering sounds in the back room, along with at least one muffled voice. I waited for another ten seconds or so, but no one came out to meet me. I could hear the cardinal chirping outside on the porch, but nothing else.

Time to fish or cut bait. I started moving toward the back room, past the staircase. I glanced up to the second floor as I passed by, but I didn't see anything up there. I put my hand on my pistol, but I didn't want to draw it if I didn't have to. I wasn't here to start any trouble—I reminded myself that I just wanted to talk with Billy. And I reminded myself that I was doing this all wrong.

I moved cautiously along the hallway toward the back of the house. A bathroom doorway was open a crack to my left, and what looked like a closet door was closed on my right. "Billy?" I said again, as I nudged the bathroom door open with my toe. The room was empty. More shuffling sounds in the back. I gripped the pistol at my side, but I kept it in its holster.

"Billy?" I said again. "I'm just here to talk with Billy..." Something heavy fell on the floor down the hallway and past the kitchen in front of me. I took a deep breath and stepped toward the kitchen.

"You don't want to go in there..." a voice said from behind me. Instinctively, I drew my pistol and whirled around to face the speaker. It was Billy the Kid. He jumped back, laughing, with his hands up in the air.

"Are you gonna shoot me, Chapel?" he laughed.

"I just might..." I said, letting out the breath I'd been holding and re-holstering my pistol. "Where were you?"

"I was upstairs, finishing some stuff up," he said. "Sorry to scare you, there…"

I nodded back to the kitchen. "So why don't I want to go back there?" I asked. Billy just looked at me for a few seconds, then smiled again.

"You here for an arrest or to talk with me?" he asked.

"To talk with you," I answered.

"Then you don't want to go back there," he said again, with a little chuckle. He turned back toward the living room and waved me over to follow him. I took another deep breath and went in there with him. He took a seat on the couch, pushing an old pizza box out of the way to make room. I leaned against the side wall so that I could face every exit and entrance to the room. I never felt even the smallest bit safe the entire time.

"So what were you going to tell me the other day, Billy?" I asked.

"Why'd you hang up on me?" he responded. I sighed before I answered.

"Actually, my cell phone ran out of battery…" I said at last. Billy just laughed.

"Gotta love that modern tech, right, Chapel?" he chuckled. "What did we do before we had cell phones to screw us up?"

"Before that, we had to miscommunicate in person."

"I guess…" he said, sitting there, looking at me. I pulled out my notebook and waited for a minute before repeating my question.

"What were you going to tell me about Hector Flórez?"

"Oh, yeah…" he said, almost as if he'd forgotten why I was there in the first place. "My man Hector apparently ran across something *real* interesting." I waited for a few seconds again, until I realized that Billy was making a game of it—he was dangling it in front of me and making me have to jump for it, just for kicks. Hector Flórez was dead—his brother ID was dead—but to Billy, it was more about having fun with it than it was about really helping in my investigation.

"I don't like playing games, Billy—what are you talking about?"

The smile faded a little from his face, but not entirely. "Okay, okay…" he said. "But you've got to promise me that you're going to take this seriously. It's kinda hard to believe."

Really? At this stage of the game, I was becoming pretty open-minded about most everything.

"Try me."

"Okay," he said, sitting up and leaning forward. "Word on the street is that the Orquestra Albany is messing with a new drug—something called '*Prisa*'—that totally jacks you up."

"What do you mean, 'jacks you up'?"

"I mean, it speeds up your metabolism," he said. "You're supposed to be really strong and really fast, for, like, an hour," he said. "Like *super*-much—you move fast, you heal fast, you break bricks with your thumbs. But it burns you out—messes with your head and tears your body to shreds."

All of a sudden, I felt a weight in the pit of my stomach. I felt like maybe I was too quick to come to a conclusion earlier. Maybe science fiction was the right answer after all.

"So why would anyone use it, if it's so dangerous?" I asked.

"Are you kidding me?" he laughed. "Why do I smoke cigs that I know are going to rot my lungs out, if I live to get old? Why do guys drop acid or get wet with angel dust or snort coke? It's the *experience*, man! Wouldn't you risk your life to live for an hour as a superhero?"

"Not in a million years," I replied.

"Well, then, you wouldn't understand, would you, Officer?" he said, shrugging his shoulders.

"And you're saying that Hector was killed because he found something out about this drug?"

"That's what I heard." I made some notes in my notebook.

"What does that have to do with the old woman?"

"What old woman?" he said, looking like he genuinely had no idea what I was talking about. "All I know is that Hector messed with totally the wrong people." I closed up my book and slipped it back into my pocket.

"You realize, of course, that el Buitre has a different story, right?" I responded. Billy started laughing again.

"You mean that whole blood-sucker thing?" he said, snickering. "Does he expect anyone to actually believe that crap?"

I didn't respond to that. I felt stupid enough already.

"So what are the ID's planning to do?" I asked at last. Billy let his laughing subside, wiped his eyes, and let his voice get very quiet.

"We're already doing it, man…" he said.

"What?"

"We're looking for their stash of this Prisa stuff," he said very solemnly. "And when we find it, we're going to use it to kill every OA in Chicago."

Background
**From *Historia Rerum Anglicarum* (William of Newburgh, 1196,
trans. J. Stevenson)**

It would not be easy to believe that the corpses of the dead should
sally (I know not by what agency) from their graves, and should wander
about to the terror or destruction of the living, and again return to the
tomb, which of its own accord spontaneously opened to receive them,
did not frequent examples, occurring in our own times, suffice to
establish this fact, to the truth of which there is abundant testimony. It
would be strange if such things should have happened formerly, since we
can find no evidence of them in the works of ancient authors, whose vast
labor it was to commit to writing every occurrence worthy of memory;
for if they never neglected to register even events of moderate interest,
how could they have suppressed a fact at once so amazing and horrible,
supposing it to have happened in their day? Moreover, were I to write
down all the instances of this kind which I have ascertained to have
befallen in our times, the undertaking would be beyond measure
laborious and troublesome...

A few years ago the chaplain of a certain illustrious lady, casting off
mortality, was consigned to the tomb in that noble monastery which is
called Melrose. This man, having little respect for the sacred order to
which he belonged, was excessively secular in his pursuits, and—what
especially blackens his reputation as a minister of the holy sacrament—
so addicted to the vanity of the chase as to be designated by many by the
infamous title of "Hundeprest," or the dog-priest; and this occupation,
during his lifetime, was either laughed at by men, or considered in a
worldly view; but after his death—as the event showed—the guiltiness
of it was brought to light: for, issuing from the grave at night-time, he
was prevented by the meritorious resistance of its holy inmates from
injuring or terrifying any one within the monastery itself; whereupon he
wandered beyond the walls, and hovered chiefly, with loud groans and
horrible murmurs, round the bedchamber of his former mistress. She,
after this had frequently occurred, becoming exceedingly terrified,
revealed her fears or danger to one of the friars who visited her about the
business of the monastery; demanding with tears that prayers more

earnest than usual should be poured out to the Lord in her behalf as for one in agony. With whose anxiety the friar—for she appeared deserving of the best endeavors, on the part of the holy convent of that place, by her frequent donations to it—piously and justly sympathized, and promised a speedy remedy through the mercy of the Most High Provider for all.

Thereupon, returning to the monastery, he obtained the companionship of another friar, of equally determined spirit, and two powerful young men, with whom he intended with constant vigilance to keep guard over the cemetery where that miserable priest lay buried. These four, therefore, furnished with arms and animated with courage, passed the night in that place, safe in the assistance which each afforded to the other. Midnight had now passed by, and no monster appeared; upon which it came to pass that three of the party, leaving him only who had sought their company on the spot, departed into the nearest house, for the purpose, as they averred, of warming themselves, for the night was cold. As soon as this man was left alone in this place, the devil, imagining that he had found the right moment for breaking his courage, incontinently roused up his own chosen vessel, who appeared to have reposed longer than usual. Having beheld this from afar, he grew stiff with terror by reason of his being alone; but soon recovering his courage, and no place of refuge being at hand, he valiantly withstood the onset of the fiend, who came rushing upon him with a terrible noise, and he struck the axe which he wielded in his hand deep into his body. On receiving this wound, the monster groaned aloud, and turning his back, fled with a rapidity not at all inferior to that with which he had advanced, while the admirable man urged his flying foe from behind, and compelled him to seek his own tomb again; which opening of its own accord, and receiving its guest from the advance of the pursuer, immediately appeared to close again with the same facility. In the meantime, they who, impatient of the coldness of the night, had retreated to the fire ran up, though somewhat too late, and, having heard what had happened, rendered needful assistance in digging up and removing from the midst of the tomb the accursed corpse at the earliest dawn. When they had divested it of the clay cast forth with it, they found the huge wound it had received, and a great quantity of gore which had flowed from it in the sepulchre; and so having carried it away beyond the walls of the monastery and burnt it, they scattered the ashes to the winds. These things I have explained in a simple narration, as I myself heard them recounted by religious men.

Chapter 13
Bringing Home a Stray

The doorbell rang, and Joanna answered it because I'd been in the kitchen with Chelsea and the twins, making dinner for everyone. But I made it out into the hallway to see her open the door, and there was Pieter Durant, dressed impeccably in a dark blue Canali suit and a long, black, Belstaff overcoat roughly the same style as his gray one—which I presumed had been ruined by all of the blood from the night before—and carrying an ancient-looking bottle of wine. He had that same sort of powerful sense of presence that he'd had when he'd first strode into the police station, and Joanna stepped back instinctively as the waves of intensity washed over her. His eyes darted around the entryway, taking in everything in an instant, and then he greeted Joanna formally. She stumbled around something in response that I didn't quite hear and invited him inside, but I could tell from the sound of her voice that she was feeling more than just a little bit overwhelmed by him. But the irony of it all was that when it came to talking with Joanna, he actually seemed more uncomfortable than she did, like he'd forgotten how human interactions like this were supposed to be handled—like it was a dance he'd learned in childhood and he was having a hard time remembering the steps.

I wiped off my hands on a dish towel as I came down the hall, and I introduced the two of them officially, which seemed to help. "And this would be for you," he said, awkwardly shoving the bottle he'd brought with him into her hands. "I believe that I should thank you for opening your home to me this evening."

Actually, as it turns out, I should probably clarify that it wasn't just a bottle of wine—it was a bottle of Château Climens, 1811. I wouldn't be surprised if the thing had been worth thousands of dollars—but then again, I thought, if Durant really was who he *said* he was, maybe he'd bought it for a franc back when it was first bottled and had just kept it stashed somewhere for over a couple of centuries. Either way, the gift was breathtaking.

"We'll just have to have it with dinner…" Joanna said, showing me the bottle in shock. Funny how receiving a bottle of wine possibly worth more than our car can make a woman turn from "Am I expected to feed him?" to "So what would you like for dinner?" in a mere matter of moments. But I guess that life often comes down to putting our experiences into distinct contexts—what would offend us in one instance flatters us in another one. Our perspectives on our situations are built on deciding whether this moment or that action fits well within the present context or not.

"Actually, I should think it more of a dessert wine," Durant corrected gently. "If I remember it aright. It has been some time since last I drank the vintage, though I actually preferred it to the Château d'Yquem…" Joanna asked if she could take his coat, but he politely declined. Another moment of awkwardness. I was about to invite him into the living room, but my cell phone rang. It was Jenkins.

"Excuse me for a second," I said, stepping away to take the call. I knew that Joanna was almost definitely going to chew me out later for leaving her with Durant like that, but since Jenkins was probably calling me *about* Durant, I thought that I should take it immediately. I expected her to take him into the living room, too, but instead, she asked if he would come into the kitchen with her to help her open the wine. Maybe it was just me, but he looked like he stutter-stepped in following her. This was not a man who was used to feeling anything other than completely in control of his situation, and this was not what he'd planned. I would've said something, but by then, I'd already opened my phone.

"What's up?" I asked.

"Detective Chapel," he said. "I did what you asked."

"Thanks, Jenkins. What did you find?"

"I—I'm actually getting a little uncomfortable with what you've been asking me to do," he said. "I mean, this isn't really what I'm supposed to be doing."

"I know, Jenkins," I replied. "But it really is important." I heard glassware clanking in the kitchen, and I could hear Joanna rummaging through the drawers, looking for our corkscrew. I couldn't help but feel decidedly uncouth, with us fumbling around in cluttered kitchen drawers so that we could open the wine bottle worth a fortune from the possibly immortal man in the designer suit.

On top of that, I'd made Chelsea her favorite dinner that evening—a peanut butter and banana sandwich, with a glass of milk to wash it down. Someone told me once that it was Elvis' favorite dinner, too, but I don't know about that. All I know is that if Chelsea's got a gooey PB&B in front of her, all's right with the world. So the last time I saw her, her face was covered in peanut butter. I'm sure that something like that would go over really well with someone like Durant.

"I checked a bunch of connections between Inspector Durant and the initials you gave me," Jenkins continued, "but I didn't really find anything. I think I'd like to stop doing this now."

More muffled voices from the kitchen, more fumbling in the drawer.

"Isn't there anything else that you can check out?" I asked him, putting the pressure on him. It wasn't the fair thing to do to the poor guy. I knew that. But I needed to know whether or not I could trust Durant. After talking with Billy, I suddenly had two equally improbable explanations for the current, thoroughly unbelievable situation.

"Well," he said, obviously hedging, "not *really*, no..."

"'Not *really*' means that there's something else that you think might work, right?" I heard him sigh an uncomfortable sigh on the other end of the line.

"Well," he said, a little unenthusiastically, "you did say that he might have used an alias, so maybe his face might be easier to find than his name."

"So what are you thinking of checking...?" I asked. There was silence on the other end of the line. "Jenkins?"

"I suppose that I could cross-link the search engine that I've been using with our facial recognition software, and then I could input Durant's face from the security camera footage we have in the office."

"You can *do* that?" I asked.

"Well, I'm not *supposed* to do that..." he said.

"But that's one last thing that you'd probably *like* to try before throwing in the towel, right?"

From the hall, I could see Chelsea sitting at the kitchen table with her mouth smeared with peanut butter, just staring at Durant, as he was explaining something to Joanna about the need to decant the wine. Chelsea didn't look frightened, like everyone else is when they first meet Durant—she just looked intensely curious, in her own four-year-old style. As I talked on the phone, I couldn't help but watch the interaction between all of them with great interest. Joanna was actually beginning to warm up to him, impressed by his knowledge and his obviously cultured demeanor. The twins were busy experimenting with smearing what might have been smashed apricots on their faces. Chelsea scratched her nose and kept on looking at Durant, not even appearing to be interested in her sandwich any more. At first, Durant didn't appear to notice her, and he stood near the table, straight and stiff as the proverbial board, trying desperately to focus on his talk with Joanna about the wine.

Finally, he turned to Chelsea and asked quite politely, without the slightest degree of agitation, "Is there something with which I could help you, young lady?" She just shook her head (actually, when Chelsea shakes her head, she tends to shake the entire upper half of her body), and continued to stare at him. He turned from her and looked back to Joanna, who was beginning to smile at the absolute ridiculousness of it all. And, if it was even remotely physically possible, I think that he actually stiffened all the more.

"Aren'tcha gonna drink your milk?" Chelsea asked at long last, pointing to the glass on the table. Technically, it was *my* milk that I'd poured for myself, but those sorts of distinctions are often lost on four-year-old minds.

Durant turned back to her and cleared his throat. "Actually, I am not really much of a milk drinker, my dear. Would you be so kind as to drink it for me?" he offered, pushing the glass in her direction.

Chelsea shook her head (and everything else) again. "Nope," she replied. "I already drunk mine. But Mommy says you gotta drink your milk or when you get old, your bones'll break up into pieces."

Durant nodded cordially. "I am already quite old, young lady."

Chelsea sat quietly for a long while, obviously thinking about that. Then she cocked her head to the side and asked, "Then don'tcha think you better drink your milk?"

That's when I told Jenkins that I'd have to call him back.

*   *   *

First things first—the wine was *amazing*. It was like having your first steak at a Morton's or Ruth's Chris or something, expecting to have a really good steak and discovering for the first time in your life that you had no idea what *really* constituted a really good steak. It was so much better than anything I'd ever tried before that it was almost criminal to drink it, since every sip you took was one less sip of that wine that could be enjoyed on the planet.

But more importantly, Joanna ended up taking the children to bed, and Durant and I adjourned to the backyard to talk in private. And yes, we took the wine with us.

"You have a lovely family," Durant told me. I was surprised, because he actually seemed to really *mean* it. It wasn't just him being polite or cordial or whatever. As much as I'd felt like a guy like him would have to have seen us as unwashed and unimpressive, he seemed to be genuinely complimenting me on them.

"Well, they're better when they're not covered in food," I chuckled.

"Loveliness is not an expression of appearances," he said. "It is an expression of the purity and sincerity of the heart. Your children are not lovely because of their table manners—they are lovely because they are sincerely loved, and because they sincerely love."

I confess that I was totally speechless. This was not what I'd expected from Durant. He took a sip of the wine and looked out at the full moon, but his face suggested that he was actually thinking of something very different.

"A family such as yours is a gift, Detective Chapel," he said. "To be given a wife who loves you and to be given children who love you and to be given a home where the atmosphere is saturated with the reality of love is a blessing from God beyond compare. You should thank him on a daily basis for his generosity."

"I guess I probably should," I said. "I don't really often think of it quite like that. Not often enough, at least."

He turned his gaze back to me, and his eyes seemed to bore into me. Not with anger, really, but with… what…? earnestness?

"Today was a gift, Detective," he said. "It will never come again, it will never be duplicated, and once it is past, it is past forever. Your children will only smile that particular smile once—the rest will be mere echoes of it. Your wife will only give you this kiss once—the rest will be their own gifts to you. Your family is entrusted to you only for a time. It may seem like the present will go on indefinitely, but that is only an optical illusion brought on by a nearsighted life. So treasure every moment that you have with those whom you love, and those with whose love God has blessed you. And thank him every day, so that you never forget that every day is a gift. But, like manna, it is a gift which can only be opened in that one, singular moment."

He just stood there, unblinking. And I just stood there, transfixed. I mean, this was *Durant*, the clothes-horse killing machine that a roomful of cops were consistently terrified of—the guy who bit a man's ear off the last time I saw him, and then chopped him up into pieces. And now, he's telling me to hug my children every day. I thought to myself, "This may be the deadliest version of Mr. Rogers that the world has ever seen…"

But he was waiting for a response from me, and eventually, I think that I burbled out something like, "Um, I'll do that." He sighed, and then pulled out his pocket watch to check the time. In the glint of the porchlight, I saw that it was engraved: *"Notre amour est immortel—C, 1790."* More to the point, I realized that Durant was focusing more on the inscription than he was on the time.

"That's a beautiful watch," I said. Durant immediately snapped it shut, and shoved it back into his vest pocket.

"Indeed," was all he said in response. That was obviously all that he was *going* to say.

I realized that I'd made him self-conscious, and that's not what I wanted to do that evening, so I tried to change the subject. There really wasn't an easy way to segue from that conversation to vampires, so I just tossed out a provocative question.

"So," I asked him, "ever heard of 'Prisa'?" I watched to see if he would change his expression, or if he would show any sign that I'd cracked open the secret that he knew more than what he'd been telling me. If he knew anything about the drug, then he had the best poker face that I'd ever seen. He just cocked his head, thought for a second, and then nodded.

"A corporation in Spain, isn't it?" he replied. "They own various media—television channels, periodicals, and such."

"I wouldn't know," I said.

"Then why did you ask?"

"I'd heard the word today, and I just wondered if you'd heard of it."

He cocked his head back the other way, with the smallest bit of a smirk rising in one corner of his mouth.

"Have you ever heard of 'Cnemaspis goaensis'?" he asked.

"I couldn't even pronounce it," I said. "What is it?"

"A rare lizard, found in Cotigao-Canacona, in India," he replied. "A species of gecko, in fact."

Now it was my turn to look at him and wonder. I stood there, watching him, and waiting to see if he was going to explain that any further. But he just stood there, watching me watching him.

"What does that have to do with anything?" I finally asked, more than just a bit confused.

"Oh, I had heard of the creature once, and I just wondered if *you* had heard of it," he said. And now I understood his meaning. "But if I left that as my final response to you, I should think that you would find that... insufficient at best. Obviously, there would either be no reason for me to connect you with Cnemaspis goaensis—in which case, it would be irrational for me to bring the creature up in our casual conversation—or there would exist some sort of logical reason for me to connect you with Cnemaspis goaensis—in which case, it would be the height of games-playing to pretend otherwise." He looked at me as if he were disappointed with me, like I was a little boy who'd just lied to his first-grade teacher... *badly*... "Are you a games-player, Detective Chapel?"

"No," I said, embarrassed. "No, I'm not." I took a deep breath and faced him straight-on. "I found out today that Prisa is a new street drug that apparently amps up your metabolism." His expression didn't change. "It makes you run really fast, heal really fast, ratchets up your adrenaline and boosts your strength. Now, do you see where I'm going with this?" I asked him. "Or are *you* going to play games?"

"You believe that what you saw last night was due to this drug, Prisa," he said.

"I believe that's a distinct possibility," I replied. "And it has the benefit of seeming a lot more rational than my other options—and a lot less cheesy, too."

"Cheesy..." he repeated quietly, with a pained expression on his face. "You find this situation to be cheesy?" Durant paused for a moment, then reached into his *got uechan* and brought out a small plastic evidence bag. In it were a number of small granules—not a powder, really, but more like a rough-ground cornmeal.

"What's this?" I asked, wondering if Durant might have somehow gotten himself a sample of this Prisa already.

"The Navajo call it *'áṅt'į*," he answered. "An element which they used in black magicks."

"I've never heard of a Navajo vampire," I said, incredulously.

"Nor have I," Durant replied. "Though I have heard of an *Apache* rogue whose acquaintance I should very much like to make at some future time." He looked lost in thought for a moment, but then returned to the conversation. "But this *'áṅt'į* was not used by the vampire we're hunting—it was used by one of its minions."

Do real people actually use the word "minions" these days? Durant apparently does.

"Used to do what?" I asked.

"Used to murder Karen Gage," he answered. Suddenly, this conversation just went from fairly kooky to deadly serious in my mind. Either he was telling the truth or he was yanking absolutely the wrong chain in me. I remembered that Durant had slipped something into his pouch at the murder scene—something that he hadn't wanted to explain to me or to anyone else that day. But he was going to explain it to me now.

"It's a poison?" I asked.

"Not... precisely..." he replied.

"So what *is* it, precisely?"

"There are various preparations, of course," he answered, "but the most powerful magicks come from *'áṅt'į* prepared from the ground-up bones of murdered children—preferably twins, and preferably those whose birth had been the result of an incestuous assault against the mother..."

"More information than I really wanted to know, there, Durant."

"My apologies for offending your tender sensibilities, Detective," he snapped. "Does it bother you greatly to understand the true level of depravity of the enemy you face? I should think that, after years as a police detective, you would be more prepared to handle this sort of thing. Does all of this still strike you as 'cheesy,' or do you begin to see the gravity of the situation?"

I don't know that I can honestly say that I believed him at that moment, but the sheer intensity of the sincerity with which he held to his convictions was palpable. None of this was really answering my questions about Prisa and its role in what I'd experienced the night before, but Durant seemed to think that what he was saying was genuinely relevant, so I decided to hear him out.

"If this stuff had anything to do with Karen's death," I said, "then

I'll shut up and listen. But you'll have to show me the connection, because I'm not seeing it."

"The 'áńt'į is used to, for lack of a better word, 'curse' an individual," he continued. "The practitioner of the magicks place it on their victim's person without their knowledge, or in their food, or under their pillow, or so forth, and the 'áńt'į draws their life-force from them, bit by bit. The more powerful the 'áńt'į, the more quickly it takes effect."

"But you found this stuff by her body in the lobby," I said. "So it wasn't put under her pillow or into her food."

"No, obviously not," he said. "Someone undoubtedly slipped some into her purse at some point during the day. It was from there that it had spilled onto the floor of the lobby."

"But when?" I asked. "She was with cops all day, at the precinct. Besides, she always kept her purse locked in her desk drawer, so she wouldn't have even had her purse *with* her until she'd left for home that day."

"If that is the case, then obviously, someone must have given her the 'áńt'į on her way home," he said. "Perhaps in an elevator, or in the station lobby, or on the bus, or even on the sidewalk." Suddenly, I remembered the texts she'd sent me. "teens kp bmpng me n laffng. ltl scry." Could *that* have been when she was poisoned with this stuff? On the L on the way home? By teenagers who were blithely laughing about killing her? While she was talking with me?

"But if so," I said, not wanting to dwell on that last part, "then all of this had to have happened within the span of only an hour or so. If the speed this 'áńt'į stuff works depends on how powerful it is… then there must have been some seriously bad juju-mo-gumbo in that stuff."

"*Very* seriously bad juju-mo-gumbo, as you say," he replied.

"Then, um…" I didn't know quite how to put it. "Should we really be *handling* it, if it's that toxic?"

"This 'áńt'į is absolutely safe for us to handle," Durant answered, "because it was not intended for us, any more than it was intended for whomever it was who had placed it on Ms. Gage's person. The only person in any danger was Ms. Gage herself." Then he leaned in closer to me. "But please understand—all of the toxicology reports in the world will never find any trace of 'áńt'į in someone's system, since it was never a *part* of their system. It is thus the perfect weapon to use in order to remove someone from a situation without making their removal appear to have been the result of a murder."

And so we were back to the "I can't / won't prove anything to you, so you'll have to accept what I'm saying on faith" argument again. Then again, it would explain a lot about how Karen could be so quickly and so dramatically killed—and why she'd looked so drained of life—while all that Saunders and Kingery and their team could conclude was "heart failure" from their autopsy. I don't much like Bill Saunders, but that's not because I think he's incompetent at his job.

"So you're saying that this is a Native American thing, then?" I asked, putting the various pieces together in my mind. "I've heard that Roscoe Village is still a locus of ancient Indian spiritualism, even today…"

"Not really, no," he responded. "Most people—and I would think that, from your reaction, you are apparently one of them—believe that magicks are localized. This is Native American magick, that is Chinese mysticism, or this other is Jamaican voodoo, or the like. The truth of the matter is that all dark power comes from the same place, across every continent. It takes different forms, of course, but all of it is truly directed by the same diabolical force. The core of the magicks do not reside in their form or in their name, but rather in their *heart*—this is a form of magick based on the suffering of the innocent, used to cause still more suffering for others. Its heart is a *dark* heart, and thus its use can ultimately bring about only darkness."

"Garbage in, garbage out…" I muttered.

"Just so," he said. "Worshipers of dark things have used forms of 'áńt'į around the world for centuries. The Chinese ground up what they saw as *lónggŭ*—dragon bones—for both curses and medicines. The Bible speaks of the *doresh el hammethim*—those who use the bones of the dead for their magic. And in Romanian *vrăjitorie*—a form of necromancy—they make use of what they call *oase rău*—'cursed bones.' But these oase rău are really simply a different iteration of 'áńt'į from another continent."

"Thank you for the recitation, Inspector," I said, beginning to become a bit frustrated. "But what I'd really like is some sort of way to follow up on all of this 'death powder' here in Chicago."

"I know of a powerful vrăjitorul from Romania who has made expert use of oase rău—or 'áńt'į, call it what you will—and who has worked on behalf the vampyri in his native land," Durant replied. "I had heard that he had recently come to the United States—specifically, to Chicago—so I had sought him out, since he had almost certainly not come here seeking a reputable fresh start in the New World. When I saw the 'áńt'į on the lobby floor, it confirmed his involvement in this case, and I thus resolved to use him to stir up the hornet's nest." He paused to let the weight of his next statement sink in.

"His name is František Yevhen Sydor."

Background
From *Die Geschichte die Vampyren* (Hieronymous A. Vordenburg, 1872, trans. F.W. Murnau)

from Liber II.

It has been the sad responsibility of my family for generations to hunt and destroy the night haunts known to the peasantry throughout Europe as the *upyr* or *strigoi* or *vampyr*. It was, in fact, one of my very own ancestors who cleansed Styria of their foul menace in the dim past, though he himself was not originally from our region. Though there are many different forms which a vampyr may take, and many different powers and abilities which the vampyr may employ in order to subdue and murder its victims, there are some elements of vampirism which appear to be true for almost all of the monsters. But I must confess that even the most learned studies of vampirism over the centuries—many of which I have made careful use of in both my own adventures as well as in the preparation of this volume—are consistently inconsistent in these matters. One can never be entirely certain of anything when it comes to dealing with the undead, and keeping that uncertainty in mind has preserved my life on more than one occasion...

The vampyr is a creature of true evil. It is created by the infestation of a newly-dead corpse by a demon which uses the corpse to hide itself amongst the living, like a predator hiding in the tall grass.[1] The demon takes hold of the body upon an infectious bite, wherein they draw blood as sustenance for themselves to maintain the illusion of life in that form. But due to the mystical nature of this infection (since it is not a disease like those known by mortals to infect one another), a single bite is not always enough to spread the infection effectively. But if a victim *dies* by the vampyr's bite, then they will most certainly rise from their graves on

---

[1]   *In 1657, Father François Richard wrote (in his* Relation de l'Isle de Santerini) *of how Satan is able to animate corpses in order to attack the living, and describes personal knowledge of several cases of documented vrykolakes, including Alexander of Pyrgos, Patino of Patmos, and Ianettis of Santorini. This view is upheld and elaborated upon by Philip Rohr in his* Dissertatio Historico-Philosophica de Masticatione Mortuorum *(1679).*

the third evening as a nascent vampyr. This is why it is utterly essential to destroy the infecting vampyr *prior* to the death of its victim, for if the vampyr is destroyed before the victim expires, then the infected person is mystically freed from the curse, and may live out a normal life, and die a normal death. Otherwise, their fate is sealed, and they, too, will extend the curse to other innocents, their souls fettered in limbo,[2] and ever in torment. The demon possessing their body draws from their thoughts, their memories, in order to hunt its prey by night. This must needs add to the horror of that bound soul, to know that he or she is actually *enabling* the demon to work its terrible predations on the people whom that person had loved in life. One can only shudder to think on the shambling Hell which must confront those bound souls on a nightly basis.

It is therefore not at all uncommon for the vampyr to so totally assume the aspect and character of the life of the corpse which it possesses that even the victim's family members are unable to readily distinguish the vampyr from their now-deceased loved one. In point of fact, this is undoubtedly part of why the vampyren are so often found hunting the loved ones of their victims, although the sheer foulness of the action must not be ruled out as well as a drawing point for their lusts.

I should comment, however, of particular situations in which a vampyr—in attempting to create a "bond" of sorts with a particular victim—has actually seduced or forced that victim into drinking the foul black ichor which flows through the veins of the vampyr itself, thus sharing blood back and forth between them. This is apparently a rare occurrence, however, and should not be seen as common practice, as such a "bond" could easily be used against the vampyr as well as in its service. The demon must be certain of its hold over its victim, or else the connexions between them could well expose the vampyr in the process, and the vampyren are notoriously averse to exposure.

It is said that not only are they themselves, by their *nature*, creatures of shadows and hiding places, but they also regulate themselves in a manner not entirely known to us. Except for episodes in which covens[3]

---

[2]   The word Vordenburg uses here to describe this is "Schwebe" and not the more anticipated "Vorhölle"—this is not a dimensional purgatory in the religious sense, but rather an almost physical sense in which the soul of the vampiric victim is eternally suspended, yearning for release but bound to the soul of the demon infecting his corpse, until freed by the vampyr's destruction. The impression one is given of the victim is a sense of horrific uncertainty, of a lack of hope.

[3]   Here, Murnau has translated Vordenburg's "Bande" as "coven"—though Vordenburg never used "Hexenzirkel" or any of its synonyms in his writings to describe the vampiric community. Having said that, there is much to be said regarding the connexions between vampirism and witchcraft, even

of vampyren have convened for their own purposes—and never, it seems, to hunt together—the vampyr is an essentially solitary creature. Supposedly, this is due to rules instituted by their vampyr lords for unknown reasons…

In rare circumstances, people may become one of the vampyren after their death if they have given themselves over to Satan in a futile attempt to achieve eternal life through vampirism… In some particular instances, even a suicide can become a vampyr after their death—as was the case of a notorious vampyr from the Karnstein family—if they were driven to that suicide by the visitations of a demonic haunt at night before their deaths, which is, itself, a spectral form of vampirism. This is yet another reason why the victim of a vampyr's bite should never seek to end their own lives, since this will almost certainly yield the same result, and they would join the ranks of the undead…

As to the nature of the infection itself, it seems that frequent infusions of the blood of their victims are necessary for the vampyren to maintain the corpses in the illusion of life. In truth, it is not at all uncommon to perceive a vampyr's appearance to become much younger or more vital after it has fed than before. If a vampyr has gone several days without feeding, it may appear aged or desiccated, and if a vampyr has gone more than a week without feeding, it may very well start to show signs of decay and begin to more clearly reflect the corpse that it truly is, since maintaining the outward picture of life requires constant energy and vigilance on the part of the vampyr. Thus also it is that the vampyr must rest throughout the day in a state of torpor to conserve its energy and to process the blood which it has ingested. If it does not have the opportunity to rest in the dark and away from the sunlight, then its energies will be greatly taxed and reduced.

It is a common misconception that a vampyr cannot survive in the sun's rays, but that is not true. Except for the most recently converted vampyren, most of the creatures can exist in the daylight as well as in the nighttime. However, it is unable to make use of many of its demonic abilities during the daytime, and this leaves it in a relatively vulnerable state. Though the vampyr is still much stronger and physically powerful than a living being, even during the day, it will be unable to change its form until sunset, and it is often quite sluggish. In fact, if you can come upon a vampyr while in the midst of its torpor during the day, it will often be so sluggish that it cannot defend itself, or even appear to be aware of its surroundings at all. It takes time for the creature to rouse itself, and thus, the most intelligent vampyr hunter hunts in the daylight

---

etymologically—the Romanian word for vampyrs, "strigoi," comes from the same root as the Italian word for witches, "strega;" the common Eastern European word for vampyrs, "upyr," derives from the old Tatar word for witch, "ubyr;" etc.

hours.

Therefore, the vampyren will tend to attempt to find burrows for themselves during the day—safe havens where they may rest and conserve their energies until they may hunt and protect themselves at peak efficiency after sunset. There is a superstition that the vampyr must rest in its coffin and on the soil in which it was originally interred, but I have personally seen the vampyr literally burrow into the earth like vermin to find its hiding place until sunset. Perhaps the legends that it must at least find its *native* soil are more accurate, or perhaps the creature only has to return to its original soil on a regular basis rather than every day, or perhaps there is no basis for the superstition in the first place. Again, it can often be helpful to maintain a certain incredulity when attempting to make use of the knowledge gained through folklore, as many of the legends not only change from region to region, but also from one telling of the legend to the next.

But there is one aspect to hunting the undead which is absolutely certain in every description and in every interaction which I have personally had. They are demonic beings, and as such, are under the authority of Our Lord Jesus Christ. Thus, a genuine faith and trust in the power of the Lord will protect the living and drive away the vampyr. Even today, you will see in most villages crosses posted on almost every building, or rosaries dangling from the windows, or prayers against the undead written on the doors to private homes, such as this common Slovak one: "Krista, nášho Pána, ste trpel a bol pokúšaný. Ste silný prísť na pomoc z tých, ktorí sú napadnutá diablom, pre vás sú podporu kresťanského ľudu. Ó Pane, chrániť pravou rukou tí, ktorí dôveru vo Vaše meno. Vyslobodil ho od zlého, a poskytnúť im večnej radosti. Amen."[4]

It may appear to the unenlightened cosmopolitan to be mere superstition on the part of their rural counterparts, but it is in fact a matter of survival for these villages. And it is no mere outward appearance of faith which they demonstrate—nor *could* it be, since it is not the simple *demonstration* of a semblance of faith which drives off the vampyr, but the sincere *application* of a *living* faith. As the Slovak prayer asks, when translated, "protect with Your Right Hand *those who trust in Your Name*," and not just those who merely *use* the Name. The Name and cross and power of Our Lord Jesus Christ are not simply fetishes or incantations which can be used to ward off the creatures of evil, but expressions of genuine faith in the God Who has authority even

---

[4]   *A prayer from St. Gregory of Khandzta: "Christ our Lord, You suffered and were tempted. You are powerful to come to the aid of those who are assailed by the devil, for You are the support of Christian people. O Lord, protect with Your Right Hand those who trust in Your Name. Deliver them from the Evil One, and grant them everlasting joy. Amen."*

over Satan and his demons. The pagan thus has no real defense against the demonic, any more than the Mohammedan or the Buddhist would—save that it might suit the demons to give this false impression for one reason or another in a given situation—since it is not merely "a faith" that saves us, or even the *appearance* of faith in the Christian God, but rather a genuine faith in the Lord Jesus Christ, against which even the strongest vampyr or demon cannot stand.

Thus it is that a vampyr may not cross into holy ground (such as a churchyard or cemetery or the like, unless it has been desecrated), or enter a home protected by genuine faith, or advance in the presence of the Host or holy water or a crucifix, when it is being held by even the weakest person with a real faith, since at that moment, that man is standing in the very authority of the Lord Jesus Christ...

The only way to incapacitate a vampyr is to pierce its heart (preferably, with a stake made from the wood of the ash, or hawthorn)—although too many have attempted this after sunset, when the vampyr is free to change its shape to that of the evening mist, and thus escape destruction... and too many others have stopped at this point and mistaken the vampyr's incapacitation for death, only to find that someone else eventually removes the stake from the creature's chest years later and begins the curse all over again.[5] I have also heard that a bullet blessed by a priest can also incapacitate a vampyr, or that the creature may be drowned in running water, or that iron spikes may be driven into its mouth and eyes, but I have never attempted such actions myself, as I am not wont to test an unproven theory at the risk of losing my own life in the process.

To *destroy* a vampyr with absolute certainty requires that one decapitate the monster and remove the head from proximity with the body. One must then fill the mouth cavity with apotropaics such as fresh garlic, wolfsbane, or wild roses—though some legends tell that the chest cavity must be similarly filled as well. Finally, the vampyr's heart should be removed from the chest cavity, since that is the lone organ which continues to function within the body of the deceased. To be absolutely certain, the head and the body should be burned—in separate piles—completely to ash and scattered to the winds. Though it is perhaps possible to skip some of these steps and still destroy the vampyr, it is strongly advisable to follow each step to the letter in order to have absolute certainty that the creature has been fully destroyed. The

---

5   *Armand Tesla references this fact in his* Supranatural şi Manifestările sale *(1727), noting "I once heard tell of a vampyr who remained in its grave for nearly a quarter of a century, only to return to its undead predations when gravediggers ignorantly removed the stake from its heart." A similar occurrence was described in the 20th century within the notes of Professor Walter Saunders of King's College, Oxford (circa 1942).*

vampyren, it seems, like our own little *Blattella germanica*,[6] are quite difficult to truly finish off…

---

[6]   *a species of cockroach commonly found in central Europe*

Chapter 14
An Invitation to the Danse

So we were on the road to Roscoe Village again. Everything seemed to keep bringing us back to Roscoe Village, one way or another—this time, to check out Sydor's apartment, which was easy enough to find by checking on his visa and employment records. He was renting a little place by the month, and his landlord said that he'd put down a big enough deposit that he hadn't required him to sign a lease. To me, that suggested that he wasn't planning to stay around too much longer—or, at least, that we couldn't depend on him to.

But then, I didn't know if I could really trust Durant, either. Did he really not know anything about this Prisa, or was he just lying through his teeth about the whole thing? No matter what was going on—sci-fi or supernatural—I knew that it was beyond me. And that meant that, at least for now, I figured that the best thing that I could do would be to stick close to the freaky guy with the sword. If he was lying, then I didn't want to let him out of my sight—and if he wasn't lying, then I'd be an idiot to let myself wander out of *his* sight.

But I still couldn't get past how bizarre the situation was. I'm driving in my car—my normal, everyday car that I've had for years—but today, my passenger may be an immortal vampire-slayer who'd been a knight of the round table... and who was, at that moment, looking out the window as we drove past a gas station. How surreal is that?

"So," I said, breaking the tense silence in the car. "You knew, like, Arthur and Lancelot and everyone, huh?"

"Lancelot is a fiction," he responded, still fixing his gaze out of the window at nothing in particular.

"Excuse me?" I asked.

"A fabrication," he said again. "There *was* no 'Lancelot' at Caer Mallet..."

"What about all the stories?" I asked. "And what's 'Caer Mallet'?"

He sighed heavily (actually, I was beginning to notice how often he did that), and turned at least toward the front of the vehicle to continue the conversation.

"Arthur's personal castle was called 'Caer Llion'—the castle of the legions. It was one of the last defensible fortifications left behind by the Roman legions which had been stationed in Britain, attached to Hadrian's Wall. But, wherever Arthur lay his head, that place was known as 'Caer Mallet'—the castle of the hammer—whether that should be in a fortified citadel or the tiny hovel of a supportive peasant. Wherever Arthur was, there was Caer Mallet."

"Or Camelot…" I said, finally making the connection.

"A popular corruption of its title, yes," Durant confirmed.

"So Camelot was like Air Force One," I said.

"Excuse me?" he asked

"Everyone always thinks that Air Force One is a specific aircraft," I explained as we crossed under the metra tracks into Roscoe Village. "But the truth is that whatever plane the President gets on is officially re-christened 'Air Force One' for the duration of the flight. He just has a special plane that he usually flies in, designed and outfitted just for him—and since he's the only one who ever uses it, it's just *always* 'Air Force One' when people talk about it."

Durant looked genuinely surprised, and maybe just a little impressed. It was always a little hard to tell with him, what with the poker face.

"I was unaware of that," he said at last, nodding slightly.

"Learn something new every day," I replied. "So, you were talking about Lancelot…" I said, trying to get him back on track.

"Pfah!" he snarled, suddenly a bit more interested in talking with me about this stuff. "You will notice that the first that anyone had ever heard of this fictional 'Lancelot' was when a French author invented a French knight who was more accomplished than every English knight at everything—and so courtly and handsome and charming that he might actually be able to steal the greatest English king's wife away from him. Absolute rubbish…"

"So Lancelot's a myth, but the rest is real, huh?" I said, chuckling.

"I can, with utter confidence, assure you that nothing and no one on God's good earth could have stolen Gwenhwyfar's heart away from Arthur. The royals were utterly devoted to one another. When Arthur died at Camlann, in her grief, Gwenhwyfar retired to a convent for the rest of her life. The Queen of England, shut away in a convent…" His brow furrowed as he thought about that, reliving a pain that obviously still hurt.

"What about you, Durant?" I asked, changing the subject. "Have you ever been married in all that time, wandering the earth?" I thought of that crucifix around his neck, and the pocket watch that he'd obviously taken such good care of for so many years.

"Yes," he said, turning back to the window. No more details coming from *that* angle.

"Okay," I continued, trying to lighten the mood. "Any *little* 'Durants' running around out there? What with what you said about family back at my place, I bet you have grandchildren of your grandchildren's grandchildren all over the world."

It was a while before he responded to that—long enough that I realized that I'd done nothing to lighten the mood at all. If anything, I'd succeeded in pushing him deeper inside of himself. "No," he said, finally. "I have no family left on the planet."

"Well…" I said, trying to lighten the mood, but mostly because I didn't know what else to do other than to keep beating the dead horse I was on. "All I have on the planet is Joanna and the kids, too. Everyone else in my family is gone now. But my wife and kids—like you said, they're a gift. They help me remember that I'm a cop, not a soldier." Somehow, that statement made him take notice again and rouse himself.

"In what way?" he asked, turning back toward me again.

"I mean, don't get me wrong—there's a lot of overlap in a lot of ways. Both cops and soldiers carry weapons, and both of us talk about defending one group and taking a stand against another group. We even have a lot of the same training. But when it comes right down to it, at the end of the day, a soldier is a guy who fights *against* the *bad* guys, and a cop is a guy who fights *for* the *good* guys. Military occupations in places like Vietnam and Iraq show just how hard it can be to ask a soldier to try to act like a cop—but it's just as dangerous when a cop starts to think like a soldier, like he's at war with criminals. He starts thinking less about protection and more about destruction."

"And you see your role differently, eh?" he asked.

"Well, yeah," I said. "I'm not out here to kill the enemy. I'm out here to make the streets safe for people like my family."

"The vampyri are already dead, and they must be destroyed," he concluded, coldly. "Perhaps you should take the time to restructure your thinking accordingly."

"No doubt," I said. "But then again, maybe it's worth asking yourself *why* you do it in the first place. Are you an exterminator or a custodian? Are you killing the vermin, or cleaning the house so that it's safe for human habitation again? I mean, do you hunt these things because you *hate them*, or because you *love* the *people* they're *hurting*? It's the 'why' *behind* the 'what' that I'm talking about."

Durant pulled out his watch and made a show of looking at the time, but I knew what he was really looking at. He was quiet for a moment, lost in one of his centuries-year-old thoughts.

"I am an exterminator of vermin," he said curtly, snapping the watch shut.

*   *   *

Sydor's room was a dump. The building's super didn't do much more than collect the rent—I probably could've gotten him to open up the room for us for a five as easily as I did for a badge—and the room itself was sparsely decorated, with a bare light bulb in the overhead socket. To be honest, I didn't think that Roscoe Village still *had* any places like that, now that it had gotten "trendy" in the past couple of years. There weren't even any lights in the hallways. Sydor's few belongings—including his ancient-looking suitcase—littered his room haphazardly.

Durant immediately growled, "There is nothing here," and turned to leave.

"Wait a sec," I said. "You're good with your sword. Let *me* do *my* thing…" I put on a pair of gloves and started poking around, starting with the suitcase.

"You guys got, like, a warrant?" the super asked half-heartedly as I set the suitcase on the bed.

"Go away," Durant clipped. "Now." And, with a cough, the guy was gone.

"Is that how you guys do things at Interpol?" I asked him, opening the case. It was empty, but I still checked around the edges. I'd seen cases like it before, used by smugglers.

"It is how *I* do things at Interpol, yes," he responded, obviously impatient with the whole process. Sure enough, as I suspected, a compartment popped open along the edge of the suitcase. Durant was surprised, and leaned in to look more closely.

"Nothing in here now," I said, searching it carefully before closing it and setting it back down where it had been before. "But I'd be willing to bet you that this is how your guy smuggled in his oase rău powder stuff. If it was just bone fragments, no drug-sniffing dog would've checked it twice."

"How does that assist us?" Durant asked.

"I dunno yet," I answered. "Maybe it will later, maybe it won't. Maybe something else will. But investigation isn't really about looking for something specific—it's about looking at *everything* and seeing how the pieces fit together. So just hold your horses and let me look around a little." I looked around the room for a moment to see where next to go.

"So just how important *are* you at Interpol?" I asked him, deciding to do a bit of fishing. "Important enough to get Saunders and Chacon dancing around for you, I guess…" I walked over to the desk next. Durant absent-mindedly began looking through Sydor's drawers.

"You mask your investigation of me by disguising it as idle banter," he said. "I should very much appreciate it if you were more direct and less deceptive." He stopped and looked at me. "I have chosen to trust you, Detective. Why is it so difficult for you to reciprocate?"

I paused for a second in the middle of the room and debated about answering him, then thought better of it and kept walking to the desk, shaking my head. I mean, he tells me that he's the Tooth Fairy, and then he wonders why I struggle to accept it? Please...

"For the record," he said, going back to the drawers, "I helped to *found* the International Criminal Police Commission in 1923, in large part to facilitate investigations such as this one." He pulled a sock out of the drawer and looked at it as if it were an alien thing. "*That* would be how important I am at Interpol..." He let the sock drop back into the drawer.

"Make sure that you put it back the way you found it," I said. I purposely didn't turn around when I said it, but I noticed the look of surprise and minor offense on Durant's face in my peripheral vision. To his credit, though, he reached back down and rearranged the sock appropriately. Score one point for the rational modern man over the grumpy immortal.

I started to go through the garbage can. Frankly, garbage cans are often the best resources for evidence that a detective could dream of. You'd be surprised at the things that people just throw away, as if no one in the world would ever think to look in the garbage can for any evidence. It's like they think that throwing something away is functionally the same thing as destroying it, because then at least it's out of *their* world—so it's *kind* of like it's out of the *real* world. Garbage cans, internet histories, and phone records—the footprints of our lives that we just forget exist.

In Sydor's trash can, though, there was very little. There was an empty cup of coffee from Starbuck's, along with a soiled napkin. There were two wrappers from some candy that I didn't recognize. And there were the charred remains of a bit of notepaper. Sydor had burnt a note to hide its contents from prying eyes. So he'd expected that someone might check his room? Probably just because Durant had roughed him up the other day, and so he got careful.

But *how* careful? I checked through the desk drawer, and found a notepad there, with the first several pages ripped out. But I could still see the barest outlines of some writing on the blank page on top, from when someone had written on the previous page in the pad and pressed too hard. I pulled it out, set it on the desktop, grabbed the sharpest pencil I could find, and began lightly feathering the side of the pencil lead across the surface of the paper. Little by little, the white indentions of the letters became more distinct against the darkening background.

"You have got to be joking," Durant said when he saw what I was doing.

"I know, I know...," I said, working carefully. "It's done to death in all of those hokey old detective novels. But the reason that every hack writer uses it in their books is because it actually really does work." Sure enough, a message began to appear.

At first, I thought that the note might have been written in code, but I quickly realized that it was actually in a foreign language—which just made sense, since Sydor was Romanian. The only portion that I could make out read, "la faţa locului, de obicei în spatele bibliotecii." I showed the sheet to Durant, who read it and nodded.

"'At the usual spot, behind the library...'" Durant mumbled, mostly to himself. "Very good work, Detective."

"You read Romanian?" I asked. He cocked his head and frowned a little, as if surprised that I would be surprised at that.

"Of course I do," he replied. *Of course* he did.

"Well, if he has a regular meeting place with someone—"

"Perhaps even our quarry," Durant interjected.

"Maybe," I said. "But if they've got a usual spot to meet, and Sydor hasn't come back here to take his stuff..."

"Then he may go there again to meet with his master..."

"Or he may even be there right now," I said. Durant slammed the drawer shut and ripped open the door to the outer hallway.

"Make haste, Detective!" he bellowed, and headed out. I smiled at his excitement. It was almost like watching a child getting ready to run out to recess when the bell rang. I tore the page I'd shaded out of the notepad, and replaced everything the way we'd found it. We didn't want Sydor to know that we'd been there.

I followed Durant into the hall and that's when things went south.

*   *   *

Durant was standing in the middle of the hallway, his head tilted as if he were listening to something that I couldn't hear.

"What's up?" I asked, wondering why he wasn't already in the car, impatient for me to get going to the library.

"Prepare yourself, Detective..."

"For what?"

He didn't respond, but instead, reached under his jacket and pulled out some sort of stick—actually, more like a short staff. The stick itself was rough-hewn, but the top of it was beautifully carved into the head of a cat.

"Where do you *get* this stuff?" I asked. "That was *not* in your coat!"

"I got it in Devonshire, actually..." he said, cryptically. He spun the staff in his hands slowly, almost absent-mindedly, waiting for what was coming. He didn't have to wait for long.

"Revenants..." he whispered.

I didn't know what to expect, but I'm pretty sure that I wouldn't have expected this. Before I saw anything, I heard the sound—a dry, crackling, skittling sound, like a thousand angry cockroaches. And then, a hissing, not so much like a snake as it was like someone slowly letting the air out of a tire. It began quietly, but then rose steadily in volume until the whole hallway was filled with the sound. And then, in the darkness, I saw movement.

It was like the floor and the walls and the ceiling were alive—like the darkness itself was alive, and moving toward us. Durant stopped spinning his staff. "Stay behind me," he said soberly, and he squared himself against the coming darkness.

The first revenant came close enough that I could finally see it. Its hair was long and shaggy, and it was dressed in tattered rags. Its face was covered in grime, and yellow bile dribbled from its cracked lips. Dark red eyes seemed to glow from its sunken sockets, and it skittered along the floor on all fours like a lizard. A dozen more revenants followed after it, clinging to the walls and the ceiling, crawling over one another like flies covering a dead thing. And hissing.

I didn't like standing in the middle of the hallway, facing that, so I turned to see if we had a more defensible position behind us. Instead, I saw more movement, and heard more hissing.

"This was another trap, Detective," Durant said. "This must have been why I was allowed to find the 'áṅt'į near Karen Gage's body—to lead us here and into this." He was gritting his teeth. For the first time, I saw Durant getting angry—not at the fact that he was about to be attacked by a horde of undead things, but at the fact that he had been played by the vampire he was hunting.

"But how…?" I asked.

"Damnable creatures…" Durant snarled.

"We know thee, Huntsman…" one of the revenants hissed at Durant, its mouth frothing with bile. "Thou art the Walker in the Daylight, the Living Ghost…" It began to cackle a wet cackle, deep in its throat, and its brethren joined in. It was a chorus of unholy laughter.

"Let the man go," Durant said to them. "He is not a part of this."

His request was met only with another round of cackling. Then I heard more skittling and hissing coming from Sydor's room—they must have come through the window behind us.

"We know thee as well, little policeman…" the lead thing rasped, pointing a taloned finger toward me. "And we know of the tender little morsels which thou hast kept and hast fattened for us in thy home…" The revenants behind it gurgled in their throats. "Our very own larder…"

I pulled my pistol and pointed it at the thing.

"You leave my family alone!" I yelled.

"Put the gun away, Detective," Durant said quietly. "It will not help you here."

"I think I'll keep it," I said. "Thanks anyway."

With that, the revenants rushed at Durant. He spun and kicked the first one away, while he swung the staff at another. The first seemed to crack under his foot, but the *second* one—it's like it *crumbled* where the staff struck it, or maybe more accurately, it *melted* like soft wax. Another spin, and the staff struck another revenant in the skull, which squished beneath the blow and dissolved. Then he threw himself into the midst of them, growling like a wild animal and gliding like a dancer. The way he moved, it was an angry ballet of killing.

I turned to the revenants coming up from behind us. I fired at the first one, but it barely even seemed to notice the bullet that struck it. All that happened was that where the shot hit, a yellow-green goo began to ooze out. I fired again and again, but nothing seemed to make a difference.

"Detective!" Durant yelled. "Drop the gun! It's distracting you!" But I kept firing into the crawling, writhing mass of revenants out of instinct—still, to no effect. One of the things lunged toward me, but Durant moved forward in a blur, and, in one fluid motion, both smashed through its body with the staff and yanked the gun out of my hand. "Here!" he yelled, throwing me the staff. "Take the Matteh ha Shelomoh!"

"Take the *what*?" I yelled back, catching it.

"*Hit* them!" he yelled. In another blur, he moved on to the next nearest revenant, driving his knee into its chest as he brought his elbow down hard, crushing its skull with a sickening crunching sound. Yellow goo splattered everywhere.

I swung the staff like a baseball bat, hitting a revenant that had come up alongside of me. I had expected it to feel like hitting a human body, or like smacking a punching bag with a stick—but the staff went straight through the thing's body, as if it had all the density of a banana within a crunchy shell. I didn't have time to be overly shocked, however, since more of the things attacked me from above. I just started swinging at everything that moved—flailing even. But with this staff, everything was a kill shot. The sound of squealing and crackling was everywhere all at once.

I turned to see how Durant was holding up, since I'd taken his weapon. Again, he moved too fast for me to see too many of the details, but I could tell from the flashing silver that he was using that sword of his. Though where he'd pulled that thing from again was still a mystery to me.

While I was watching Durant, one of the revenants jumped me from behind. It dug its sharp talons into my shoulder, and I could smell its foul breath as it leaned in to sink its teeth into my neck. I twisted and let myself fall to the floor, and the thing was now above me, tumbling. But as it fell onto me, I brought the staff up into its belly, and punched all the way through its back in the process. Its corpse fell on top of me, spilling its gelatinous innards all over my body. It smelled like rotten eggs and rancid meat, all mixed together.

I pulled its talons out of my shoulder and tried to push its corpse off to the side, only to see another revenant leap at me from the wall, hissing. I couldn't get the staff up in time to block it, and I genuinely thought that this was it—that I'd die at the hands of an undead thing in a dirty hallway in Roscoe Village.

Suddenly, though, the thing was dispatched by a blinding blur of silver that sliced it cleanly in half. Durant slowed down enough that I could finally see him clearly.

"Get up, Detective," he said.

I pulled myself to my feet, bracing myself for another attack, but the remaining revenants were pulling back, skittering down the hallway and back into the darkness, dragging their dead with them.

"I guess they had enough…" I said.

"Not at all," Durant corrected me. "Their master simply realized that they would not win this battle, and called them away for another one at a future time."

I leaned against the wall to catch my breath, and Durant took the staff back from me. He walked back into Sydor's room and cleaned it off, using the bedspread. I guess we were kind of past that whole "not wanting him to know that we were here" thing.

I came into the room behind him, still huffing and puffing a bit. He set the staff onto the bed, and began cleaning his sword the same way.

"How did they know about me and my family, Durant?" I asked.

"Apparently, the vampire whom we are hunting has been actively researching us as well," he said. "All the more reason to dispatch the fiend quickly."

I was going to press the issue, but I realized that Durant was right— it just meant that we had to get this guy as soon as possible. I pulled out my phone to call Joanna and tell her to take the kids to her mother's house right away. There was always the possibility that the revenants had just retreated to go to my house instead.

"So, you got this thing in Devonshire, huh?" I asked, glancing at the staff while I dialed. It sure didn't look British to me.

"Yes," he answered me, taking it and sliding it under his coat. "In 1610, at the deathbed of a good friend and kindred spirit who was dangerouser than a wolf…"

"Uh-huh," I said. "And what *is* it? Because it's a *lot* more than just a stick."

"It is indeed," he agreed, placing the sword under his coat as well.

"It is the *Matteh ha Shelomoh*, the Staff of Solomon. It was a gift to Solomon from God himself, which the king used to rid Israel of the last remnants of the vampiric plague which had begun in Assyria—namely, a creature which was an unnatural cross between the Lilitu and the Sutekh-Apopheratu, and which Solomon called the *Muthim Chayim*—the living dead. If you intend to use the staff again, perhaps I should teach you the same bataireacht moves that I taught to Edward William Barton-Wright..."

Joanna didn't answer her phone, so I left her a message. No packing—just go. Hopefully, she'd get it and act on it immediately, before something could happen... if it hadn't already. I couldn't imagine these things invading my home and getting to the people I loved. I didn't *want* to imagine it.

"Your family is safe for this evening, Detective," Durant assured me.

"How do you know?" I asked.

"Because they serve as a bargaining chip," he replied. "Killing them now would only galvanize your resolve, not deter you. Our enemy wishes to stop us, not to encourage us."

"So, 'Walker in the Daylight,' huh?" I said, changing the subject. "What was that about?"

"Every society has its bogeymen, Detective—even the society of the undead." Durant took off his overcoat and examined it, sighing at the globs of yellow goo that had stained the expensive fabric. "The waking world fears the vampyri, and the vampyri... well... *they* fear *me*..."

I couldn't help but notice that the coat just draped over his arm—there was neither a sword nor a staff anywhere inside of it.

Background
From *Die Geschichte die Vampyren* (Hieronymous A. Vordenburg, 1872, trans. F.W. Murnau)

from Liber IV.

There are those who question the vampyr's existence as if it were merely a modern phenomenon, or one which has not been attested to by countless historians over the centuries. But, as Baudelaire has written, "la plus belle des ruses du diable est de vous persuader qu'il n'existe pas."[1] The truth is that history is replete with documented evidence of the undead hunting the living, and only those who wish to remain willfully blinded to the facts will fail to acknowledge them. Following is but the merest fraction of what could be said about the vampyr in history.

In the 11th century, the Abbot of Burton spoke of two peasants who had died mysteriously, and yet were seen the very night after their burial, carrying their own coffins throughout the town. According to the Abbot, the two men could change form from men to dogs or bears at will, eluding any pursuit taken by the townspeople. They began to prey upon the living, night after night, and villagers began to succumb one by one to the wasting effects of their nightly predations. Eventually, the townsfolk dug up the corpses of the two vampyren and performed the rites to destroy the creatures once and for all, cutting off their heads and removing their hearts. Immediately, the victims of the vampyren became well again, and no other outbreaks of vampirism within the village were reported. This episode is a matter of official record within the Catholic Church.

In the 12th century, chronicler William of Newburgh wrote[2] of the "Hound Priest" who rose from his grave in Melrose to hunt the living. He had been such a rogue before he died that it is difficult to say whether he succumbed to the bite of a vampyr, or whether he himself had given his soul over to Satan in order to continue his amorous pursuits, even

---

[1]   *"The greatest trick of the Devil is to persuade you that he doesn't exist,"*
      from Le Joueur Généreux *(1864, Charles Baudelaire)*
[2]   *in* Historia Rerum Anglicarum *(1196, William of Newburgh)*

after his death. He continued to predate women in his former diocese, including the woman of stature for whom he had served as chaplain before his demise. It took two powerful men of God—two friars from the nearby monastery—to track the creature down and wound it with an axe, deep into its chest. Even then, the Hound Priest made its way back to its tomb in order to regenerate during the daytime, but the two friars were able to capture the vampyr during its time of torpor, and drag it out and burn it, scattering its ashes, as they should.

Newburgh also wrote of another vampyr near the castle of Anantis which had been laying waste to an entire town. He documented that two brothers finally made their way to the cemetery to end the fiend once and for all. "Snatching up a spade of but indifferent sharpness of edge, and hastening to the cemetery, they began to dig; and whilst they were thinking that they would have to dig to a greater depth, they suddenly, before much of the earth had been removed, laid bare the corpse, swollen to an enormous corpulence, with its countenance beyond measure turgid and suffused with blood; while the napkin in which it had been wrapped appeared nearly torn to pieces. The young men, however, spurred on by wrath, feared not, and inflicted a wound upon the senseless carcass, out of which incontinently flowed such a stream of blood, that it might have been taken for a leech filled with the blood of many persons. Then, dragging it beyond the village, they speedily constructed a funeral pile; and upon one of them saying that the pestilential body would not burn unless its heart were torn out, the other laid open its side by repeated blows of the blunted spade, and, thrusting in his hand, dragged out the accursed heart." These cases are well-documented, and it was not uncommon in medieval times for villages to bury those who died under suspicious circumstances face-down, so that, should they try to dig themselves out of their graves, the vampyren would only dig themselves deeper into the earth.

In that same century, Walter Map wrote[3] of a "wicked man" in Heresford who rose from the dead and went through the streets at night, hauntingly calling out names of his intended victims. No matter what attempts were made to protect the people, the vampyr continued to kill at will. In this case, even decapitation and holy water—the proscribed method given by Bishop Gilbert Foliot—did not stop the creature, and it required a sword blow to the head (which had somehow reattached itself since its decapitation) to cleave the skull itself in twain and finally finish off the vampyr. Again, one must always be prepared to change one's tactics and assumptions when dealing with the undead.

Beginning in roughly the 13th century, Eastern Europe became infested with the vampyr plague, particularly amongst the nobles,

---

[3]   *in* De Nugis Curialium *(1190, Walter Map)*

perhaps because many of them were already known for cruelty and bloodthirstiness in their rules even without the vampyric influence. One Prince Antonin Wojciech[4] came to nominal power in a small princedom in Hungary as part of the Árpádok dynasty sometime before the invasion of the Mongols in 1241. Known as much for his mane of golden hair as for his charisma, Wojciech fought—and lost—alongside Count Palatine at the battle of Verecke Pass, their entire garrison slaughtered by Batu Khan and his Golden Horde. Dying on the battlefield, Wojciech was supposedly visited by an angel who promised him eternal life, if he were to but sell his soul to Satan. Foolishly, he accepted, died from his wounds, and rose again on the third night as a vampyr. He was content for months to prowl the Carpathian Mountains, attacking unfortunates who wandered into the wilderness at night, but when Béla IV pushed the Mongols out of Hungary in 1242,[5] Wojciech returned to his own princedom in or near Szörény, and used his position and the pretense of life to satiate his foul needs. In particular, the "Golden Vampyr" (as he had become known) was renowned for somehow seducing even the most happily married young woman, then debauching himself with her. Sometimes, he would allow the woman to return to her home and husband, wracked with guilt and shame; but more often, he would torture her afterwards and mutilate her body, hanging her corpse upon his castle wall. In 1308, when the first Angevin king, Károly Róbert,[6] came into power and removed several of the petty provincial Árpádok dictators, Wojciech was run out of his own territory, disappearing again into the Carpathian Mountains. It is believed that, over his nearly 70-year, iron-fisted rule of his province, he had butchered nearly 9,000 of his own people—most of whom were young wives and mothers (thus earning Wojciech his more familiar nickname, "Özvegycsináló").[7] There were vague rumours that the "Golden Vampyr" had been seen in later centuries in France, but we shall do well not to indulge unsubstantiated claims such as these. The boundary between superstition and history can sometimes be a faint one, but often

---

[4] *Other sources name him Anton or Antal Wojtek (both spellings of the name mean, "He who enjoys war")*

[5] *Arguably, the Mongol withdrawal in 1242 was as much—if not more—due to the death of Great Khan Ögedei as it was to any of the relatively ineffective efforts of the defending native troops (with the possible exception of the Croatian soldiers), even though Béla subsequently became regarded by his people as the "Második Honalapító" ("Second Founder of Our Country"), and Vordenburg attributes their retreat to him accordingly (though that title was earned more by Béla's forward-thinking social policies than it was by any substantial military victories).*

[6] *King Charles I of Hungary (1308-1342)*

[7] *"The Widower-Maker"*

nonetheless a critical one.

At the beginning of the 15th century was born the vile knight of Brittany called Gilles de Rais (or de Retz), a bloodthirsty, evil madman who sold his soul to Satan in a ritual conducted by Francesco Prelati in 1432, and was thus turned into a vampyr by his own request. A friend of the court and a hero of France, the Seigneur and Baron de Retz had an almost unlimited ability to do as he chose within his own lands, and he fell into the habit of luring young children to his estates in Champtocé and Machecoul in order to torture, debauch, and ultimately murder them, to satisfy both his own blasphemous lusts and the personal tastes of the demon lord he served. He found particular delight in the horror of his victims, and thus did all that he could to increase it, bringing himself to satisfaction upon their persons at the height of their terror. Even after decapitating or disemboweling them, he would often make use of their wounds for his pleasure, saying at his eventual confession that he found their corpses "beautiful" in his eyes, and that he "took delight at the sight of their inner organs; and very often when the children were dying he sat on their stomachs and took pleasure in seeing them die and laughed," drinking their blood at the end of their torments, and then burning their bodies slowly in his fireplace so as to avoid both discovery and the creation of new vampyren to threaten his free hunting. In all, de Rais murdered almost 600 innocents in this manner in the eight years before he was captured in 1440 for assaulting a churchman from the Church of Saint-Étienne-de-Mer-Morte. But this was not the end for de Rais, nor for his killing.

His bloody swath of child murders *would* have ceased at his execution on October 26, 1440, but his pious-sounding and persuasive gallows speech touched the tender-hearted bishop, and his body was not thrown into the fire after his hanging as he had been sentenced to be, and as his compatriots in his crimes suffered. Instead, four women of the community whom de Rais had seduced with his charm and money took his body from the gallows before it could be burned, and had him buried with honors… not realizing that he would soon rise from that grave and continue his depraved work across France and Belgium over the next 300 years. Little is known about the final fate of de Rais, except that according to the Count of St. Germain, he appears to have met his demise here in Austria at the hands of Gerard van Swieten, the personal physician of the Empress Maria Theresa, who was sent in 1755 to once and for all put an end to the vampyr menace which swept Eastern Europe in the 18th century. Though several contemporary historians attest to this fact, it is important to note that van Swieten himself discounted the story in his book, *Abhandlung des Daseyns der Gespenster*[8]—although it is

---

[8]   Discourse on the Existence of Ghosts *(1768, Gerard van Swieten)*

generally believed that van Swieten wrote the book to consciously downplay the existence of the vampyren which he himself had destroyed, so as to better alleviate the public panic.

Later on in the same century, Vlad III (also known as Vlad Țepeș Drakulya[9]) was made voivode of Wallachia, defeating not only the Turkish incursion during the height of the Ottoman Empire, but also the existing voivode, Vladislav II, and taking the throne for himself. Drakulya's life was a complex weave of conspiracies and personal torments, and he learned cruelty at the hands of the Turks while being tortured as a young captive. He particularly despised the boyars, the ruling elite who had turned him over to the Turks in his youth, and he vented much of his bloodlust on them and their families. Under Drakulya's rule, it was not uncommon for him to impale whole boyar families, or even whole villages of Transylvanian Saxons containing hundreds of men, women, children, even infants—or to torture his own peasants when in a particularly foul mood. For instance, we're told that, when he overheard a peasant complaining that his trousers were too short, and that his legs thus became cold when working his fields in the winter, Drakulya had the peasant's feet chopped off just above the ankle, so that the trousers now fit accordingly, and the peasant would remember before he complained the next time. In still another recorded episode, when a gentleman failed to doff his cap as Drakulya passed by, the voivode had the man's cap nailed to his head. In the end, though the Turks occupied Drakulya's capital city of Târgoviște, he successfully continued to wage war against them, and turned them back in a pivotal battle outside of Buzau in 1462. The Pope and many of the Christian leaders of Europe declared the retreat of the Mohammedan Turks to be a miracle from God, but the truth was exactly the opposite. In actuality, the bloodthirsty Drakulya had given his soul to Satan for the power to rout the Turks (much as Antonin Wojciech had done two centuries before him), and had thus been turned into a vampyr—which arguably changed his personal disposition very little. In his life, he had slaughtered nearly 80,000 souls, many through torture. After his death, his slaughters continued, especially during the Ottoman control of his kingdom under the puppets Basarab Laiotă cel Bătrân and Basarab Țepeluș cel Tânăr, keeping the region in political instability for nearly a decade after his death. Drakulya appears to have taken great and particular delight in attacking the turncoat Wallachians who had followed Laiotă and Țepeluș, even more so than the Turks themselves. But once Drakulya's brother, Vlad Călugărul, took the throne in 1482, the creature apparently faded into obscurity into the mountains of his homeland. But there are still enduring claims that Vlad Țepeș Drakulya yet haunts the Carpathian

---

[9]   *"Vlad the Impaler, Son of the Dragon"*

Mountains of Transylvania, aided by a dwindling band of faithful gypsies who worship him as their dark god.

From the 16th century comes the well-documented story of Erzsébet Báthory, the "Blood Countess" who murdered young women unrepentantly in an attempt to remain eternally young and beautiful. From her castle in Trencsén, she oversaw the torture, mutilation, devouring, and bloodletting of over 600 young women from her estates in Hungary, before the Palatine eventually arrested and imprisoned her, after years of petitions from a local Lutheran minister. An unusual form of vampyr, Báthory did not hunt her victims or always *drink* their blood, but rather *bathed* in it, as it poured over her from slits in the floor from the torture chamber situated above her specially designed bathtub. She particularly wanted the blood of beautiful young girls, since she felt that their blood was especially effective in maintaining her own beauty—but then, she also apparently took great pleasure in destroying their good looks through branding, biting, or otherwise mutilating their faces and womanly parts, so perhaps she envied them their looks as well. The Palatine even discovered that Báthory had kept a journal in her own hand of her atrocities, presumably to read and re-read, so as to enjoy them during times of repose between murders. In the end, though hundreds of witnesses—including the Palatine himself and his arresting officers—corroborated the heinous actions of the countess, King Matthias chose to imprison Báthory rather than to execute her, since he decided that the execution of a beautiful noblewoman might be more of an embarrassment to his reign than even her hundreds of foul murders had been—and it was noted that, even at age 50, she still appeared as young, fair, and beautiful as a teenaged maiden at her trial. She was walled into her rooms at Csejte, and apparently died four years later—but since the people of Csejte refused her burial at the local churchyard, she was quietly buried in the family crypt at Ecsed. If she rose from the crypt to continue her crimes—or if, indeed, she had become one of the undead years before, and had only fallen into a deep state of torpor, awaiting freedom from her prison so that she might feed again—is unknown, but some stories claim that even as late as 1796, she was still seducing young maidens into her home and bathing in their blood, as beautiful and youthful in her appearance as on the day of her wedding in 1575.

Also in the late 16th century was born another noble who ended his life as a vampyr, William Ruthven, the youngest son of the first Earl of Gowrie, the fourth Lord Ruthven. Though he had taken no part in his elder brothers' failed attempt to kidnap and ransom King James VI of Scotland (who later became King James I of England) in 1600—echoing a similarly failed plot undertaken by their father in 1582—he was nonetheless implicated in their treachery.[10]   Upon the deaths of the conspirators, John and Alexander, William attempted to flee with his surviving brother, Patrick, to England. But as they were racing through the moors that night, they were set upon by a vampyr, and neither youth ever saw the light of an English dawn in his lifetime. Patrick's neck was broken in the initial scuffle, but 18-year-old William died at the fangs of the foul creature, only to be found and buried the next morning by local villagers who had no knowledge of the identities or cause of death of the two lads.

Rising from his shallow grave three nights later, Ruthven began to stalk the countryside, eventually making his way southerly into England. Supposedly, by 1635, a vampyr hunter named Drake was so close to destroying him that Ruthven changed his name and fled to the American colonies aboard Captain Issac Bromwell's ship, the *Assurance*, taking on the alias William Ruffin. Thus, he was to elude capture and notice for several generations, feeding primarily on the natives of that country and breeding aquatic, reptilian vampyren which they refer to as the "apoyamkin."[11]   But as wanderlust overcame Ruthven, he began to travel the world again sometime in the early part of this century, eventually making his way into London society by use of his original title. As Lord Ruthven, he made the acquaintance of a young man named Aubrey, with whom he traveled for a time. But Aubrey soon recognized the character of this fiend, who routinely seduced young women and slaughtered them throughout Europe. In fact, Ruthven— under yet another alias, the Earl of Marsden—wooed Aubrey's young sister and even married her, murdering and feasting upon her on their wedding night out of sheer sadism. Though authors such as Alexandre Dumas have romanticized Ruthven in various fictional stories over the decades, endowing him with a dashing demeanor and exotic weaponry, there have been no actual documented references to the creature since he returned to the continent in 1819.

In the mid-17th century, an Istrian peasant named Jure Grando from the village of Kringa died and was buried by the local priest, Father Giorgio. Arising from his grave later as a vampyr, over the next decade and a half, Grando quietly hunted the countryside, for some reason, feeding mostly on the blood of animals. Though it is uncertain why he changed this practice, he suddenly began hunting within Kringa in 1672, toying with his victims by smilingly warning them in advance that he was going to kill them (much like Walter Map's "wicked man" in

---

[10]   *The fact that King James already owed the eldest brother, John, several thousand pounds may have also contributed to their motivation for attempting to abduct him.*

[11]   *Most sources use the more familiar "apotamkin." See also the mid-western "mishipeshu" legends.*

Heresford had done five centuries earlier—indicating, perhaps, that Grando's corpse was being reanimated by the same demonic force). It was, in fact, Father Giorgio who finally found and stood up to the foul creature one night and, holding a crucifix in faith before him, commanded, "Evo Isuse Kriste, ti vampir! Prestanite nas muče!"[12] causing the fiend to flee. Father Giorgio led the villagers to the grave the next day, and Grando's corpse was disinterred and decapitated. Interestingly, it was apparently impossible for the villagers to pierce the creature's heart with a hawthorn stake, though why this would be the case is unclear.[13] As I have oft said, one should never assume what one thinks that one knows, when it comes to hunting the undead.

Beginning in the late 17th century and continuing through the present day, there have been reports of "Oude Rode Ogen"[14]—a jet-black creature with glowing red eyes who hunts the children of Flanders at night and drinks their blood. The fiend—which the Belgians also refer to as "De Nekker" because of its black coloring—is said by Monsignor Vincent Menten to be able to change its shape to that of a large, black hound—a beast. At one point, the people of nearby Nekkerspoel hunted down and executed a black vagrant whom they had found living near their town, skinning him alive in the process attempting to elicit a confession from him before hanging him from a gibbet, but it did not stop De Nekker's killing spree. In fact, whether or not the vagrant killed by the townsfolk was, indeed, Oude Rode Ogen, is a matter of some debate—skinning and hanging would certainly not have destroyed a vampyr—but whatever the case, the fiend remains at large.

In the early 18th century, both Petar Blagojević and Arnaut Pavle hunted amongst the eastern Austrian provinces during the plague of vampirism which was ultimately eradicated by van Swieten in 1755 at the behest of the Empress Maria Theresa. Blagojević, a peasant from Kisilova in Veliko Gradište, rose from his grave in 1725 to attack the people of his village, and the killings only ceased after the local priest and the Imperial representative dug up and examined Blagojević's remains—which, according to official Imperial records, were youthful, undecayed, and engorged with fresh blood—and had the body both decapitated and burned.

In the case of Arnaut Pavle, Pavle was an outlaw from the village of Medveđa who had fought off a vampyr near Gossowa, but foolishly did so by painting his own body with the blood of the creature in order to ward it off (a local superstition which served only to infect the intended victim, rather than to protect them in any way). When Pavle died, he

---

[12] *"Behold Jesus Christ, you vampyr! Stop tormenting us!"*

[13] *All of this is referenced in detail in Janez Vajkard Valvasor's 15-volume opus,* Slava Vojvodine Kranjske *("The Glory of the Duchy of Carniola," 1689)*

[14] *"Old Red Eyes"*

rose again to attack the villagers at night over the next month, killing four of them in the process. As with Blagojević, the Austrian officials disinterred his remains and found them to be engorged with fresh blood, and so mandated that not only his corpse, but also the corpses of his victims be decapitated and burned, and their ashes scattered. Both military surgeon Johann Flückinger and Imperial Contagions-Medicus Johann Friedrich Glaser attested to the existence and destruction of these vampyrs in their official capacities. Dr. Flückinger wrote an official report to his superiors (the now-famous *Visum et Repertum* from 1732), and Dr. Glaser wrote an article on the subject for the scientific journal *Commercii litterarii ad rei medicae et scientiae naturalis incrementum institute* (also in 1732), in which he wrote the following: "Mortui nimirum humati illaesis surgentes sepulcris vivos enecant, hique necati et sepulti similiter surgentes alios interficiunt; quod sequenti contingit modo: Mortui nempe dormientes noctu adoriuntur, sanguinemque ex illis exsugunt, ut cuncti tertio exspirent die. Huic autem malo hucusque nulla medela inventa est."[15]

Less than half a century ago, in 1824, a young veteran named Antoine Léger sequestered himself in the woods of de la Ferte, where he lived in a cave in the rock of the Charbonniere, ate gooseberries and roots, and drank rainwater from the crevices. Somewhere during this time, Léger went quietly mad, and began holding conversations with a demon at night. On August 10, he spied a 12-year-old girl named Aimée Constance de Bully near a vineyard and he abducted her, dragging her back to his cave and violating her in multiple heinous ways, finally drinking her blood and devouring some of her flesh. Very soon after, he was apprehended and then tried by the Court of Assizes at Versailles, at which time, it is said, "his countenance displayed profound apathy, even an air of gaiety and satisfaction…" and his face "far from betraying any emotion, seemed rather to sparkle with increased satisfaction" as his crimes were described. He was executed on December 1, 1824, by hanging… and arose on the evening of December 3 as a vampyr. His first victim was another young girl named Jaceline Petit, whom he found tending to her family's horse outside her home in Guyancourt. He not only drank her blood, but committed other atrocities upon her person in the process, apparently delaying her death until just before dawn. Over the next two weeks, he attacked at least six other women—most of them under the age of 17—killing four of them. The villagers, eager not only to stop the menace, but also to do so before Christmas, spent three full

---

[15] *"People that are certainly dead rise from undisturbed graves and kill the living, and these killed and buried people similarly rise and kill others; it happens in the following fashion: At night they attack sleeping people and suck out their blood, so that they all expire on the third day. Against this evil no remedy has been found."*

days hunting through the vast Forest of Rambouillet for the creature, finally trapping Léger in—ironically—a cave, and driving an oaken stake through its heart. They then decapitated the corpse and burned both the head and the body in separate piles.

Around six years ago, a Portuguese sailor named James Brown attacked and killed two of his shipmates aboard the *Atlantic*, and was found drinking their blood by other sailors. He was arrested and taken into custody, and was sentenced to death for his crimes, but—for reasons which I do not comprehend—his sentence was commuted by the American president, Andrew Johnson. He remains incarcerated in an asylum in the United States to this day, occasionally attacking his fellow prisoners to drink their blood. Whether Brown is a true vampyr or simply a madman is a matter of current debate.

Another example, however, is not. Only two years ago, in the town of Kantrzyno, Franz von Poblocki died in his home from tuberculosis.[16] Being a pillar of his community, von Poblocki was buried in the churchyard with full Christian honors. But two weeks later, his son, Anton, also died from an unusually fast-moving form of tuberculosis.[17] And soon, other members of the family were beginning to waste away as well, experiencing horrific visions in the night about haunting visitations from the elder von Poblocki, and then awakening ever-more fatigued and pale. Calling on a vampyr hunter named Johann Dzigielski, they decided to decapitate Anton in order to prevent his becoming a vampyr as well, and then disinter the corpse of Franz to cease his predations. Though the local priest, Father Block, attempted to prevent them from doing so, they brought von Poblocki's body out from their family tomb and discovered that it was robust-looking and engorged with blood—far *more* robust-looking, in fact, than it had appeared in life. They decapitated his corpse, and then reburied von Poblocki in the tomb. Ironically, the priest reported them to the officials, and they were brought up on charges for this action. Dzigielski was sentenced with four months in prison, but the von Poblocki family argued that they were acting in self-defense against a vampyr, and the charges were dropped.

Even as this volume goes to print, the disposition of one Vincenzo Verzeni is being debated in Bottanuco, in Lombardy. Dubbed "il Vampiro di Bergamo"[18] by the press, Verzeni has confessed to the stalking and murder of two young women, and the attempted murder of

---

[16] *The word Vordenburg uses here is actually* "Auszehrung," *which literally means* "wasting" *(like the English archaism,* "consumption"*), and could easily be describing the slow death arising from repeated vampyric attacks*

[17] *Interestingly, the phrase Vordenburg uses here is* "Galoppierende Schwindsucht" *(literally,* "galloping lung disease"*), which was almost certainly a misdiagnosis of death by vampyric bite*

[18] *"The Vampyr of Bergamo"*

four more, beginning with the horrific attack on Giovanna Matta, aged 14. After murdering her, he mutilated her corpse, drank her blood, and then attempted to hide her body under a pile of straw in her own family's barn. Later, he similarly murdered Elisabetta Pagnoncelli, her body hacked into pieces after her blood had been drained and consumed. Prior to these successful murders, young Verzeni had attempted an attack on his own cousin, Marianna, while she slept, as well as attacks on several young women, named Barbara Bravi, Margherita Esposito, Maria Galli, and—the day before the murder of Elisabetta Pagnoncelli—Maria Previtali. The eminent Dr. Cesare Lombroso has quoted Verzeni as proudly saying, "I have really butchered some of the women, and I have tried to strangle a few more, because I take immense pleasure in these acts. The scratches found in the thighs weren't the product of my nails, but of my teeth, because after the strangulation I bit her and sucked the blood that dripped out, which I enjoyed very much."

To deny the existence of these fiends in the face of such overwhelming evidence is not only ludicrous, but foolhardy—it is precisely such willful ignorance that allows the vampyren to thrive, both throughout history and even into our modern age.

Chapter 15
Ironclad

Now, we didn't know exactly *which* library to be looking for. I mean, was it a *public* library? And if so, was it the Lincoln Belmont branch, or the Logan Square branch, or the Lincoln Park branch, or some other branch entirely, on the other side of Chicago? No way to know for sure. But I was betting that it was close by, since Sydor wouldn't know the city that well—and, since the public library branches were all in relatively busy areas, I figured that the note was probably talking about the Richardson Library on the DePaul University campus. Between the parking lots and the wooded areas around St. Vincent's Circle, there were lots of places where two people could talk in private, without ever being seen. It was a gamble, but we had to pick one—and I couldn't very well ask cops to stake out public libraries, just in case a vampire might use one to talk with a desk clerk from a local condo. I did decide to put some surveillance on Sydor's place, however, just in case he went back there. It would be easy enough to justify, what with all of the "gang violence" we'd just experienced there that night. I picked up the phone to make the call.

"To be truthful," Durant clarified, as we drove away from the scene, "the title 'Walker in the Daylight' was not the creation of the undead." He was still picking at the goo in a vain attempt to clean his coat, and I held off on the phone call for a second. "It was in fact originally coined by the young son of a friend of mine. Young Christopher—little 'Kit'— often called me that." For a flashing moment, he actually smiled a small, nostalgic smile—but only for a moment. "You must understand that, by the time that I knew Kit, I had already been hunting the undead for a thousand years. To him, I was as much a legend as I was a favorite 'uncle' to him."

"That—that actually sounds *nice*, Durant," I said, surprised by his sliver of warmth again.

"It was *quite* 'nice,' as you say, for a time," he said. "In his innocence, Kit played out the youthful fantasy that he himself was his 'Uncle Walker,' the immortal Huntsman, the Living Ghost, lunging around the decks with his wooden sword, defending the innocent against the wicked, century after century. To his mind, I suppose that all of this seemed rather glorious…"

"The decks?"

"Hmm?" he asked, finally giving up on his coat and looking out of the window at seemingly nothing. "Yes. Christopher served as cabin boy aboard his father's ship, the *Mary Elwyn*." His eyes glazed over a bit, recalling a long-lost grief. "Both were lost when their ship was sunk by pirates in the Indian Ocean nearly five centuries ago."

"I'm sorry," I said, and I really meant it. He seemed to continually have the weight of the world on his shoulders. The idea that he'd found some respite for a time in a family who had cared about him, only to lose them to such a meaningless death—it was tragic. "I guess you've had a lot of people die on you over the years, haven't you?"

His brows furrowed into a deep frown, and I saw his teeth clench tight—and I realized that I might've just been more tactless than I'd meant to be. "Quite so," he answered in a clipped, terse tone. He sat in silence for a time, continuing to gaze out of the window of the car. After a while, I picked up the phone again and dialed Jenkins.

"Stop the car, please," Durant requested as it started ringing. We were near the Clybourn Market, so I just pulled the car over into the parking lot and stopped. I started to ask why he needed me to stop here, but Durant just opened the door of the car and got out before I could. As it turned out, that was okay, since Jenkins answered right at that moment.

"Detective Chapel?" he answered excitedly. "I-I've been afraid to call you."

"Why afraid, Jenkins?" I asked. "What's going on?" I watched as Durant walked back down the street from the parking lot we'd parked in. I had to twist in my seat to see where he was going.

"It's just that, I don't know what to do—now that I…" Jenkins trailed off, his voice shaking.

"Talk to me," I said. "What?"

"Okay," he responded, taking a deep breath before continuing. "Remember when I said that I was going to try something for you?"

"Yeah, the face recognition thing." Durant walked directly up to a business now darkened and locked, and that's when I saw the homeless guy passed out and curled up in the doorway. To be honest, I've never really understood why more of them don't take advantage of the missions and shelters around. I know that some of them aren't the safest places in the world to sleep, but I've got to think that they're still better than being out alone on the cold street. We weren't that far from the Lincoln Park Community Shelter, or even from Anawim—the Catholic shelter down by Holy Trinity that reaches out specifically to Native Americans. I shook my head just thinking about it.

"That's right," Jenkins continued. "I took some shots from the security cameras until I found the clearest one, and then I ran it through the recognition software. I didn't get any hits against any criminal databases or anything…"

"Uh-huh…" I said, watching Durant. He hunched down next to the guy, and I wondered what he was going to do to him.

"But then I expanded the search, and that's when I actually got a hit."

Now that made me sit up and focus. "You did?" I asked. "What? What did you find?"

Jenkins cleared his throat before answering. "You're not going to believe me, sir."

"You'd be surprised," I responded. I turned back to see Durant laying his coat over the homeless guy. "I'm actually getting more open-minded by the second."

"Well," he said, "I found a photograph of him standing in the background with a bunch of other guys…"

"Uh-huh—and…?"

"Sir, the photograph was from 1862."

I actually started to chuckle. I mean, I'd been coming to the conclusion that Durant had actually been telling me the truth about his immortality, but this was the first actual confirmation of it. "Are you sure it was *him*?" I asked, just to make certain.

"I'm positive," he said. "I mean, it's the clearest picture I've ever seen from the Civil War, and it's either him or he looks exactly like—and I mean *exactly* like—his great, great, great grandfather."

I smiled as I turned back to look at Durant again, and then I saw him do something that shocked me almost more than anything else I'd seen that night—I watched as he put his hand on the guy and *prayed* for him. Durant's… well, he's *Durant*… but he actually put his expensively-manicured hands on this dirty, smelly derelict and *prayed* for him.

That's when I realized that I didn't really know Pieter Durant at all.

"Hey, family resemblances can run deep," I assured Jenkins. "I mean, otherwise, the guy's a century and a half old, right?"

"I *know*! How can he be that old?" Jenkins replied. "What do we do about this, sir? I mean, how *can* he be that old?"

I watched as Durant pulled a card out of his vest pocket and set it in the man's hand, closing his fingers around it. He then stood up and started walking back to the car.

"He can't, Jenkins," I said. "Obviously, he's some kind of spook with Interpol, and this is bigger than you or I should get involved with. He's just a spook who happens to look exactly like another guy in 1862."

"But—"

"Seriously, Jenkins," I interrupted him. "Let it go. I'm sorry I got you chasing your own tail there for so long. Maybe we both need to get more sleep, huh?"

"I-I guess so…"

"Unless you really think that people live for hundreds of years, right?" I laughed. "I mean, that'd be crazy, wouldn't it?" Jenkins laughed with me, but I could hear that he was forcing it.

"It sure sounded crazy to me," he said, uncertain.

"Yep," I said again, as Durant got back into the car. I told Jenkins the address to Sydor's apartment, and I told him to ask Tony to set up a team to put a watch on it. He told me he would, but then asked why I didn't ask Tony myself.

"Because then he'd want to know where I was…" I said, and hung up. Durant looked out the window, back toward that doorway and the man sleeping in it.

"So, you gave that guy your coat, huh?" I asked him, putting the phone away.

"Hmm? Oh, it was ruined anyway," Durant said, dismissing the question and glossing over the action that I was obviously trying to point back to. "No dry cleaner would have been able to sufficiently get those stains out for me to be comfortable wearing it again. It would have been a terrible waste simply to throw it away."

"Uh-huh," I said, remembering the tenderness with which Durant had laid the coat over the man, and the warmth of his prayer. I wasn't buying the tough guy crud he was dishing out now. "And what was that card all about?" Durant cleared his throat.

"I happened to have a gift card for a supermarket on my person," he said, uncomfortably. "They do not sell alcohol—but they *do* sell *food…*" He just *happened* to have one on his person. Right. I wondered how many of those "happened to have" gift cards Durant has handed out over the years. "Exterminator of vermin," my butt.

"Well, that was… *fortunate*, wasn't it?" I asked.

"Indeed," he said, looking out of the window again, presumably to avoid the whole conversation. So I started the car up again and pulled out onto the street, back on our way toward DePaul.

"So, I ran across something interesting," I said, deciding to change the subject. And I waited until Durant responded. He didn't for a while, until he finally realized that I was waiting on him, sighed, and turned back to me.

"And that would be what, Detective?" he asked, actively disinterested.

"A photograph of you from the Civil War." I waited to see what his reaction would be—would he try to feign ignorance, or would he become angry, or what? Instead, he smiled again, shaking his own head as he turned back to the window.

"I know this photograph," he said, gazing back out into the street.

"One of the few which I have ever allowed to be taken, for obvious reasons—since people such as yourself might recognize me in them and begin to understand that I am... different. But the art of photography was still in its infancy, and I did not fully grasp the permanency of artifacts such as photographs."

"So that *was* you in the photo?" I pressed. "What *exactly* do you *do*, Inspector Durant?"

"It was I," he said, and then he turned back to me and squared his shoulders, settling in for what was evidently going to be a long story. "The photograph in question was taken in 1862, when I found myself accompanying Philippe d'Orléans, the Comte de Paris—the rightful, albeit exiled, heir to the throne of France—back to the Americas as a personal favor to his mother, Hélène. He joined the Army of the Potomac as a captain, and thus had the misfortune to serve under General George McClellan during his wrongheaded Peninsular Campaign, with whom that particular photograph was taken. Though young Philippe acquitted himself well in the war, I cannot say the same of McClellan. I swear, that educated idiot could train an army, but he could not put it to field to save his very soul. I felt it impossible to stand in the same room with such a racist blowhard, and I recall suggesting to your President Lincoln that he should consider getting himself an actual *soldier* to lead the army in place of such a preening martinet. But I digress..."

I got a mental picture of Pieter Durant barging into Abraham Lincoln's office and growling at him about McClellan, and wondered if that was what had pushed Lincoln into removing him from the position, even though he didn't have a replacement for McClellan available at the time.

"It was for this reason that I was in the Americas during an historically profound, if tactically indecisive, battle between two new ships—the USS Monitor and the CSS Virginia, the first American ironclad ships of war. The result of their battle was under-impressive, to say the least. And yet, I defend that it was historically profound not only in that it ushered in a new age of maritime combat and rang the death-knell of wooden warships, but moreso because it strikes me as perhaps the most historically perfect example of a stand-off of complementary firepower. The Virginia carried ten guns in fixed positions, while the Monitor carried only two, though on a moveable turret—and yet, the Monitor's two guns were each of a larger caliber than any of the Virginia's guns, and she was quick and agile, while the Virginia took upwards of an hour to complete a full turn. In that first battle at Hampton Roads—due to a lack of complete confidence by her designers and handlers—the Monitor's guns were loaded with only half the charge that they should have been, and the crew of the Virginia had never thought to bring along any armor-piercing ammunition, so the two ships spent the entire day barely denting one another's iron hulls."

"So you're saying they were evenly matched," I summarized, not completely understanding why we were having this conversation in the first place.

"They were *not* evenly matched—they were complementarily empowered," Durant corrected me. "Greater overall firepower was negated by a smaller and more agile target, while mobility was negated by the need for greater firepower. Do you understand?"

"I guess so," I said, turning the corner onto Fullerton. "So how long were you here in America?"

"Actually, I was called back to Europe that very same year by King Maximilian II himself to help investigate the theft of the Kalakistan fragment from Das Museum für Gefährliche Bücher und Papiere in Munich. I was thus unable to participate at great length in your war, nor was I able to continue to aid the Comte de Paris in his service here."

"That's a shame," I said sarcastically.

"Indeed," he said, and then he added with one last snort of disdain, "Ironically—due to the vicissitudes of European politics—within the decade, I found myself fighting *against* the French alongside the Prussians under Prince Friedrich Karl, after that fool Trochu refused to accept the help of the Orléans princes. C'est la guerre…"

"I guess…" I said. "But what does any of this have to do with… well, with *anything*?"

Durant looked back out of the window again. "My apologies, Detective," he said. "I had thought I was being clear. Please forgive the imprecise ramblings of a man unused to conversation. I was trying to use your photograph in order to explain the concept of complementary power, and thus to answer your question as to what exactly I 'do'."

Right. Amazing that I hadn't followed all of that.

"Okay, how so?" I asked him again. He turned back to me to answer.

"The world is full of unholy things, Detective," he said with a solemn tone. "A great horde of vile bastardizations of Creation, seething in power and with terrible intent. Consider them to be as the CSS Virginia was—strong, but ultimately cumbersome. Thus, to combat their vile infestation of His world, our Lord created a complementary power, quick and focused, much like the USS Monitor."

"And that would be…?"

"Consider me the 'ironclad' of our Lord," Durant clarified, "if such a metaphor is not too ridiculous to your ears." I stopped at the stoplight at the Southport intersection and turned toward him.

"So you're God's Monitor against Satan's Virginia?" I asked, laughing.

"Not to put too fine a point to it," he replied, "yes." I stopped laughing because of the seriousness of his response. That's what he actually believed—that he'd been, like, chosen by God to fight the things that go bump in the night. I was thinking to myself about just how nuts this guy must be, when Durant pointed ahead of us. "Your light has changed, Detective." Sure enough, it was green.

I pulled ahead and tried to wrap my head around what he was saying. The truth was, he obviously wasn't normal—and thanks to Jenkins, I was now sure that he'd been around for a long, long time. Was it really such a stretch to attribute his abilities and longevity to God? Well, kinda, yeah…

"By the way," Durant commented, almost casually, "we are still being followed."

I screeched on my brakes and looked behind me as I peeled right into the parking lot of the little MCL Center on the corner of Wayne. But I didn't see anyone behind us. At that time of night, it was all pretty calm there on Fullerton. I waited for a second, but no one appeared.

"What are you *talking* about?" I asked. "I don't see any cars anywhere!" Durant sighed one of his patented sighs.

"I was concerned that you had not noticed," he said, "and you have not disappointed my lack of confidence in you. We are not being followed by a car."

Okay, I was officially confused. "If not a car, then what's following us?"

"The same korrigan which has been following us for the past few days," he said. "Have you not been looking out of the same windows that I have? Did you not see her when we stopped at the *last* parking lot, when you made your phone call?"

"What's a 'korrigan' and no I didn't see anything and what are you *talking* about?" I barked. I wasn't even remotely surprised when he sighed again before answering.

"A nain rouge, a lutine, a water witch," he answered. "Have you learnt nothing from history?"

"Apparently, I was busy learning about *not* 'crazy world' history in history class," I said.

"At the moment, she is in the form of a red bird, resting on that ledge across the street," he nodded subtly, without gesturing. I looked, and—sure enough—I could barely make out a red bird across the street in the dark. "When I stepped out of your automobile to surrender my coat, she was in the form of a red cat in an alleyway, watching."

"This 'water witch' of yours," I said, incredulously. "And she keeps changing into birds and cats, huh?" Durant turned and looked at me, with the most serious expression I've ever seen.

"You are an imbecile, Detective," he said, completely without emotion.

"Why?" I asked. "Because I find it hard to believe that there's a shape-changing witch following us just because you saw a bird?"

"No," he replied, obviously disgusted with me. "Rather because you have not seen the continuous procession of red-furred and red-feathered creatures which have been following you, undoubtedly ever since you began investigating this case, even though you are a trained and talented observer—because your observational abilities are hampered by your rationalism. That, and because you now believe in the vampyri and in revenants and in immortal swordsmen, and yet continue to stumble over your own ignorant skepticism whenever you run across another supernatural creature with which you have not yet made acquaintance." He snorted and turned ever-so-subtly to look at the bird again. "This is no mere bird, Detective," he said again.

Was he right? Was that why he was always looking out of the window of the car? I'd just assumed that he was avoiding interacting with me or thinking about other stuff, but what if he was right? I started wracking my brain to remember if I'd seen any red animals before then. I looked back at the bird myself, but it was gone.

"Where did it go?" I asked, looking around.

"A good question," he answered. "She flew up and above your vehicle, and I can no longer see her myself. I've little doubt that she is still watching us, however."

"Then let's give her something to watch," I said, opening my door and getting out of the car. "If that bird really is a witch, and she really is working for the bad guys, then we sure don't want them to know where we're going tonight."

"You believe that going to the library is still a good idea, do you?" he asked.

"I do indeed," I said. I stood in the center of the parking lot, looking up, looking over, looking everywhere. Was that a red bird in the tree across the street? Was there a red rat behind it, in front of the discount laundry? Suddenly, the world was all about looking for red animals.

Durant stepped out of the car and walked up next to me.

"What are you attempting to do, Detective?" he asked.

"I'm trying to catch our tail, Inspector," I said. He snuffed a little and almost sighed again. I could hear it—he really did want to sigh again.

"She will not have been this surreptitious to this point, only to show herself now," he said.

"I dunno about that," I replied, continuing to scour the landscape for anything red. "She's been surreptitious because she figured that it would work. But if we make it clear that it's not working any more, maybe she'll change tactics." Durant shrugged and stood near me, looking around himself. Nothing happened. Nothing happened for several minutes.

"Hey, korrigan!" I yelled, but there was no movement from anything around us, at that time of night. "Hey, lutine! Nain rouge!"

"I doubt this course of action to be wise," Durant said at last.

"Maybe not," I said. "But I'm hoping that it's fruitful…"

And then I heard the lights blow out across the street. We spun around, and saw that everything was dark underneath the big, heavy stone archway of the Altgeld Club across Fullerton from us. I'd driven past it dozens of times before, of course. The Altgeld Club was built in the 1990s, providing condos for DePaul faculty and rich college kids, but up until then, it was nothing special. But right then, at that moment, that was the scariest dark archway I'd ever seen. Because right then, at that moment, I saw something moving in the darkness.

At first, I couldn't tell what it was—just that it was movement. Nothing else was moving anywhere—there wasn't even any traffic on the streets. But little by little, we could see that two figures were definitely moving under that stone archway. They moved just close enough to the light that I could begin to see some details, though not very clearly.

The taller figure looked like a woman—a pretty, but somewhat plain Native American woman, dressed in skins. Her face was smiling, but I realized that she wasn't looking at me—she was looking directly at Durant. Next to her was a large, panting, red-furred wolf. The wolf was looking at me.

"Pierre…?" the woman called out to Durant. Her voice was soft, but hollow—almost like an old-fashioned recording. "Est que vous, Pierre?"

I thought about everything I'd ever heard about the ghosts of the Native Americans who haunted Roscoe Village at night, and I suddenly believed everything that Durant had said to me—even that I'd been blinded my whole life by what I thought I'd understood. Somehow, there's a whole world out there, going on around us, right in front of us, that we don't really see—reality, just barely glimpsed out of the corner of our eyes, but dismissed by our rational minds.

"Who is *that*…?" I found myself whispering, almost reflexively.

"*That*…" Durant answered unexpectedly, "would be my *wife, Catherine*…"

Background
From *On the Road: A Personal Travelogue of Illinois* (1992, J. Cunningham)

from *Chapter 7: "Will We Play in Peoria?"*

Traveling north from Lincoln on Interstate 155, we aimed the car for the city of Peoria, located on the banks of the Illinois River. Most people don't realize what a rich history the city of Peoria has—even those who've lived in the state all their lives don't always appreciate the local color of the oldest settlement in Illinois and the state's third largest metropolitan area.

In its day, Peoria has seen missions and forts, burlesque and open-tent revival meetings, the underground railroad and organized crime. The city weathered the Depression of the 1930s and the Recession of the 1980s by thinking outside the box, and changing the ways they did business. Today, the "city-in-the-middle-of-a-cornfield" is a happening place. *Business Week* has now officially declared that Peoria is "in" while New York is "out"—so I guess it must be true.

Traditionally known for its background in vaudeville and burlesque (which spawned the familiar catchphrase, "But will it play in Peoria?" as a gauge for how well an act strikes at the core of the American psyche), Peoria now boasts over 350,000 people in its Metropolitan Statistical Area; professional baseball, football, and hockey teams; a thriving medical center (with a burn unit that even *Chicago* flies patients down to); its own symphony orchestra; a $64 million Civic Center; and a road on a high hill overlooking the river that none other than Teddy Roosevelt himself called "the world's most beautiful drive." I'd also heard that they have the best gyros in the state at a little restaurant called Haddad's, and that was one of the main reasons why Peoria was our next scheduled stop. As Mayor Jim Maloof—formerly the owner of one of the largest real estate agencies in the area—has said, "We can offer anything in Peoria that the big cities can offer. Besides, we have no rush hours."[1]

Peoria's current economic well-being can be traced to two recent

---

[1]   *As quoted in* The New Corporate Frontier *(David Heenan, 1991)*.

mayors—Richard Carver, who worked to clean up the prostitution and corruption in the downtown area in the late 1970s, and then to bring in new businesses and industries to broaden Peoria's infrastructure; and Maloof himself, who's spent most of the last decade not only as mayor, but also as a sort of "goodwill ambassador" for Peoria to the rest of the world. We had the chance to meet him on our third day in the city, and between his white hair, cherubic smile, caterpillar-bushy brows, and pudgy little frame, he reminded me of a beardless, Lebanese Santa Claus. He even gave us each a mug that said, "London, Rome, Paris, Peoria" (and I'm drinking my coffee out of it right now as I write this— thanks, Jim). All in all, Peoria is an excellent place to start up both a family and a business.

It can be hard for some people to understand why a city like Peoria is so inviting to its citizens—it has an unfair reputation for being a Podunk little town in the middle of nowhere. But the "feel" of downtown Peoria is decidedly metropolitan, even if the outskirts of the city are decidedly Mayberry-esque. It's as if someone chopped out a chunk of downtown Chicago and plopped it into the middle of a bunch of cornfields, so you get a lot of the big city amenities without many of the big city headaches—and that draws a lot of people out of the metropolises and into the countryside.

As University of Washington professor Jack Lessinger argues, American history is all about migration—and not just migration from Europe to the New World in the first place. The first move was a north-south one within the colonies; the second was a western move to the Mississippi; the third was an urbanization that followed the Industrial Revolution; the fourth was a *sub*urbanization that followed World War II; and the fifth migration is going on right now—into a "penturban" environment of "small cities and towns, and subdivisions, homesteads, industrial and commercial districts interspersed with farms, forests, lakes and rivers."[2]   Peoria stands as a perfect example of the sort of "penturban" area that Lessinger is talking about.

Actually, Peoria's history was all about migration, too. French Jesuit missionary Father Jacques Marquette and Canadian explorer Louis Jolliet were the first Europeans to come to the Peoria area in 1673 to bring God to the Native American Illiniwek tribes, as part of an evangelistic mission that took them all the way from Quebec down to the Gulf of Mexico (in fact, we had reservations waiting for us in the swanky Père Marquette hotel in Peoria, named after its famous discoverer—but more on that later on). Following their trail, more French explorers built the first settlement in the Peoria area in 1680—a fort they called "Fort Broken Heart" ("Crèvecoeur") because of all of the

---

[2]   *In Lessinger's* Regions of Opportunity *(1986).*

pain and hardship that they'd gone through to get there. Even today, a town called Creve Coeur is still a suburb of Peoria, just across the river from the city proper.

Another little-known fact is that it was a Peorian who founded the city of Chicago. A hundred years after Marquette and Jolliet had wintered in the Chicago area before coming down to Peoria, another Frenchman named Jean Baptiste Point du Sable came up to Chicago from Peoria to become the first European to settle there. Almost as if to set the stage for Peoria's future rowdiness, Point du Sable himself had a checkered past—he may not be French, and his name might not even have been Point du Sable. It looks like his real name might have actually been Pierre Dandonneau, but even that was probably just another alias. He may have been a white Frenchman who'd migrated down to Peoria from Canada, or he may have been a black Haitian who'd migrated up to Peoria from the south—no one knows anything about him until he started working as an *engagé* (a fur trader licensed by the British government) in the 1770s. But even that was apparently just a cover for his *real* work—he was really a spy for Col. George Rogers Clark (older brother of the explorer from the later "Lewis and Clark" expedition) against the British in the Revolutionary War, and he helped the Colonial Army capture settlements like Kaskaskia, Cahokia, and Vincennes.

After the war, Dandonneau (or Point du Sable) took his Potawatomi wife, Kittihawa (who also called herself "Catherine"—because apparently everyone had two or three different names to go by back then) and their children, Suzanne and Jean Jr., up to the Chicago area to settle. When the Delaware, Wyandot, and other tribes officially lost the Northwest Indian War in 1795, they signed the whole area over to Gen. "Mad Anthony" Wayne and the United States government. That paved the way for the government to build Fort Dearborn there in 1803 and cement the white man's presence in Chicago (even though Dandonneau himself had abruptly sold his land and left the area in 1800, and Fort Dearborn itself was later burned to the ground in the War of 1812).

By the way, no one knows what happened to Dandonneau / Point du Sable after he left Chicago, or why he left in the first place. He was supposedly an unusually well-educated man for a fur trader, so maybe he just lost himself in a major city somewhere; other sources say that he returned to Haiti and died there; still another popular theory is that he moved to St. Charles, Missouri (then part of Spanish Louisiana), where he died penniless in 1818. Of course, since his grave in St. Charles Borromeo Cemetery actually has no body in it at all, that's probably a red herring, too—one last joke on history from the life of the Peorian founder of Chicago…

Background
From *Recollections of an Illinois Fur Trapper* (1804, Ezekiel Clyburn)

I done kilt[1] me my share o' redskins in my day, them's fer sure an' fer certain. But 'twas allers in a fair fight, an' I got me my own fair share o' whuppin's as well, with the scars ta prove that ta be the God's truth. But them Odaawaas is a dark people, an' they goes ta war with jus' about any feller what comes their way, be them French or English or Americans or even other Injuns. An' they's crazy fer religion too, crazier than any circuit-ridin' Methodist preacher, I says. Chief Pontiac an' that Delaware medicine man o' his gots them all ta thinkin' what that the Great Spirit was fixin' ta give them the scalps o' ever white man in the territory, jus' like it was Christmas mornin'. That's what got all them Odaawaas in a frame ta start up their warrin'. Seems Detroit is allers in their sights, though God in His mercy keeps them vile fellers from ever gettin' inside them walls.

Far as I kin recollect, there's none o' them redskins what kin say what happened that day at Parent's Crick.[2] I heared tell o' dern near five score redcoats got theyselves chopped up in the waters there;—others count it more'n that, 'course, but there's no tellin' that now. But what one soldier what lived through the horribleness told ta me hisself still makes me chart a wide course 'round Detroit, even if'n I was ta go 'round themabouts today. Seems there's a white man what was helpin' the redskins agin his own kind, an' he was availed o' some powerful unholified magic. With that scoundrel's conjurin', Pontiac got hisself a passel o' critters what I never seen nor heared of in all my years in the West. Ask ol' Roger Picking what he seen that day, an' he should tell you 'bout a band o' redskins what weren't strictly redskins. They din't just scalp them redcoats that day in the Crick;—they cut them up an' ate

---

[1] *The editor (Simon Goodnight, 1976) of this memoir has sought to preserve Clyburn's colorful speech patterns, and thus has refrained from correcting his poor diction and spelling. He did, however, correct much of the punctuation and paragraph breaks.*

[2] *Clyburn is referencing the Battle of Bloody Run, fought outside of Detroit on July 31, 1763.*

their bones an' drank their blood, much as lions does.

Now, I knowed o' some men what had been out in the big wild fer too long, lost in the winter, an' had ta do what they had ta do ta keep livin'. But this here was men din't need nothin' o' the sort, but did it on account o' they liked it. They made the whole Crick red with blood, an' drank it all up like dogs or the like. Picking done said they was as strong as a moose, an' he swears that he shot one o' them fellers smack in the chest an' it ain't done nothin' ta him but make him surly as all get out. Now, I been huntin' with Picking since then, an' I cain't speak as ta how's his shootin', exceptin' that he never did no harm by me, nor missed a buck what he was aimin' fer. If'n he says he shot that big Odaawaa, then I'd put a penny on it fer a pound.

So people in them parts says that Pontiac an' the redskins in his party was all set fer ta take on Detroit itself, exceptin' that they got all beat at the last bit. No one knows the whys nor the wherefores, but I heared about some continental European what kilt them all hisself, din't never even fire a shot nor nothin' o' the sort. What a European was doin' helpin' them British ain't rightly somethin' I can purport ta understan' myself, nor how he kilt all them moose-strong Indians when them redcoats wasn't able ta. It's a powerful mystery stands ta this day, an' Detroit folk loves ta speak up a mystery a mite ta make it more interestin' at the dinner table or o'er a jug, so who's ta tell what really done happened? But without them monsters ta help them, the rest o' them redskins just started ta leave ta go back home, I reckon. Weren't three or four months later, Detroit was freed up agin.

Couple years after that, them Injuns what follered Pontiac turned back on him an' kilt him theyselves in the streets o' Cahokia.[3] Now, old Mike Henson says it were that Delaware cuss what kilt him out o' spite, but One-Toe down ta Fort Dearborn swears that it were that blamed white-skinned medicine man was behind the whole thing. I ain't rightly one ta say one way or t'other, though all it done was ta set off another war with them Peorias an' their confederates. Same year, them Odaawaas trapped some Illini up on La Rocher an' starved 'em out an' kilt 'em all as well.[4] Ain't really no way ta tell with redskins, but I think them Odaawaas just like lettin' blood.

I never did hear tell o' none o' them monsters what kilt them soldiers at Parent's Crick no more, but I also ain't gone 'round Detroit since that time, neither, nor never shall.

---

[3]   *Pontiac was killed on April 20, 1769, by the nephew of Makatchinga, a chief of the Peoria tribe. He was 49 years old.*

[4]   *The butte subsequently became known as "Starved Rock" to the white settlers of Illinois.*

Chapter 16
In Pace Requiescat

"Your *what*?" I asked, but Durant began walking toward the two figures in the archway, almost as if in a daze. I caught up with him and grabbed him by the sleeve. The muscles underneath the fabric were like knotted iron. I tried to grab his attention away from the two... things... across the street. "Waitaminute—do you mean 'Catherine,' as in the 'C' who gave you the pocket watch in 1790?"

Durant turned and glared at me, half in surprise and half in indignation.

"What? I *am* a *detective*..."

He turned back to face the archway and began walking again. Since I couldn't stop him, I walked with him. The Native American woman kept watching Durant and smiling the most pleasant, relaxing smile that I've ever seen—the big red wolf kept watching me.

"Venez à moi, mon amour..." the woman said, opening her arms toward Durant and smiling with even more emotion. I have to admit, *even I* was beginning to like the woman. Her voice was like warm honey, and I found myself feeling just a little bit sleepy, listening to her. "Je suis revenu pour vous," she said to him, tears of joy brimming in her chocolate brown eyes. "N'ai-je pas vous dire que notre amour est immortel...?"

Durant was almost across Fullerton by now, an inscrutable look hanging on his craggy face. As he approached, the wolf stepped back into the shadows, though she kept her eyes fixed on me the whole time. As concerned as I was about the wolf, I couldn't help but feel excited that Durant would be reunited with his lost love, after more than two centuries. In fact, my concern about the wolf was almost completely gone by the time we got to the other side of the street. All that I felt was warmth and safety and contentment. Now that we were with this woman, everything would be all right.

She took one step toward Durant as we hit the sidewalk, and I barely noticed the wolf disappear completely into the shadows. I expected Durant to reach back to her and embrace her. Instead, with a blur of motion, he reached into that pouch of his and pulled out what looked like an arrow, though shorter and thicker. With a speed that defied my eye's ability to keep up, he whirled the arrow toward her and plunged it into her chest. The look of fear and pain and absolute sadness that flashed across her face as the arrow went in broke my heart. I was so hurt by her death myself that I literally crumpled to the ground, as if I'd just seen my own wife murdered before my eyes.

But then I saw her features begin to melt, and her body began to bloat in size. As she died, fangs grew out of that beautiful mouth, and her eyes darkened and turned red. Her slender body bubbled and grew, and I saw that it was massively muscled and covered in a shaggy, dirty fur. Long, clawed hands sprouted from her thick arms, and a thick tongue flickered in and out of her broad mouth. By the time she hit the ground, nothing remained of the woman I'd seen as Catherine.

"Damn you…" Durant whispered at the thing on the ground. And then he gazed into the darkness under the archway. "Damn you!" he growled louder, and I knew that he was growling at the wolf hiding there. Suddenly, in a flurry of movement, a red bird emerged from the darkness and began flying away as fast as it could. Durant's hand darted back into his pouch and brought out a dark-colored knife, which he threw at the bird with such force that I swear, it sounded like a whip's crack. It went straight through the bird's left wing and through the leaves of the nearby tree and then lodged into the building behind the tree, buried into the brick up to its hilt. I looked back at the bird, expecting to see it falling, but instead, I saw only a ladybug, flittering wildly through the air, until I lost it in the blackness of the night sky.

"Damn you, Rhiannon…" he whispered again, and then he hung his head down. "Damn you to Hell…"

I realized that all of this had happened in the span of only a few seconds. I'd gone from utter bliss to utter despair to utter shock in rapid succession, and I found myself out of breath, sitting there on the street. Durant walked over to the thing on the ground and pulled the arrow out of its chest. He wiped the gory tip against the shaggy fur of the thing's side, then carefully began to put it back into his pouch—which I realized was much shorter than the arrow was.

"Wh-what's going on?" I asked. "What *was* she? And what's with the arrow? And what's with that stupid pouch of yours?"

"'It,'" he corrected me. "Not 'she,' but 'it.' And this is a crossbow bolt, not an arrow."

"But why'd you stab her—*it*—with a crossbow bolt?"

"Because I hadn't the time to organize a proper crossbow."

He honestly seemed to think that was an appropriate answer. I shook my head as I got up to my feet and walked over to the thing. It had to have been at least seven feet tall, and probably weighed something in the neighborhood of four hundred pounds. At first glance,

I'd thought it was an ape or something, but looking at that face, with its curved tusks sticking out of its mouth from above and below, I realized that this thing wasn't a primate at all.

"It is called a *Rakshasa*, Detective," he said, answering the question bouncing around in my mind, "and whomever it is that we are hunting, he is apparently using all of his apparently not inconsiderable resources to thwart us."

"A Rakshasa…" I repeated. "Is that another Indian thing?"

Durant almost chuckled, in dark sort of way. "Yes, Indian…" He leaned down onto his haunches and examined the body more closely.

"Am I missing something?"

"The Rakshasas are demons from India—Sri Lanka, more precisely," he said, as he poked at its fangs. "Ali Lakshmi and I stirred up a nest of these monsters in New York back in 1974, with the help of a young woman named Lakota. When they scattered, we had to split up our forces to hunt them down. Lakota destroyed the one which she hunted in Rutland, Vermont, with the help of that occult investigator for whom she had begun working. Ali followed the two juveniles here to Chicago, and—though it took me almost a year to find them—I finished the rest of the nest off in Amityville, after their particularly gruesome rampage." He stood back up and took in a deep breath, composing himself.

"I had assumed that Ali had destroyed both of the Rakshasas which he had tracked here in Chicago—it would not have been like him to have missed one. But…" his brow furrowed in grief, "but then, he was getting on in years. He was no longer the young man whom I had taught to hunt, sixty years earlier in Madurai. I should never have let him go off alone… to die alone…"

He looked lost for a moment, and I could only imagine what was going through his head. I knew he was mourning an old man, dying alone here on a hunt in the streets of Chicago, but I also thought that he might be picturing running through the jungles of India with a young man—a boy who laughed and played, as if life were still a great adventure to be enjoyed. I wondered if he had made Durant remember that feeling, if only for a time… or if Durant had seen the youth's energy and idealism and—even then—had been reminded that young Ali would certainly die some day, just as young Kit had, just as Catherine had, just as everyone had whom he had ever known. I felt like reaching out and putting a hand on his shoulder, to try to empathize with him, but seeing the tenseness of his muscles, I didn't dare approach him. Instead, I tried to break the tension.

"So *that* was a *juvenile*?" I asked, getting back to the Rakshasa on the sidewalk.

"Did you hear it speak?"

"Yes."

"Then it was no longer a juvenile." As I suspected, correcting me actually made Durant relax, and he became more... himself...

"They are thieves, Detective," he said, sliding into his instructive mode again. "Scavengers of battlefields and predators of playgrounds, looking for easy meat—and the only way to destroy them is with a crossbow bolt." He reached into his pouch and pulled out a small flask. "They steal from your mind, you see. They take the appearance of someone whom you love, someone whom you trust, ripped from your own thoughts. And then they counterfeit that appearance to make you trust them and draw you close enough to them that they may devour you."

"For you, it was your wife..." I ventured.

"For you," he asked, pouring the contents of the flask over the body, "would it have been yours? Or would it have been Detective de Tullio?" He cocked his head and looked at me. "Or would it have been Miss Gage?"

I felt that surge of guilty spite rising in my guts again. "Have you been talking with Tony?"

"What on earth could possess me to subject myself to that particular horror?" Durant replied, putting the flask away and pulling out something else. Somehow, the irony of him saying that while standing next to a huge, shaggy thing that had just tried to seduce and eat him made me start laughing. In fact, I couldn't *stop* laughing—adrenaline rush, I suppose. But there I was, laughing like an idiot.

Durant lit the match in his hand and flung it onto the body of the Rakshasa. The thing burst into flames so hot, they burned blue.

"Why'd you do that?" I asked.

"Would you like to explain the corpse of a Rakshasa to your Lt. Chacon?" he asked, and I have to confess, I saw his point. I wasn't sure how I was going to explain any of this, actually, especially since, once we crossed the river, I wasn't even in my own jurisdiction any more.

"So can I ask you something?" I asked him, my gaze lost in the flickering blue flames. "How did you know that it *wasn't* your wife? I mean, with all of this other weirdness, maybe what she was saying made some sense. Couldn't she have found a way to immortality, just like you did?"

He sighed, and pulled out his watch. "You have asked me about this watch before, Detective," he said quietly, stroking the metal lightly with his fingers. He opened the watch and showed me the inscription that I'd seen earlier. "My Catherine gave this to me as present on our daughter's wedding day, celebrating our own twenty years together." He smiled for a moment—a thin, pale smile. "She had the watch sent up all the way up from St. Louis. That may not seem like anything particularly special by modern standards, but at the time…"

"That would've been like importing it from Europe today," I suggested.

"Quite so," he said, nodding. "Quite so…" He stroked the watch one more time, then carefully put it back into its pocket. "Catherine was a Bodéwadmi, you see, and though she died twelve years before the Fort Dearborn Massacre and the subsequent Peoria War, her… her *people* were not well loved by the growing white population in the area—particularly by General Tony Wayne and his bloody Legion." Again, his mind seemed to drift back to another time, and his teeth gritted together ever-so-slightly in a long-remembered anger.

"We had thus chosen to keep our cabin far from the white men's encampments—which turned out to be a tragic error in judgment on my part." He sighed again, and then continued. "The year was 1799, and I had been called away briefly to Tennessee to consult with Governor John Sevier, who had found armored skeletons in some caves which seemed to confirm what an old Cherokee chief named Oconostota had told us nearly twenty years before, about the territorial war between the Welsh and the Cherokee in late 12th century Alabama…" I tried not to let that little revelation distract me from what he was trying to tell me about his wife.

"I came back to my home after having been away for almost a month, and saw my wife at a distance in the shallows of Lake Michigan, washing out some clothes. She turned and waved at me, with much the same smile that you saw on the Rakshasa's face here this evening. She never saw the mishipeshu break the water's surface behind her."

"What's a 'mishipeshu'?" I asked.

"The North American cousin to the ceffyl dŵr—such as the afanc that I killed near the bridge of Bryn Berian over a millennium earlier…" he said simply, as if that actually clarified everything. "Though that one wielded a ffechwaew…" I didn't ask anything more, given the context of the information, and resolved to look it all up myself later. For the record, there are "lake monster" legends all over the world, with the "mishipeshu" here in Illinois, the "afanc" in Wales, the "muš-huššu" in Babylon, the "kelpie" in Scotland, etc.—not sea serpent-type creatures like the Loch Ness monster, but what the Welsh called a "water horse" or the Midwestern Native Americans called a "water panther"—an aggressive and bizarre predator that looks like a cross between an alligator and a deranged elk. I'm not making this up. Apparently, Durant's seen these things at least twice on at least two continents, so who am I to argue?

"I watched my wife ripped apart by a mishipeshu in the shallows of Lake Michigan two centuries ago, Detective," he said. "I was too far away to help her—even as fast as I am, she was dead by the time I reached the water's edge. The irony is, mishipeshu avoid large human settlements, so if we had lived closer to the white men…" his voice trailed off as his eyes closed. "Then she would have died hereafter, nonetheless," he said, nodding to himself. His eyes opened again, and he looked at me.   "I do understand the concept of loss, Detective Chapel. I buried my wife's body with my own hands in the dark brown earth behind our cabin. I carved her name in stone, and I knew that I would never lie beside her again—in life *or* in death. There is a curse that comes along with the blessing of the Grail."

I'd never really thought about long life being a bad thing—I guess everyone kind of wishes that they could live forever. But when I think about Chelsea and the twins, would I really want to watch them grow old and die, their *children* grow old and die, their *children's* children grow old and die, while I still kept going on and on?

"I have walked away from so many gravesides over the centuries," Durant said, his voice suddenly sounding quite old. "Death comes to *all* men, save *one*—and in my very long life, notwithstanding all those whom I have saved, I am still haunted by those far too many loved ones whom I was *not* able to save…"

Durant took one last look at the ashes of the Rakshasa on the sidewalk, which the night breeze was already beginning to blow away. He leaned down, and whispered something—luckily, I was close enough to hear him say, "It's over now, Ali." And then, in an even quieter voice, breaking with emotion, he added, "I… *miss* you, Catherine… In pace requiescat…"

Rest in peace…

*   *   *

We positioned ourselves near St. Vincent's Circle, behind the Richardson Library on the DePaul University campus. We had a pretty good view of most of the area behind there, and we figured that we'd be able to see Sydor if he showed up there. It was a longshot, I know, but it seemed worth a try.

We sat in silence for probably half an hour, just watching. After a while, I became aware of a little scuffing sound. I turned toward Durant to see him whittling on a small piece of wood with a little pen knife.

"What are you doing?" I whispered.

"Hmm?" he replied, roused from his simple reverie. "Oh, an old habit," he whispered back, continuing his work with the little knife. "I used to carve things when I was a boy, and I suppose that I've never truly ceased to do so. I do awfully despise waiting, you see." I started to laugh, and then stifled it and kept quiet, but Durant actually smiled a little, too. "You would think that, after all of these centuries, I should have learned more patience, yes?"

"That's kind of what I was thinking, yes," I said.

"And yet, I have not," he replied. "I still have the keen awareness of the inexorable passage of every minute, every second. Even with so many seconds behind me, I know that there are yet only a finite number of seconds in every day, and that every day sees its time, and then is gone forever. 'If you can fill the unforgiving minute with sixty seconds' worth of distance run, yours is the Earth and everything that's in it'—"

"'And—which is more—you'll be a man, my son!'" I finished the quote. Durant looked surprised. "My dad's favorite poem," I explained to him. "He used to bellow parts of it while walking down the halls in our house, as if he was giving a recitation in some old-time town hall. We all laughed at him when he did it, because he sounded so crazy."

"And was he?" Durant asked.

I smiled. "Not one bit."

"Just so," he said, and he began carving some little detail into the top of the little block of wood. "Wisdom should be shouted from the rooftops, not relegated to musty conversations between creaky, learned men in salons and pulpits. I applaud your father's efforts."

So do I, I realized. And I made it a point to remind myself that, when I got back home, I should start shouting some Kipling through the rooms of our home, too. Chelsea would love it, but I'd probably have to explain it to Joanna. Of course, maybe half the fun would be in *not* explaining it. I looked back to our hunting grounds again, searching for any movement, but I didn't see anything. Maybe Sydor wasn't coming? Maybe we had the wrong library after all?

"You know, our Lord was a carpenter by trade," Durant said, finishing his whittling and blowing off the bits of shavings from the wood. "I have often wondered if, while sitting by the evening fire with his disciples along the dusty roads of Judea, he himself may have often carved a piece of wood not unlike this one." He held up a little figure of a knight in armor, with a sword held in his hands, its tip resting on the ground. It was beautiful, actually. I smiled and nodded in appreciation.

"My grandfather was a carpenter, too," I said, trying to connect with him.

"So, obviously, this information about the library was another trap," Durant said, breaking the happy little moment as he set the figure down onto the ground next to him. "We are wasting our time here, do you not agree?"

"No, I don't think so," I countered, more than just a little frustrated—in part because he might just be right, and that was the most frustrating part. Durant frowned and turned to me. "Look, Sydor burned the note before he threw it away because he knew that we would come to his room to check up on him," I said. "*That* was the *trap*, right?"

"That was *a* trap, yes."

"But he *burned* the note," I continued. "That means that the information that we were able to salvage from the notepad is probably righteous. I mean, if the thing about the library was another false lead, then they wouldn't have destroyed the note, right? They would've *wanted* us to find it."

"Unless they fully expected your ridiculous trick with the pencil, and *counted* on it," he responded, with more than just a little disdain in his voice.

"And may I say 'You're welcome' for that ridiculous trick of mine that *got* us our next lead," I said. "*You'd* never have done it..."

"That is correct."

"So even if they figured I might try something like that, what are the chances that we'd have come to the room together? Could they have counted on *that*? You wouldn't have checked the notepad—you wouldn't have checked *anything*, apparently—" I added, becoming more frustrated with him as I spoke, "and I don't know how to read Romanian. If we hadn't *both* been there, then we wouldn't be here right now. That suggests to me that it's a righteous lead."

Durant was silent for a moment. I couldn't tell if he was debating about the logic of my thinking, or if he was just reluctant to admit that I was making sense.

"I see your point," he finally commented... quietly...

"You know, you're copping a pretty bad attitude for a guy who brought me into your little psycho world specifically because of stuff like my ridiculous pencil trick," I grumbled. "Detective work is what I do."

"Indeed," he said, looking away into the night. "And I do appreciate your skills, *overall*..." and it was his emphasis on that last word that turned his little compliment into a backhanded rebuke. "But perhaps we should reconsider the investigation. This is not at all the manner in which I usually conduct my hunts..."

"Well, that could be good *or* bad," I countered. "But maybe you're right—maybe we should be more proactive in this. Maybe we should do what we do with *human* suspects and figure out how to get them to turn on one another—convince one that it's in their best interests to rat out another one."

Durant snorted at the suggestion. "These creatures are not like the 'perpetrators' with whom you regularly deal, Detective," he chided. "They are corpses animated by demons—they do not reason as men do..."

"I can see your point," I admitted. "But then again, isn't that supposedly why the demons fell from Heaven in the first place? Because they selfishly turned on one another out of jealousy?"

Durant turned to me and cocked an eyebrow in surprise.

"What?" I responded. "I went to Sunday School…" Durant shook his head and turned away again.

"Think about it," I continued, pressing the point. "If *human* criminals are prone to turn on one another when it looks like they're up against the wall, don't you think that *demonic* criminals are likely—maybe even more likely—to do the same? The only real differences are in the level of evil and the degree of weirdness. Look at Dracula." I offered, trying to appeal to what little I actually thought I might know about vampires. "I mean, he was a prince in Transylvania once, right?"

"A voivode," Durant corrected.

"Anyway," I continued, "he traded his soul for power and eternal life. And that worked for a while. For a while, he had armies and retainers and treasures and all of that, but by the time Stoker's book comes around, that's all gone. I mean, after a couple of centuries, even Dracula was reduced to the ratty clothes on his back, living in a broken-down castle, getting by each day until he could get his next 'fix' so that he can get by until his *next* 'fix,' day after day. Whether we're talking about blood or cocaine, the point's still the same. He lost everything and everyone and all of the trappings of power that he'd *used* to think were important back when he was alive—all of the stuff that I assume he traded his soul to hold onto forever in the first place—but in the end, none of that was as important any more to him as his addiction was. Dracula may have lived in a castle and still had piles of gold lying around, but for all of his power, he was still reduced to the same quality of life that any crack-head is living today—a slave to the addiction that *he* thinks makes him feel strong, hiding alone in his hole because all that matters to him is the next 'fix'…"

Durant furrowed his bushy brows and pondered this. The guy is a millennium and a half old, but I think I actually got him to think about something that he'd never considered before. Chalk up one for the mortal guy.

"It was for precisely this sort of insight that I sought you out, Detective Chapel…" he said at last, with an uncomfortable grimace on his face. "But even so, you are still ever the modern rationalist…" he said, shaking his head and picking up another piece of wood to whittle. We were both quiet for a while again, waiting for something to happen. But nothing did.

After a few minutes, Durant spoke up again. "Do you know why it was that, in the Middle Ages, people thought that there were trolls in the hills?" he asked, continuing his carving.

"Because they were superstitious about the wilderness?" I ventured. "Because they'd spent so many generations trying to scare their children into not wandering too far from home that they'd begun to believe their own ghost stories? Because they were ignorant, illiterate and dirty, and they put their faith in fairy tales? Am I getting close?"

"No," he said. "It was because in the Middle Ages, there were still trolls in the hills. I *know*, because I was *there*." He blew on the piece of wood, and then went back to whittling.

"What's your point?" I asked.

"My point is that not everything in this world fits into the paradigms which mankind cleverly constructs for itself," he replied. He whittled in silence for another minute or so, then continued. "For instance, whilst I was traveling through Tibet with Brian Houghton Hodgson in 1830, we found the lost city of Iolkos, hidden away in a valley deep in the Himalayas. The only reason that we were able to communicate with them at all was due to my familiarity with Greek, albeit a dialect quite removed from their own significantly evolved version of the language. They had been descended from the members of the armies of Alexander, you see, and had maintained their culture by embracing his more idealistic concepts—and far more successfully than had the Nuristani in Sikandergul, I might add."

I frowned, wondering what any of this had to do with anything.

"But I digress," he said—and I agreed. "No one believed that we could have found a lost Ionian culture, still thriving in the mountains of Tibet after all those centuries, because such a possibility did not fit into their conception of rational reality." He blew more shavings away, and then continued whittling as he spoke again. "For that matter, on our way back out of those mountains, Hodgson and I also saw a migou at a distance, though no one believed that, either."

"What's a migou?" I asked, since we were stuck in this conversation anyway.

"It literally means, 'wild man'—the word which our Tibetan guides used to describe what others referred to as a 'yeti' or a 'mirka'—a large, bipedal anthropoid which lived on the slopes of the mountains."

"You saw an Abominable Snowman?" I asked, chuckling.

"No," he replied, deadly serious. "I saw a migou. The native bearers saw a migou. Hodgson believed it to be some sort of orangutan, but it walked on two legs for too long a stretch—and there are, of course, no orangutans in Tibet..." he blew more shavings away. "But there are quite obviously migou..."

"So you're saying that it's really real?" I asked again, more than just a little doubtful.

"Are orangutans real?" he asked me. "They were considered by the scientific community merely creatures of superstitious myth—the 'wild man of the forests' in Malaysia—until a Westerner finally authenticated them at the turn of the 18th century, and thus made them *real* to the rationalists. Are mountain gorillas real? And yet *they* were considered a native myth as well, until Hauptman von Beringe from the Totenkopf Hussars shot and killed two of them at the dawn of the 20th century, photographing the corpses and bringing back the remains for authentication by the rationalists. And yet, rather than admit that there are more things in Heaven and earth than are dreamt of in science, humanity continue to assume that, though the 'wild man' of Sumatra succeeded in becoming scientific fact, the 'wild man' of Tibet must be the result of so much superstitious hysteria, and the 'wild man'—the Sésquac—of your own Pacific Northwest must be equally as fictitious. You assign ridiculous names to them, like 'Abominable Snowman,' and 'Bigfoot,' so that they are more easily dismissed in your minds—your self-righteously *rational* minds."

Okay, I never would've thought that a guy like Durant would get so passionate about believing in Bigfoot. "You've got to admit," I said, "it's still kind of hard to believe." Then again, the moment the words tumbled out of my mouth, I thought of the lutine, the mishipeshu, the Rakshasa, the vampires, the revenants, and all of the other things that I hadn't believed in up until recently, and I realized that I was still just as instinctively closed-minded as I had ever been.

"On that same expedition to Tibet, Hodgson also discovered 39 species of mammals and 124 species of birds which had not been described previously by science," Durant replied. "And yet, for some reason, the world still utterly discounts his assertion that he saw a migou as well. Why might that be, Detective?"

Because we're stupid, I thought to myself. Or, more accurately, because we like remaining ignorant about the things that would frighten us to death if we believed that they were really out there.

"I don't know…" was all I actually said in response.

"Then remind me not to tell you about the reptilian kongamato I saw flying over Shiniama on the Luapula River in Northern Rhodesia in 1915…"

I was about to say something snarky in response to that, when I looked back toward the library and saw a figure of a man standing, back-lit against the streetlight. I put my finger to my lips and whispered, "Shh…" pointing to the silhouette. Durant nodded.

The figure was right next to a tree, standing without moving. That's not quite true—it was like he was swaying slightly in the night breeze. We watched for a few moments, and then I noticed that even his *feet* were swaying, just a bit—he wasn't quite touching the ground. His head was cocked at a strange angle, and I began to have a bad feeling about all of this. Okay, an *even more* bad feeling about all of this than I'd had up to that point, and *that* was saying something.

"Something's not right here," I said to Durant.

"Which *part*?" he replied. I stood up from our blind and started to move toward the figure. "Get down!" Durant whispered hoarsely, but I kept on.

"Watch my six," I said, pulling out my gun and moving in closer, hugging the treeline as I approached. After a few more steps, I confirmed my suspicion that the man was actually dead, hanging from the tree with a noose around his neck… and hanging low enough that he obviously hadn't been *killed* there—he'd just been *left* there. But who had left him there, and who had they left him to be found by? I had another very bad feeling about that.

I pulled back into the trees, looking up, down, right, left. No one around that I could see, other than Durant behind me. I stepped forward again and looked closer at the hanged man, and that's when I recognized who the victim really was. And yes, it was exactly what I'd been afraid of.

I was looking at the body of František Yevhen Sydor.

Background
**Abraham Van Helsing, from Mina Harker's *Journal*, as reprinted in
Dracula (Bram Stoker, 1897)**

There are such beings as vampires; some of us have evidence that they exist. Even had we not the proof of our own unhappy experience, the teachings and the records of the past give proof enough for sane peoples. I admit that at the first I was skeptic. Were it not that through long years I have train myself to keep an open mind, I could not have believe until such time as that fact thunder on my ear. "See! see! I prove; I prove," Alas! Had I known at the first what now I know—nay, had I even guess at him—one so precious life had been spared to many of us who did love her. But that is gone; and we must so work, that other poor souls perish not, whilst we can save.

The nosferatu do not die like the bee when he sting once. He is only stronger; and being stronger, have yet more power to work evil. This vampire which is amongst us is of himself so strong in person as twenty men; he is of cunning more than mortal, for his cunning be the growth of ages; he have still the aids of necromancy, which is, as his etymology imply, the divination by the dead, and all the dead that he can come nigh to are for him at command; he is brute, and more than brute; he is devil in callous, and the heart of him is not; he can, within limitations, appear at will when, and where, and ill any of the forms that are to him; he can, within his range, direct the elements; the storm, the fog, the thunder; he can command all the meaner things: the rat, and the owl, and the bat— the moth, and the fox, and the wolf, he can grow and become small; and he can at times vanish and come unknown.

How then are we to begin our strife to destroy him? How shall we find his where, and having found it, how can we destroy? My friends, this is much; it is a terrible task that we undertake, and there may be consequence to make the brave shudder. For if we fail in this our fight he must surely win; and then where end we? Life is nothings; I heed him not. But to fail here, is not mere life or death. It is that we become as him; that we henceforward become foul things of the night like him— without heart or conscience, preying on the bodies and the souls of those we love best. To us for ever are the gates of heaven shut: for who shall open them to us again? We go on for all time abhorred by all; a blot on the face of God's sunshine; an arrow in the side of Him who died for man...

All we have to go upon are traditions and superstitions. These do not at the first appear much, when the matter is one of life and death—nay of more than either life or death. Yet must we be satisfied; in the first place because we have to be—no other means is at our control—and secondly, because, after all, these things—tradition and superstition—are everything. Does not the belief in vampires rest for others—though not, alas, for us—on them? A year ago which of us would have received such a possibility, in the midst of our scientific, skeptical, matter-of-fact nineteenth century? We even scouted a belief that we saw justified under our very eyes.

Take it, then, that the vampire, and the belief in his limitations and his cure, rest for the moment on the same base. For, let me tell you, he is known everywhere that men have been. In old Greece, in old Rome; he nourish in Germany all over, in France, in India, even in the Chersonese; and in China, so far from us in all ways, there even is he, and the peoples fear him at this day. He have follow the wake of the berserker Icelander, the devil-begotten Hun, the Slav, the Saxon, the Magyar.

So far, then, we have all we may act upon; and let me tell you that very much of the beliefs are justified by what we have seen in our own so unhappy experience. The vampire live on, and cannot die by mere passing of the time, he can flourish when that he can fatten on the blood of the living. Even more, we have seen amongst us that he can even grow younger, that his vital faculties grow strenuous, and seem as though they refresh themselves when his special pabulum is plenty...

He throws no shadow; he make in the mirror no reflect... He has the strength of many of his hand... He can transform himself to wolf... He can be as bat... He can come in mist which he create... He come on moonlight rays as elemental dust... He can, when once he find his way, come out from anything or into anything, no matter how close it be bound or even fused up with fire—solder you call it. He can see in the dark—no small power this, in a world which is one half shut from the light. Ah, but hear me through.

He can do all these things, yet he is not free. Nay; he is even more prisoner than the slave of the galley, than the madman in his cell. He cannot go where he lists; he who is not of nature has yet to obey some of nature's laws—why we know not. He may not enter anywhere at the first, unless there be some one of the household who bid him to come; though afterwards he can come as he please. His power ceases, as does that of all evil things, at the coming of the day...

It is said, too, that he can only pass running water at the slack or the flood of the tide. Then there are things which so afflict him that he has no power, as the garlic that we know of, and as for things sacred, as this symbol, my crucifix, that was amongst us even now when we resolve, to them he is nothing, but in their presence he take his place far off and silent with respect. There are others, too, which I shall tell you of, lest in our seeking we may need them. The branch of wild rose on his coffin keep him that he move not from it; a sacred bullet fired into the coffin kill him so that he be true dead; and as for the stake through him, we know already of its peace; or the cut-off head that giveth rest. We have seen it with our eyes. Thus when we find the habitation of this man-that-was, we can confine him to his coffin and destroy him, if we obey what we know…

Chapter 17
Rumors of Wars

"So this *was* a trap," Durant said, looking at Sydor's body.

"This was *a* trap," I clarified, "but not for *us*. If it was a trap for us, it would be *our* necks in that noose." No, this was something else—cleaning house and leaving a warning to be found. I called it in, and that was a pain in the butt in and of itself, trying to explain to the Area 3 Detective Division why an Area 5 detective was stomping around their turf and stumbling over a murder victim. Obviously, I never mentioned the Rakshasa. I hung up the phone and pulled out my notebook as Durant began walking away.

"Where are you going?" I asked.

"The man is dead," he replied. "We have other things to do."

"The dead still teach the living," I said, starting to make notes about the blue nylon cord he was hanging by, and about the knot it was tied with—a slipknot, not a hangman's noose. It looked to me as if someone had slipped it on him from behind and choked him, since it didn't look like his neck was actually broken. Durant looked exasperated, but he stayed put. I figured that I had at least a few minutes before the CSI guys would get there, and/or before I'd wear out Durant's dwindling patience altogether.

The cord was new—probably purchased specifically for this killing. There were no markings or other identifiers on the cord, but I could still have Jenkins run a check on the basic brand to see where a length of it had been recently bought, and by whom. Or, to be fair, I figured that the Area 3 guys should do that, since I was stepping on their toes already.

"The Chicago Outfit used to do something like this, as a warning," I said, poking around Sydor's pockets carefully. I wanted to keep Durant involved, connected. "They'd take mice from pet stores, tie little nooses around their necks, and then dangle them from your rearview mirror, windshield wipers, whatever. You'd go out to your car in the morning or after work, and you'd see them hanging there—immediate freak-out. It was their way of telling people to back off."

"I knew something similar in Māzandarān, on the coast of the Caspian Sea," Durant replied, still obviously wanting to be on the move, rather than standing still.

"How so?" I asked, trying to engage him.

"Wajid Ali Shah was a vile ruler, but he considered himself cultured, aesthetic. Thus, he thought it ironically appropriate that his chief torturer and assassin was a Frenchman of music and refinement—albeit a horribly disfigured one, with a soul as hideous as was his face. The fiend's favored weapon was the Punjab lasso made of catgut, and he would loop its noose around his victim's neck unexpectedly, from out of an alleyway, or a darkened stairwell, and then leave the body hanging outside of the homes of their compatriots as a warning that they had incurred the Shah's wrath."

"Sounds like a nice guy," I said, a little frustrated at the lack of anything in Sydor's pockets. I hunched down to look at the ground around his feet.

"Indeed. The Shah called him *'Aka Mainyu'*—the 'Evil Ghost'— but he referred to himself as *'le Mort vivant'*—the 'Living Dead.' This nomenclature was, itself, the 'noose' which Lord Aberdeen used to pull me into the conflict and involve me in the destabilization of the Shah's power in Oudh, as I had interest in neither the Crimean War nor any of the politicking surrounding it."

"So this Aka Mainyu guy was a vampire, huh?" I asked, still trying to keep Durant occupied while I investigated.

"Not at all, as Lord Aberdeen knew full well," he replied. "He looked to me like a walking skeleton, with yellowed, parchment-like skin, and scant wisps of hair floating around his skull-like face—but he was only a man. He was, however, as very nearly separate from humanity as a mere human could ever hope to be… though the local daroga seemed quite impressed by him."

"The what?"

"The daroga. Think of him as the chief of police there in the province of Māzandarān. He told me that the Ghost was a gifted architect, and that he could have been a man of some influence in his native France, had he not been born so disfigured. In fact, he seemed quite taken with the fiend, focusing on his better qualities and thus, his lost possibilities. Apparently, the Ghost was quite the musician as well."

"And Hitler loved his dogs…" I muttered, standing back up again.

"What was that?"

"They say that Hitler loved his dogs," I repeated. "He played with them, he took pictures of them, the whole shmear. No one is *totally* evil—or, for that matter, a total *saint*. But none of that really makes up for the six million Jews he killed or that whole 'trying to take over the world' thing. So who cares how operatic a singing voice the professional torturer has?"

"Just so," Durant said. "I was quite taken aback when the daroga helped the Ghost escape from our clutches."

"Why would he do that?"

"He felt an empathy for the man, whose own family disowned him at birth. He enabled the fiend to escape from us, and, I understand, facilitated his return to Europe during the Anglo-Persian War a few years later, when Wajid Ali Shah was deposed. Lord only knows what a vengeful genius such as the Ghost would do, if loosed upon an unsuspecting France..."

I scribbled down some final notes just as a blue-and-white patrol car drove up. Some uniforms and detectives came over, and I had to come up with the same vague excuses again for them that I'd used on the phone. But this time, Durant was actually helpful. Just as one of the detectives was starting to put the screws to me, Durant exploded into the conversation, flashing his Interpol identification, and informing them that I couldn't tell them any more about the incident without jeopardizing an ongoing international operation. He told them that they'd have to contact Lt. Chacon for more information, and then pulled me away from the scene.

"Thanks," I said, as we got back to my car. Durant grunted and nodded. "To be honest," I continued, "I'd kind of forgotten about that whole Interpol thing—it sure comes in handy sometimes, doesn't it?"

"Indeed," he replied. "Again, such was one of my primary motivations for forming the organization in the first place."

*   *   *

I called Tony and asked him to meet us at the office ASAP. It was only after I'd hung up the phone that I realized that it was almost 2:30 in the morning. Tony was not going to be a happy man.

But as we drove, I kept coming back to how the tunnels weren't lining up in my mind. We've been chasing this lead and that, but never quite catching a break. Our perp had been throwing this and that at us, but never quite taking us out of the equation. Why?

"It's a distraction," I said finally, more to myself than to Durant.

Durant grunted back at me a grumbling, "What did you say?"

"It's all a distraction," I repeated. "I mean, all of this is keeping us from really looking back at the original question of why anyone would kill both Amanda Cairns and Hector Flórez..."

"Perhaps because the killer is an undead creature who feeds on human blood to survive," Durant suggested. "That would seem to be motivation enough..."

"But he *didn't* feed on Amanda Cairns," I reminded him. "He killed her for some other reason, and then chased Hector Flórez down and killed him as well—and *that's* when he fed."

"And your point would be…?" he sighed.

"That the key issue here—the key issue to *everything*—is answering the question, 'Why did he kill Amanda Cairns?' And he's trying to distract us from that." Durant sat up more in his seat, his brow furrowing in thought.

"And why not just kill us?" I continued.

"Has he not tried to do precisely that?" Durant asked. "And on multiple occasions?"

"Well, yeah," I admitted. "But I mean, instead of sending a lone vampire or a Rakshasa or those revenants, why not just have twenty vampires come to take us out? I mean, fighting even that one vampire back in the warehouse was a legitimate fight for you, wasn't it?"

"I can easily handle a vampire such as that one," he snorted. "I've not been truly bested in combat but once in the past seven hundred years—damnable Muramasa blades…"

"Uh-huh. But could you handle *twenty* of these things?" I asked again.

"Probably not, but that is not an item for concern," he answered.

"And why is that?"

"Because of the Danse."

"The what?"

Durant sighed, and turned to face me. "As part of a means of trying to control a population of ravenously hungry, thoroughly self-absorbed monsters, the vampyri have created the Danse—a subculture of their own, a set of rules by which they nominally govern themselves. For instance, a vampire may not convert a human into another vampire without the approval of the Lord of the vampires in that region."

"So that's why Hector Flórez isn't up and biting people on the neck right now?" I asked.

"Precisely," he replied. "He was not bitten, and thus he was not infected—he was ripped open and sucked dry, so that he would not subsequently join the undead as one of them. Another of the rules of the Danse is that no more than one vampire may engage a victim—or an opponent—at one time."

"That seems like a bizarre rule," I said, chuckling to myself.

"Perhaps," he said. "But it has nonetheless prevented my own demise on multiple occasions. I suspect that it serves both to prevent mass deaths that would draw attention to a vampire coven, as well as to force each vampire to strengthen its own abilities, rather than to rely on its compatriots, *en masse*. They are an odd combination of cowardliness and combativeness—they strike from the shadows, even when they far outmatch a victim, but they also prize strength and power in their own members. Only the strongest vampire in a region may become the Lord of that place."

"But that still doesn't really answer my initial question," I said again. "Why kill Amanda Cairns, if it had nothing to do with feeding on her?" I stopped at a stoplight. "She was killed because of something that she did, or something that she knew."

"You speak of this more as a murder than a predation," he said.

"Absolutely," I said, driving into the intersection once the light turned green. "I don't care whether a perp is a human or a vampire or an alien—there's always a motivation for a killing. And if that *isn't* sustenance, then it's something else—something important enough to kill for."

"Killing a human is inconsequential to a vampire," Durant said.

"Is it?" I asked. "You just said that they didn't want to draw attention to themselves. What was so important about killing an old woman that it was worth drawing our attention to the existence of our vampire? Something else is going on here, and all of these little side-trips are distracting us from it."

*   *   *

I was right. Tony was mad.

"What'd you an' Monty Python here get me outta bed for?" he growled at us. Not "Hello," or "What's up, Tom?" but a full-on growl, first thing.

"Hey, 'Our day starts when yours ends,' remember?" I said, reminding him of the homicide detectives' motto. "You want a day job, be a teacher."

Tony grunted, and slurped up another sip of Coke.

"It's morning," I said, pointing to the can. "I thought Coke was only for after lunch…?"

"It ain't mornin'," he replied, finishing off the can. "It's real, *real* late at night. An' I already had a late night ta start with."

"How so?" I asked, tossing my keys onto my desk and plopping down into my chair. Durant was getting himself a drink from the water cooler nearby.

"Ya didn't hear?" Tony asked. "Man, you *are* outta it these days…" he slammed his body down into his own chair, across from mine. "Nate Kingery's still tryin' ta ID a bunch o' OA's what got found hangin' on a fire escape in Bucktown tonight."

"What?!?" I asked, leaning forward. "What happened?"

"Dunno yet," he said, popping open another can. "All's I know is that seven Orquestra Albany punks got 'emselves strung up by rope in an alley in Bucktown. Rodriguez an' Taylor is on it."

I leaned back in my chair again to drink it in. I noticed Durant looking at me out of the corner of my eye.

"Rope, or blue nylon cord?" I asked.

"Huh?" Tony sputtered into his new can. "How'd ya know 'bout that, if ya didn't even know they was dead?"

"Because I found another dead body, hanging the same way over at DePaul tonight," I replied.

"DePaul?" Tony growled. "So you was sniffin' 'round there again, huh? Why didn't ya call me? I coulda come back ya up!"

"Durant was with me," I answered him, and I noticed Durant's stare becoming more of a scowl. Tony snorted again.

"Well, them OA's had Insane Deuce crap spray-painted all over 'em," he said. "An' we're already seein' the town goin' crazy in response. The OA's 're out there, taggin' buildings an' garage doors, spray-paintin' 'Insane Deuce Killer!' on 'em. An' I heard from a buddy of mine over at the 13th that the ID's are doin' about th' same thing. We got us a war brewin'…"

Great. *That* won't be a distraction at all. I knew that Billy had been spoiling for a fight with the Orquestra Albany over this Prisa thing, and I wondered if he and Mojo were all right.

"Oh, an' I found a connection 'tween Hector Flórez an' Amanda Cairns," Tony said. "That is, if ya even care any more 'bout *our* murder case…"

"What's that supposed to mean?" I asked, feeling a tinge of guilt mixed in with indignation.

"Well, you an' yer Eurotrash buddy jus' seem ta be more interested in whatever he's doin' here than in findin' the ol' lady's killer."

Okay, Tony had a point. But I couldn't explain to him that what Durant and I were doing was directly related to the case—other than just to say it that way.

"You have to believe that what we've been doing is directly related to the case," I said, though I knew that wasn't going to be nearly enough to satisfy Tony.

"Uh-huh…" he said, rolling his eyes and slurping on his can again. "Whatever…"

"So what did you find out?" I asked, trying to refocus the conversation. "What's the connection between them?"

"Well," Tony began, taking one more loud sip before launching into things. "Apparently, Amanda Cairns used ta tutor young Hector in art, when he was jus' a *lil'* juvenile offender. He an' th' neighbor kids'd come to her apartment an' paint flowers an' crap."

I thought about that young Hector Flórez—the one who fought with his father in the kitchen, and who, at one point, wanted nothing more than to escape his hellish little world through his art. I pictured him painting in that little apartment with a lonely old woman who filled her days helping other people's children, since she'd never had any of her own. I remembered the smell of oil paints and thinners and wondered how long it had been since Hector had painted with a brush instead of a spray can. And I wondered what had brought Hector back to that apartment again, after all these years.

"So why would that be a reason for murdering either one of them?" I asked. Tony just belched and shrugged his shoulders.

"I jus' said I found a connection—I didn't say I found a motive."

"Well, keep on it," I told him. "Oh, and while you're at it, have you ever heard of a drug called, 'Prisa' on the street?"

"Nope," he said, shaking his head. "Am I *supposed* ta 've?"

"Just keep an ear open for it," I asked. "It may be important." He nodded.

"So what're we gonna do 'bout this war?" he asked.

"We'll have to go see el Buitre and the Angel again," I said, "and then maybe whoever's in charge of the ID's these days." I scribbled a note to that effect in my notebook, then looked back up at Tony. "Who *is* the jefe over there nowadays?"

"I dunno," he replied. "That's across the river in Roscoe Village…"

*　　　*　　　*

Durant asked me to drive him over to Roscoe Village before I went back home to crash for a while. I was fine with that, because I had a question or two more to ask him about what had happened to us that night. I started with the most obvious one.

"So who's Rhiannon?"

"Rhiannon?" he repeated the name, feigning a certain ignorance… badly…

"Now who's playing games, Durant?" I asked. "You called that witch 'Rhiannon' when she was getting away. Who *is* she?"

Durant actually looked a little sheepish about his pretense, and he cleared his throat.

"She has gone by many names over the centuries," he said. "When I first met her at the Gorsedd Arberth—the Hill of the Immortals—she was called, 'Rigantona.' A fiery beauty, that one, the daughter of Eveyd Hen." He took another deep breath before continuing. "She… *endeared* herself to me, by use of magicks which I did not at that time understand. It is a fearful thing to find oneself tumbling into those green eyes, Detective…"

I thought about how I'd felt—even for a moment—listening to that Rakshasa, with the red wolf standing next to her in the archway on Fullerton. I could only imagine what it would be like to have the witch pouring it on full-steam, with no experienced Durant there to pull me out of it.

"The last time that I saw her in person was nearly three centuries ago, when she was in the service of the Baron de Retz, in Vienna. She was going under the name of 'Raina du Vilaine' at that time." He sighed that patented Durant heavy sigh. "She is a water witch, remember. She had always been tied to Brittany in general and to the river Vilaine in particular, so when de Retz was turned to the undead in 1432 and eventually became the Vampire Lord of that region, she became his own personal korrigan—his creature. I had thought her destroyed when I had fought de Retz in the newly opened Viennese orangery at Schönbrunn Palace, but such was not the case. Later, she reappeared in the fog outside of Detroit in 1812. I sought her out there, and then followed her back to Europe in close pursuit, only to lose her at last in Leipzig. Again and again over the centuries, the malignant creature has both haunted and eluded me."

"Man, you've seen a lot of monsters over the years, haven't you?" I said.

"Indeed..." he said. "All manner of beastly things..." His eyes glazed over as he turned to look out of the car window again. I could only imagine the tapestry of oozing, skittering, blasphemous monstrosities that flashed across his mind's eye, as he remembered century after century of hunting the things that drive the rest of humanity to our nightmares. One man, quietly holding the night back from devouring us, all alone in the dark... forever. "Over a thousand years ago," he continued, "I fought against the damnable Erik Bloodaxe over Northumbria, and against the mad úlfhéðnar first created by his father, Haraldr hárfagri. We tried in vain to hold on to the hard-won peace and unification of the whole of England that we had obtained under good King Æthelstan, but the northlander hordes poured into Britain in wave after horrible wave, and Æthelstan's weak son, Edmund, was simply not up to the task of protecting that which his father had won for him. Thus, between those filthy Uí Ímair mongrels like Amlaíb Cuarán and the invasion by Erik's great heathen army, we had to settle for holding them to that northernmost kingdom, instead of driving them back into the sea as we should have done..."

Now, I confess, he might as well have been speaking Greek to me right then and there. I had no idea what he was talking about, except that it appeared to include Vikings. But one thing I did notice was that his story didn't seem to include anything about monsters.

"Okay, so how is that about supernatural creatures again?" I asked.

Durant seemed disoriented for a moment, as if he was no longer in the conversation we'd been having, but instead a million miles away. He looked at me as if he didn't know me—just for a second—and then literally shook himself back to reality again.

"Forgive me, Detective Chapel," he answered at last, his face looking drawn and suddenly much older. "I have seen much in my time, and much of it still holds onto my soul, as surely as a child holds onto his father's sleeve. I feel, at times, as if the memories themselves fear being lost, and that they cling to me as if, in doing so, they might gain a degree of immortality along with me. As if they fear that to be forgotten would be to have been as if they never were at all." A slight smile recovered itself on his haggard face again. "Or to be blithely relegated to the mists of myth…"

I had wondered about how many of those memories bouncing around in that skull of his—all of those battles and lost loves and pain and triumphs—had just became a fuzzy collage in his mind, like the way you or I might think of our time in elementary school. Yes, there are moments here and there that stand out, but most of it is just a blurry photograph in my memory. But extend that over centuries, millennia, and what must that be like? But listening to him speak about them, a lot of his memories are still apparently just as sharp now as they were way back then. Maybe, instead of just being custodian of our survival, Durant was also something of a custodian of our history.

"But to your query," he said at last, visibly relaxing into the seat. "You have heard, I presume, of the bear-skinned bärsärkars who fought like demons amongst the Viking hordes?" I nodded, vaguely remembering at least that we get our word "berserk" from how crazy they were when they fought. "Well, Detective, there was a reason for their fearlessness in battle. They received their strength through the demon, Odin, who imbued them with a sliver of his power when they turned themselves over to him, body and soul."

"Wait a minute," I interjected. "I always thought Odin was some sort of a Norse god…"

"You shall find—should you live long enough—" and here he bent his neck and leaned toward me, emphasizing his words as a gentle nonverbal chiding, "that a great number of the things which you have always thought to be true must needs be reconsidered." He sighed again, and sat back into his seat. "There is but *one* God, Detective," he said at last. "He gave himself on our behalf on the cross, and conquered death and sin to save us from the terrors which we all have brought upon ourselves—an unwavering faith in this fact on your part will be an absolute necessity for our task ahead. Odin, however, was the Demon Lord of Scandinavia—a one-eyed Prince of the Kingdom of the Air— and a devout servant of the Evil One."

He paused here, as if to let the full impact of the weight of his words sink in, and I confess that I found myself chuckling at the thought.

"You're talking about, like, the Devil, right?"

"I find it fascinating in the extreme," he replied, "that you should be able to convert your paradigms enough to intellectually accept the existence of the vampyri, and yet continue to find the truth of the existence of their creator still beyond your ability to grasp. Why should this be?"

The man had a point.

"The bärsärkars received their strength, speed, and ferocity in battle—as well as their tremendous constitution and ability to withstand attack—from anointing themselves with an unction distilled through certain arcane rites performed by their sorcerers, and then wearing upon their bodies the pelts of bears. Through Odin's demonic magicks, they gained the strength and power of bears, as well as their bestial nature. It was not at all uncommon for them to bite their shields, growl, and howl as they entered the fray. I myself saw them more than once shrug off blows that would have killed an ordinary fighter. King Haraldr's úlfhéðnar were his own derivation of that hellish sorcery to use against us in Northumbria, but wrapping his warriors in the pelts of timberwolves instead of bears..." He paused for a moment, frowning as if making a connection that he hadn't considered before. "This is not unlike the rituals which Richard Verstegen and I made note of being used in England nearly seven centuries later... hmm..."

"So, these úlfhéðnar—how did you guys stop them?" I asked, breaking his concentration to get him back to his story.

"Hm?" he said, rousing himself from his thoughts. "Oh, the Northumbrians most certainly would not have been able to defeat them on their own. Those creatures were foul, heartless things, and they had given themselves and their humanity up so completely to their evil that neither their life nor limb any longer seemed important to them. I once saw one úlfhéðinn continue to battle seven Northumbrians, even after having lost one of his arms in the conflict. He never even seemed to notice..." Durant paused, picturing the moment again in his mind. "But as fortune and God's providence would have it, Christian England did have its own supernatural force to counter Satan's."

"And what was that?" I asked. He turned to me and cocked his head as if surprised at the question.

"Me, of course."

Of course, I thought. But I have to admit, he didn't seem to say it with any kind of pride or braggadocio—he just said it as if it were a simple matter of fact. The Vikings had an army of deadly, superhuman, pseudo-werewolves, and England had Durant, and that's why England beat them. Like, *of course* England would beat them. But then, knowing Durant even for as short a period of time as I had, I began to believe it. If he hadn't have beaten them, then he wouldn't have been sitting there chatting with me. He didn't strike me as the sort of man who would leave before a fight was finished, particularly when that fight involved an enemy whose strength was supernatural in its origin—and as time went on, I found quite dramatically that I was right in that assumption.

"So there's no such thing as a *real* werewolf?" I asked, almost sorry to hear it, now that the concept was on the table as something potentially factual.

"No, there certainly is," he assured me. "In fact, a protégé of mine—a young Spaniard named Esteban de Navarra—was cursed to become a wolf by night by a corrupt French bishop in 1208 because they both loved the same woman. I would have helped the lad, but I myself was languishing in an oubliette in Nottingham at the time, having been cast there by the sheriff, Gerard de Athies. An oubliette," he continued, obviously picking up on the fact that I had no idea what that word had meant, "was a pit within a dungeon, into which unusually... *unruly*... prisoners were thrown to die slowly. It was a particularly and ironically perilous situation for one such as I, who would be *incapable* of dying, and thus in danger of spending the rest of human history there. As luck would have it, however, de Athies later threw into my oubliette a forest outlaw whom he had captured at St. Mary's, and we were both eventually freed by one of the outlaw's men—a giant of a man named John."

"What happened to Esteban?" I asked.

"Oh, by the time that I became aware of his situation, he had already freed himself and his love from their curse—killing the bishop with the longsword which I myself had presented to his great-great-grandfather, Rodrigo, over a century before in recognition to his service under King Sancho the Strong during the War of the Three Sanchos. In fact, I fought alongside Esteban only a few years later at the battle of Las Navas de Tolosa, against the Almohads, which was the first time that I had heard of his unfortunate previous circumstances."

"So is that when you got that pouch that you wear at your side?" I asked, trying to slip the question in under the radar, hoping that he'd finally explain it to me, now that he was in "lecturer" mode again.

"As I told you," he replied. "It is the *got uechan*." And that's all he seemed prepared to say.

"Oh, come on," I asked again. "What *is* the *got uechan*? It's not any kind of *normal* bag, is it? Where did you *get* it?"

"It was a gift," he answered me. "Ironically, from Rhiannon—long, long ago."

"That really doesn't answer my main question," I pressed him. "All you're saying is that it's an old bag. I knew that much already. But I've seen—at least, I *think* I've seen—you pull a whole sword out of that thing, a crossbow bolt, a big old stick—"

"The Matteh ha Shelomoh..." he corrected.

"The Matteh ha Shelomoh," I continued, "and everything short of a small elephant out of that little thing at one point or another. Just what exactly does the *got uechan* do?"

"It holds things," he said simply.

"*What* things?" I asked, exasperated. He sat there in uncomfortably tense silence, hesitant about whether or not he really wanted to answer me. "Come on!" I pressed him. "*What* does it hold?"

"*Everything...*" he replied.

Background
From *The Mabinogion* (c. 11th-13th century, trans. Lady Charlotte Guest)

Pwyll[1] Prince of Dyved was lord of the seven Cantrevs[2] of Dyved...[3]

Once upon a time, Pwyll was at Narberth, his chief palace, where a feast had been prepared for him, and with him was a great host of men. And after the first meal, Pwyll arose to walk, and he went to the top of a mound that was above the palace, and was called Gorsedd Arberth. "Lord," said one of the Court, "it is peculiar to the mound that whosoever sits upon it cannot go thence, without either receiving wounds or blows, or else seeing a wonder." "I fear not to receive wounds and blows in the midst of such a host as this, but as to the wonder, gladly would I see it. I will go therefore and sit upon the mound."

And upon the mound he sat. And while he sat there, they saw a lady, on a pure white horse of large size, with a garment of shining gold

---

[1] *Gillian Rhys-Jones has persuasively argued (in her* Chwedlau Hynafol Cymru, *1984) for a re-conflation of* The Mabinogion's *stories of Pwyll and Peredur. "The overwhelming number of similarities between the two heroes strongly suggests that they both diverged from a common source, an historical 'proto-Peredur' within the Arthurian cycle," a conclusion which expands on Jorge Cortázar's similarly hypothetical historical character in* Rey Arturo y los Caballeros de la Mesa Redonda (*1963) —whom Ifor Williams (in his* Pedeir Keinc y Mabinogi, *1930) associates with Pryderi. John Whitehead (*Guardian of the Grail, *1993), further argues that Pwyll literarily morphed into both the Fisher King and Sir Pellinore—whom Malory (*Le Morte d'Arthur, *1485) actually names as Sir Percival's father.*

[2] *Wales was at one time divided into "cantrevs"—small kingdoms ruled by minor kings. The word "cantrev" literally just means, "one hundred homesteads."*

[3] *Welsh territory inhabited by the Déisi (Latin "Demetae"). According to genealogist Lewis Dwnn, writing during the time of Queen Elizabeth, "The kingdom of Dyved formerly extended between the rivers Teivy and Towy, from Llyn Teivy and the source of the Towy to St. David's, and the centre of this kingdom was the Dark-Gate, in Carmarthen." It was later combined with Seisyllwg to form the kingdom of Deheubarth.*

around her, coming along the highway that led from the mound; and the horse seemed to move at a slow and even pace, and to be coming up towards the mound. "My men," said Pwyll, "is there any among you who knows yonder lady?" "There is not, Lord," said they. "Go one of you and meet her, that we may know who she is." And one of them arose, and as he came upon the road to meet her, she passed by, and he followed as fast as he could, being on foot; and the greater was his speed, the further was she from him. And when he saw that it profited him nothing to follow her, he returned to Pwyll, and said unto him, "Lord, it is idle for any one in the world to follow her on foot." "Verily," said Pwyll, "go unto the palace, and take the fleetest horse that thou seest, and go after her."

And he took a horse and went forward. And he came to an open level plain, and put spurs to his horse; and the more he urged his horse, the further was she from him. Yet she held the same pace as at first. And his horse began to fail; and when his horse's feet failed him, he returned to the place where Pwyll was. "Lord," said he, "it will avail nothing for any one to follow yonder lady. I know of no horse in these realms swifter than this, and it availed me not to pursue her." "Of a truth," said Pwyll, "there must be some illusion here. Let us go towards the palace." So to the palace they went, and they spent that day. And the next day they arose, and that also they spent until it was time to go to meat. And after the first meal, "Verily," said Pwyll, "we will go the same party as yesterday to the top of the mound. And do thou," said he to one of his young men, "take the swiftest horse that thou knowest in the field." And thus did the young man. And they went towards the mound, taking the horse with them. And as they were sitting down they beheld the lady on the same horse, and in the same apparel, coming along the same road. "Behold," said Pwyll, "here is the lady of yesterday. Make ready, youth, to learn who she is." "My lord," said he, "that will I gladly do." And thereupon the lady came opposite to them. So the youth mounted his horse; and before he had settled himself in his saddle, she passed by, and there was a clear space between them. But her speed was no greater than it had been the day before. Then he put his horse into an amble, and thought that notwithstanding the gentle pace at which his horse went, he should soon overtake her. But this availed him not; so he gave his horse the reins. And still he came no nearer to her than when he went at a foot's pace. And the more he urged his horse, the further was she from him. Yet she rode not faster than before. When he saw that it availed not to follow her, he returned to the place where Pwyll was. "Lord," said he, "the horse can no more than thou hast seen." "I see indeed that it avails not that any one should follow her. And by Heaven," said he, "she must needs have an errand to some one in this plain, if her haste would allow her to declare it. Let us go back to the palace." And to the palace they went, and they spent that night in songs and feasting, as it pleased them.

And the next day they amused themselves until it was time to go to meat. And when meat was ended, Pwyll said, "Where are the hosts that went yesterday and the day before to the top of the mound?" "Behold, Lord, we are here," said they. "Let us go," said he, "to the mound, to sit there. And do thou," said he to the page who tended his horse, "saddle my horse well, and hasten with him to the road, and bring also my spurs with thee." And the youth did thus. And they went and sat upon the mound; and ere they had been there but a short time, they beheld the lady coming by the same road, and in the same manner, and at the same pace. "Young man," said Pwyll, "I see the lady coming; give me my horse." And no sooner had he mounted his horse than she passed him. And he turned after her and followed her. And he let his horse go bounding playfully, and thought that at the second step or the third he should come up with her. But he came no nearer to her than at first. Then he urged his horse to his utmost speed, yet he found that it availed nothing to follow her. Then said Pwyll, "O maiden, for the sake of him whom thou best lovest, stay for me." "I will stay gladly," said she, "and it were better for thy horse hadst thou asked it long since." So the maiden stopped, and she threw back that part of her headdress which covered her face. And she fixed her eyes upon him, and began to talk with him. "Lady," asked he, "whence comest thou, and whereunto dost thou journey?" "I journey on mine own errand," said she, "and right glad am I to see thee." "My greeting be unto thee," said he. Then he thought that the beauty of all the maidens, and all the ladies that he had ever seen, was as nothing compared to her beauty. "Lady," he said, "wilt thou tell me aught concerning thy purpose?" "I will tell thee," said she. "My chief quest was to seek thee." "Behold," said Pwyll, "this is to me the most pleasing quest on which thou couldst have come; and wilt thou tell me who thou art?" "I will tell thee, Lord," said she. "I am Rhiannon,[4] the daughter of Heveydd Hen, and they sought to give me to a husband against my will. But no husband would I have, and that because of my love for thee, neither will I yet have one unless thou reject me. And hither have I come to hear thy answer." "By Heaven," said Pwyll, "behold this is my answer. If I might choose among all the ladies and damsels in the world, thee would I choose." "Verily," said she, "if thou art thus minded, make a pledge to meet me ere I am given to another." "The sooner I may do so, the more pleasing will it be unto me," said Pwyll, "and wheresoever thou wilt, there will I meet with thee." "I will

---

[4]   *Almost certainly another name for the Celtic sorceress or korrigan known as Rigantona. It is unclear, then, whether Heveydd Hen is truly her father (thus making her half-human), or yet another human male placed under her supernatural control—or if, as Rhys-Jones (1984) suggests, both Heveydd Hen and his palace were perhaps entirely illusory in the first place.*

that thou meet me this day twelvemonth at the palace of Heveydd. And I will cause a feast to be prepared, so that it be ready against thou come." "Gladly," said he, "will I keep this tryst." "Lord," said she, "remain in health, and be mindful that thou keep thy promise; and now I will go hence." So they parted, and he went back to his hosts and to them of his household. And whatsoever questions they asked him respecting the damsel, he always turned the discourse upon other matters. And when a year from that time was gone, he caused a hundred knights to equip themselves and to go with him to the palace of Heveydd Hen. And he came to the palace, and there was great joy concerning him, with much concourse of people and great rejoicing, and vast preparations for his coming. And the whole Court was placed under his orders.

And the hall was garnished and they went to meat, and thus did they sit; Heveydd Hen was on one side of Pwyll, and Rhiannon on the other. And all the rest according to their rank. And they ate and feasted and talked one with another, and at the beginning of the carousal after the meat, there entered a tall auburn-haired youth, of royal bearing, clothed in a garment of satin. And when he came into the hall, he saluted Pwyll and his companions. "The greeting of Heaven be unto thee, my soul," said Pwyll, "come thou and sit down." "Nay," said he, "a suitor am I, and I will do mine errand." "Do so willingly," said Pwyll. "Lord," said he, "my errand is unto thee, and it is to crave a boon of thee that I come." "What boon soever thou mayest ask of me, as far as I am able, thou shalt have." "Ah," said Rhiannon, "wherefore didst thou give that answer?" "Has he not given it before the presence of these nobles?" asked the youth. "My soul," said Pwyll, "what is the boon thou askest?" "The lady whom best I love is to be thy bride this night; I come to ask her of thee, with the feast and the banquet that are in this place." And Pwyll was silent because of the answer which he had given. "Be silent as long as thou wilt," said Rhiannon. "Never did man make worse use of his wits than thou hast done." "Lady," said he, "I knew not who he was." "Behold this is the man to whom they would have given me against my will," said she. "And he is Gwawl the son of Clud, a man of great power and wealth, and because of the word thou hast spoken, bestow me upon him lest shame befall thee." "Lady," said he, "I understand not thine answer. Never can I do as thou sayest." "Bestow me upon him," said she, "and I will cause that I shall never be his." "By what means will that be?" asked Pwyll. "In thy hand will I give thee a small bag," said she. "See that thou keep it well, and he will ask of thee the banquet, and the feast, and the preparations which are not in thy power. Unto the hosts and the household will I give the feast. And such will be thy answer respecting this. And as concerns myself, I will engage to become his bride this night twelvemonth. And at the end of the year be thou here," said she, "and bring this bag with thee, and let thy hundred knights be in the orchard up yonder. And when he is in the midst of joy and feasting, come thou in by thyself, clad in ragged garments, and holding thy bag in thy hand, and ask nothing but a bagful of food, and I will cause that if all the meat and liquor that are in these seven Cantrevs were put into it, it would be no fuller than before. And after a great deal has been put therein, he will ask thee whether thy bag will ever be full. Say thou then that it never will, until a man of noble birth and of great wealth arise and press the food in the bag with both his feet, saying, 'Enough has been put therein;' and I will cause him to go and tread down the food in the bag, and when he does so, turn thou the bag, so that he shall be up over his head in it, and then slip a knot upon the thongs of the bag. Let there be also a good bugle horn about thy neck, and as soon as thou hast bound him in the bag, wind thy horn, and let it be a signal between thee and thy knights. And when they hear the sound of the horn, let them come down upon the palace." "Lord," said Gwawl, "it is meet that I have an answer to my request." "As much of that thou hast asked as it is in my power to give, thou shalt have," replied Pwyll. "My soul," said Rhiannon unto him, "as for the feast and the banquet that are here, I have bestowed them upon the men of Dyved, and the household, and the warriors that are with us. These can I not suffer to be given to any. In a year from to-night a banquet shall be prepared for thee in this palace, that I may become thy bride."

So Gwawl went forth to his possessions, and Pwyll went also back to Dyved. And they both spent that year until it was the time for the feast at the palace of Heveydd Hen. Then Gwawl the son of Clud set out to the feast that was prepared for him, and he came to the palace, and was received there with rejoicing. Pwyll, also, the Chief of Annwvyn,[5] came to the orchard with his hundred knights, as Rhiannon had commanded him, having the bag with him. And Pwyll was clad in coarse and ragged garments, and wore large clumsy old shoes upon his feet. And when he knew that the carousal after the meat had begun, he went towards the hall, and when he came into the hall, he saluted Gwawl the son of Clud, and his company, both men and women. "Heaven prosper thee," said Gwawl, "and the greeting of Heaven be unto thee." "Lord," said he, "may Heaven reward thee, I have an errand unto thee." "Welcome be thine errand, and if thou ask of me that which is just, thou shalt have it gladly." "It is fitting," answered he. "I crave but from want, and the boon that I ask is to have this small bag that thou seest filled with meat." "A request within reason is this," said he, "and gladly shalt thou have it. Bring him food." A great number of attendants arose and began to fill the bag, but for all that they put into it, it was no fuller than at first. "My

---

[5]   Or "Annwfn." A supernatural Otherworld, which Pwyll supposedly ruled
      for a year in an earlier legend.

soul," said Gwawl, "will thy bag be ever full?" "It will not, I declare to Heaven," said he, "for all that may be put into it, unless one possessed of lands, and domains, and treasure, shall arise and tread down with both his feet the food that is within the bag, and shall say, 'Enough has been put therein.'" Then said Rhiannon unto Gwawl the son of Clud, "Rise up quickly." "I will willingly arise," said he. So he rose up, and put his two feet into the bag. And Pwyll turned up the sides of the bag, so that Gwawl was over his head in it. And he shut it up quickly and slipped a knot upon the thongs, and blew his horn. And thereupon behold his household came down upon the palace. And they seized all the host that had come with Gwawl, and cast them into his own prison. And Pwyll threw off his rags, and his old shoes, and his tattered array; and as they came in, every one of Pwyll's knights struck a blow upon the bag, and asked, "What is here?" "A Badger," said they. And in this manner they played, each of them striking the bag, either with his foot or with a staff. And thus played they with the bag. Every one as he came in asked, "What game are you playing at thus?" "The game of Badger in the Bag," said they. And then was the game of Badger in the Bag[6] first played.

"Lord," said the man in the bag, "if thou wouldest but hear me, I merit not to be slain in a bag." Said Heveydd Hen, "Lord, he speaks truth. It were fitting that thou listen to him, for he deserves not this." "Verily," said Pwyll, "I will do thy counsel concerning him." "Behold this is my counsel then," said Rhiannon; "thou art now in a position in which it behoves thee to satisfy suitors and minstrels; let him give unto them in thy stead, and take a pledge from him that he will never seek to revenge that which has been done to him. And this will be punishment enough." "I will do this gladly," said the man in the bag. "And gladly will I accept it," said Pwyll, "since it is the counsel of Heveydd and Rhiannon." "Such then is our counsel," answered they. "I accept it," said Pwyll. "Seek thyself sureties." "We will be for him," said Heveydd, "until his men be free to answer for him." And upon this he was let out of the bag, and his liegemen were liberated. "Demand now of Gwawl his sureties," said Heveydd, "we know which should be taken for him." And Heveydd numbered the sureties. Said Gwawl, "Do thou thyself draw up the covenant." "It will suffice me that it be as Rhiannon said," answered Pwyll. So unto that covenant were the sureties pledged. "Verily, Lord," said Gwawl, "I am greatly hurt, and I have many bruises. I have need to be anointed; with thy leave I will go forth. I will leave nobles in my stead, to answer for me in all that thou shalt require." "Willingly," said

---

[6]   *The common medieval means of catching and subduing badgers involved scooping them into a heavy bag and then bludgeoning them. A variation on this activity still exists today in a Scottish game called "Beat the Badger," where boys run through a gauntlet comprised of other youths, who beat them with sticks as they pass by.*

Pwyll, "mayest thou do thus." So Gwawl went towards his own possessions.

And the hall was set in order for Pwyll and the men of his host, and for them also of the palace, and they went to the tables and sat down. And as they had sat that time twelvemonth, so sat they that night. And they ate, and feasted, and spent the night in mirth and tranquillity.

Chapter 18
Faith, Hope, and Love

Durant didn't go into any more detail than that. *Of course* he didn't. He was the unchallenged champion of the tantalizingly dangling statement.

Then again, I knew that what he'd said more or less agreed with what I'd already figured out. Somehow, whatever Durant put into that *got uechan* of his, *fit* into it. Sword, stick—sorry, *Matteh ha Shelomoh*—carving knife, Buick, whatever, if he put it in there, it all fit. My old roommate in college (Joe, the *Star Trek* geek who could quote every sci-fi movie ever made) would have called it a "pocket dimension" or something. The old knights in shining armor would've called it magic. I don't know what I'd call it.

To be honest, what bugged me more was how he just reached in and pulled out the thing he was thinking of, without even having to fish around for it. It takes my wife roughly an hour to find anything in her purse, and that thing is only a couple of cubic inches in volume—how is it that Durant just reaches in and automatically grabs whatever it is that he needs? That's not right.

But let's face facts—this is a guy who's been hacking up monsters for centuries with his magic stick and shiny sword, and who's the guardian of the Holy Grail. Who am I to say what isn't right?

I dropped him off at Roscoe Village to do whatever it was that he wanted to do there (he refused to tell me any details, and by then, I was fine with that). I pictured him beating people up and biting off ears and generally doing the "Durant" kinds of investigating that no other Interpol agents actually do, and I turned around and drove home. It was approaching dawn by then, and I needed to get some sleep. Funny how I was finding my sleeping habits to more and more mirror the monsters we were hunting. Maybe that's normal, I dunno. But I found myself watching for red birds all the way home.

As I drove, I thought about why a vampire would kill both a senior citizen and a gang-banger in one night, other than just to feed. He didn't kill Amanda Cairns for food—he killed her for some other, more *human* reason. Well, why does *anyone* murder someone else?

A crime of passion? Maybe, but I'm hard-pressed to picture anyone having "passion" for a little old lady like Amanda Cairns that would drive him to murder.

To cover over a theft or some other crime? The woman had nothing of any *real* value in her home, and what little she had was still there. The only thing missing was that portrait. Why would someone kill over a portrait?

Sadism? She'd been *engaged* to William Raffey, who was the prime suspect in the torture and murder of Connie Dillard back in 1961. I hadn't spent much time following up on that—I'd left it to Rodriguez and Taylor, mostly—because I couldn't picture a seventy-something-year-old man ripping her and Hector Flórez up like that. But if William Raffey was like Durant, if he was an *immortal*, even a *vampire*, then maybe he really *was* the one we were looking for. Raffey liked hurting people—hurting women in particular—and not just *hurting* them, but *humiliating* them. But then, why would he wait fifty years to do it? And why would he kill Hector Flórez? None of that fit his M.O.

Tony said that Hector had known Amanda Cairns when he was a kid. She'd taught him to paint. He'd been in her apartment years ago, when she was one of the few adults who'd cared for him. Had he gone there that night to protect her from something? Had he known that Raffey was coming for her, somehow? Or did Raffey come for her *because* of Hector Flórez for some reason?

Could the murder have been about revenge, somehow? Why would anyone care that much about revenge half a century later? If Raffey had been turned into a vampire in 1961, then what did Amanda Cairns have to do with it? Why hadn't he just killed her fifty years ago?

The pieces were all there, but they still didn't fit together in my mind. Too many tunnels to follow, with too many possibilities, and not enough definite answers. But I made my mind up to talk with Rodriguez and Taylor the next chance I could get, just to find out what they'd found out.

There was one key thing somewhere that connected Amanda Cairns and Hector Flórez and that led to both of them being murdered by an undead monster. I knew that. And I knew that I'd find it.

I kept looking for red birds.

*   *   *

When I finally got home, I was exhausted, and I really needed some sleep, but I needed to see my family even more. I needed some sort of a connection to sanity and normalcy. So I sat there in the early morning hours, watching with my bloodshot eyes from the dark in the other room as Joanna and the kids came into the kitchen for breakfast. I wanted desperately to shut my eyes and retreat into a deep and hopefully dreamless sleep, but I still sat there, distant and disconnected from them, watching. There was something in the routine of it all—the simple *sameness* that day as it had been on any *other* day—that was comforting to me.

Chelsea padded into the kitchen in her pajamas, rubbing the sleepiness out of her eyes (mostly unsuccessfully). She plopped down into her chair, and sat facing the table, as if entranced by her empty cereal bowl. Joanna didn't even know I was there, so she cheerfully babbled with the twins as she put them in their high chairs, and they craned their heads to keep their eyes on her every movement. Chelsea just kept looking at the bowl.

Ordinarily, of course, I would step in and tell them that I was home. I'd give Joanna a hug and a kiss, and I'd help get everyone some breakfast. But that day, I just needed to watch from the safety of the dark. I watched as Joanna prepped out the twins' food, and then handed Chelsea the box of cereal. I watched as Chelsea did nothing with it.

"You're awake now, honey," she reminded our daughter, and Chelsea nodded, vacantly. As Joanna started pouring the milk for everyone, Chelsea started pouring her cereal. She even got a decent percentage of it into the bowl, and I chuckled in spite of myself to see her frowning at the overflow, as if confused about what to do about it. She sat there for almost a full minute before it dawned on her to pick each piece of cereal up off of the table and begin to put them into her mouth.

And that's when Joanna stopped her and announced that it was time to pray. She and Chelsea helped the twins put their chubby little hands together—as if they had any clue what they were doing by the action—and then they each bowed their heads.

"Dear Lord," Joanna started. "Thank you for this new day, and thank you so much for this food that you've given to us. Help us to eat with happy hearts, and to love one another well today. In Jesus' name we pray—*Amen*." Chelsea nodded and said "*Amen*" with her, but the twins just looked at both of them with an innocent obliviousness. Joanna smiled and clapped for them nevertheless. "Good praying!" she cheered them on, and they smiled because she had smiled. With that, they all began to dive into eating their various breakfasts. Chelsea had awoken enough by that time that she began a combination of chattering and mumbling as she ate, but I couldn't tell you now what she was talking about. All I heard was the comfortable drone of her tiny little voice, and the gentle chuckles of her mother in response. Tears welled up in my eyes, and I felt an immense weight on my shoulders.

I don't know if I'd never really thought about it until then, or if I was just unusually sensitive at that moment because I was so tired, but I confess that I was profoundly moved by that prayer time between my wife and children. I don't mean that the prayer itself was profound—or then again, maybe it was, in its own simple way. All I knew was that Joanna really *meant* it, and so did Chelsea. They really thought that they were talking with a God who actually cared about the fact that they were sitting down and eating cereal. Joanna prayed that same stupid prayer every morning, but she *meant* it every morning. And Chelsea was young enough that she still saw God as a big, loving Daddy who was always there to protect everyone and provide for everyone—the perfect version of the kind of Dad that I tried to be… and yet so consistently fell short of. For her, praying to God was as real as me talking to you over a cup of coffee.

What affected me so profoundly was that I realized right then that I didn't know what I believed about God at all. Here Durant kept telling me how important it was to have faith—real, solid faith—to fight these things that had suddenly entered my world, and I didn't know what I believed. I mean, I figured that I believed that there was a God out there, somewhere. I'd spent my whole life more or less going to church, though I hadn't been with Joanna and the kids for a while. Sure, I believed that God was the source of the morality that showed the good guys to be good and the bad guys to be bad, even if I'd quietly long since given up any hope of seeing God do much about any of that. But part of me began wondering who I was more like when I prayed with the family at the dinner table or at bedtime—Joanna and Chelsea, who really *believed* in what they were doing, or the twins, who were just going through the motions because it seemed so important to their mother. I realized that I prayed those family prayers more out of habit or *social inertia* than out of any kind of active faith. The last *real* prayer I prayed was a little throw-away one that Karen would be safe, and God didn't seem to care about *that* prayer at all…

And then I thought of Durant, kneeling beside a vagrant that he'd never met before, praying like *he* meant it. There wasn't anything rote or "throw-away" about that prayer. Vampire-slaying, monster-hunting, immortal dealer of death, pouring his heart out to God to take care of some old burn-out that he had no reason to care about. He and Joanna actually *believed*, actually felt like God was real and that he wanted to talk to them as much as they wanted to talk to him. For some reason, at that moment, I felt more empty than I'd ever felt in my whole life, and I didn't even know why.

But I did know—at that moment, I knew for a *fact*—that if I'd held a cross out to a vampire right then, the thing would have laughed in my face.

*   *   *

I slept long and hard all day. I awoke sweating and panting, my heart beating like a jackhammer in my chest—I'd had a horrible nightmare, but I couldn't remember what it was about. All I knew was that I was terrified beyond belief... and filled with a horrible, unwavering sense that something very bad was going to happen very soon. It was irrational, I know, but I couldn't shake it. And given the past several days of my life, who was to say what was irrational any more?

There was a voicemail waiting for me on my cell phone from Tony, telling me that he'd set up a meeting with el Buitre for this evening in Bucktown. El Buitre, it seems, liked having meetings in public restaurants, over food. I didn't know if it was because he felt safer that way, or if it was because he thought it made everyone less jumpy, of if it was because he just loved food that much. Whatever his reasoning was, it was fine by me, since there was a lot less chance of gunplay and mayhem in a public place. It seemed more neutral ground, somehow, and that was comforting to me.

Anyway, I knew that it was probably pointless to try to call Tony back—if he wasn't right at his desk, right at that moment, there'd be no way to find him. I decided to clean up and just catch up to him at the meeting in Bucktown. Joanna and the kids were all gone somewhere. I'd never even talked with them that morning—I couldn't break into that serenity I'd been watching with the sound of my voice. It's like it would've broken the spell or something. So I'd just slipped away into the bedroom and drifted off to sleep without saying a word. Joanna must have seen me when she'd gotten dressed, but she'd just let me sleep. The funny thing is, as much as I hadn't wanted to talk to anyone that morning, I desperately wanted to talk with her at that moment. I hit the speed dial for her cell phone on mine, but then I hung up before it had a chance to ring.

What was I going to say to her? "Hi, honey—I just wanted to hear the sound of your voice because I love you and I'm having vampire problems that give me bad dreams..."? When it came down to it, I really wanted to *hold* her, not just to talk with her from a distance. I had the most unsettling feeling that I'd lost a crucial chance to talk with her that morning, to *be* with her—a chance that I might not get to have again. I shuddered reflexively.

I realized that my schedule had been so erratic lately that I hadn't actually showered for a while, so I took the time to let the water wash over me. Joanna likes her showers hot enough to melt iron, but I tend to like mine cooler—it seems more refreshing, and a warm shower always leaves me feeling kind of groggy afterwards. That day, I ran the water about as cold as I could stand it. I wanted to be awake and alert... but more than that, I wanted to feel *alive*. I needed to know that my pulse was pounding and that my lungs were breathing. I needed to *feel* it, on a deep, visceral level.

On top of that, I needed to feel clean. It's like all of the dirt and grime and sweat and heaviness of the city had settled on me over the past few days, and I needed to feel like I was clean again, down to the bones. My *soul* needed cleaning. At least for the length of a shower, I didn't want to think about vampires or revenants or red-haired witches or Pieter Durant.

Of course, I spent the entire shower thinking about how much I didn't want to think about any of those things.

Getting dressed, I grabbed my gun and my cell phone and headed out the door. I didn't realize how cloudy it was until I'd already gotten to the car, and that's when I noticed Chelsea's pink plastic umbrella, still sitting in the back seat next to my black one. I smiled. Even when they weren't with me, my family could still make me smile—even when I was on my way to talk with a gang jefe to try to stop an impending gang war, even in the midst of a murder investigation that involved vampires, even when it was about to start raining on my head. I could still smile. I opened the back door to reach for my umbrella, and that's when I noticed that it wasn't the only thing there.

There was also the Matteh ha Shelomoh.

For a moment, I thought that Durant may have forgotten it and left it there by accident. But then I reconsidered the man I was thinking about. Durant didn't do *anything* by accident. He'd left it there for me, so that I could use it to protect myself. He was confident that I'd know how and when to use it.

Now, realistically, up until that point in my life, the sum total of my experience with the concept of vampires had been learned from late-night cable-TV schlock horror movie hosts like the Son of Svengoolie and Peter Vincent. The fact that a real-life "fearless vampire killer" would trust me with his special, God-given, vampire-slaying stick was morbidly heartwarming. He *trusted* me.

I set the staff up in the front seat, suddenly acutely aware of how awfully nice it would be to have my own *got uechan* to put it in. The thing was over three feet long, with that carved cat's head on the top, and it stuck out like a sore thumb. Suddenly, the pink umbrella didn't seem so ridiculous-looking in comparison.

*   *   *

El Buitre was eating at Babylon, on North Damen Avenue, just north of Armitage. That's where the meeting was set up. I had to admit, it was a good place for it—deep in Bucktown, with nice, big windows out front so that everyone could see everything going on. To be honest, I kind of wished that he'd been at Coast Sushi, just up the street. I hadn't had one of their nama-sake salmon rolls in forever, and I suddenly realized how hungry I'd gotten, since I hadn't eaten all day.

By that time, the rain was coming down pretty hard outside, and the sky was black with clouds. Nonetheless, Tony was there on the sidewalk, under his umbrella, waiting for me... alongside the four OA's who were outside, standing guard. Funny how none of them seemed to mind the rain. They were footsoldiers for Buitre and the Angel, as loyal to the Orquestra as they were hateful toward everyone else. Luckily, I was able to park in front of the barber shop next door, so I could just make a rush for the door, and I didn't have to take my umbrella with me—or even Chelsea's pink one. Somehow, I thought that it might make the wrong impression on Buitre and his posse... not to mention Tony. For a moment, I almost instinctively grabbed the Matteh ha Shelomoh, but then I thought better of it.

Tony grumbled something undoubtedly obscene at me as I approached, but between the rain pouring down and the cars passing by on North Damen, I couldn't make it out. Just as well.

I was about to ask if Buitre himself was inside, but then I looked for myself through the big windows and saw him there, big as life, already eating.

"You ready, partner?" Tony asked. I didn't answer right off, but just kept walking toward the door. I was surprised that the four guards didn't pat us down like last time. Was that an indication of acceptance? Or of defiance?

"Just let me do the talking," I said, as we went inside together. "They don't much like you."

"Mutual..." he growled.

Inside, we shook the rain off of our coats, and Tony closed his umbrella. There was el Buitre, sitting his big frame at one of their little tables, wolfing down a shawarma, with an appetizer of baba ghanouj. And right beside him was his resident goon, the big ape from before, with his arms perpetually crossed. No civilians were in the restaurant, as usual, but what surprised me was that I didn't see the Angel anywhere, either. Scratch that. It didn't just surprise me—it *concerned* me.

"Whassup, ese?" Buitre said between mouthfuls. "You wan' talk wif me *again*, eh? You mus' be, like, un fanático, no?" The ape smiled, and two other OA's behind us laughed out loud. "Acérrimo..."

"That's right," I replied, smiling back. "I'm your biggest fan..." The OA's laughed louder.

"Genial!" Buitre laughed, spitting tahini everywhere as he did so. "Hey, Ramon—you get mi acérrimo some dolmeh or somethin', eh?" One of the OA's behind us jumped forward, since he'd been leaning against the wall, and walked over to the counter.

"That's okay, Buitre," I said. "I'm good."

"You eat some dolmeh, you be better than good, no?" I couldn't tell whether that was an offer or an order, but either way, I figured that the best move for me would be to just eat the food he was giving me and like it. A lot.

"Then thank you," I said. "I'd love some." I debated about sitting down, since we were all being so friendly with each other, but I noticed that no one else was sitting. Just el Buitre. So I decided against committing some sort of faux pas and risk offending the very guy we were here to see. "We wanted to talk to you about the Insane Deuces," I said, trying to get straight to the point. "This is turning into a war, and nobody really wants that…"

El Buitre wiped his mouth on his greasy napkin, and turned his bright, blue eyes to me.

"Who say that, eh?" he chuckled. "Who say we don' wan' that, eh? Maybe we wan' una guerra *enorme*, eh? Maybe tha's good for bidness, no?"

"Good for business?" I asked. "Maybe in some ways. People will fear you all the more, that's true. But how many troops will it cost you? How many are going to die? And how many are going to get locked up for murder?" He cocked his head, but didn't answer. "And how many of the businesses like the one you're sitting in right now are going to get shot up or firebombed or worse? Even if you end up *winning* the war, do you really want to be king of a ruined kingdom?"

"*Even* if I win?" he growled, standing up from the table. Man, he was huge! "*Even* if I win? Que hijo de—" He was so angry that he couldn't even finish swearing at me. Ironically, that's just when my dolmeh was ready at the counter.

"Listen," I said, trying to calm him down. "I'm just saying that—"

"No, *you* lissen, paco!" he started yelling, pounding his fist against the table so hard that his drink spilled over. I saw Tony twitch as he considered reaching for his gun. But then he thought better of it and stood still. "I give you some dolmeh, but you don' show me no respec'! No puedo creer… Tha's no righ', paco. So I gonna have to *teach* you some respec', no?"

What happened next happened very, very quickly. Buitre yelled, "Tomar estos idiotas de atrás!" and I saw the two OA's behind us reach for their guns, so both Tony and I started to crouch and pull out our weapons as well. The ape stood where he was, and el Buitre just glared at us.

That's when I heard the glass shattering behind me. At first, I thought maybe one of the guards outside had seen what was going on and started shooting at us through the window. But that's when I saw the *body* of one of the guards outside go flying past me, surrounded by shards of flying glass.

Durant! I thought. No one else could throw a 200-pound, armed thug through a commercial window like that. When a second guard came crashing through the window only a second later, I knew that it *had* to be Durant.

The OA's in the restaurant immediately turned toward the front and started firing toward the windows. Tony and I spun around and ducked away from the falling glass. It wasn't until we'd safely slid under one of the tables and got our bearings that I actually saw the fear on their faces, and then what was actually going on outside.

It was *Mojo*, of all people, looking ashen gray in complexion, holding a struggling guard above his head. The bullets coming out of the restaurant ripped through him, but they seemed more like annoyances to him than anything else. With a jerk, he yanked the guard down to his face, taking a huge bite out of the man's neck and gulping down the blood that started spraying out.

Mojo had been turned.

What's more, I saw Rhiannon standing there behind him, outside on the sidewalk in the rain, her arm held in a green silk sling—the broken wing from the impact of Durant's strange, iron knife the night before. She was smiling, watching Mojo in action. Actually, that's not entirely true—she was smiling, looking at *me*. I saw her lips moving, and I could hear her voice, even over all of the gunfire and shouts and broken glass, though I couldn't make out any words.

Buitre grabbed a gun from under the table and started shooting Mojo himself, but the vampire just finished sucking blood out of the open wound from the guard and flung his corpse to the side as if it were an old, wet towel. He roared at the OA's in the restaurant, snarling like a wild animal. From what Durant was saying before, I figured that meant that he'd only recently been turned—that this was maybe his first kill. He certainly wasn't like this the other day, the last time that I'd seen him.

I could hear the screams and the cries and the crashing sounds all around me in the restaurant, but I realized that it was like it was on a television show that someone was watching in another room—distant, both physically and emotionally. *Maybe it's shock or adrenaline,* I thought.

Mojo leapt through the window, amidst more broken glass, and mauled one of the OA's shooting at him from the other side of the room. Tony was yelling something at me, but I couldn't really hear him. I found myself thinking that Rhiannon's voice sounded the way that satin feels. She looked so beautiful standing there, smiling, in the rain.

By this time, Tony was shooting at Mojo as well, for all the good that it was doing. His body was covered in blood, his clothes were tattered by gunfire, and his eyes were nothing but pale points of light within a bloodshot red. He smiled at Buitre with teeth that were sharp and caked with gore. Mojo then grabbed the other OA standing there in shock, and threw him so hard at the ape that I heard bones cracking—both of their bodies crumpled together against the brick wall behind them with a wet sound.

I swear that I could smell caramel when I heard Rhiannon's voice. It was intoxicating.

El Buitre threw his gun to the floor in frustration, and pulled out the single biggest knife I've ever seen. "Vete al infierno, demonio!" he screamed, and lunged toward Mojo, swishing his blade in the air with a terrible fury. I'd never seen him fight before—he moved like a freight train, and probably hit about the same as one, too. But Mojo caught him by the neck in a flash, lifted him off the ground like a baby, and swatted the knife out of his hand with ease.

Tony started shaking me, yelling something at the top of his voice, but I didn't really care—I *couldn't* really care. All of my thoughts were out there on that sidewalk, with Rhiannon. I couldn't stop looking at her warm smile, or listening to the music of her voice. I realized right then and there that, whatever else might be true, I was now absolutely, hopelessly in love with her…

Background
From *Les Histoires Traditionnelles de la Bretagne Ancienne* (ed. G. Chabrier, 1938, trans. R. Louati)

from *L'Homme Noir et le Sorcière Rouge*

Once upon a time, there was a good young girl named Gabrielle, who lived in the forest near the village of Plouezoc'h, on the sea, with her grandfather. Her grandfather was a woodcutter, and though they were very poor, they were also very happy together.

Every morning, Gabrielle would rise early to pick wildflowers for their meager table, and arrange them in the little vase that had belonged to her mother. That way, there was a new bouquet awaiting her grandfather each day when he woke up, and it made him smile to think of how much his little granddaughter loved him. She was so much like her mother, so full of life, that all who knew her loved her.

Once a week, every Saturday morning, Gabrielle would go into town to buy bread for them. She would put the bundles of wood that her grandfather had cut onto the back of their very old horse, which her grandfather had named Foudre. They would walk together, Gabrielle singing to Foudre, down the forest path, past the little stream that fed eventually into the river Vilaine, down the slope of the hill that led down to the sea, and into the village itself. There, she would go first to M. Desmarais the blacksmith, who would give her a coin for half of the wood, and then to Mdme. Blanchard the innkeeper, who would give her a two coins for the other half... and perhaps a little wheatflour pancake or two, if some were left over from breakfast. Then Gabrielle would take all of the coins to the bakery, where fat M. Armand the pâtissier would give her the loaves of bread that they needed. Because she was such a kind girl, he would often give her a tarte or a blancmange as well, just to see her smile at the sweet taste of his craft.

But her favorite part of the trip each week was when she would take the bread—still warm in its basket—and visit old Captain Laurent in his little house on the edge of town. For the price of one of their little loaves, Captain Laurent would tell her stories of the great battles in which he had fought against the English, in exciting and exotic-sounding places like Vernuil and Patay. The best but saddest stories he told her were about that horrible day on the plain between Tramecourt and Agincourt, when the English king, Henri, had slaughtered ten times as many soldiers as he himself had lost. Every time he told her a story about that day, she cried. And yet, every week, she asked him to tell her another.

For as much as Gabrielle loved her grandfather, and all of the people in Plouezoc'h, she also longed to see the rest of the world. She dreamt of far-off places like Paris or the Pyrenees in Spain, or even Captain Laurent's own nearby homeland in Anjou, and how wonderful it would be to see them, to drink their differences in. It was not that she wanted to escape where she was, so much as that she fervently wished to experience where she had not yet been.

Gabrielle felt sorry for old Captain Laurent. He lived alone, and he spent most of his time in his little chair by the fire, praying his rosary and waiting for someone to come speak with him... but no one else ever did. For such a man, who had apparently been so dashing and impetuous in his youth, to have to spend his final days alone and without adventure seemed tragic to her. He seemed to light up whenever she came around, however, and she felt like her mere presence was a service to him, and one which she was all too happy to perform. Perhaps someday, when her grandfather had finally passed away, she, too, would leave the forest and travel to someplace more exciting than this one. To Gabrielle, there was nothing so horrific in all the world as the possibility that she would never see anyplace but home.

One Saturday morning, as she traveled with Foudre down the forest path, she saw a little oxcart by the side of the path, and a woman sitting at the stream nearby, weeping. Gabrielle went over to her and introduced herself.

"Why are you crying, madame?" she asked.

The woman wore a long, red cloak, with a heavy hood, but even so, Gabrielle could tell that the woman was beautiful, even though tears left their tracks across her pale cheeks.

"Good morrow, my pretty one," replied the woman. "Thou art kind to think to stop and help a stranger." Gabrielle enjoyed the woman's fancy way of speaking, and found herself liking the woman on the spot... if for no other reason than that she was so obviously from somewhere else. "Dost thou live nearby, my child?"

"Yes," said Gabrielle. "If you need a place to stay, I'm sure that my grandfather would let you stay with us for a while." The woman reached forward and stroked the girl's cheek—not once, or even twice, but three times.

"What a pretty morsel thou art..." she whispered into Gabrielle's ear, making the girl blush at the compliment. As Gabrielle turned to lead her back up the path toward their little cabin, the woman stopped and took her arm as they passed the oxcart. "I should need my things as well, my love," she said, pointing to the large crate that rested on the cart. It looked as big as a man, and Gabrielle knew that there was no way that she could carry it, even with the woman's help.

"Can't your box wait here until my grandfather can come back to help us?" she asked.

"Oh, my," said the woman, tears welling up in her deep, green eyes. "But should a bandit stray by, all which I own would be lost to them…"

"But, it's too heavy for us to carry, and far too heavy for Foudre to pull, old as he is…"

"But is that not what beasts of burden are for, my child?" the woman asked, and Gabrielle had to admit that she was right. Why should they keep old Foudre around, if not to do the chores which were too heavy for her or grandfather to do? She hooked him up to the oxcart, and they started back toward her cabin. Foudre strained against the weight of the cart, and halfway home, he began to wheeze and whine. But Gabrielle found that each time she began to feel sorry for her old friend, she would immediately find herself frustrated with his complaining. For the first time in her life, she actually struck him.

"Get along now!" she commanded, slapping his bony rump. He whinnied and continued up the path, frothing at the mouth, with the woman in the cloak walking behind them all the way.

When they reached Gabrielle's home, they found her grandfather outside, chopping up some wood. He was surprised to see his granddaughter home so early on a Saturday, and he asked her if she'd gotten the bread that they needed.

"No," she admitted. "But I found something far more important—someone we've never met before!" And with that, she introduced the woman in the cloak. Grandfather was unsure at first, wondering how they were going to feed a third mouth when Gabrielle hadn't even gotten enough food for the two of them, but then the woman began to speak.

"Thy kindly granddaughter hast been kind enough to reach out to a weary traveler along a lonely path. I thank thee both for the hospitality of thy home." He was struck by her courtly manner, as well as by her beauty, and he welcomed her inside their home.

The woman told them that she was a servant, awaiting her lord, the Baron, along the road. He was a great hero, she said, of many battles. The moment that she said that, Gabrielle's eyes began to sparkle at the thought of meeting such a man.

"Is he an old man?" she asked, thinking of Captain Laurent.

"Not at all," said the woman. "He is young and handsome. Alas," she said, taking off her cloak and letting loose her mane of curly, red hair, "he has no wife with whom he might carry on his line…"

Immediately, Gabrielle began to fantasize. What if the dashing young Baron would come to their home, see how beautiful she was, and want to marry her? What if he took her off to his château in some exotic part of France, where she and her grandfather could live in grandeur for the rest of their lives? What a story she could have to tell old Captain Laurent then!

As evening fell, they heard a rap at the door. The woman smiled and said, "That should be my lord now..."

Gabrielle had brushed out her hair and put on her prettiest dress in preparation to meet their new guest. *Two guests in one day!* she thought to herself. *And one a Baron!* She opened the door, and there in the dark of the sunset stood a tall, handsome man. His dark hair was pulled back from his high forehead, and his thick, dark moustache and beard were well-trimmed, framing his angular face perfectly. Gabrielle decided that she had never in her life seen a more beautiful man than this baron.

"Please, come in, milord," she said, and she curtsied, just as her mother had taught her before she died. The Baron smiled warmly, and ducked his head as he entered the doorway.

"A fine, young child," he said in response. His voice was deep and rich, as if someone could take the low rumble of a bull and somehow turn it into human speech. Gabrielle smiled at the sound, as it filled her down to her core.

"You've done well, Raina," he said to the woman by the fire, who nodded in silent response. "She shall do very well for my needs, I think."

When Gabrielle heard those words, her heart skipped a beat. The Baron wanted her! He loved her as she had hoped! But her grandfather heard something else in his words, and he asked his guests to leave. Gabrielle turned to her grandfather with trembling lips and tears in her eyes. Why would her grandfather steal from her the one chance that she would ever have for true happiness?

"Leave this place at once!" he demanded of them. The woman by the fireplace just smiled, but the Baron laughed out loud.

"Perhaps we shall," he said to the grandfather, "taking this child with us." Gabrielle beamed with joy when she heard this. Her Baron wanted her!

With this, her grandfather grabbed for his axe, and held it high above his head. Gabrielle barely noticed, lost as she was in the timbre of her Baron's voice. The Baron nodded at his servant, and the red-haired woman glided over to Gabrielle's grandfather.

"Dost thou *truly* wish us gone?" she purred, as she reached out to touch him. "Wouldst thou not prefer us to stay?" Her eyes were so green, so deeply, emerald green, that the grandfather found that he could no longer remember why he'd picked up his axe. The woman leaned in and kissed him, gently, over and over. Her lips touched his, brushed his cheek, filled his every thought. Her eyes and her lips became his whole world.

"Dost thou *truly* wish us gone?" she asked again, whispering into his ear.

"N-No..." he answered back dreamily. "Please stay with me... forever..."

The woman smiled again, and turned her gaze back to her lord. The Baron smiled back, baring his fangs. He nodded, and the woman turned back to face the old man.

"Wouldst thou not wish to watch us take your granddaughter?" she cooed to him. "Wouldst thou not wish to *join* us?" She touched his cheek with her slender hand, and it felt to him as if her hand was on fire. "Dost thou not *love* me?" He nodded, not truly comprehending what he was doing.

"Chop her with that axe of yours!" cried the Baron, clapping his great hands together with a vile, rapturous joy. "That would be great sport to watch you do it!" The woman gazed into the grandfather's eyes and beckoned to him, and the grandfather stepped forward toward his granddaughter, his axe in hand.

Gabrielle only knew that she would be leaving this place and seeing the world, and doing it at the side of the man whom she loved—whom she had *always* loved, it seemed to her. When she saw her grandfather coming toward her slowly, she only knew joy and happiness.

"My child," the Baron's deep, sonorous voice called out. "My child, it's time to awaken..."

Suddenly, Gabrielle saw the room in a different light. She remembered poor Foudre covered in sweaty foam, and she remembered how he'd collapsed when they'd gotten back to their little home. Why hadn't she remembered that before? Why hadn't she cared? She saw her grandfather coming toward her with his axe raised, a lost look in his vacant eyes. She turned in horror to see the Baron's eyes gleaming red with excitement, his mouth full of long, sharp, yellow teeth. His breath was foul, and his clothes were torn, and caked with earth and dried gore. Why had she not seen all of this before? She screamed in terror, realizing the nightmare that she had become lost within.

The Baron giggled with a high-pitched squeal at her horror, and his strong hands held her fast as she struggled. The more she squirmed, the more she screamed, the louder and more energetically he giggled—in fact, he began to pant like a dog on a hot summer's afternoon. Her grandfather kept walking toward her, the red-haired woman's hand on his shoulder the whole way.

"No, Grandfather!" she screamed. "Please, dear God, no!"

With that, her grandfather swung his axe down upon her with all of his strength, cleaving her skull in two. Her brains and blood burst forth, and the Baron screeched in delight, finally letting her body collapse upon the floor of the little cabin. The grandfather just stood there, mindless, while the red-haired woman stroked his neck with her long fingers.

Just as the Baron leaned down onto the floor to feast upon her blood and body, the door burst open, and in came old Captain Laurent, his rusty old sword in his trembling hand.

"My God!" he cried, surveying the scene. "What happens here?"

The Baron spun to face the old man, angered at the interruption. He flashed his fangs to him and snarled a hideous snarl.

"I-I *know* you," the Captain said with a tremulous voice. "I saw you hanged in Nantes a decade past!"

The Baron found himself giggling again at this, excited as he already was by the killing of the beautiful child. "Some lives continue on, even after such trivialities..." he quipped, batting away the Captain's sword as a man might swat away an insect. He smiled again, and Captain Laurent saw the teeth once more.

"Foul fiend!" he cried, stumbling back toward the doorway. The Baron advanced toward him, but the Captain pulled from his pocket the rosary which he kept always with him, holding it out toward the vile thing in the cabin. The Baron had been lunging toward him with such great speed that his hand ran straight into the crucifix, and burst into flame at the touch. He howled in pain, clutching his flaming hand, and called for the woman to come away with him.

"Let us fly!" he growled. "I've had my fun, if not my fill..." And with that, the two creatures just seemed to fade from sight like a morning mist, never to be seen in those woods again.

Trembling still with fear, the Captain approached the grandfather, who was just waking from his dreamlike state. The Captain took the axe from his hands, and slowly, slowly, the grandfather began to remember the events of the recent past.

"When your granddaughter did not come to visit me today," the Captain said, laying the axe aside, "I came to see if all were well with you two. She has never missed a Saturday, in all these years, you see..." His gaze turned from the old man to the lovely girl who lay dead on the floor of the little cabin. "I have grown to love her as if she were my own child."

The grandfather's growing realization of what he'd done began to tear at his sanity. He saw the body of his beloved Gabrielle at his feet, and he cried out in pain and anguish. He lunged for the axe to end his own life, but the Captain grabbed his arms and stopped him. They grappled for a moment, and then sobbed in each other's arms for the life of the girl whom they both had cared about so dearly.

"How could I have done this thing?" wept the grandfather at last.

"Such is the fate of all those who would love a witch," said the Captain. He raised his rosary to his lips and kissed the crucifix suspending from it. Crossing himself, he went back to the body of little Gabrielle, scooped her up in his arms, and carried her outside.

That night, two old men buried a young girl in the earth near the little cabin. By sunrise, the deed was done, and the Captain said a simple but sincere prayer over her grave. Then the two men slowly parted, each to live lonely and alone, never to speak of this night to anyone, even to one another.

The grandfather stumbled back into his cabin, exhausted, only to find blood-spattered flowers in the little vase on a table. He cried for an entire day, and never picked another flower for the rest of his life.

Chapter 19
A Cold, Hard Slap of Reality

Somehow, I found myself on the sidewalk. I don't remember walking out of the restaurant—I don't even remember standing up from the floor. But there I was, on the sidewalk. I was vaguely aware of Rhiannon saying something to Mojo about el Buitre, and slightly more aware of Tony grabbing at my sleeve, but everything seemed coldly distant next to the warmth of Rhiannon's musical voice. Her eyes seemed transfixed on mine, and her gaze drew me to her like a moth to a flame.

I wish I could explain it better. It was like I was watching someone else move my feet, or like the desires of my heart were making them move instead of the thoughts of my brain. I wanted to be with her, so I was moving closer to her—not that I'd *planned* it that way, or *thought* about walking to her, but just that I'd wanted to be next to her, and so I was just automatically moving that way.

Tony was shouting in my ears now, and I made out a word here or there—many of which were profane. But mixed in were things like "crazy," and "snap out of it," and "Tom," none of which seemed to sink much deeper than the shallowest level of my attention, like noticing something out of the corner of your eye and then forgetting it. But then he said one more word that registered—one that made me stop and think, stop and decide for myself where my feet were going to go. He said, "Joanna." I found myself rousing just a bit, like *almost* waking up from a deep sleep.

But now, with every golden word coming out of Rhiannon's perfect mouth, I began to feel uncomfortable. Every yearning of my heart toward her started to feel wrong, off-kilter, askew. The more I drank in the shape of her body, the deep green of her eyes, the moistness of her lips, the more guilty I began to feel. I knew that I was in love with her, but then, I *also* knew that I *wasn't*. I was lusting after her, and that's a different thing. She began to frown, realizing that something had changed, and that frown helped rouse me all the more.

I started feeling increasingly... *dirty*... somehow. And that led me to do something that I hadn't done in years—I prayed for help. It wasn't a grand prayer, or an eloquent one. It was just mostly saying, "God, help me. I'm doing what I don't want to do, and I can't seem to stop myself."

Increasingly, I started picturing Joanna. I saw her on our wedding day, when the doors opened from the church foyer and there she was in her dress. I saw her as she dug her fingernails into my hand while she was giving birth to Chelsea. I saw her after our first kiss, with her eyes still closed and her face just beaming. And the more I thought of her, the louder and clearer Tony's voice became.

"Are you gonna let 'em kill yer whole family?" he was shouting. And suddenly, I was back.

"Wh—What are you talking about?" I asked, realizing that I'd just missed something crucially important. Rhiannon had stopped talking, and now she was glaring at us full-bore.

"She jus' told that freak to kill ya an' then yer family next!" Tony yelled. "Wasn't ya listenin'?"

I realized that I had only been listening to the sound of her voice, and not to her words. I turned to see what was going on in the restaurant, and the scene made me almost sick to my stomach. Mojo had flayed Buitre like butchered meat, and had pinned him to the wall with splintered wood from the tables and chairs. He was feasting on Buitre's blood with a crazed excitement, and I shuddered when I saw Buitre's head move slightly. He was still alive… at least for another moment or two.

"Cover her!" I yelled, and I bolted for the car, only a few feet away. Behind me, I heard Tony yell something frantic, and then fire two shots, but I didn't turn to see why. I was focused on only one thing—a very special stick sitting in my front seat.

I ripped open the door and grabbed the Matteh ha Shelomoh, and then I turned back to survey the scene again. Tony was firing a third shot at a red cat that was awkwardly leaping across the sidewalk and into the alley beside the framing store, gingerly holding one of its forepaws close to its body. I was still feeling a little groggy, but what bothered me the most was how much it bothered me that he might hurt Rhiannon. I had a sudden urge to grab his arm and stop him before he could hit her— an immediate, protective instinct. I shook it off and looked back into Babylon.

El Buitre was quite definitely dead now, and Mojo was gone.

Now, I knew that he hadn't given up, so that meant that he was either heading to my home to kill my family, or that he was trying to find an angle to pounce on me from. Maybe he instinctively knew that the Matteh ha Shelomoh was dangerous for him—otherwise, I can't see why he wouldn't have just attacked us both from the front, full-on.

Suddenly, the street lights—*all* of the lights, actually—on the block went out. On the plus side, that suggested that Mojo was going to try to hit me now, instead of going after Joanna and the kids first. Thank God for small favors, right?

I knew that he was going to try to jump out at me from the shadows somewhere, and that he'd do it right now, before our eyes could adjust to the dark. I only had a split-second to make a decision—he was so terrifyingly fast now. He obviously wasn't in the restaurant in front of me, so the smart move would have been for him to lunge at me from one of the alleyways to the sides—I'd only have one shot at a 50-50 chance of guessing which side he'd come from, and with my luck, I'd probably guess wrong and end up as dead as Buitre and his OA thugs. Then again, Mojo wasn't really the sharpest crayon in the box *before* he died, and it didn't look like death had helped him much with that.

So, anticipating his next move—and hoping that I'd anticipated correctly—I spun around and swung the staff with all of my strength *behind* me. And I prayed again. I really, sincerely prayed.

The staff connected with Mojo's head, just as he was dashing in for the kill. It felt like hitting ten pounds of raw, ground hamburger with a baseball bat, and it went through it about the same way. His skull just caved in like an overripe melon, and the staff came out the other side. Strangely, there wasn't even any blood—his head just fell apart, like he'd been made of clay. But Mojo's momentum made his body still hit mine with a crushing force that still knocked me back onto the sidewalk. I lay there for a second, panting, with Mojo's headless corpse lying on top of me.

Tony looked—well, I've never seen Tony scared before. Not really. In all the years we've been together, I've seen him wary, and I've seen him befuddled, and I've seen him jacked up on so much adrenaline in a fight that he was bug-eyed and half-crazy. But I've never seen him really terrified, like he looked right then. I can only imagine that it was roughly the way that I'd looked a few nights before in that warehouse on Clybourn, the first time that I'd run across a vampire.

"Wh-wh-wha—?" Tony was stammering.

"Vampire," I answered, still lying under Mojo's corpse.

"A vamp—?" he started. "Yer freakin' kiddin' me!"

"No, he is not," I heard a deep voice say from above me—*Durant's* voice. *Durant?* "Can you extricate yourself, Detective, or must I help you?" he asked. I pushed Mojo off of me, and scrambled to my feet. Durant kicked what was left of Mojo's head over to the rest of him.

"Wha's *he* doin' here?" Tony asked, even more confused.

"Eliminating complications," Durant responded, and pulled a familiar-looking little flask from his bag. He poured the contents onto Mojo's remains, and then pulled out a match.

"I asked a question!" Tony growled.

"And I answered it," Durant calmly replied. He lit the match against the brick wall, and then flipped it onto Mojo's corpse, which then burst into those bright blue flames that filled the evening with an uncomfortable warmth.

"You can't do that!" Tony yelled, pushing past me to get to the body. By the time he got there, it was almost turned completely to ash. "Tom, he can't do that!" With that, my phone started ringing.

"He's Interpol, Tony," I said, flipping my phone open. "He can do anything he wants…"

Tony stomped over to Durant and the two started grumbling at each other surprisingly quietly while I took the call. It was from someone at Chicago Police headquarters—a Lt. Bainbridge in the Organized Crime Division.

"Detective Chapel," he said, his voice clipped and angry, "have you been involving yourself in the conflict between the Orquestra Albany and the Insane Deuces?"

"Yes, sir," I said, knowing that if he's calling me about it, there's no reason to deny it. "The gangs are both within my jurisdiction here in Area 5," (which was mostly true), "and my involvement is actually part of an ongoing murder investigation regarding—"

"I'm aware that you're a homicide detective, Chapel," he interrupted. "But I was unaware that you had joined the Organized Crime Division, too."

"No, sir," I tried again. "But like I said, the only reason that we're involved with the—"

"My office, Detective," he interjected again. "*Now*." And then he hung up.

To be honest, I can't tell which part of the evening made me feel the most tired—fighting Mojo, fighting off Rhiannon's influence, or listening to that one word, "*Now*." I knew that I'd overstepped my jurisdiction, and I knew that there was no way to explain why I had done so, without sounding like a complete idiot or psychotic. I looked at the caved-in front of the Babylon restaurant, filled now with the corpses of eight OA's, and at the pile of ash that had, at one time, been an Insane Deuce named Mojo, and which was already starting to blow away from the sidewalk. I watched Durant sigh as Tony's voice kept getting higher and higher.

"I never even heard o' no black vampires!" I heard Tony bark at him.

"Oh, I've seen several, actually," Durant replied at last. "Most pointedly in 1914, when I traveled back to Africa when the silent city of vampires resurfaced near Kôr. It was a moral imperative to deal with it myself, as a personal pledge to an old friend—the very friend, in fact, who had given me the Matteh ha Shelomoh in the first place, so very long before." He nodded to the staff in my hand.

"Thus, not even Kitchener could keep me in Europe at that point," he continued. "Actually, Kôr was itself quite near the village where my friend had originally received the staff from a juju man—an ancient old pagan witch doctor who had no idea whatsoever of its true significance, its true origins... or its true power..." I looked at the staff, and somehow, it felt heavier suddenly. I wondered if Tony even had a clue what Durant was talking about, and I could tell from the tone of Durant's voice that this wasn't him telling one of his stories to help me understand something—this was Durant just trying to mess with Tony's mind.

"I fought the vampires alongside a strange jungle sentinel whom the East Africans called *'Kivuli,'* and an Englishman who had been raised by animals. Ironically, they both also claimed to be functionally immortal, as had the ancient white queen of Kôr whom the savage Amahagger natives called, *'Hiya'.*" He stopped for a moment, seemingly quietly amused at the details of his own story. "In truth, there was a terrifyingly conspicuous confluence of Caucasion immortals in the jungles of Africa at that time in history..."

Tony just stood there in stunned silence for a minute, drinking it all in. "What th'...?" he started at last. And then he turned to me. "Is he fer real, or is he some kinda nut?"

"I'm not sure that it's an either/or question," I replied, sighing myself. Durant scowled at me, but he didn't respond. "We've got a problem, Tony."

"Yer tellin' me!"

"No, I mean *another* problem," I put my hand on Tony's shoulder and looked him straight in the eyes. "Tony, this is what I've been doing with Durant for the past couple of days, and this is why I couldn't tell you about it—I didn't want to get you involved. But now you *are* involved, and now I need your help." Tony's bushy eyebrows knotted up, and for a second, it looked like he was going to tell me off. Then, he took a deep breath and his eyes softened.

"Whaddya need, Tom?" he said, nodding.

"I have to be in three places at once, Tony, and I need your help with that. I've gotta go to CPD headquarters down on Michigan, but I've also got to make sure that my family is safe. Do you understand?"

"Ya want I should check on 'em, right?"

"I need you to, Tony," I said, as seriously as I could. "I don't trust anyone in this world like I trust you." I handed him the Matteh ha Shelomoh, and Durant stiffened.

"Wha's this?" Tony asked, obviously confused.

"Your gun isn't going to be much good against a lot of the crap out there," I explained to him. "I want you to take this staff and use it if you need to." He shifted it in his hands, feeling its weight. "That thing's a couple thousand years old, and it's really important—please don't lose it."

Durant winced, just hearing that.

Tony saw how uncomfortable Durant was getting with the concept of him holding the Matteh ha Shelomoh, and that seemed to help. He smiled and nodded again.

"Ya can trust me, Tom," he said. "I promise that yer wife an' kids'll be jus' fine." But then he added, "But I thought ya said *three* places…?"

"That's right, Tony," I replied. "I'm going to swing past the ID house near DePaul on my way to meet with Lt. Bainbridge. I want to check on Billy. Our… perp… seems to be targeting both the OA's *and* the ID's, and I need to at least try to warn him. And I want to know why Rhiannon brought Mojo here first."

"He was sent to kill this Buitre fellow, obviously," Durant said. "I should assume that our Vampire Lord wanted him out of the way to further his purposes."

"Our *who* wanted 'im outta th' way ta *what*?" Tony asked. "Who's the perp here, besides Mojo and the hot chick?" And that's when a horrible thought crept into my mind—one that made several of the tunnels connect in the case.

"Who had the most to gain here this evening?" I asked, starting to put the pieces together. "Who would've benefited from el Buitre being suddenly out of the way? Who'll become jefe now that he's gone?" Tony's eyes got big as it started making sense to him as well. "And who *wasn't here* at the meeting tonight?"

"Camacho!" he snuffed.

"The Angel," I agreed. "Keep an eye out on him—in fact, let's put an APB out on him as a person of interest in this hit tonight. Call it in and explain it, Tony. Just don't say anything about Mojo being… you know… a *vampire*."

"'Cuz that'd be bad, right?" he said, rolling his eyes.

"That would be bad, right," I replied. "Just say it was a hit from the Deuces. That's more or less true anyway."

"The Deuces and a kitty-cat," he snorted.

"Yeah," I added. "Leave out the cat, too."

"You got it, Tom," Tony said, hauling himself back toward his car. "But when this's all over, you an' me is gonna have a long talk, lemme tell ya…"

I turned to go to my own car, and motioned for Durant to come with me. "I could really use your help, both with Bainbridge and with anything else that might try to eat me tonight."

"Of course," he replied. "Now that you have tossed away one of the most powerful weapons on Earth and are left defenseless." He gritted his teeth as he walked to the car. "I entrusted you with the staff of King Solomon himself. You used it once, and then you handed it over to an orangutan."

"You could've stopped me."

"No," he said, shaking his head. "Once given, it's for the recipient to use as he sees fit." He stopped in his tracks, a thought striking him. "That idiot will probably use it to play cricket…"

"Naw," I assured him, opening up the car door for him. "He plays softball, not cricket."

"Oh, you really ought to take your dolmeh," Durant said, pointing back to the counter. "You've still not eaten, and you will need all of the strength you can get."

"Waitaminute!" I barked, closing the car door again.

"No love for grape leaves?" Durant responded.

"Don't be funny," I replied. "How did you know that it was *my* dolmeh? How did you know that I haven't eaten?" My frustration with Durant built the more I thought about the implications. "*Why* are you *here* at *all*? Just how long have you been tailing me tonight?"

"Since before you awoke this afternoon," he replied, nonchalantly. "I had assumed that you would stumble into the hornet's nest—and we *needed* the nest to be stirred up—so I simply allowed you to do what appears to come so naturally for you to do."

"You used me as bait… *again*."

"Well, it did work rather well the last time," he said, scratching his beard with perhaps just the slightest hint of a guilty conscience. But then he pulled himself straight up to his full, intimidating height. "Face the truth, Detective," he said, glowering at me gravely. "These fiends tend to run after you, and they tend to run from me. Since I am, in fact, *hunting* them, what would you suggest that the intelligent strategy might be?"

"But you *watched*—you just stood there, hiding, and *watched*—as Mojo killed all of those people, as he tried to kill me!"

"Yes."

"You could've saved them!"

"I shall lose no sleep over the deaths of murderers and rapists, Detective," he said. "I wanted to see if you could handle yourself, and you did. Quite well, in point of fact. I would have stepped in, had you or Detective de Tullio ever been in any real danger."

"Mojo leaping at me from behind to kill me wasn't enough 'real danger' for you?"

"Detective," he replied, with more than just a little consternation growing in his deep voice. "I once engaged a thief to steal the Mona Lisa to further a mission. I have never been one to shrink back from a necessary ruthlessness. Are you telling me that you have never made use of undercover police officers, or of decoys, or of other, as you say, 'bait,' for criminals?"

"Not without telling them!" I yelled.

"You've warned every pusher, every informant, every thug whom you've placed in harm's way to catch the 'bigger fish,' that they were acting as your bait?"

"No," I admitted. "But that's different. They weren't on the job—they weren't on the team."

"I am on no one else's 'team,' Detective," Durant said, walking past me and opening the car door himself. "If you only knew what human beings have done to one another over the centuries, foolishly and ineffectually trying to stand against these horrors, you would applaud my restraint." He paused at the open door and waited, looking at me. "I am only doing what I must, using what I must—and whom I must."

I thought about what he was saying, and it hurt. I'd thought that we were kind of like partners by that point, that he had trusted me with his magic stick and everything. But I was reminded again that Durant was playing this on his own level—that he was thinking like a soldier instead of a cop. If he lost a few of his pawns along the way, it didn't matter, so long as he could claim his checkmate at the end of the game.

Then again, though I still think that it stinks, it did make a little more sense as I thought about it. This is a guy who's lived, what, twenty or thirty lifetimes? How long can you live before you see the life spans of all of the normal people around you as less like people and more like fruit flies? I mean, if you let yourself care about every life that you came across—like a good cop does—then how many centuries of death before that would drive you crazy? I didn't like it, but I could see his point.

"You put it back, right?" I asked at last, walking over to my side of the car.

"Hmm?"

"You put the Mona Lisa back, right?"

"Good Heavens…" he replied, shaking his head and getting into the car.

Background
From *Geschichte des Deutschen Volkes seit dem Ausgang des Mittelalters* (Johannes Janssen, 1878-1894, trans. M.A. Mitchell)

A witch-trial which deserves special notice on account of its unique nature took place in 1597 in the imperial city of Gelnhausen. "At this trial," says a report, "it was learnt for the first time by the testimony of the sorceress that, added to all the rest of the craftiness which Satan practised with witches, he could actually appear and act in the shape of fleas and worms."

Clara Geisslerin of Gelnhausen, widow of a day-labourer and 69 years of age, had been denounced by a condemned witch as "a prostitute who was in league with three devils and who had dug up from their graves several hundreds of innocent children and murdered numbers of people." After the application of the thumb-screw, all sorts of questions were asked her, but, hardened by the Devil, she stubbornly persisted in her denials. When, however, her feet were crushed and her body stretched out to greater length, she screamed piteously and said all was true that they had asked her; she drank the blood of children whom she stole on her nightly excursions, and she had murdered as many as sixty. She named some twenty other witches who had been with her at the dances; she said the wife of the late mayor was the president on the journeys and at entertainments; also she had a devil always with her in the shape of a cat with which she, also in the shape of a cat, rambled about the roofs at night.

Released from the rack, she retracted all these statements wrung from her by torture and said it was all invention and not a word of it true. She begged "in the name of God and the Lord Christ" that they would have pity on her, she had suffered much from illnesses, and her head was often in a whirl in consequence. As to what she had said about others, she did not know it herself, but had only heard it said by other people; she begged that they too might be spared. The honourable inquisitors thereupon resolved that "the delinquent must first be kept in prison" in order to see whether "her paramour the devil would feed her," but that meanwhile "some of the witches she had accused must be arrested and questioned mildly, or if needs be with torture." When one of the latter told the very wickedest things about Clara Geisslerin, far worse and more inhuman than what she herself had confessed under torture, the unhappy woman was again put on the rack and again she said "yes" to all that was asked her; but after she was released again recanted everything, and "so demented did she become that she actually invited judges and attendants to the judgment seat of God."

At a third bout of torture which lasted several hours and was characterised by "the utmost severity," she confessed that "for forty years past, she had committed immorality with numbers of devils that had come to her as cats, dogs, often even as fleas and worms;" she had murdered over 240 people, old and young, had bred about seventeen children with the devils, had murdered them all, eaten of their flesh and drunk of their blood; far and wide and for a long time, she had caused terrible tempests; had nine times poured fire on to houses; had wanted to set the whole town on fire, but one of her demon paramours, the devil called "Bursian," had dissuaded her from doing it because there were some more people in the town whom he wanted to turn into witches and receive homage from.

During the torture, she became paler and more exhausted, and after it was ended, she sank lifeless on the ground. "The devil," so ran the judicial report, "would not let her disclose anything more and so wrung her neck."

Her corpse was burnt.

Chapter 20
Obsessions

As we drove to DePaul, I couldn't help chewing on what Rhiannon did to me. It was like a violation—not physical, but mental, emotional. She took my brain and played with it. She made me a toy, and she was going to kill me and everyone I loved, and I would've let her do it, if it wasn't for Tony. I found myself grinding my teeth in frustration.

"You are thinking about Rhiannon, yes?" Durant asked, eventually. I was surprised that he'd be able to tell—or that he'd even care.

"How'd you know?"

"I have owned mirrors in the past, Detective," he replied. "I know the look all too well."

I glanced over to him, and he almost looked... concerned? But I was still mad at him, and I didn't really want to let him into this portion of my psyche. I didn't want him talking about *her*.

"I don't need your help dealing with Rhiannon," I grumbled. "I can handle her on my own."

"Ah, the foolishness of youth," he laughed coldly. "You will need all the help that you can possibly find, and far more, Detective. My experience has been that humans who try to deal with these creatures alone tend to end quite badly. Rawlins and Kilcoyne lost everything, but never did succeed in destroying the monster whom they hunted. Norliss disappeared after stumbling across the Danse in California, as did Dürrenmatt in Germany. For all anyone knows, Mears is still haunting the hills like a guerilla. And Aubrey ended up confined to a particularly ghastly asylum."

I kept driving. I didn't know who any of those people were, of course, but it sounded bad. I could imagine how easy it would be to find yourself in over your head with all of this.

"The problem is, there is only one of you, and a great host of them. And they have no compunctions against attacking your loved ones to get to you, or simply leaving the field of battle and hunting elsewhere, robbing you of any victory or closure. And they can simply *outlast* you—even if they cannot successfully kill you, if they can merely *avoid* you for a few decades, they will have won by mere attrition. But their greatest strength, of course, is the fact that *no one believes that they exist.* You will continually be alone in this fight, and as much at odds with the living as with the undead in the battle. Is that what you truly want? To watch your family suffer, and to spend the entirety of your short lifetime in a pursuit whose main fruits will be pain, frustration, and failure?"

"Of course not," I grumbled again. "I just can't stop thinking about... about *her*..."

"Allow me to share with you a bit about obsession, Detective," Durant said, leaning back in his seat. "Back in 1906, I had steak, tomatoes, and a surprisingly good stout at Delmonico's in New York City with my friend, Lieutenant Gullivar Jones. He and his older brother had been born in Scotland, both of them sons of a long line of naval men—though some sort of unfortunate incident with bilge rats had soured a young Henry on the navy. Having spent long hours discussing history with me as a lad, Henry thus chose to stay with his mother and go to university at Oxford to study medieval literature, while Gullivar came here to America with his father."

"Gullivar was a man of the world, and yet, he wished to be even more..." Durant said, sighing one of his sighs. "Over dinner, he told me a fantastical tale about visiting the planet Mars by use of no less than a magical carpet, which had fallen from the sky in front of him on a New York City street."

I almost slammed on the brakes, hearing that. "You're kidding me!" I said, laughing. "That's the most ridiculous thing I've heard from you, and that's saying something..."

"I know, and I agree," he said. "But Gullivar adamantly defended the veracity of his story, and desperately wished to return to the red planet. He spoke of his fruitless search for an obscure French scientist named Dr. Oxus or Oméga or somesuch—I forget the name now—who was apparently working on a device which could afford interplanetary travel. Both Henry and I thought him at least fairly obsessed—the entire Jones family tended toward such intensities, of course—but he dismissed our concerns with a quick, 'If only you'd been there, old man!' and a flippant wave of his hand."

"As we continued our meal, he told me that he had read about a whaling station on Liverpool Island which had discovered an alien creature in the ice in 1904, and that he wished to travel there to discern if the thing had left any secrets to interplanetary travel in the ice with it. I countered, of course, by suggesting that planning a trip to Antarctica to see an empty hole in the ice was hardly the contrivance of a rational man, and he grudgingly admitted that I was probably right. We finished our dinner, spoke of politics in Europe, and I thought no more about it."

I turned down Fullerton, heading down toward DePaul. Ironic that we'd have to drive right past the Altgelt Club building again to get there, I thought to myself. In fact, I actually found myself debating about whether or not to take another route, but I wouldn't let myself give in to fear. I knew that it's not really the building that's the problem.

"Unfortunately," Durant continued, "as it turned out, he could not stop thinking about traveling to Mars. Ironically, Robert Darvel succeeded in doing precisely that two years later, but that is neither here nor there..."

"What?" I interjected, coming up on the intersection with Ashland. "You're telling me that a man went to Mars in 1908? On a magic carpet?"

"Of course, not," he said—and then he added, "Darvel voyaged in the ship which he had built with the monks of Chelambra," as if that detail made it as believable as if he'd just said that a man had sailed to France. "But pray, let me continue." I bit my lip and let him go on.

"In 1918, having long since resigned his commission, Gullivar signed on aboard the *Toreador* under Captain James Lawton and Tom Billings when he heard that they were sailing to an uncharted island very near Liverpool Island, looking for a lost American named Bowen Tyler. When Billings flew a seaplane ashore, Gullivar apparently used the distraction to steal a lifeboat from the ship, intending to reach the whaling station on his own. No one ever saw him again, though the lifeboat was found at Liverpool Island in 1964, so I do have some small hope that he did, indeed, make it that far. Of course, by then, the Norwegians had made it a protectorate of their own sovereign nation and had renamed the island 'Bouvetøya'..."

"Okay, so you're saying that his obsession was irrational and pointless," I summed up. We were passing by the Altgelt Club archway at that moment.

"Actually, quite the contrary, as things turned out," he corrected. "I myself made it a point to travel to Bouvetøya in 1979, because I had heard of another alien thing which had been found in the ice by a Norwegian scientific expedition there. Suddenly, Gullivar's fanciful tales had taken on at least plausibility, and I felt the need to know for myself—particularly since I had so casually dismissed him seventy years earlier. I found not only the abandoned whaling station from earlier in the century, but also the Norwegian research station, similarly abandoned and partially destroyed. The only physical evidence I found at first was a chunk of ice with a large hole in it. The Norwegians had apparently taken both their helicopter and their sled dogs, though they had left all of their supplies and equipment. But as I continued to search, I also found the dead bodies of several of their expedition, and indications that they had been frantically attempting to combat something in their last moments. I can only imagine that the

Norwegians in their helicopter had made good their escape from their harrowing experience. But, knowing that there was also an American research station relatively nearby, I made up my mind to continue the search in that direction—only to come across something which I had never expected to find."

"And that was…?"

"Before I could reach the American installation, I came upon a large ship, the likes of which I had never seen before, hovering above the ice. From it came a creature quite alien indeed—a hunter of sorts, from another world.   Apparently, these creatures bring various other dangerous alien monsters into harsh environments on other worlds so that they might hunt them down for sport. They seemed particularly fond of hunting various shape-shifters…"

"What happened?"

"We battled—first on the ice, and then aboard its craft, which flew into the air and across the ocean at great and increasing speed. When I finally committed the killing blow, the creature had just enough time to activate what I recognized—too late—to be a Brahmāstra of the same sort which I had once liberated from a very unique warehouse in Moscow in 1830."

"A Brahmāstra?"

"Yes. An ancient explosive nuclear device of what I obviously then learned had been alien origins. Apparently, these creatures have visited our world many times in the past, and have, upon occasion, left their artifacts behind."

"So how did you stop it?"

"As I said, we battled and I killed the thing."

"No, I mean the nuke—how did you stop the nuke?"

Durant cocked his head to the side, as if what I was asking made no sense to him. "I was unable to simply 'stop the nuke,' as you say. I dove from the ship, into the icy waters of the Antarctic, and watched as the craft exploded nearly a mile away."

"So you survived a nuclear explosion?"

"I was not in the immediate vicinity, as I said," he replied—again, as if that made everything perfectly normal. "Yet even so, it took nearly two full days to completely heal from the experience…"

Two full days to heal from being nuked. And here I was, shooting at him the other day with my pistol. Yeah, that was gonna work…

"And so, this Jones guy," I said, trying to figure out what Durant's point was in all of this. "What you're saying is that his obsession with Mars was fruitless and self-destructive, right?"

"No, Detective," he replied. "I am saying that his obsession was *fruitful* and self-destructive. The danger with obsession is not that it is unrequited, but that it is ultimately self-digesting. Obsession always consumes the one who obsesses. Whether or not one's ends are achieved is incidental."

I chewed on that for a while. And then something sprang to mind and out of my mouth before I could even consider whether or not to say it. "What about you?" I asked. "Aren't you the most obsessive man who ever lived? You've spent 1500 years doing the same blasted thing and nothing else. You're so obsessed with killing things that you've lost the ability to care for living people!"

Durant was silent for a time, and then turned to look out of his window, watching the buildings pass by. "Then you should accept that I know how unassailably true my assertion is…" he said quietly. And all of a sudden, I felt really bad about bringing that up.

"So it sounds like this Bouvetøya is kind of a hotbed for alien activity," I chuckled, trying to change the subject. "A regular Roswell of the Antarctic."

"Not at all," he replied, still looking out the window. "The aliens who crashed in New Mexico in 1947 were from a completely different species altogether."

I really couldn't tell if he was joking or not.

"But with regard to Bouvetøya," he continued, sighing again, "I suspect that all of the 'alien activity' to which you refer stemmed from the original crashed vessel from which those remains frozen in the ice had come in the first place. I have even heard that there had been two alien seed pods found a few years earlier on the island by a British research team, undoubtedly brought to earth on that same ship. Lord only knows what would have happened, had those seeds been allowed to germinate."

"So," I said, as we finally turned down the street towards Billy's house. "You said that you stole one of these nuclear bombs from a warehouse in Moscow…"

"No, I said that I had *liberated* one from the warehouse," he corrected me. "The contents of the warehouse were being packed up for shipment to London, and—as I was passing through Russia on my way back to England from my excursion to Tibet—I did not believe it wise to allow them to continue the possession of such a dangerous device. The artifacts in such warehouses have historically had a decidedly nasty habit of getting loose into the world…"

"So whatever happened to it?"

"To the Brahmāstra?" he asked, and I nodded. "Why, it's in my *got uechan*, of course…"

"Waitaminute!" I bellowed, slamming on the brakes instinctively, as if jumping out of the car would make any difference if the thing happened to go off. "You're saying that you have a *nuke* in your fanny pack?!?"

"No," he responded calmly, "I have a Brahmāstra in my *got uechan…*"

*   *   *

I decided that it wasn't worth asking Durant any more questions. It seemed increasingly like the more he told me about things, the less comfortable I became. I kept thinking that I had a handle on the guy, and then he'd talk some more, and then I'd realize how little I actually knew about him… and how little I really *wanted* to know about him.

As we approached the house, I saw a bunch of young guys playing basketball at a public court. I pulled over on the other side of the street to get a better look at them. Sure enough, I saw Billy and several of his Insane Deuce posse there, shooting hoops as if nothing was wrong in all the world.

"There he is," I said, pointing to Billy. Durant didn't even look over, but kept looking out of his own window, toward the university. "Are you coming?" I asked him.

"Do you really need my help to try to save more murderers, Detective?" he asked, turning toward me at last.

"You know, you're really starting to get on—" I stopped when I saw the look on Durant's face. He was actually pale as he looked over my shoulder toward the basketball court. "What? What is it?" I asked.

"That man there," he said, his voice low and quiet. "The pale one in the green shirt."

"That's Billy Rivers," I replied. "What about him? Do you know him?"

"I *knew* him," he answered, his eyes now beginning to grow angry instead of shocked. "But the creature appeared a great deal older and more distinguished when it wore its beard."

I looked back again at Billy, playing a stupid basketball game on the school court. He sure didn't look like anyone unusual—just a kid who should've been going to college instead of running the streets. Maybe Durant was off on this one.

"Are you sure that he's who you *think* he is?" I asked. "I mean, you've run into a lot of people over the years. Maybe you knew of a relative who looked a lot like him. I mean, Billy can't be older than, what, *twenty* at most?"

Durant never moved, and I realized that his eyes hadn't blinked since he first saw Billy across the street. "No," he growled quietly with his broken glass voice. "I know this one all too well…" And that was the end of the matter. I'd never seen Durant looking so intense, and that's saying something. But it was more than just intensity—it was out and out *hatred*.

"Okay, then who is he?" I asked at last.

"The creature was born in 1582," Durant said quietly, his tone cold and hard and measured. "Its given name was William Gowrie, Lord Ruthven. I had thought that young Van Helsing had destroyed the fiend well over a century ago—and it is, most certainly, the Vampire Lord which we have been hunting."

With that, Durant proceeded to tell me another story...

Background
Abraham Van Helsing Attends a Wedding

When Van Helsing ran, it was a colorful sight. He was not fat by any means, but he was a square, stocky man. And with his ruddy face framed by a mane of bristling red hair and his thick red mutton chops, his blue eyes glistened like sapphires in the midst of glowing orange. Watching him run was not unlike watching a live coal tumbling out of the fireplace and onto the hearth.

On the evening of June 21, 1874, he had good cause to be running through the Smithfield Market in London. It was the evening of the wedding day of Sir James Ribault and his pretty young bride, Elizabeth Tisdale—and that meant that Elizabeth was probably going to die within the next few hours. Luckily for Elizabeth, she had been unswerving in her desire to be married in the afternoon rather than in the evening, as her groom had so severely pressured her to agree to. She had, however, finally assented to his desire to be married outside in the fresh air, instead of in a church, as she had originally desired. Sir James had told her stories about his disastrous childhood memories of the corrupt parish in Shoreditch, of which his family had been part, and of his subsequent and adamant aversion to all things religious. He begged her not to taint his enjoyment of their nuptials with such painful associations with things he so despised. He would not even allow a cross to be present at the ceremony, nor any Scripture to be read, nor any Christian hymns to be sung, nor any prayers to be spoken. And it was held on a Sunday, which was absolutely unheard of in that day and age.

It was all quite irregular, but they were young and beautiful and in love, and so her family had dismissed it all as the mere eccentricities of a well-bred gentleman—much as they did his keeping apartments in Shoreditch, dilapidated though they had become. It was rumored that Sir James' family had been Huguenots who had made their fortunes two centuries earlier in the silk trade and bought their nobility with the weaving of a worm's excrement—though, arguably, that is still more noble a price than many a gentleman can claim for his own lineage. When the Ribaults had apparently first moved to the area in the latter half of the 17th century, it had been Hackney's most fashionable neighborhood, with booming industry and beautiful homes. But by 1874, it had become a debauched echo of its former opulence. Few gentry found their way to Shoreditch in those days, save perhaps to have a lark with a fourpenny tart to warm them for a few moments on a chilly evening—and even then, there was more than a good chance that someone would try to pick their pocket in the meantime. But again, the Tisdale family were so desperate to connect themselves through Elizabeth to the nobility which their own considerable wealth had still lacked, that they saw in Sir James' decaying rooms—filled with faded paintings and rich but worn furniture—merely the detritus of former glory, the evidence of noble histories, and the foundation for their own future family pride. As Elizabeth's mother had once apparently encouraged her, "All that Sir James really needs is the right woman to bring his household back up to its former standards"—almost certainly referring more to his family line than to his rooms. More's the pity for young Elizabeth, who had certainly done nothing in her short life to deserve the horror which awaited her later that evening.

The couple had been wed at Hyde Park, not far from Sir George Gilbert Scott's newly opened Albert Memorial (of course, this was before the statue of Albert himself inhabited the Memorial), just off of Exhibition Road. Though the ceremony was held some distance from Sir James' apartments, the grounds were conveniently close to Miss Tisdale's family's home in Kensington, and it was a beautiful location for a wedding, carpeted with cool, green grass and surrounded by a well-kept treeline. Nearly everyone of their second-tier distinction in central London society was in attendance, even though holding the service on the Sabbath was an almost unforgivable social taboo—or perhaps precisely *because* it was an almost unforgivable social taboo. Sir James was renowned within his social set for being both charming and risqué, both blithely urbane and fashionably uncouth. This was an age of social repression, as well as an age of winking disregard for that repression— so long as that disregard was expressed in an engaging fashion. This was a time when courtly men and women attended brothels dressed in tails and opera gloves, and respectable bank presidents bred pit bulls and ratting terriers to fight in illegal pits against their Cockney cousins on the East End. So indeed, perhaps it was not in spite of but rather *because* of Sir James' shocking behavior that his wedding was the social event of the mid-Summer... a fact which actually served to help Abraham Van Helsing slip in amongst the guests all that much more easily. No one really seemed to notice the burly Dutch gentleman with the intense stare, because all eyes were on the bride and her stunning gown. All eyes but Van Helsing's.

It had been a warm and pleasant June Sunday, filled with sunshine and singing birds and all of the accoutrements of the perfect wedding.

The bride's white lace and tulle gown was fashioned by Worth in Paris (or, at the very least, it was an excellent *copy* of a gown fashioned by Worth in Paris), with a long train and a coronet of orange blossoms crowning her lace veil, while her bridesmaids wore roses on theirs. Around her neck, she draped an expensive, antique necklace given to her specifically for the occasion by Sir James, interweaving diamonds and pearls into a long and elaborate pattern. In all, she was a stunning sight, and she all but glowed from her innocent excitement.

But no less stunning was her groom. Sir James—ever an unnaturally *beautiful* man—wore a double-breasted vicuña frock coat of the deepest Navy blue, particularly fashionable in this case because they had been out of fashion for years. His lavender cravat was tied in a Ruche knot, and perfectly matched his lavender gloves and his lavender doeskin trousers. He wore an orange blossom in his lapel, and—strangely—topped his ensemble off with a broad-brimmed black coachman's hat, which was popular enough amongst the young gentlemen of the day, but never worn with such formal apparel at such an important function. He said that it was to protect his sensitive skin from the sun—and indeed, his skin was always quite pale and smooth—but the effect of the costume as a whole was as disconcerting as it was striking.

Nonetheless, many of those in attendance found themselves in awe of the young man, particularly most of the females in the congregation. His grey eyes, though hooded by the broad brim of his hat, still bore down on everyone upon whom he rested his gaze—even though they never seemed to express much interest in anything they perceived. In all, he was an unsettling mixture of boiling intensity and shallow ennui that the upper-middleclass bourgeoisie found entirely compelling.

Van Helsing himself watched the groom with a grim intensity. He watched as Elizabeth came into view and, though everyone else in the congregation gasped and wept at her beauty, Sir James barely batted a grey eye. He watched as Sir James allowed himself the slimmest, grimmest sneer of a smile when he took her white-gloved hand in his. And he watched as they stood together before the Tisdale family and the cream of social London and vowed to love one another for the rest of their lives. Van Helsing watched because he knew that, unless he acted quickly, Elizabeth's young life would be measured in hours. He watched because he knew that Sir James Ribault was a complete fabrication, hiding the *true* identity of the man holding Elizabeth's hand—a man who had been born almost three centuries earlier in Scotland as William Gowrie, Lord Ruthven.

In fact, Van Helsing's research had uncovered that it was Ruthven himself who had purchased those apartments in Shoreditch six decades earlier, under the guise of the Earl of Marsden. Van Helsing found that, as Marsden, he had moved back to London in 1816 after almost a century of wandering the world, and had—after a sadistic custom of his—wed a young woman named Aubrey, only to murder her on their wedding night. The necklace worn that day by Elizabeth Tisdale was the very same one which he had given to at least nine other women over the centuries, including the unfortunate Miss Aubrey. For, though Ruthven fed on lovely young girls on a regular basis to sustain his own unholy semblance of life, he found particular pleasure in *winning* them with his charms, feigning an amorous interest in and commitment to them, and then dashing their hopes after they have completely given themselves to him in the seeming purity of the marriage bed. The sheer horror that they felt upon their realization of his true depravity was to him like a fine wine. Simply knowing that, by his beautiful appearance and overwhelming charisma, he could so completely debase something as utterly holy as matrimony, that he could completely abuse something as compellingly pure as a bride, was perhaps the only true enjoyment that the fiend still possessed... and he relished the anticipation. It was, in fact, this cruel anticipation which Van Helsing had seen in his eyes when the monster had looked at Elizabeth.

*   *   *

The young Dutchman and I had hunted a vampyr[1] before, during the cold siege of Paris at the close of the Franco-Prussian War. Under that damnable Jules Favre, the French had disregarded the armistice signed by their own emperor, Napoleon III himself, and their military discipline had begun to break down. Our troops were beset by their francs-tireur guerillas on a nearly nightly basis, and it was during that time that General Louis Jules Trochu attempted a rather unorthodox means of attempting to break the siege—Trochu enlisted the aid of a vampyr.

Actually, I had first met the young doctor a few months earlier at the Battle of Spicheren, when we both fought in the Second Army under Prince Friedrich Karl (alongside of whom I'd fought against the Austrians a few years earlier at Königgrätz—a battle which, arguably, actually precipitated the Franco-Prussian War). Van Helsing had been attached to the army as a surgeon, but he saw an unusually high share of combat on that hot August day at Spicheren, since his ambulance corps were tending to more and more Prussian wounded, and he himself was forced into the fray at one point to rescue those who were trying to save others. He fought valiantly and passionately that day with his long knife, if not entirely skillfully (in point of fact, I was forced to come to

---

[1]   *I have retained how Durant would have spelled it here—he once told me that he favored "vampyr" over "vampire," for reasons which, I'm sure, made complete and utter sense to him.*

his aid finally when two French cavalry officers bore down on him from behind, but that is another story). I was impressed by his unflappable Dutch determination in the face of the horrors of the battlefield, and I have always respected intensity and passion in a warrior—even an inexperienced one.

That winter, at the siege of Paris, I happened to run into the good doctor again. Trochu's vampyr began attacking the Prussian pickets alongside their francs-tireurs that icy January, and I was sent by Prince Friedrich Karl from Le Mans to destroy the monster. So when I found that Abraham Van Helsing had been brought in to help with the growing number of tuberculosis victims within the besieging Prussian forces, I already knew that he was a man in whom I could place my confidence in a difficult situation, and I appreciated his assistance in my task. As it happened, the creature was only a newly turned vampyr—a former peasant by the name of Bernard-René Gourlier—and so, though he hunted with impunity for the first few weeks of his spree through those icy white woods outside of Paris, it was relatively easy to destroy him once I arrived on the scene and enlisted the aid of Van Helsing. Ironically, we found that the thing had killed nearly as many French soldiers as Prussian ones, prowling around those misty, snow-covered pine forests—in fact, a young French officer named Léonce Patry actually helped us set a trap for Gourlier within three days of beginning the hunt, using himself and his patrol as bait for the creature. Van Helsing and I shadowed the patrol on its far right flank, and I recall thinking again and again how horrible it would be if Gourlier had decided to attack from the right that night, since we trained our senses completely on the French patrol, and would have been caught completely unawares. But, as fortune and Providence would have it, the beast came upon the men from the rear left, and set upon a young Basque before we could reach the group, ripping his throat out ere any of us even knew he was there. But Patry was prepared, and thrust at Gourlier with his saber, giving us enough time to close in and engage the monster. As I grappled with Gourlier, Patry drove a stake through his heart and pinned him to a pine tree until I could finish him off. Van Helsing then filled the mouth of his severed head and the cavity of his chest with garlic, and the deed was done.

That night was the last time that I saw Van Helsing until nearly the turn of the century. What I did not know through those intervening years was that he had continued not only his medical career, but also— apparently taking his cue from his time with me outside of Paris—his growing obsession with hunting down and destroying the creatures of the night. It was apparently Van Helsing who later institutionalized the werewolf, Bertrand Caillet, during the Paris Commune of 1871. And it was Van Helsing who had begun hunting Lord Ruthven the next year in

Gascony while I was off in Styria, finally catching up with him in London two years later in 1874, on the day of his wedding to Elizabeth Tisdale.

*   *   *

As the foul creature now calling himself Sir James Ribault slipped the ring onto her finger, the cruel, slender smile again flickered across his pale lips. Ruthven knew that, in a few short hours, once the sun had gone down and the couple were back in his apartments in Shoreditch, his foul hungers would be satisfied, and the thought almost warmed his cold heart. Van Helsing vowed that he would not allow this to happen... but then, the doctor had never gone up against such a powerful creature as Ruthven before, and he had no idea what was to happen to him when he confronted the vampyr later.

The wedding concluded, and the couple received their guests at a supper in the park, complete with caviar, oysters, beef consommé, pâté de foie gras, a rare selection of fine wines, brandy, and other liqueurs, and dainty confections such as éclairs and sugared eggs, spread out over multiple courses. The Tisdale family spared no expense in making this a memorable occasion for all those involved. But just how memorable it would ultimately be depended entirely upon Abraham Van Helsing. Out of the corner of his eye, he saw a constable who was taking a shortcut through Hyde Park on his rounds, and a plan began to coalesce in his mind. He slipped away from the meal and caught up with the constable near the Memorial.

"Come with me!" he called to the young officer. "There is a trouble which I have find here in the park, and have placed young woman in terrible jeopardy!" I confess that I do not know all of Van Helsing's argument to the constable, but he apparently painted Ruthven / Sir James as a madman who had been slaughtering young women across the continent, eluding the greatest policemen in Europe, and had now set his sights on young Elizabeth—which was not altogether far removed from the truth, as it happens, but nonetheless avoided the more supernatural elements of the case, for fear of demonstrating *himself* to be the madman. He also fumbled through his satchel until he found some sort of papers which invested in him the full confidence of Prince Friedrich Karl—not that young Constable George Lestrade could have read or understood the German documents, but he was certainly impressed by their royal seals.

"Don' 'at jus' take th' biscuit!" he exclaimed.

If Lestrade had been older and more experienced, he would have no doubt called in support from other officers—or dismissed this charge entirely as the ravings of a foreigner who was besmirching the character of a knight of the realm—but Lestrade was still young and hungry to demonstrate his own ability as a police officer, and he saw this situation as the chance to make his name in the department. Above all else, Lestrade was desperate to become an inspector someday and to be involved in important cases filled with dramatic personages, and Van Helsing appeared to be his in-road to this end.

So the gaunt young constable made his way back to the reception with the stocky Dutch doctor, and together, they stood on the outskirts of the supper. Van Helsing watched as "Sir James" made merriment with all those around him, brazenly feeding bits of sugared eggs to his bride, while subtly flirting with the bridesmaids. He watched for some time, and never saw Ruthven actually eat any of the food set in front of him— bits of it were fed to Elizabeth with the illusion of affection, or cheerfully tossed to the birds nearby, or handed to a bridesmaid to enjoy, or otherwise disposed of, but all in ways that deftly drew no attention to the fact that he himself ate nothing. No attention, save that from Van Helsing.

Lestrade, on the other hand, was taking advantage of the situation to eat as much as possible. While the doctor stood silent vigil, watching the groom but also the sun as it lowered itself across the darkening London skyline, the constable was picking at nearby plates of food. To be fair to him, he had never been this close to filet mignon, or truffles, or foie gras, and the temptation was simply too great for him to withstand. After sampling several of the exotic foods, he piled a mound of caviar onto a truffle, then stuffed the whole thing into his mouth… only to immediately spit it back out in disgust.

"So 'ow does 'em swells gag 'is scabbers down?" he sputtered to Van Helsing.

"It is acquired taste," the doctor replied, never moving his gaze away from Ruthven.

"Whussat, then?"

"It means that the wealthy man display his wealth and excess by eating expensive food what he does not like, until he grow so used to it that he is eventually believing that he actually like it."

Lestrade stood still, squinting disbelievingly at Van Helsing for quite some time, then spat the last bits of caviar out of his mouth. "Well, 'at's *barmy*, 'at is…" he said, sticking a fork into another cut of filet mignon to cleanse his offended palette.

The last few guests were taking their little boxes of cake home with them, just as the sun was beginning to touch the rooftops, and Van Helsing watched Ruthven watching its descent. The groom leaned over and whispered something in Elizabeth's ear, which made her giggle and blush, and the two began to walk toward Ruthven's carriage, awaiting them on Exhibition Road.

"Quickly!" Van Helsing barked. "We must the carriage to find for ourselves to follow! We have not a moment to lose!"

O, that the good doctor had not placed his faith in such a sallow, immature young man! But then, I suppose, Lestrade did have his important part to play in this as well... and God, in His Providence, used Lestrade's youthful ineptitude to set the stage for an even larger and more crucially important vampyr hunt in the decades to come. But I am getting ahead of myself.

Lestrade gulped down his bite of meat and quickly stuffed some éclairs into his pockets for later on, then ran off to the street. Van Helsing moved through the dwindling crowd toward the newlyweds, watching Ruthven pick up his own pace in anticipation. The bride's parents met them right on the edge of the road, wishing them good fortune and happiness, and Van Helsing could see the hunger and impatience growing in Ruthven's eyes as his intended victim innocently smiled and hugged her family, ignorant of his true plans for her. He had neither fed nor rested all day long, and his vampiric needs were impressing themselves upon him greatly—but Van Helsing knew that he would wait, even though his hunger gnawed at him, until he could get Elizabeth back to his apartments in Shoreditch. As with many of these sorts of killers, there was a liturgy to his madness, and there was a sad and horrific elegance that must be fulfilled. He'd taken all of this time to woo and win her, and he would not waste that effort, just to kill her like any of the common trollops he'd fed upon on a nightly basis. This was not to be a crime of hunger, but one of wanton malice—he'd desire his bride to be broken and destroyed emotionally before he finally fed upon her coursing blood. But that prolonged wait was leaving him both increasingly agitated and increasingly excited.

Eventually, the Tisdales stepped aside, and Ruthven all but pushed Elizabeth into the waiting carriage. He turned and said something witty to her parents that *almost* assuaged them, and then tapped the roof for the driver to begin. Van Helsing was becoming desperate, since Lestrade was not back yet with a vehicle to use in the pursuit. The carriage was moving at a leisurely pace—obviously, at Elizabeth's insistence—but there was no way that he could follow them long on foot. Fortunately, the carriage turned northward on the Exhibition Road, and deeper into the park, instead of southward toward the Carriage Drive and into town. Van Helsing could follow them into the park and eventually lose them as his endurance gave out, or gamble that they would turn onto the Serpentine Road and make their way to Mayfair—and take a more direct route there himself to cut them off. With seconds to choose, he turned southward, away from the carriage, and prayed to God that his decision did not doom the poor young bride to a gruesome and horrible end.

Van Helsing took one more look down toward the street, hoping against hope to see Lestrade somewhere, but he was nowhere to be found. With a deep breath, he broke away from the road and onto the paths of the park, heading due east with as much speed as his stout legs could muster, his satchel banging against them as they pumped along. He could not help but notice that the sunlight was turning a deep orange around him, and he knew that with every minute that the sunlight lessened, Ruthven's strength would be growing. But he also knew that, since he had been unable to spend the day resting and restoring his strength, Ruthven would be able neither to change his shape (even in the darkness) nor exercise as much of his unnatural strength and speed as he would normally have been able to on any other night. At least, that was what he kept telling himself as the dayglow faded around him.

He broke through Belgravia at a slower pace, finding himself huffing far more than he would have wanted to, knowing that there was much left to do on this night, and praying that he would have the constitution to accomplish it. As luck would have it, his gamble had paid off, and he arrived at Hyde Park Corner less than a minute before the wedding carriage itself came down the Serpentine Road and out of the park. Unfortunately, he also realized that he had no strength left in either his legs or his lungs to follow it any further, and his heart sunk with the knowledge that he had failed not only Elizabeth, but all of the young women whom Ruthven would kill in the months and years ahead. With wheezing breaths, he stepped out into the street, searching against all hope for a handsome cab that he could flag down, but none was visible. The girl would die a horrible death, and all because of him.

Suddenly, rounding the corner from the west at great speed, came a water-cart, roaring out of the deepening shadows. But instead of the carman one would expect to find on its seat, there sat the young constable Lestrade, cracking the whip and barking at the horse as if possessed. Van Helsing waved at him frantically, but Lestrade was singularly engaged on the street itself, and didn't see the doctor. In desperation, Van Helsing lept into the street, waved his arms, and shouted, "HALT!"

The horse reared up, and the cart all but tipped over, splashing its contents as the constable brought it to a sudden stop. "There y' is!" he yelled back to Van Helsing. "This 'ere's all's I could find, gov'nor, but 'e's a fine 'orse, ever I seen one, 'e is…"

"He is the most magnificent thing ever I have seen in my life!" the doctor exclaimed as he climbed aboard next to Lestrade. "We must be off! The carriage he is direct ahead of us!" And with that, the chase began.

Ruthven's carriage picked up speed as it hit Piccadilly, but the water-cart was easily able to match it and follow at a discrete distance. The sun officially went down as they passed the Royal Academy of the

Arts, but, though Van Helsing let slip that the darkness concerned him, Lestrade assured him that the lamplighters had lit the streetlamps, and that there was no chance that they could lose their quarry now. Van Helsing did not explain his concerns further.

The carriage passed through Piccadilly Square, and moved on to Shaftesbury Avenue at the same pace, but somewhere outside of Covent Garden, near the Palace Theatre, it suddenly lurched into high speed. Either Ruthven's thirst was overwhelming his enjoyment of the anticipation, Van Helsing thought, or he had finally realized that he was being followed. Either way, the situation had turned toward the desperate, and he called for Lestrade to pick up their pace to catch up.

In a daring move, Ruthven had the coachman race the carriage to its limits, and then, amongst the traffic of the intersection, make a high-speed turn off of Shaftesbury and eastward onto High Holborn. Van Helsing had expected him to go up to Theobald's Road and then on toward Shoreditch directly, but Lestrade's keen eye caught the carriage's turn, and they followed them onto High Holborn in close pursuit. Fortunately, neither the carriage nor the driver had been built to sustain such speed, and they could not maintain that manic pace. Van Helsing and Lestrade were now close enough to the carriage that they could actually hear Ruthven's voice, barking at the driver of his carriage—and Van Helsing thought that he could also hear the frantic cries of Elizabeth as well. His resolve was greater than ever, and Lestrade pulled out his whistle and began blowing it, then shouting for the driver to stop, then blowing his whistle again.

The volume and irritation of Ruthven's voice continued to rise until, just as the carriage passed Charterhouse, he grabbed his bride and leapt from the moving vehicle. Lestrade assumed that it was a trick of the lamplight that made the leap look so unnaturally smooth and powerful, but Van Helsing knew better. He knew that, even though halved or quartered by his lack of rest, the vampyr's strength was still far beyond that of any normal man, and that their chances of defeating him at night were slim at best. But the only other option was to lose Elizabeth to his vile depredations, and he utterly refused to do that.

The now-empty carriage continued on Shaftesbury, but the water-cart turned down Charterhouse and continued to follow the monster and his victim. Ruthven was no longer even attempting to make a pretense of normalcy, and dragged the young bride through the streets at such speed that she could no longer keep up—at which point, he picked her up and tossed her over his shoulder as easily and casually as a normal man might sling his overcoat. But still, the frothing horse of the water-cart was gaining, and Van Helsing knew that they would quickly be upon them. He drew his pistol, loaded with silver bullets blessed by Cardinal Manning himself, and prepared for the fray that would soon come.

In an effort to lose his human shadows, Ruthven made for the Market on Charterhouse, with Van Helsing and Lestrade right behind them. They entered the Central Market through the Grand Avenue, past the bronze dragons and stone griffins lit in shifting shadows by the gaslight around them. The tall, arched ceiling stretched above them, but the building was darkened for the evening, awaiting the early Monday morning hubbub that was to come in just a few more hours. They stopped for a moment to adjust their eyes to the dimmer light, and to listen for sounds of movement from the fugitive and his victim, but they heard nothing beyond the normal nighttime street noises behind them.

"You are armed, Constable?" asked Van Helsing, gripping his pistol tightly.

"I 'aves me cudgel, I does," responded Lestrade with an ignorant confidence, and he steeled himself, thinking again about the important arrest which awaited him somewhere in the shadows of the Smithfield Market ahead of them.

Van Helsing sighed, and said, "This cudgel may not be enough." He drew his long knife from his satchel and handed it to the constable. "When this you use, you aim for the heart, yes?"

"As good a place as any, I'd wager," replied Lestrade.

"Nee! The heart! The heart it must be, you understand?"

"Sure, gov'nor, sure…" the constable agreed, taking the knife for himself. Together, the men entered the deepening gloom. They moved quietly, cautiously, into the darkness, straining to hear even the slightest noise from within. As they crept along, Van Helsing thought of that night in the icy forest outside of Paris, and that sinking feeling that the fiend might very well attack from an unknown quarter and slaughter them before they even realized what was happening. The creaking of every crate, the skitter of every rat in the darkness, became in his mind the prelude to a sudden attack from the vampyr from the shadows of the Market. But they continued along the arcade toward the Central Market, wanting to inch along as slowly as possible, and yet knowing that every second they wasted here, Ruthven could be getting that much farther away with his innocent bundle. The agony of those steps would haunt Van Helsing for the rest of his life.

Once inside the Central Market, they realized that every stall could contain the fiend, lying in wait. And yet, Ruthven might not even *be* in the Market any longer—he may have dashed through to one side or the other and made his way back to Charterhouse, or on to Smithfield Road, or into one of the buildings nearby. Elizabeth may have already been slaughtered, for all they knew. Van Helsing found himself ironically counting on Ruthven's sadism, his desire to torture the poor girl prior to murdering her—he hoped that, even cornered, Ruthven would still try to retain that satisfaction for himself, and not rush to feed so quickly.

Just then, they heard movement ahead, and saw a shape emerge from one of the stalls. It was a man's shape, and it stood just outside the stall, watching them. They stood still, it stood still, and no one said a word or moved a muscle. Van Helsing wondered if they were somehow hidden from sight by something he could not perceive, or if something behind them was obscuring their outlines from detection. But it seemed, for a time, that they were nearly invisible to the lurker before them.

Suddenly, they were struck by a light ahead—by a lantern trained on them by the figure standing before them.

"Oy!" the figure shouted. "Who's over there?"

"An' jus' who'd *you* be?" Lestrade answered back, more than just a little bit shaken.

"It is the night watchman," Van Helsing suggested to the constable, recognizing at once that it certainly wasn't their quarry. "He is of help to us, I would think."

Lestrade shouted back that he was a constable, but before he could begin explaining why they were there and for whom they were searching, the watchman turned his lamp to the side and into the hallway leading to the West Market.

"Cor!" he yelled down the hallway. "What're *you* doing over there, then?"

Van Helsing saw a blur of motion in the lantern's glow—a flash of deep blue and lavender across the beam of light. In an instant, the watchman's body was gone—gone, in fact, before the lamp hit the ground with a clank and its light went out. The men were momentarily stunned by shock, but were brought to their senses quickly by the sound of the watchman's screams. Lestrade had never heard a man scream like that, and it chilled him to his core. Van Helsing, however, had heard the very same sort of terrified, hopeless sound in those dark, snowy forests around Paris... and it chilled him even more than it did Lestrade. But to both men's credit, they broke into a sprint toward the sound.

By the time they got to the intersection and looked down the hallway, their eyes had adjusted better to the dim light of the lowered gas lamps situated along the great halls. Lestrade picked up the fallen lantern to re-light it, and Van Helsing saw the smear of blood that led down the hall toward the west. The medical man in him recognized that, as a cold comfort, a man could not live long, having lost that much blood that quickly—the watchman was surely dead.

But Elizabeth need not be. Lestrade finished lighting the lantern, and they ran in the direction of the blood, leading them through the West Market and out to the construction of the new Poultry Market beyond. Here and there, starlight broke through the unfinished roof, and stacks of lumber and stone lay round about, awaiting the masons and carpenters who would arrive in the morning. There were places open in the ground as well, where the workers were still building bits of the foundation and working to cover over the connections with the underground which lay beneath the Market. There, lying amidst the shafts of soft starlight, the two men saw the body of the night watchman, crumpled in an uncompleted stall like a discarded doll in the corner of a little girl's room. The head was dangling to the side by a few sinews, and the ribcage had obviously been crushed in and split open. Van Helsing was repulsed, but Lestrade was in shock.

"Mother o' God!" he gasped, crossing himself.

"Yes, this is appropriate to do," said Van Helsing. "The one whom we follow have done this thing, and evil he is to the very soul of him." The doctor took out some wafers from his satchel and, breaking them, whispered quickly, "Accipe, frater, Viáticum Córporis Dómini nostri Jesu Christi, qui te custódiat ab hoste maligno, et perdúcat in vitam aetérnam. In nómine Patris, et Fílii, et Spíritus Sancti, exstinguátur in te omnis virtus diáboli per impositiónem mánuum nostrárum. *Amen...*"[2] as he tossed the pieces into the wounds, and then crossed himself.

"Bollocks!" Lestrade snorted. "But 'ere's no bloody way any man done this! An' us jus' talkin' wif th' bloke not a mo' ago..."

"No," answered Van Helsing solemnly, moving deeper into the construction site, "not a man..."

Lestrade did not follow this time—in fact, he seriously considered leaving. He was no coward, but the sheer weight of the situation was beginning to hit him with great force. He was away from his patrol area, alone, in the middle of a darkened and uncertain terrain, facing something far more powerfully evil than he had originally imagined. There was *criminal* evil, the evil of *madness*, and then there was the evil of whatever *this* thing was. And the only real weapon he was carrying was a long knife. He suddenly felt woefully inadequate... which, indeed, he was.

But then they heard the young woman's scream from nearby, piercing the night air. And both men bolted in that direction, all fears immediately forgotten. Lestrade blew his police whistle continually as they ran, hoping that some other constable would hear it and join them in the fight, and Van Helsing drew from his satchel a small crucifix, clutching it in his fist.

As they turned down a small hallway filled with new stalls, they glimpsed Lord Ruthven, again carrying his flailing bride on his shoulder, darting toward one of the openings to the underground.

---

[2]   *"Receive, brother, the Viaticum of the Body of our Lord Jesus Christ; and may He keep you from the malignant foe, and bring you to life everlasting. In the Name of the Father, and of the Son, and of the Holy Spirit, let there be extinguished in you all power of the devil by the Imposition of our hands. Amen."*

"Lord Ruthven!" shouted Van Helsing. "Stop in the name of Our Lord Jesus!"

Though Lestrade would never have expected it to, that tactic actually worked. For some reason, the fiend stopped in his tracks, and turned around to face them, in all of his bloody horror.

"What name did you call me?" he hissed, the watchman's gore still dripping from his lips and whiskers. "What was that name?" Seeing the two men approaching, Elizabeth fainted from relief, and Ruthven dropped her to the ground.

"Your name I called you," answered Van Helsing, advancing toward the monster with the crucifix held before him, and Lestrade only a half-step behind him. "The name of your birth, William Gowrie, Lord Ruthven of Scotland!"

"How do you know me, sir?" the vampyr asked, as if he were speaking to an acquaintance on the cobblestones on a sunny afternoon. "You've done your studies, I see..."

Van Helsing and Lestrade continued forward, undeterred by the conversation. "You have not stop out of curiosity or sociability," Van Helsing said, "but by command by the name of the Lord. Even with all of your strength, you are yet under His command."

Ruthven snorted at this, and wiped the blood from his mouth with his sleeve. "I serve none, nor shall I ever—and certainly not the Nazarene. You are much mistaken, my continental friend." And yet, he still did not move one inch toward them nor one inch farther away.

"So you say," said Van Helsing, approaching now almost close enough to touch the creature, but not quite. "And yet, His name you do not speak." He heard Lestrade breathing heavily behind him, but he found his own breathing almost alarmingly regular at this point. He realized that it was his faith that sustained him now—his absolute assurance that, in Jesus Christ, he actually possessed more power at this point than the vampyr did. And thus, even in the midst of the deadliest moment of his life, Van Helsing was unafraid.

More's the pity, then.

For at that moment, Lestrade called out, "This'll do ye!" and lunged forward clumsily, trusting more in the long knife than in what appeared to him to be mere words passing between the two strangers next to him. Van Helsing pivoted out of the way, but, losing his concentration, also lost his control over Ruthven, who easily parried Lestrade's assault, laughed deeply, and flung the constable back against the doctor, sending both of them falling backwards into the nearby stall. Lestrade leapt back to his feet, but was surprised to see blood on his knife, since he knew that he had not touched Ruthven in any way. But then he looked down and saw the long, bloody gash on Van Helsing's leg.

"C'est la vie, good sirs," the vampyr cackled, collecting Elizabeth from the ground again, "though I salute you for coming closer to stopping me than anyone has in over a century." He began to move again toward the opening to the underground, when Lestrade—whether caught up in the fire of the moment, or overwhelmed by his own ineptitude which had led to the injuring of his fellow—again struck out at the creature and unexpectedly connected, slicing the monster's right wrist. But instead of blood, only a thick, black ichor began to ooze out.

Ruthven whirled in anger and pain and struck Lestrade across the chest, cracking his collarbone and smashing him to the ground, breathless and stunned.

"For that, little mortal," he hissed, "you shall die slowly!"

But by that time, the bleeding Van Helsing had dragged himself to his feet again, and, leaning against the wall of the stall, took aim and fired his pistol. The silver slug grazed the vampyr's shoulder, and Ruthven howled in pain and terror.

"Damnable Dutchman!" he growled, and spun again toward the hole to the underground, disappearing with Elizabeth down into the tunnel. But Van Helsing limped behind him, flinging himself into the hole with a wild abandon, already light-headed from blood loss. He tumbled down the shaft and into some foul, standing water, just missing smashing his skull into the Snow Hill railway tracks in the fall. Somehow, even in the midst of his fall, he had kept the presence of mind to hold the pistol up and away from the water, and he sat bolt upright, prepared to fire.

The creature heard the splashing behind him, and turned to see Van Helsing rising from the oily pool. "Enough of this!" he snarled, and dropped Elizabeth into the water at his own feet. He began to sprint toward Van Helsing, but the knee-deep water slowed him down enough that Van Helsing was able to get off a shot, striking Ruthven in his stomach. The creature howled again, and crumpled back, falling into the water and splashing around as if the wound were on fire.

Van Helsing tried to rise to his feet again, but almost blacked out in the process. He splashed down into the grimy pool himself, barely able to keep the pistol above the waterline. Ruthven's face was contorted with pain and rage, and he pulled himself up to his feet, digging at his stomach for the bullet lodged there, black ichor spilling out, mixed with the red, fresh blood of the watchman. As he dug at himself, he splashed closer and closer to Van Helsing, who increasingly perceived the tunnel around him growing darker and darker. Finally, the vampyr climbed out of the water and onto the tracks above Van Helsing, who himself was scrambling backwards, up out of the filthy pool and back toward the tunnel wall. Elizabeth was stirring somewhere down the tunnel as well, but Van Helsing realized that he could no longer see that far.

"Damn you!" hissed the vampyr as it lunged toward Van Helsing.

"Verdomme!" Van Helsing yelled back, squeezing the trigger. The bullet hit Ruthven square in the chest, and Van Helsing saw the body fall backwards, onto the railway tracks, even as his own world went black. "Moge je voor eeuwig branden in de hel..."[3] he muttered, and he could have sworn that he heard the sound of a train coming down the tunnel toward them. But then he heard nothing at all.

*   *   *

It was almost by chance that Van Helsing survived this encounter. Lestrade was found by a carpenter the next morning, unconscious, and taken to nearby St. Bartholomew's Hospital. But since he *remained* unconscious for several days, he could tell no one about the doctor who had fallen into the dark railway tunnel beneath the Market. Elizabeth, emotionally shaken and scarred, but otherwise unharmed, was found wandering on Fann Street the next afternoon. She could not remember anything about the night before—in point of fact, she barely remembered her own name—and was taken back to her family's home in Kensington to convalesce. And so Abraham Van Helsing lay, sliding in and out of consciousness, covered in grime, near the Snow Hill railway tracks for nearly two days. His surgeon's instincts had kicked in somewhere along the line, and he had tied a tourniquet around his leg to stop the bleeding. When he was conscious, he remembered to loosen it and tighten it, but gangrene was beginning to set in when fortune—or Providence—stepped in once again.

On June 23, a stonemason fell into the same hole through which Van Helsing had chased the vampyr, breaking his leg in the process. A young doctor named John Seward, who was studying at St. Bartholomew's Medical College at the time, happened to be passing by on his way to the hospital when he saw the man fall, and he rushed over to help them pull him back up and out. While he was down in the tunnel, he saw Van Helsing's body as he lay in the half-light, and immediately began treating him.

Not only did Seward's serendipitous intervention save Van Helsing's life (and his leg), but it also began a lifelong bond of mentoring friendship between the two doctors—and one which would have a profound impact upon the world some twenty years afterward. Though the ordeal of his fight with Ruthven had convinced Van Helsing to give up his vampyr hunting and go back to both his medical practice and—ultimately—his native Amsterdam, he nonetheless began tutoring his young friend in the more esoteric sciences of the occult.

Years later, when Dr. Seward stumbled across a particularly bizarre ailment which strongly resembled some of the more fanciful-seeming

---

[3] *"Damn you... May you burn in Hell forever..."*

stories of his mentor, he called upon Prof. Van Helsing to come to consult on the case—if nothing else, as an expert on blood disorders. Very quickly, the good doctor recognized Lucy Westenra's case for what it truly was—the slow death of repeated vampyr attacks—and assembled around him the team of friends who would help him ultimately destroy Count Dracula. But that is another story…

Chapter 21
Enlightenment

"This fiend we see before us is quite definitely *undead*. The way it moves, the strength and agility which it obviously holds back while it plays with the humans—but only just enough not to be noticed. The pale delicacy of its features, the cruel coldness of its eyes, even when it smiles..." His voice trailed off while his gaze burned down towards Billy. Again, I was shocked at the sheer level of hatred rolling off of Durant as he watched the game.

I looked more carefully, and I have to confess, I slowly began to notice how strangely Billy moved. Durant was right—it was like he was just a hair faster than everyone else, but still only moving at half-speed. And though that three-pointer he just threw while I watched was a long shot, it looked like he made it with the barest of physical effort. The more I watched, the more alien Billy Rivers was becoming in my perception. But then I noticed the detail that most disturbed me.

Everyone was caked in sweat... everyone except Billy Rivers. And, though even the Latinos were red-faced from exertion, there wasn't a hint of color to Billy's pale face. I've never seen anyone that pale not have their cheeks flushed with pink, running around like that in the cool night air. It wasn't... well, *natural*.

I felt the pieces start to come together in my brain. Billy was a vampire. No, Billy was *the* vampire—the Vampire Lord—and he had been all along. The irony is, here I was, trying to find Billy and save him from Mojo's fate, when it was Billy who'd turned Mojo in the first place...

Suddenly, in one huge flash, the tunnels in my mind all lined up, and the case finally began to make sense to me. That's the answer to the question—*Why would a vampire care about a portrait?* Because the portrait was of *him*, and it would betray his identity, just like that photo of Durant from back in 1862. Billy Rivers, William Ruthven, William Raffey—all the same man. And both Amanda Cairns and Hector Flórez would have recognized him... but as totally different people, decades apart.

Amanda Cairns had known him as William Raffey, the dashing

young man whom she'd fallen in love with in the 1960s. But the murder of Connie Dillard would've put the police on his tail, and he couldn't stay to do *whatever* it was that he had been planning to do to Amanda. So she pined for him for years, never knowing what a monster he really was, and she even lovingly painted his portrait and hung it in her apartment. And that's what signed her death warrant fifty years later.

Hector Flórez knew him as Billy Rivers. Hector had spent time in Amanda Cairns' apartment as a child, where he'd had to have seen that portrait that she'd painted of Billy dozens of times. But it wasn't until years later that he'd have met Billy Rivers, so he didn't recognize him at first. Or maybe he did, but didn't know from where. Somehow, probably recently, he'd finally made the connection between the Insane Deuce that he knew as Billy Rivers and the painting of the man Amanda Cairns had known as William Raffey fifty years before. How freaked out would he have been to realize that Billy hadn't aged in all that time?

I don't know if Hector had been dumb enough to confront Billy about it—probably not, or the creature would've killed him right then and there. So I'm thinking that he probably went to Amanda Cairns' apartment that night to make sure of what he thought he remembered. Somehow, either Billy or Rhiannon had caught wind of it, and Billy—or I guess I should say, *Ruthven*—went there after him. And that's when it all went down.

Carmine Wisniewski had heard Hector Flórez climb up the stairs to the apartment that night. I don't know what happened in that half an hour before Ruthven had arrived, but I assume that it had included awkward re-introductions, reminiscences about the past when Hector had learned to paint in that apartment as a boy, etc. And then, Hector took the time to look at the portrait—really *look* at it and remind himself. Judging from the quality of Amanda's work, I'm assuming that Hector recognized the subject of the painting immediately, and it confirmed his suspicions. Maybe he already knew what that meant about Ruthven, or maybe all his suspected was that something was definitely wrong, and that "Billy" wasn't at all who he'd claimed to be. Maybe Hector had tried to talk with Amanda about it, trying to find out what she knew, and that's why he was still in the room thirty minutes later.

And that's when Wisniewski heard the second set of feet climbing the stairs—Ruthven's feet. He couldn't have just followed Hector there, or he would've caught him *before* he'd entered the apartment. So he must've heard about Hector's plans somehow—again, probably from Rhiannon. He entered the apartment, and immediately started destroying the place.

But he didn't start with Hector Flórez—he started with Amanda Cairns. Why? Because he thought that he could somehow control Hector later? Probably not, since he just ended up killing him anyway.

And he didn't feed on the old woman—he just ripped her apart and flung her around the room.

This was a crime of passion. By definition, any time that someone crosses that line and commits murder, it's out of a strong, emotional need—even if it's only the need to *feel* an emotion. You're breaking the law and placing yourself in the highest jeopardy in order to forcibly end another human being's existence. It's always going to be an emotional thing. But this time, even after hundreds of years of torturing and killing—this time, it was a very personal murder.

Was it an unrequited love thing? Had Ruthven actually fallen in love with her, fifty years before, and thus couldn't handle the thought of them both being alive, and yet separated? Not likely. That sort of reaction does happen every once in a blue moon in a psychotic personality, but it doesn't fit the profile, of either William Raffey or William Ruthven. Raffey toyed with women—he hated them and saw them merely as instruments of his own, sick pleasure. They weren't human beings in his mind—they existed only to be hurt, emotionally as well as physically, so that he could derive personal satisfaction. I don't think that it's possible for someone who thinks like that to actually "fall in love" with a woman. Besides that, Durant told me that vampires aren't really people any more—they're demons who infest a dead body and trap the victim's soul so that they can twist and defile it into a template for them to use as their vampiric personality. William Ruthven had been a messed-up guy before he became a vampire, so the vampire became a caricature of everything dark and tainted about the original Ruthven, and a corruption of anything that had been good in him. Again, outside of sparkly romance novels, a vampire isn't capable of loving anything but itself.

No, far more likely is that Ruthven couldn't handle Amanda Cairns being "the one that got away," and her mere existence caused him pain. He'd wanted to torment her, hurt her, when she was a beautiful young woman, and that pleasure had been stolen from him. To the true sociopath, though they literally can't feel any remorse for the pain and suffering they cause to others, their own pains are magnified a hundred-fold. They can murder an entire family and feel no anguish at all, but if someone scratches their favorite DVD, they're inconsolable with grief. That's what I'm guessing happened in the apartment that Monday night. Hector Flórez had screwed up Ruthven's plans by remembering that portrait, and Amanda Cairns had screwed up his plans by still being alive, and so he exploded in a self-pitying rage. He didn't get what he wanted, and he couldn't handle it.

So he tore an elderly woman apart like a ragdoll and sprayed her blood all over her room. In essence, he destroyed not only her life, but also her world, just as he felt that she'd destroyed his by not letting him torture her half a century earlier. And while Ruthven was lost in his orgy of rage, Hector Flórez escaped the carnage and ran down the stairs, for all the good it would do him.

Ruthven took his time before following him. Obviously, part of that time was spent finding and taking the portrait, but that would not have taken more than a moment or two. Did he want to give Hector a head start, to taunt him like he had taunted countless victims over the centuries? Did he stay in that blood-stained room to absorb the full impact of what he had done? Did he walk through the rooms, looking at mementos and remembering the life they'd had together? No—we would have found bloodied footprints in the carpet, or bloodied fingerprints on items in the apartment. Perhaps he just stood there for a time, drinking in the obvious years that Amanda had mourned losing him, and trying to gain at least some satisfaction from the *length* of the pain he'd caused her, if not the *depth* that he'd wanted to have relished. We may never know, in large part because men like Carmine Wisniewski don't care enough to check on an old woman who lives on another floor.

I couldn't help but suddenly think of Pieter Durant, laying his coat over the sleeping form of a perfect stranger on the street.

So Ruthven followed Hector Flórez out into the streets, chasing him down the alley where he'd lost his shoe, and over the rusty fence where he'd torn his shirt and jeans, and finally catching up to him behind the deli, where he ripped open his throat and drank his blood. He then tossed the body down into the pile of boxes, as if it were just another piece of garbage.

People aren't people to Ruthven—they're cattle. No, worse than that. They're just *things*. You devour them, you make them squeal and use them for your pleasure, but it's not like they're real. Having been dead for so long, he'd forgotten what it means that a human being is a living thing. Or maybe he'd never cared about that at all.

*　　*　　*

Durant was still watching Billy on the basketball court while all of this went through my mind.

"Prisa…" I mumbled.

"What's that?"

"Prisa. It was Billy that told me about Prisa—that drug that I asked you about." I sighed an almost Durant-ish sigh as I thought about how many hours I'd wasted, trying to figure out what to do about that particular lead. "He led me on a wild goose chase and made me actually *worry* about him, when all the while, he's been behind everything."

"Indeed," Durant said, shrinking back into his seat to avoid being seen. "He excels at that sort of deception. A great number of people over a great number of years have been seduced in one way or another by that evil creature."

I shrunk down a bit, too. The light was such that I figured he wouldn't be able to see us in the car, even if he looked over at us—but then again, Durant warned me not to underestimate a vampire's senses. But Billy kept playing, obviously oblivious to our presence.

"Even his sword was evil," Durant said at last, watching without blinking. "Its name was *Chi no Yokubō*, and its soul was as dark as Ruthven's own. I knew it well, from its previous owner."

"The sword has a name?" I asked. "And a soul? How can a piece of metal have a soul?"

"*That* is perhaps just a piece of metal," he chided me, pointing to the wrought iron fence next to the car. "But a sword is more than just the sum of its materials, just as a painting is more than just a smear of paint across a piece of linen. The soul of the artist—or at least an echo of it— is instilled in the work. In the case of, say, Da Vinci, his warmth and genius became a part of every drawing, every painting, every invention which sprang from his imagination. But in the case of Muramasa…" his voice became low and cold as he spoke that name. "Muramasa was a madman, sold out to evil to a degree which I've seen but seldom among mortal men. His darkness infused every blade he ever forged and folded. I have watched men go mad, simply unsheathing one of Muramasa's swords."

"My roommate in college was into Japanese swords," I offered, wanting to join in. "He said that katanas were the best swords the world has ever produced."

"The argument could be made," he said, shrugging. "The first time that I myself held a katana, it was actually one which had been made by another master swordsmith—Masamune himself, no less," he said. "Thus, I confess that the sheer perfection of that blade somewhat spoiled me for every other katana which I have made use of, over the years."

"So you were hunting vampires in Japan?"

"Actually, oddly enough, it was in Spain," Durant replied, almost wistfully. "I was there to help Fray Martin Casteñega deal with an outbreak of vampiric children in the early 16th century. Emperor Charles V gave us free rein to hunt them down and eradicate them— primarily, I believe, because he felt that the Emperor of the Holy Roman Empire should not be seen to have been bested by a pack of demonic children." He almost smiled when he said that sentence. Almost.

"I found it odd at first when he insisted that his foppish chief metallurgist join us on the hunt, but Don Juan turned out to be an exceptional individual in many respects, not the least of which was his considerable skill with a blade. It was actually *his* Masamune katana— and Lord only knows how a Spanish nobleman had come by such a masterpiece of Japanese sword-craft in those days—with which I finally destroyed the loathsome bruxa who had created the little monsters in the first place. It was almost a shame to return it to him when the matter was concluded." He sighed and settled back into his car seat.

I thought again about the long centuries that Durant had been out there, hunting the monsters that the rest of us tried to pretend weren't real. I wondered how many people he'd confided in, the way that he was confiding in me. He'd been so quiet about everything when we'd first met, playing everything so close to the vest. But then, after he started sharing with me, it was like that bottle just kept coming uncorked, and his whole life just spilled out in large gushes.

"I'd spent my youth believing that he who talks too much commits a sin," he'd once told me, "and commitment to that belief succeeded in causing me great grief at one point, when I'd foolishly held my tongue." So I wondered if he'd shared like this with other people over the years, or if he just finally decided to let loose with me for some reason, after corking it all up for centuries at a time.

"So you've never actually been to Japan, huh?" I asked, breaking the silence again and trying to encourage him to tell more of his stories.

But Durant simply kept quietly watching Billy on the court and only furrowed his bushy brows in response. In fact, his silence on the subject was deafening.

*   *   *

I waited another fifteen minutes or so before speaking again. Durant was obviously dealing with more than just the vampire in front of him, and I wanted to give him a little time to do so. But then, I tried to break the tension again.

"I don't know what to do about Tony," I said at last. "He's going to complicate things."

"Kill him," Durant said, without missing a beat. For a second, I almost thought he was serious.

"No, the paperwork on that alone would be even more complicated," I replied. "And I've got enough hot water to swim through with Bainbridge down at HQ." I looked at my watch. "In fact, I really need to get going, or it's just gonna get worse."

Durant sat up in his seat when I said this, surprised.

"You mean that you actually intend to leave, now that we have finally uncovered the Vampire Lord whom we seek?" he asked, shocked. "Your entire investigation has led to this moment, and yet you would abandon it to placate a bureaucrat?"

"My career is going down the drain, Durant," I said in response. "I need to catch this guy, but let's be honest—there's no way that we're going to *arrest* him. So even if we do get him, you're just going to burn his corpse up with that stuff of yours, right?"

"The body will undoubtedly simply crumble on its own, after all these centuries," he replied.

"Whatever," I said. "Either way, I won't have anything to show for any of this, and I've still got to try to pull a paycheck next month, next *year*. I've got a family to feed. So yes, I was kind of thinking about actually following orders at least once this week, and going down to the Organized Crime Division while you continue the stakeout. See, the rest of us have to deal with real life, even after you've had your melodramatic swordfights and then left the continent to go on the next hunt. But I guess I shouldn't expect you to understand that..." I added with a snort.

Durant sighed. "I do indeed understand that concept, Detective. All too well, in fact." I could hear another story coming on in his voice. Sure enough, after a brief pause, he continued. "I recall a time around 1813, I believe. I was hunting the vampire de Retz, who had reappeared in Leipzig around the same time that Napoleon's forces clashed there with... well, with everyone else. I had traveled there myself with von Klenau's forces, at the advice of my friend, Sir Andrew Ffoulkes. He himself, of course, had grown too old for the sort of adventuring which he had devoured so lustily in his youth, dashing about the French countryside, saving families of aristocrats from the guillotine alongside my namesake and their League."

"Your namesake?"

"Hmm?" Durant asked, jarred to have been interrupted in mid-story. "Oh, yes. I had saved Sir Algernon Blakeney and his pregnant wife, Joan, from a rather nasty fate in Sussex in 1760, so in return, they had named their newborn son after me—Percival. Quite an interesting fellow in his own right..."

I felt a tangent coming on, so I jumped in again. "But you were talking about this Ffoulkes fellow." Durant frowned a bit, to have been interrupted twice in succession.

"Not really, no," he corrected. "That was actually the last time that I ever saw the man, though I later worked with one of his descendents during the Yambuku outbreak in 1976. Ironic that, since one could argue that Sir Andrew would have beeen seen as something of a terrorist by the French Republic, and Rufus was a specialist in *counter*-terrorism. Odd duck, that fellow..."

A tangent off of a tangent off of a tangent. "He who talks too much commits a sin," I guess...

"But I was actually going to speak about my time in Leipzig. The fiend de Retz had already killed several people there by the time I arrived on the scene, including a delightful old widow named Kunhardt whose deceased husband I had known years before—but my investigations were hampered not so much by the Napoleonic wars going on around me as by a mad French officer who continued harassing me until I should fight a duel with him."

"Why did he want to fight a duel?"

"The matter in question was never quite made clear to me," he answered, frowning again. "It had something to do with his horse, I believe, and a perceived slight which I had apparently done him regarding the animal. But I suspect that it had far more to do with Fournier than with his horse…"

"Fournier?"

"Yes," he responded. "An annoying little man from Sarlat-la-Canéda with a scar across his forehead. I understood his real name to be François Fournier-Sarlovèze, though for some reason beyond my ken, he formally served under the name of 'Féraud' within the military. Quite possibly, he was hiding under that name to avoid prosecution for earlier dueling elsewhere…"

"So did you end up actually fighting him?" I asked.

"In the end, I had no other choice," he replied. "You have to understand the social climate of the day. To have refused to fight him would have been to validate his insanity and to call myself and all those with whom I associated cowards and blackguards."

"Yeah," I said, snorting again. "You couldn't have *that*…"

"No, Detective, I could not," he replied sharply. "And this is the point that I was attempting to make here. I would only be in the area for a short time, engaged in my 'melodrama,' as you say. But for those who had already helped me in my hunt, avoiding the duel would have meant a lifetime of shame for them that would have made it impossible for them to maintain their businesses and livelihoods, to receive the promotions to higher rank which they had earned, or to otherwise function in that society. Do not judge past centuries by the shifting social mores of the present one, sir. I could not destroy the lives of good people, simply because I refused to kill a ranting idiot."

"But the man didn't stand a chance!" I barked. "You basically murdered the guy!"

"Oh, good Lord!" Durant replied, rolling his eyes in disgust. "Killing him would have been akin to murdering an ill-mannered child!" He murmured something under his breath that sounded a lot like, "though a man such as Fournier would have certainly deserved it," but I can't be sure. "No," he continued on at full volume, "I parried with the fool for a few minutes, then allowed him to stab me through the heart, just to make an end of it. In fact, the hardest part of the whole affair was lying in the grass and keeping still while he prattled on to his fawning friends about his honor and his skill with a blade," he said. "The man knew nothing of honor—he merely vented his spleen on those whom he felt he could badger into fighting him."

"What was he so angry about?" I asked.

"Being alive, I should think," he answered, matter-of-fact. "But as a result of that idiotic waste of time with Fournier, de Retz had the opportunity to elude me once again." His voice developed an edge again as he said that, but then softened as he continued. "Nonetheless, I did recognize the importance of considering the lives of those around me, which would continue long after I had left." He looked straight at me, those clear grey eyes boring into me under those heavy, black brows. "So do not lecture me on what I do or do not understand."

Apparently, it was at precisely that moment, when Durant turned to look at me, that the game finished—or at least, that Billy had brought the game to an end. Because when I turned around, all of the guys were grabbing their gear and toweling off. I caught a glimpse of Billy stepping out of the lights of the court and into the darkness beyond—and I swear, it looked like, at that last second, he smiled at us.

"The point is moot, Detective, and the game is afoot!" Durant growled, whipping open the door to the car and stepping out. "The fiend now knows that I am in pursuit. Go on your way to see this Bainbridge fellow, and I shall find you later!"

"Wait!" I shouted, as Durant slammed the door behind him. I opened my own door and jumped out to follow him. "Let me come with you, if you're actually going after him now."

Durant turned and faced me with another shocked expression.

"I commend your courage, Detective," he replied, shaking his head. "But for someone like you to pursue a Vampire Lord—*at night*—in his own hunting grounds? That would be folly of the highest order. In truth, you would be more of a hindrance than you would a benefit to me."

With a blur of motion, Durant was gone. I couldn't even tell which direction he'd gone in, he was so fast.

I'll be honest—my first thought was to be offended by all of that. I mean, I'd done pretty well for myself over the years, and I'd held my own fairly competently throughout all of this craziness with Durant and the vampires. I'd even taken out Mojo all by myself, thank you. But the more I've thought about it since that night, the more I realized that Durant probably saved my life right there.

Mojo was a newly-turned vampire, so that made him about as low-level a vampire as they come, whereas Ruthven was a Vampire Lord—by definition, the strongest vampire in the whole region. Even though their "Danse" thing dictated that he would only fight us alone, he'd still be the most powerful thing that I'd ever faced, and he'd be in his own element. And from what I'd learned, a vampire is at its strongest in the night-time, and able to shift its form to a wolf, or a bat, or mist, or probably a dozen other weird things that I'd never even considered. And finally, though I'd never admit it to Durant, I'd probably been more than a little stupid to give the Matteh ha Shelomoh to Tony—and that would make it *totally* stupid to face Ruthven without even the weapon that had saved me from Mojo in the first place.

I thought of a big, young, ruthlessly aggressive fighter like Hector Flórez, and how easily Ruthven had killed him that night in the alleyway. Realistically, the monster would've probably killed me before I even realized what had happened. But all of that still doesn't mean that I had to like being left behind on my own collar.

The guys had pretty much vacated the court, and the streets were empty. I took a deep breath, mustered up a whole different kind of courage, and got back into the car to drive down to Michigan Avenue and face Lt. Bainbridge and the full fury of the Organized Crime Division. Somehow, it seemed scarier to do that than it would to try to follow Durant and Ruthven into the dark. I mean, at least then, it would be an exhilarating chase, followed by a big, cathartic fight. But any time that you're essentially called down to the principal's office, you know that it's going to be a joy-sucking journey to get there, followed by an excruciating interrogation that won't just end there—you know that you're going to be dealing with the ripple effects of that talk for a long, long time.

Unlike vampires, you just can't smack your superior officer with a stick and make an end of it. And the world is a sorrier place as a result of that fact.

I turned the key in my ignition and looked forward before pulling out. There, in my headlights, stood Raphael Camacho—the Angel— with a pistol pointed at my head.

And behind him, with her hand on his shoulder, stood Rhiannon, wrapped in a green satin gown that clung to every curve.

What scared me most of all was the sheer joy I felt in seeing her again...

Background
From *Dissertation Sur Les Apparitions Des Anges, Des Demons Et Des Esprits: Et Sur Les Revenans Et Vampires* (Dom Antoine Augustin Calmet, 1746, trans. H. Christmas)

Men, it is said, who have been dead for several months, come back to earth, talk, walk, infest villages, ill use both men and beasts, suck the blood of their near relations, destroy their health, and finally cause their death; so that people can only save themselves from their dangerous visits and their hauntings, by exhuming them, impaling them, cutting off their heads, tearing out their hearts, or burning them.

These are called by the name of d'oupires or vampires, that is to say, leeches;[1] and such particulars are related of them, so singular, so detailed, and attended by such probable circumstances, and such judicial information, that one can hardly refuse to credit the belief which is held in those countries, that they come out of their tombs, and produce those effects which are proclaimed of them...

It is true that we remark in history, though rarely that certain persons after having been some time in their tombs and considered as dead, have returned to life. We shall see even that the ancients believed that magic could cause death, and evoke the souls of the dead. Several passages are cited, which prove that at certain times they fancied that sorcerers sucked the blood of men and children, and caused their death.

I undertake to treat here on the matter of the vampires of Hungary, Moravia, Silesia, and Poland, at the risk of being criticised, however I may discuss it; those who believe them to be true, will accuse me of rashness and presumption, for having raised a doubt on the subject, or

---

[1]   *Calmet's "oupire" is an obviously French transliteration of the Russian "upyr'," Polish "upiór," or Czech "upír" (and his "vampire" surely translates the Magyar "vampyr"). Calmet's translation of these words as "leech," however, is problematic, since, for instance, the common Polish word for a leech is "pijawka," the common Russian word is "piyavka," the Czech word is "pijavice" (or, sometimes, "felčar"), etc. Even the compound word, "blood-sucker," would be "krovopiĭtsa" in Russian. All of these terms are more likely carryovers from "ubyr," the Tatar word for "witch," brought to the Slavic states through interaction with the pre-Ottoman Turks.*

even of having denied their existence and reality; others will blame me for having employed my time in discussing this matter, which is considered as frivolous and useless by many sensible people. Whatever may be thought of it, I shall be satisfied with myself for having sounded a question which appeared to me important in a religious point of view. For, if the return of vampires is real, it is of import to defend it, and prove it; and if it is illusory, it is of consequence to the interests of religion to undeceive those who believe in its truth, and destroy an error which may produce dangerous effects.

The revenants of Hungary, or vampires, which form the principal object of this dissertation, are men who have been dead a considerable time, sometimes more, sometimes less; who leave their tombs, and come and disturb the living, sucking their blood, appearing to them, making a noise at their doors and in their houses, and lastly, often causing their death. They are named vampires, or d'oupires, which signifies, they say, in Slavonic, a leech. The only way to be delivered from their haunting, is to disinter them, cut off their head, impale them, burn them, or pierce their heart.

Several systems have been propounded to explain the return and apparition of the vampires. Some persons have denied and rejected them as chimerical, and as an effect of the prepossession and ignorance of the people of these countries, where they are said to return.

Others have thought that these people were not really dead, but that they had been interred alive, and returned naturally out of their tombs.

Others believe that these people are truly dead, but that God, by a particular permission or command, permits or commands them to come back to earth, and resume for a time their own body; for when they are exhumed, their bodies are found entire, their blood red and fluid, and their limbs supple and pliable.

Others maintain that it is the demon who causes these revenants to appear, and by their means does all the harm he can both to men and animals...

Vampires in their graves returned to life after a certain time, and their soul does not forsake them absolutely until after the entire dissolution of their body, and when the organs of life, being absolutely broken, corrupted, and deranged, they can no longer by their agency perform any vital functions. Whence it happens, that the people of those countries impale them, cut off their heads, burn them, to deprive their spirit of all hope of animating them again, and of making use of them to molest the living.

Pliny, mentioning the soul of Hermotimes, of Lazomene, which absented itself from his body, and recounted various things that had been done afar off, which the spirit said it had seen, and which, in fact, could only be known to a person who had been present at them, says that the enemies of Hermotimes, named Cantandes, "burned that body, which gave hardly any sign of life, and thus deprived the soul of the means of returning to lodge in its envelop" ("donec cremato corpore interim semianimi, remeanti animæ vetut vaginam ademerint")[2]...

The grand difficulty is to explain how the vampires come out of their graves to haunt the living, and how they return to them again. For all the accounts that we see suppose the thing as certain, without informing us either of the way or the circumstances, which would, however, be the most interesting part of the narrative.

How a body covered with four or five feet of earth, having no room to move about and disengage itself, wrapped up in linen, covered with pitch, can make its way out, and come back upon the earth, and there occasion such effects as are related of it; and how after that it returns to its former state, and re-enters underground, where it is found sound, whole, and full of blood, and in the same condition as a living body? Will it be said that these bodies evaporate through the ground without opening it, like the water and vapors which enter into the earth, or proceed from it, without sensibly deranging its particles? It was to be wished that the accounts which have been given us concerning the return of the vampires had been more minute in their explanations of this subject.

Supposing that their bodies do not stir from their graves, that it is only their phantoms which appear to the living, what cause produces and animates these phantoms? Can it be the spirit of the defunct, which has not yet forsaken them, or some demon, which makes their apparition in a fantastic and borrowed body? And if these bodies are merely phantomlike, how can they suck the blood of living people? We always find ourselves in a difficulty to know if these appearances are natural or miraculous.

A sensible priest related to me, a little while ago, that, traveling in Moravia, he was invited by M. Jeanin, a canon of the cathedral at Olmutz, to accompany him to their village, called Liebava, where he had been appointed commissioner by the consistory of the bishopric, to take information concerning the fact of a certain famous vampire, which had caused much confusion in this village of Liebava some years before.

The case proceeded. They heard the witnesses, they observed the usual forms of the law. The witnesses deposed that a certain notable inhabitant of Liebava had often disturbed the living in their beds at night, that he had come out of the cemetery, and had appeared in several houses three or four years ago; that his troublesome visits had ceased because a Hungarian stranger, passing through the village at the time of

---

[2]   *The Latin here simply echoes the translation that Calmet gives directly before it, and is quoted from Pliny's* Naturalis Historia *(c. 77-79), Lib. VII.*

these reports, had boasted that he could put an end to them, and make the vampire disappear. To perform his promise, he mounted on the church steeple, and observed the moment when the vampire came out of his grave, leaving near it the linen clothes in which he had been enveloped, and then went to disturb the inhabitants of the village.

The Hungarian, having seen him come out of his grave, went down quickly from the steeple, took up the linen envelops of the vampire, and carried them with him up the tower. The vampire having returned from his prowlings, cried loudly against the Hungarian, who made him a sign from the top of the tower that if he wished to have his clothes again he must fetch them; the vampire began to ascend the steeple, but the Hungarian threw him down backwards from the ladder, and cut his head off with a spade. Such was the end of this tragedy...

Will it be said that the devil can subtilize these bodies, and give them power to penetrate through the ground without disturbing it, to glide through the cracks and joints of a door, to pass through a key-hole, to lengthen or shorten themselves, to reduce themselves to the nature of air, or water, to evaporate through the ground—in fine, to put them in the same state in which we believe the bodies of the blessed will be after the Resurrection, and in which was that of our Saviour after his resurrection, who showed himself only to whom he thought proper, and who without opening the doors, appeared suddenly in the midst of his disciples, and said, "Pax vobis"?[3]

But should it be allowed that the demon could reanimate these bodies, and give them the power of motion for a time, could he also lengthen, diminish, rarefy, subtilize the bodies of these ghosts, and give them the faculty of penetrating through the ground, the doors and windows? There is no appearance of his having received this power from God, and we cannot even conceive that an earthly body, material and gross, can be reduced to that state of subtlety and spiritualization without destroying the configuration of its parts and spoiling the economy of its structure; which would be contrary to the intention of the demon, and render this body incapable of appearing, showing itself, acting and speaking, and, in short, of being cut to pieces and burned, as is commonly seen and practiced in Moravia, Poland, and Silesia. These difficulties exist in regard to those persons of whom we have made mention, who, being excommunicated, rose from their tombs, and left the church in sight of everybody.

We must then keep silence on this article, since it has not pleased God to reveal to us either the extent of the demon's power, or the way in which these things can be done. There is even much appearance of

---

[3]   *"Peace be to you." in the* Gospel of St. John, *xx, 26.*

illusion; and even if some reality were mixed up with it, we may easily console ourselves for our ignorance in that respect, since there are so many natural things which take place within us and around us, of which the cause and manner are unknown to us.

Chapter 22
Facere Quod in Se Est

Here's the thing, and every good detective knows it, though very few civilians ever really think about it. The truth is, detective work is often more about controlled empathy than anything else. Don't get me wrong—I'm not saying that an eye for detail isn't important, or that it doesn't require a strong stomach to deal with the kinds of things that a homicide detective sees on a regular basis. And to me, the challenge of putting the puzzle pieces of a crime scene together into a coherent picture is crucial. But when it comes down to it, a detective needs to be able to crawl into the minds and hearts of some very bad people, and yet still be able to crawl back out again.

You need to be able to care enough about a murder victim to be motivated to solve their murder, but not care so much that your emotions get in the way of your clear-headed, puzzle-solving ability. It's dangerous to care too much—not only will you be ineffective as a cop, but you'll also probably get an ugly divorce, drink a lot, and have an emotional breakdown after a while. And yet, God knows, I've seen what can happen to a detective who doesn't really care about the victims at all and only gets off on solving the case details. Those guys usually end very badly, and where the overly-caring guys usually die alone, the uncaring guys too often take other people with them.

Or when you're working with a suspect, trying to elicit a confession—that's when you need that controlled empathy the most. The Cook County State's Attorney's office is a big fan of confessions, even more than physical evidence. DNA, boot prints, fingerprints— those things are far more solid and reliable than eyewitness accounts (you'd be shocked at how malleable and untrustworthy the human memory really is), but nothing sways a jury more than an actual human being saying, "I killed her," or "I watched him kill her," and that's all that they're looking for, when it comes right down to it. We detectives are in the business of solving crimes—the State's Attorneys are in the business of convicting criminals, so all that they really want is a case that wins with the jury. That's one of the many reasons why we cops have to make sure that we're getting our facts right to begin with.

And yes, people really do confess, even to murder. Oh, it's not like on those television shows, where slick murderers hide behind unwavering lies, or where punks break down the second they start getting questioned, but it does happen. And it doesn't involve strong-arming the suspect—that never works well, at least in my opinion. It's usually a long, unpleasant process that takes hours and hours of ever-deepening layers of confessions. As a buddy of mine on the force has argued repeatedly, it almost always starts with "I don' know nuthin'" kinds of answers, where the guy denies everything—he'd deny his own mother's name, if he thought it would get him off. If you tried to beat a confession out of him then, all you'd end up with is more lies to sort out later.

No, you've got to do this careful balance act of putting enough pressure on the guy that he *wants* to tell you *something* to make it stop, and yet making him feel like you're his best friend in the world, there to help him when the rest of his posse is hanging him out to dry. After an hour or two, he'll slip with a detail that he'd meant to hide, or he'll toss you a bone, just to get the questioning over with. "Well, I guess I heard somethin' about this girl…" just burbles out.

You get the guy a Coke, because he's been talking for hours. Maybe you even sit down and eat a hot dog with him. You talk with him like he's a buddy, and you start trying to make a connection with him. Controlled empathy. You hide how much this murdering piece of filth disgusts you, and you talk about the Cubs, about growing up in the city, or about women. And that's where things get weird.

In order to get him to talk, you have to make it seem like it's *safe* for him to talk to you. Forget the tape recorder. Forget the guys watching us from behind one-way glass. Forget that every word you're saying is being scrutinized in my mind for slips and cracks and flaws. Forget all of that, and let's just talk, man-to-man. You pretend to like him, even though you suspect that he's a kidnapper, or a rapist, or a murderer, or all of the above—and you have to make part of yourself *actually* find something to like about him, or else you can't sell it. More controlled empathy.

So you talk about girls, and then a couple of hours later, you talk about how they dress, and then a couple of hours after that, you talk about how they kind of *deserve* to be hurt, what with how they tease everyone, and all the while that you're drinking that Coke with this scum, you're listening for any word, watching for any little facial twitch that gives him away. You tell him about the girl's family, and how they need closure. You point out the inconsistencies in his story, and you help him to realize that he's definitely going down for *something* here, and that you're the white knight who can save him from the worst of it. Maybe then, he remembers that, well, maybe he *saw* something—he's a *witness*, not a murderer. And he starts to tell a different story that's at least a little more like the truth.

He talks about *watching* the girl being assaulted, and that's when you find yourself having to go to the darkest places within yourself. "I bet she *wanted* it..." you mumble, terrifyingly hoping that this pointless excuse for a human being sitting across the table from you will take the bait and join in. When and if he finally does, you have to squelch that moral part of you that wants to vomit, or to leap across the table and strangle him with your own hands—instead, you smile and nod and egg him on. By that time, he *wants* to share it, he *wants* to justify himself to *someone*... and now he trusts *you*. And thanks to that trust that you've built up all day with him, you can finally betray him, trap him in his own words, and toss his hide to the State's Attorney to lock away forever. If you're lucky.

The hardest part of days like that is going back home to your family. I mean, you *yearn* for it, and they bring your dead heart back to life again, but at the same time, you're looking at their loving, smiling, innocent faces, and remembering the kind of people that are still out there in the world, waiting for them.

It can be a truly horrible job to have to empathize with the last thoughts of a victim to understand how and why she died, or to have to empathize with a murderer's motivations for killing so that you can actually find and arrest him, or to have to empathize with his feelings so that you can trap him in his own confession, and then to have to turn that empathy off at the end of the day so that you can eat a chicken dinner with your family that evening without crying, or so that you can sleep that night without nightmares. But then again, to *not* do the job is to give the world over to the kinds of people who do the kinds of things you're trying to stop, and I just can't do that.

All of this is to say that when Rhiannon turned her voodoo against me for the second time that evening and made me want her again, she picked both the easiest target and the worst one imaginable.

*   *   *

The Angel just stood there, smiling, pointing his pistol. But Rhiannon slipped from his side and began to glide toward me. Every step was the most graceful, sensuous movement imaginable—it was more like a slow-moving dance than it was simply walking. Her left arm was still cradled in that green silk sling, useless because of Durant's knife strike. Part of me ached to see her in pain—how could he have done that to such a goddess? And another part of me—the detective part—wondered why he'd used such a strange, iron knife to do it. She took another step toward me, and I saw her perfect body moving beneath her green satin dress, and I couldn't look away. I didn't *want* to look away.

She began speaking—and, just like before, I realized that I wasn't really hearing the words, so much as becoming lost in the music of them. Even though I was still in the car, and she was several feet from me, I could swear that she was whispering the words to me, and I honestly thought that I could feel her warm, breath against my ear. I smelled her dusky, perfumed scent, and I opened the door to get out of the car.

I don't know why I did it. Maybe she'd told me to get out of the car, or maybe I just wanted to get closer to her. All I know is that I got up from behind the wheel and started to walk toward her. She smiled at that, and my heart began beating like a jackhammer in my chest. That smile—that incredible, sensual smile, with her eyelids half-closed, and her tongue slowly licking the inside of her perfectly red lips. I'd never wanted anyone or anything as much as I wanted her at that moment. Her thick, red hair was shining in the light of the streetlamps and the moonlight, and her eyes were green fire. I was only vaguely aware of Angel by now—I had no idea what he was doing, and I didn't care. Rhiannon was everything in my world. As she reached out to me, I heard thunder in the background, and all I could think of was keeping the impending rain off of her perfect hair. I reflexively remembered that I had an umbrella sitting in the back seat of the car.

A pink umbrella.

A pink umbrella with a kitten on it.

A pink umbrella with a kitten on it that my daughter had given me to help protect her daddy.

"You take good care of Daddy, don't you?" Joanna had said to her in response. My wife, Joanna. My wife whom I loved, and my children whom I loved. My daughter who'd wanted to protect her Daddy from the dangers of the world with her little pink umbrella. Strange that such silly things can sometimes be so profound.

To be honest, my emotions had been jerked around a lot through all of this—about Karen, about Rhiannon, whatever—but no matter what else happened, one thing remained a constant in my life. I love my family. I love my family more than I love breathing, and nothing will ever change that—not even some red-haired freaky water witch.

Remember what I said about controlled empathy? It can be so easy for a detective to empathize with the foulest people on the planet—we're trained to do it, and we do it every day—so it can become kind of a reflex for us. Rhiannon was playing on that reflex, pumping it up to a near-infinite degree of desire for her. But then, we're also trained to turn that empathy off when we need to, so that we can get back to being the people we *want* to be and not get lost into becoming the very people we *don't* want to be. All it took for me to get back to myself was a trigger— in this case, a ridiculous little pink umbrella, handed to me by a little girl who loved me innocently and completely.

I instinctively pulled my pistol, pointing it at Rhiannon. I mumbled something about her holding still—I may have even told her that she was under arrest. I really can't recall. It was like waking up suddenly from a deep sleep, and it's all a bit fuzzy in my memory now.

She laughed coquettishly and cocked her head to the side. She said something else that I didn't catch, but the tone was dismissive and playful. I started to lower my pistol, feeling myself getting drowsy again, but then I thought of the umbrella and Chelsea's face, and steeled myself against this witch in front of me.

But where was the Angel? I spun around, remembering that the last time I saw him, he was pointing his own pistol at me. I tried to keep an eye on Rhiannon as I pivoted right and left, looking for the Angel. He was nowhere in sight. Where was he? And how long had I been listening to Rhiannon's voice, becoming lost to everything else? A minute? *Ten* minutes?

I turned back to her, but she was moving away from me, toward the sidewalk.

"Stop!" I shouted. She smiled and continued to glide away from me, saying something in her musical voice that made me want to let her go.

"Stop!" I shouted again, more to emphasize it to myself than to her. I felt my finger begin to press onto the trigger, but I didn't know if I'd actually be able to shoot her, if it came down to it. A slight frown flickered across her perfect face, and she said something else, while shaking her head. This time, I remember catching one of the words— "*family…*"

I pulled the trigger, and shot her full in the chest. No hesitation whatsoever.

Rhiannon slammed back from the force of it, banging against the fence. She yelped in pain, and her face became a mask of hatred and evil intent. She turned and glared at the fence behind her, then back at me. The bullet had gone through her, and the hole in her chest was a bloody mess, but she seemed more hurt by hitting the fence than by being shot. Why?

I fired again, but this time I missed—because where Rhiannon had once stood, now there limped a large, red wolf. I didn't even notice the change. The wolf snarled at me, and then turned away. It was obvious that she was planning to retreat again, but then she paused and turned back at me. Her green eyes narrowed, and I could tell that she was going to pounce. So I fired again, straight at her head.

Again, the force knocked her back a bit, but she seemed to just shake it off. Why had Durant's little knife done more damage to her than being shot twice with my pistol?

I didn't know all of the "how's" and the "why's," but the detective in me started trying to piece together the details. Was it the form that she'd been in? Would it make a difference whether she was a bird or a wolf? Probably not. Was it the kind of projectile—a bladed weapon versus a slug of lead? Again, probably not. Then it must have been the actual, physical material—the lead of my bullets had caused some damage, though not enough to really hurt her, but Durant's iron knife…

Iron…

That's why banging into the fence behind her had hurt her more than the bullet had—because the fence was made from wrought iron. It was rusty, bent, and twisted, but it was still iron, and that made it a weapon that I could use.

She bounded at me, but her wounded left foreleg made her attack clumsier than it should have been, and I was able to dodge to the side as she bounded past me. I jumped onto the hood of the car, and then rolled over it, onto the sidewalk. I turned back toward her, but she was gone.

I'd hoped that she'd be angry enough with me by now that she'd stay and continue the fight, rather than trying to get away again. But as I waited, all I saw in front of me was the empty basketball court. I stood there for a minute, my pistol pointed in front of me, straining to hear some sound that might tell me which direction she'd gone. I looked up, into the night sky, hoping to see a red bird or something flying there, but it was empty.

But then, a bright red alley cat leapt onto the hood of the car, favoring its left leg. There was a gash on its forehead, and blood on its chest, and its angry, green eyes burned at me as it hissed and bared its fangs. I pointed my gun at it and hoped that the cat would do something stupid. Rhiannon was a persuader, a manipulator—not really a combatant. I was hoping that, though she'd wanted to toy with me before, she now was so focused on killing me that she would be making her decisions in terms of supernatural strength, and not in terms of tactics.

The cat padded toward me, across the hood, picking up speed as it went. I backed up, away from the car, still pointing my gun at her. At the last second, the cat leapt from the hood toward me—and suddenly, it wasn't a cat in the air at all, but that wolf again, bearing down on me with all of its red, angry mass of claws and fangs and fur. I fired one more time as I jumped to the side and rolled away from her, onto the sidewalk.

As I heard her yelp in pain, I spun back to fire again, only to see the wolf's struggling body impaled on the twisted iron fence. It was a corny old trick, and I'd seen it in a dozen old movies, but it still worked. The more she wriggled, the more the iron dug into and ripped her flesh. She flung her head back and howled, and then went limp, whimpering. As I watched, her form turned back to that of Rhiannon—perfect and beautiful, even with all of the bloody wounds. Several of the gnarled pieces of iron had gashed her, but one long, sharp fencepost was sticking through her belly. She howled and wriggled, and tried to push herself off of it with her right hand, but it looked like even the barest touch of the iron was painful to her. She yanked her hand back reflexively, as if it she'd burned it.

She stopped struggling and consciously smiled at me that perfect, false smile, and said something in her singsong voice. In the back of my mind, part of me wanted to reach over and pull her to safety, cradling her in my arms and nursing her back to health—maybe then, she would *truly* love me as much as I loved her.

But this time, that thought was *only* in the back of my mind. I was beginning to feel the difference between my own mind and the part that Rhiannon was twisting with her words, and her magicks weren't going to work on me again. Rhiannon was realizing that at about the same time, and I heard the tone of her voice change, even as her face bent into a scowl. Something in the back of my mind felt dark and cold and scared, and that part wanted to run away and hide.

But I controlled that part again, pushing it down and away from me. Instead, I holstered my piece and leaned back against the car to watch her. I watched her until her body stopped moving altogether, and her voice stopped echoing in my head. I watched her until her eyes finally closed, and then I watched her for several more minutes after that.

I went over to her and checked her pulse. I took a deep, long breath, and then walked back to my car, got in, and drove away. I didn't look back, except at the umbrella still sitting in my back seat.

*   *   *

I drove down the Kennedy Expressway, then onto the Dan Ryan over to 35th Street. For some reason, it's always therapeutic for me to drive on the Dan Ryan, even when the traffic is bumper-to-bumper. Maybe it's just having grown up in Chicago, but something about it says *permanence* to me… *familiarity*. There's no other drive quite like it, especially when you're driving north across the river and you can see the Sears Tower—since that's what I'll *always* call it—up there on the right. It's not what I'd call a pretty drive, of course—not like Lake Shore Drive, or something like that. But it's just so… I dunno… so *Chicago*…

As I pulled onto 35th—that's when that warm, familiar feeling started to give way to a more eerie one. I mean, it was still relatively early in the evening, and I knew that there'd be cops all over the place once I got to HQ, but for those couple of blocks from the Dan Ryan to the HQ, there wasn't anyone on the road anywhere. Of course, there's only so spooked that you can really get, when there's a Starbucks right there on the corner at State Street, but it was weird nevertheless. Granted, it was beginning to rain by now, so I wasn't expecting many pedestrians, but unless it's three in the morning, there's always at least *someone* on the streets in Chicago.

So I passed under the train tracks and I kept looking for at least *someone* as I drove on by the De La Salle Institute, heading east. Every time I go past there, I'm reminded of how Tony loves to tell everybody that he went to De La Salle—and especially that he'd had Chet Bulger as a coach. Of course, that was before this particular building had even been built, but hey, Tony's never been one to get tripped up by little things like details.

I turned into the parking lot, and still there was no one to be seen. I wasn't really looking forward to meeting with Bainbridge, and all that I really wanted to do was go home and see Joanna and the kids. I wondered if Tony was there with them right now. For a second, I debated about calling him to find out, but then I thought better about it— the odds of Tony having his cell phone on and at hand were roughly the same as the odds of the Cubs winning the next World Series... or *any* World Series. I debated about calling Joanna, too—in fact, I even dialed her number and let it ring once, but then I hung up. What would I tell her about why I was calling? Did I even want to start that kind of conversation, right before heading inside to talk with Bainbridge? I promised myself that I'd call her as soon as I got back out to the car. A reward for going through the next few minutes.

I got out of my car and started walking into the building, carrying Chelsea's little umbrella to keep the worst of the rain off of me. Yes, I could've taken the black one and been more professional, but right then, I needed more than just to stay dry—I needed to feel loved. I was beginning to have a lot of positive associations with that umbrella.

Just about the time that I got to that funky steel sculpture that no one really likes, I heard something that made me stop dead in my tracks. For a quick second, it almost sounded like the crackling of dry kindling in a fire—almost a pleasant sound... for a quick second. But then, as it got louder, I felt a chill as I recognized it as the same, dry, skittering noise that I'd heard before, back in Sydor's building. A noise like the sound of hundreds of cicadas skittering across the same dead tree. The sound of a horde of revenants, closing in.

And there I was, without my stick.

I kicked myself yet again for giving the Matteh ha Shelomoh to Tony, especially since it meant that yet again, Durant had been right. I really hated that.

The sounds seemed to be coming from everywhere, all at once. I dropped the umbrella and drew my pistol, and then I remembered Durant telling me that the gun wouldn't do any good, that it would just distract me. I'll be honest with you—that was really beginning to annoy me. Years of practice on shooting ranges, a great handgun that I will *always* maintain is better than the Glock, and I keep finding out how useless all of that is when I'm dealing with rejects from the creature features.

The rain started picking up, but in and amidst the raindrops, I began to see movement—shadows pouring over the rooftop of the De La Salle building across the street and down its light-colored walls, like streaks of dark ink running in the rain. They skittered down the walls in wavy lines, like ants do, each following the other ones' trails. I could hear their sickening clicking and gurgling sounds getting louder, even as the rain picked up.

There were dozens of them—maybe hundreds. Even if my gun *would* be effective against them, they'd still overwhelm me in moments. I turned and began to run full-tilt toward the building. I knew that the doors wouldn't stop them, but maybe I could get a tactical advantage if I could get inside. I mean, over a thousand people work in the building during normal work hours—maybe I could at least find *someone* to help me now.

The sound of skittering, babbling, gibbering things behind me was becoming deafening. I fought the urge to turn my head, but I knew that I just needed to get to those doors. That needed to be the only thing on my mind at that moment, and turning my head would only slow me down that much more. I ran faster than I'd ever run before in my life.

I almost made it.

With a shriek, something jumped on my back and dug its nails into my shoulder. I jumped backwards, toward the Haymarket Riot Monument, and bashed it against the stone pedestal until the thing dropped off. Then I spun around and fired. The side of the revenant's head exploded with yellow bile, and it rolled onto its side, hissing. But it wasn't dead.

And while I was dealing with that one, dozens more poured onto the grass and sidewalk next to me, hopping and climbing over one another, growling and hissing, their red eyes glowing in the dark. The rain made the torn rags of their clothing glossy and black. They looked like a swarm of cockroaches, and they smelled like rotted meat.

But they didn't attack. They paused for a moment, as if sizing me up. Some climbed onto the steel sculpture to get a better view. A few more started skittering up onto the brick walls of the building, trying to get between me and the doors. I started to inch my way over there, my gun pointed at the clump of them in front of me. And then one of them began to speak.

"Policeman…" it hissed in a wet, phlegm-coated voice.

"Wh-what do you want?" I replied, trying my best to sound brave.

"The world…" it answered, and began to cough its way through a high, sick giggle. The other revenants began to laugh along with the first, clicking their sharp, rotted teeth together. "But tonight, naught but thee. Tonight is the night when all things shall come to fruition, little policeman. Tonight is the night when the Lord shall begin his reign…"

Suddenly, my cell phone rang. I jumped instinctively. Here I was, surrounded by these unholy things, and the sound of the cell phone made me jump. I whipped it out and opened it, hoping against hope that it was someone who might be able to help me. Did Durant even *have* a phone? But as soon as it opened, I saw that it was Joanna calling.

"Tom?" she yelled, panic in her voice.

"Joanna!" was all I got out before I was attacked from behind again, and the phone fell from my hands, onto the sidewalk. The revenant that I'd shot was back up and well, and it cackled as it tore at me again with its talons. It flung me to the side, and I crashed against the wall of the building. As it leapt at me again, I fired three shots into its chest, splattering more of its green-yellow goo as the creature flipped backwards into a crumpled mess on the ground. Why didn't they all just attack?

"Tom?" Joanna screamed again. "Can you hear me? Please help us!"

I watched as the lead revenant approached the phone, scrambling along the ground toward it. He reached a long, dark tongue out from between his teeth and flicked at it, leaving a thick, foul mucus on the phone. "She's a juicy dainty, this wife of thine, policeman," the thing whispered hoarsely toward me. "I should wish to taste her for myself…"

I pushed off from the wall and lunged for it, but the thing was too fast. It scooped the phone off of the ground with lightning speed, just as another revenant hopped off of the brick wall and crashed against me, smashing me into the pedestal of the memorial again. It tore a chunk out of my arm with its claws, and I dropped my gun, even as I felt my ribs cracking in my chest. I slumped down to the ground in helpless pain.

"We're at 2nd Presbyterian, Tom, but—" Joanna continued, and I heard something crash on the other end of the phone. 2nd Presbyterian Church—that was just up Michigan Avenue, only two miles to the north of me. "Dear God, what is this thing?!?" she screamed again, and I heard Chelsea screaming in the background. And with that, the revenant snapped the cell phone shut, giggling.

"I shouldst think that this is enough," it hissed at me. "To know that thy last moments have been spent, hearing thy family at sticky-sweet play with my Lord…"

I tried to get to my feet, to fight back, to do anything, but I couldn't. I could feel my head swimming from loss of blood, and my ribs stabbed at me like hot knitting needles in my side.

"Don't..." was all that I could get out.

The lead revenant laughed its horrific laugh again, and the storm broke into thunder and lightning. The night was alive with the sound of revenants clicking and cackling and coughing their bile onto one another.

"Shall I provide thee one last gift before we feast?" the thing said, cocking its head at me. "Shall I...?" The other revenants laughed in delight, urging the thing on. The creature smiled, showing its shards of broken, yellowed teeth. Bits of ragged meat were wedged between them in the cracks, and I was overwhelmed by its reeking breath as it leaned in to whisper to me.

"There *is* no 'Bainbridge'..." it hissed. It licked its face with its tongue. "Not since we devoured his carcass yesternight..." The swarm's cackling rose to a fever pitch.

So all of this was just another trap. That's why "Bainbridge" called me and demanded that I come in right away—to get me away from Durant. And to get me away from my family? They faked a call from him, all to get me here, now, and finish me off alone. Maybe they even knew that Tony had the Matteh ha Shelomoh, and I'd be defenseless against these things.

I was bleeding out, all over the place, and I watched as the revenants skittered closer, licking the blood off of the sidewalk. They were like junkies, licking cocaine out of the carpet when it spills. Durant had described them like vampire wannabes—with only some of the same strengths. But then I remembered that he'd also said *with all of the weaknesses...*

I was no vampire scholar, but I'd seen my share of movies. And I remembered that little cross on the chain around Durant's neck. With my left hand, I mopped up some of the blood from my right arm, and I painted a thick vertical line of blood onto the pedestal, above my head. The lead revenant cocked its head again, licking its lips in anticipation of my blood, but interested to see what I was up to. I mopped up more blood, and pulled my left hand horizontally, across the vertical line, *forming a cross.*

The revenants hissed and leapt backwards, as if stung by something. They were drawn toward the blood, but repulsed by the cross, and it was torture for them. I remembered what Durant had told me about why the cross worked—not because the shape is scary to them, or because it has any kind of magical powers, but because of the faith of the person *with* the cross. And that's when I realized it. That's when I realized that I knew what I *really* needed to do.

"Dear God," I said, each word making my ribs dig deeper into my side. At the sound of my praying, the revenants skittered farther back. "P-please keep my... family..." I couldn't even finish the prayer for the pain. *Please keep my family safe, somehow,* I prayed in my head.

I coughed, and blood came up. "Jesus..." I tried to pray again, but I couldn't get any more words out. But the revenants were shrieking, as if in pain. Tears welled up in my eyes. I thought of the dream I'd had, of being powerless to save the people I loved. I thought of my children's smiles, of my wife's face. "*Please...*" I whispered. My side felt like it was on fire, and I began to black out.

Background
**From *Dissertatio Historico-Philosophica de Masticatione Mortuorum*
(Philip Rohr, 1679, trans. M. Summers)**

It is certain that the devil cannot raise the dead to life. This is a dogma divinely revealed to us. It is also manifest from all the arguments and reasons of sound philosophy, for such a thing is opposed to nature.

At the same time we do not deny that it has often happened and may very well be happening to-day that by the Divine permission the bodies of some who are dead issue from their graves owing to the agency of the devil and that these corpses perform various actions, or rather seem to perform such actions, and consequently they may also partake of food. Instances of this can be seen in Kornmannus, *De Miraculis Mortuorum*[1] II, cs. x and xiii; in Johan Georg Godelmann, whose work has been translated by Georg Schwartz, Rector of the University of Marburg, as *von Zaubern Hexen und unholden*[2] I, iv, 47; and in Delrio *Disquisitionum Magicarum*[3] Liber II, qu. 29. sect. 1. post medium 308, sqq. When he has given various examples from Pagan history of dead men who were supposed to have been raised from the tomb Delrio adds not impertinently: "Of a truth many an illusion and deception can be wrought by the Devil with regard to these mysterious happenings. For sometimes he will steal away the bodies of those who are dead, and he will substitute other phantasmal forms, which move exactly as though they were human and alive. And it is not unknown that he will enter into and possess the bodies of the deceased. Nay, moreover, he will sometimes cause the very corpses to appear to live, and this is done by his power (permitted to him) when he energizes and possesses them: and just as a pilot will move a vessel so will he move them, and he will compel these dead bodies exactly to imitate the actions and gestures of living men..."

The principal cause is the Devil himself who actually causes and

---

[1] De Miraculis Mortuorum *(1610, Heinrich Kornmann)*

[2] *Rohr abbreviates the common German title of* Tractatus De Magis, Veneficis Et Lamiis, Recte Cognoscendis Et Puniendis, Propter Varias & Controversas De Hac Quæstione Hominem Sententias *(1591, Johann Georg Godelmann)*

[3] Disquisitionum Magicarum Libri Sex *(1599, Martín Antonio Del Rio)*

brings about manduction[4] *by the dead.* There can be no doubt at all as
to his desire and his will to produce such an effect, for he is indeed the
craftiest of enemies (μυριοτεχνίτης hostis), a foe who is ever seeking
every occasion and opportunity to hurt and harm poor wretched mortals.
After death hatred no longer rages in the heart of a man, but it is always
raging in the temper of the demon whose sole pleasure and delight it is
to injure and destroy the human race at any time and in any way he may
be able to do so. He betrayed his inveterate malice indeed in his
contention with the Archangel S. Michael over the body of Moses, *S.
Jude,* 9. Many of the other lying wonders which he effects show us that
he is quite well able to produce this extraordinary manduction. We do
not allow that he has that power over the soul when it is separated by
death from the body, which is attributed to him by Delrio—far too
unguardedly as we conceive *(Disquisitiones Magicae,* q. 25); but that he
has a considerable power over the human body, in so far as God permits,
we would not venture to deny. "If God will, the *demon is able to distress
us during our lives, to torment us* with *horrible* dreams and disturb our
repose, to deform and distort our limbs, nay, to afflict us with sickness
and disease." This is the opinion of S. Cyprian of Carthage in his treatise
Quod Idola dii non sint[5] and these words are quoted by Binderus in his
treatise *De Causa Pestis.*[6] The Devil, to cite Delrio's exact phrase, is
able "to perform the most marvellous things with regard to dead bodies,
and to bring to pass such extraordinary happenings that it would seem as
if the very corpses were alive again and informed by intellect and soul.
He can, for example, cause blood to flow from the wounds of a dead
man in the presence of his murderer; he can also cause dead bodies to
remain whole and entire without corruption, yet this can happen
naturally either through the art of the embalmer, or from the peculiar
nature of the place where the deceased are buried, and sometimes even
from the kind of death; and this incorruption is often effected by the
mysterious power of the demon, so that to answer his purpose for a long
while at all events the remains shall not be cremated." It is indeed quite
impossible to give any account of all the extraordinary happenings
which the power of the demon can bring to pass in connexion with dead
bodies. Nor can there be any doubt at all that he can produce
manduction, and this he causes to be accompanied by a horrible
grunting noise...

---

4   *"Manduction" refers to the act of chewing and eating*
5   Quod Idola dii non sint *is actually a forgery often wrongly attributed to St.
   Cyprian of Carthage (208-258)—and by no less luminary minds than those
   of Augustine and Jerome.*
6   Αἰτιολογικον Theologicum, de Causis Pestis, methodo Analytica explicatis
   *(1611, Christoph Binder). Binder had earlier served with theologian Jakob
   Andreae in defense of Lutheran orthodoxy at the court in Weimar in 1570.*

The instrumental cause of this manducation must logically be these human corpses.[7] It is plain that naturally the demon is unable to perform any corporeal action, because he has no body of his own proper to himself. Wherefore if he wishes to produce any such action he abuses our human nature by energizing with activity some body that is purely passive, or else he effects this by falsely vitalizing with movements certain bodies of dead men as if they were themselves of themselves endowed with motion, so that they may stimulate such effects as in the natural order of things would proceed from a body animated by the soul. In his treatise *De Causa Pestis* Binderus tells us that the Devil is able to employ natural objects and natural causes to produce the effects he desires. Accordingly the Devil cannot bring about the act of manducation unless he employ some other suitable body to whom this act is natural, as his instrument or agent, and therefore because this act is natural to a living body that most foul enemy of the human race enters those dead bodies and by these he fulfils his desire, although being dead of themselves they must remain passive and without movement unless they are moved and energized by some superior cause. Yet it seems that certain writers are doubtful whether he can be said to perform the act of manducation by means of a corpse. For example, Conrad Schlüsselburg[8] writes: "es ist gewiss dass diss Schmetzen nicht geschehe von den Cörperm der Todten in Grabe."[9] To this I reply: Technically this may be true, that is, if the act of manducation is considered as being a separate and definite operation, but none the less it is effected by the demon, as Garmann precisely states in his well-known treatise,[10] where he declares that the Devil may in a grave make curious noises, he may knock, he may lap like some thirsty animal, he may chaw, grunt and groan. But yet the demon cannot perform these actions unless he use the body as an instrument for this manducation. In the same way legend says that Pope Sylvester II,[11] who on account of his great learning in common fable was reputed to be an adept in occultism, kept certain bones in a shrine or an ark and thence upon occasion was heard to arise a murmuring and

---

[7] *For more information on chewing by the dead, see also Michaël Ranft's excellent later work,* De Masticatione Mortuorum in Tumulis Liber *(1725), where he writes of* "die schmatzenden Toten" *(the "smacking dead")*

[8] *in* Oratio Funebris: De Vita Et Obitu Reverendissimi Viri, Pietate, Doctrina, Humanitateet Constantia Praestantis Iohannis Wigandi *(1591, Conrad Schlüsselburg)*

[9] *"It is not certain how this action is performed by the corpse of the dead in the grave"*

[10] De Miraculis Mortuorum *(1670, Johann Christian Frederick Garmann)*

[11] *Gerbert d'Aurillac (served as Pope from 999-1003); a man with great scientific knowledge and integrity, who was also denounced for sorcery—he was said to have built a bronze head which spoke to him through a demon named Meridiana*

certain noise. The story is told by Schlüsselburg who says he had it from Cardinal Lodovico Simonetta.[12] However this may be, there can be no doubt that witches can exercise their power over dead bodies and raise them up so that they appear to be alive both by their walk and their gestures, examples of which may be found in many authors who have written upon these subjects. This is further confirmed by the $αυτοψία$[13] of certain authors who describe that corpses have devoured their rotting flesh and with their teeth torn to tatters the cerements and shroud. Wherefore it may very fairly be said that these dead bodies do perform the act of manducation, although they do not do this of their own initiative but by some foreign power, which is to say that they are merely the instruments that cause this operation. But if some person objects that I am allowing too much power to the demon by saying that he has influence over these bodies which, as all other things, are in the keeping of Almighty God, then will I thus make reply, (1) The power of the devil is straitly *[sic]* restricted, yea, and limited by Divine Providence; it is kept well within bounds and he is only permitted to exercise it for the just trial and the proving of good men. (2) We do not allow the demon, by arguing that he has this restricted power over dead bodies, any greater power than the Holy Scriptures allow him, for it is written that he is able most grievously to possess living men, and he on occasion may afflict even the holiest with terrible diseases. And it has been said in a Commentary upon the Epistle of S. Paul to the Galatians that if it be heaven's will we are all of us so far as our bodies and mere temporal things in the power of the demon $εις την ἀπώλειαν$, (fitted for destruction)[14]...

That the devil delights to mislead and bemuse our senses is plainly stated by Gisbert Voet in his *Disputationes Selectae,*[15] part I, "De Operatione Daemonum," and these are his words: "The devil can cheat and deceive a man's five senses and the organs of sense in more ways than one. For example the evil spirit can mock the ears by imaginary

---

12 *Bishop of Lodi in northern Italy from 1537-1568, who also presided at the Council of Trent*

13 *"autopsy"*

14 *Rohr appears here to be alluding to the Apostle Paul's* Letter *to the Romans, ix, 22-23, rather than to a commentary on his* Letter *to the Galatians, as he claims. He also appears to be spuriously equating the word which Paul used for "destruction"—"ἀπώλειαν" or "apōleian"—with the proper name of the destroyer angel/demon whom the Apostle John speaks of in* Revelation, ix, 11—"Απολλυων" or "Apollyōn"—as if Paul had been alluding to a demon in his letter (i.e.; that sinners being "fitted for ἀπώλειαν" would be synonymous with being "in the power of the demon [Απολλυων]")*

15 Disputationes Selectae *(1655, Gijsbert Voet—better known as Gisbertus Voetius, the famous Dutch Calvinist theologian who pastored at Vlijmen and taught at the University of Utrecht)*

noises, etc." ...

In some cases a wise precaution has attempted to counteract these operations of evil spirits by certain amulets and charms, and in some cases it would seem that reliance upon these periapts is merely superstitious. Since, therefore, obviously they are not all of the same value we will divide them into two general classes, the true and the false. Among the false we may at once include that old custom of the Jews which is described by Schickhardus[16] in his works upon Hebrew rites and ceremonies. For there he mentions that the Jews clasp the hands of the dead so that in their disposing they fancifully form the name of Almighty God שדי.[17] And this, the learned Buxtorf observes in his *De Synagoga Iudaeorum,*[18] xxv, inspires Satan with the greatest fear and he dare not so such as approach the body. This practice is also mentioned by the eminent Dilherrus in his *Disputationes Academicae*[19] tom. I (p. 510), where speaking of this custom of the Jews he says that sometimes they draw a long thread from the garments of the deceased and this they twist about his fingers so that it seems to represent the sacred letters שדי. Some may think this efficacious, but for my part I cannot agree with them. I can scarce believe that the letters שדי in some way impressed upon the hands of the deceased would drive away the evil spirit. Assuredly if they were impressed upon the hands of a living man the demon would not any the less spare to tempt him, to endeavour to lead him astray, and to weary him with wicked suggestions. For the same reason I should not perhaps put such faith in the consecration of cemeteries, *[loquitur Haereticus]*[20] which is treated at great length by Durandus and by Angelus Clavassius, who are quoted in the work of Kornmannus to which we have already referred. Delrio tells us that the demon has indeed a certain power over the bodies of the dead, and he may indeed take their form and appear in this shape; and his power is especially great over those which are buried in unconsecrated ground...

A practice that is not uncommon in certain districts is to place a morsel of new earth upon the lips of the dead, and in this they would seem to be following an old custom of the Jews... Some deeming this not altogether sufficient before they close the lips of the dead place a stone and a coin in the cold mouth, so that in his grave he may bite on these and refrain from gnawing further. That this custom still persists in

---

[16]   *Wilhelm Schickard (1592-1635)*

[17]   *"Shaddai," commonly used as part of the more complete title,* "אֵל שַׁדַּי" *("El Shaddai," or "God Almighty")*

[18]   De Synagoga Iudaeorum *(1603, Johannes Buxtorf)*

[19]   Disputationes academicae, praecipue philologicae *(1652, Johann Michael Dilherr)*

[20]   *"thus says a heretic"—Rohr self-deprecates as he disagrees with common theological thought of his day*

very many parts of Saxony we learn on the authority of Gabriel Rollenhagen...[21]

Theodore Thummius in his tractate that we have already quoted[22] and Johann Conrad Dammhauers[23] most excellently sum up for us the true remedies by which we may oppose these devices of Satan, by which indeed, we may defend ourselves against all these ghostly deceits of the devil as also against the power of his sworn servants and bondslaves, sorcerers and witches. The first of these remedies is to have a lively trust and firm faith in Our Blessed Lord Who hath crushed the serpent's head,[24] and withal to nourish in our hearts a purpose of amendment and a hatred of sin. The second is the Word of God, that sharp sword which the Holy Apostles have put into our hands, relying upon which weapon under the protection of God we may utterly foil and frustrate the open attacks and the dark ambushes of Satan.[25] The third protection is Prayer, the scourge of evil spirits, a sure safeguard against the wiles of the demon. The fourth protection is the help of the Holy Angels who by God's command are ever at our side to keep us safe, so that we may have no fear "of the arrow that flieth in the day, of the business that walketh about in the dark: of invasion, or of the noonday devil" (*Psalm,* Xff, 6). All these remedies are treated of at greater length in the works of our eminent Theologians.

---

[21]   *Also known as "Rollenhagius," a poet and humorist from Magdeburg most famous for his illustrated book,* Nucleus emblematum selectissimorum *(1611)*

[22]   Tractatus theologicus, de sagarum impietate, nocendi imbecillitate et poenae gravitate *(1622, Theodor Thumm)*

[23]   *Rohr is almost certainly—and again, somewhat inaccurately—referring to Johann Conrad Dannhauer's work,* Scheid- und Absage-Brief einem ungenannten Priester aus Cölln, auf sein Antwortschreiben über das zu Strassburg vom Teufel besessene adeliche Fräulein gegeben *(1654)*

[24]   *An allusion to the* Book of Genesis, iii, 13-14.

[25]   *An allusion to the sole offensive element in the armor of God in the* Letter to the Ephesians, vi, 11-17—all of the other pieces which the Apostle Paul lists as part of the armor are for defensive purposes.

Chapter 23
The Wrong Place at the Right Time

Apparently, Joanna had taken the children to eat at Eleven City Diner that night. We've always loved that place. It's a throwback to the great diners and delicatessens of the past, with great jazz playing in the background and a giant Chicago municipal flag hanging overhead. Eating there always feels like stepping back in time, to a nicer, warmer age, so we always turn off the cell phones and enjoy ourselves. Plus, the owner's mom always gives my kids suckers when we go there.

Joanna usually gets their Rubin's Reuben—arguably the best Reuben in the entire world, and I'm not kidding—but Chelsea always, *always* gets their Basil Pesto Omelette. I don't blame her, of course, but we keep suggesting that she try something different the next time we go there. Her response is always, "*Gotta* have my *petto*, Da-DEE!" and that's become a running joke in our home.

Going to Eleven City Diner has always been about family, about comfort food, about warm joy, and about innocence. That's what it had always been for us, before that night.

After dinner, Joanna and the kids had walked down Wabash to the Canady Le Chocolatier to get some gelatos. Knowing Joanna, I'd bet that she got herself a Dark Chocolate Truffle or two as well. They were walking out, under that green awning, when a teenager in a green T-shirt blocked their path.

"Yo…" he said, leering at Joanna.

"Excuse me," she said, trying to get past him. She debated about just stepping back into the Chocolatier, if he didn't move out of the way.

"My bad…" he said, stepping aside with a toothy grin. He patted Chelsea on the head as the family passed by him.

"Tha' hurted!" she said, sticking her bottom lip out at him.

"Keep moving," Joanna said to her and pulled her along the sidewalk, pushing the stroller with the twins just that much faster. She glanced back and watched the teenager step into the Chocolatier. That made her feel better—he'd been after chocolate, not her. But she was still a little rattled by the encounter. She reached into her purse and turned her phone back on, just in case.

They continued on to the parking lot where they'd parked, near the tracks on Balbo. All the way, Chelsea chattered on about how she wanted to go see the rockhopper penguins at the Shedd Aquarium again for her birthday.

"But that's what we did last year," Joanna reminded her. "Wouldn't you like to go somewhere else this year?"

"But tha's where my pengins is, Mom-MEE!" she replied, gelato smearing her face with pink. "Does somewhere else got pengins?"

Joanna started to tell her about the Lincoln Park Zoo, and how she thought that they probably had penguins, too—and lots of *other* animals as well—when she saw a couple of young men watching them from the sidewalk in front of the South Loop Club. At first, it was no big deal. There were people all over the place, even though it started to look like it was going to rain. But she saw that they *kept* watching them, and that they were both wearing green. She tried not to stare back, or to look frightened, but it was becoming increasingly difficult not to.

They walked into the lot, and got to the car. Joanna couldn't help glancing back to the Club, but the two guys were nowhere to be seen. Again, she felt better. She put the kids into their car-seats, and folded up the stroller to stow into the trunk. As soon as she popped the trunk open, she heard a gruff voice from behind her.

"Pretty girl…"

She jumped, and spun around to see a large latino standing right behind her. He was wearing a green tank-top, and his muscled torso and arms were covered with tattoos—most of them of playing cards and dragons. He was looking into the car at Chelsea, smiling, and one of his front teeth was gold.

"Th-thank you," Joanna said, trying to hold her composure. She pulled up the stroller and threw it into the trunk, then slammed it shut again. The man had walked around the car to be close to her again. "I have to go now," she said, trying to move past him. He didn't move.

"Why you gotta leave, eh?" he asked, leaning in closer to her and letting his eyes wander up and down her body. "You *bangin'*, mami…" Joanna turned to go the other direction around the car. Standing in front of her there was one of the two men from in front of the South Loop Club—the one with a green bandana.

"Whassup?" he asked with a nod. "Dis cholo buggin' you, girl?"

"N-no," Joanna responded. "I just have to get going. My husband is expecting me." She said that to somehow convince them to leave her alone, but the moment she said it, she thought to herself, *I should have said, "My husband will be here any minute…"* Not that it would have made any difference, mind you—they never believe comments like that from women they're trying to scare.

"Un tipo afortunado…" he sneered, "gettin' wi' *dat* every night…"

The larger man moved in from behind her. Joanna reached into her purse for the can of mace that I'd made her keep with her, and pulled it out as menacingly as she could.

"Leave me alone right now!" she shouted. Out of the corner of her eye, she saw a couple of guys coming out of the Club turn toward them and take notice. They didn't move to help out, but they weren't wearing green, either. "I mean *now!*" she said again, spinning to point the can at the larger man when they didn't respond.

"Whoa!" said the smaller guy in front of her, glancing over at the same guys that she'd noticed. "You don' gotta be trippin' like dat, baby!"

"Help!" she yelled over to the guys across the street. "Please help my family!" The men started walking over to them, crossing Balbo. The larger gangsta looked at the smaller one, and they both looked angry.

"We bailin'…" he said to the other one, and they both turned to leave. "But we see y'all later, *Señora Policía…*" he added with a chuckle. With that, both men started jogging away, across the lot.

*   *   *

Joanna had explained the situation to the men who'd come over to help her, and she thanked them for probably saving her life. "Ain't no thang," they said, laughing, and they offered to stick around until she was safely on her way. Then she took a deep breath and calmed her nerves before she started the car. Chelsea waved at the two men who'd helped them as their car pulled out onto Balbo, and they waved back, smiling warmly.

They took Balbo east to Michigan Avenue, and then turned south. As they made the turn, something struck Joanna. How had the gangstas known that I was a cop? And if that first guy at the Chocolatier had been in on things—and he probably had been—then how long had they been watching them, waiting for them to get off of the main street and onto some lonely side street? And why *them?* Her phone rang—a single ring. But by the time she'd fumbled to pick it up, out of her purse, it had stopped ringing. She saw that the call had come from my phone, and she debated about calling me right back, but then she figured that if I'd only let it ring once, I was probably in the middle of something. She resolved to call me back in a few minutes, once her heart had gone back to beating at a normal kind of speed.

Within a minute or two, she had begun to calm down. It was hard to worry about gang thugs under the tracks when you've got the lakeshore on your left and the towered condos of the Columbian on your right. By the time she'd gotten to 14th Street and the Chicago Firehouse, she realized that it had started raining. In fact, it was coming down fairly hard, though she hadn't noticed it yet. She shook herself and told herself to wake up and get back in the game, finally turning on the windshield wipers.

But there was something else that took another block or two for her to pick up on. By the time she passed under the tracks and got to 16th Street (and the world's tiniest Dunkin' Donuts shop), she began to notice how few cars there were on the road. It wasn't really that late in the evening, and even though the rain was coming down harder and harder, she was *still* on Michigan Avenue—there really *should* have been more cars around.

But even that didn't bother her, per se. It just struck her as odd. It didn't start bothering her until she got to 18th Street, and she realized that hers was the *only* car on Michigan Avenue. The rain was coming down in sheets, and thunder and lightning were everywhere. The twins began to cry, and even Chelsea—who *loves* a good rainstorm—was looking out of the windows with apprehension.

"Can our car float?" she asked her mother, and she pulled her stuffed bear to her chest and hugged it hard.

Joanna slowed down, because she could barely see where she was going. She considered pulling over, or going inside somewhere, but all of the businesses around were only open during business hours, and since she didn't know how long the rain would last, she hated to think that she'd be condemning the children to sit in the car for hours.

Finally, she saw La Cantina Grill coming up to her left, and she remembered the carne asada that we'd had there a couple of years ago. She pulled over, on the other side of the street, and let out a heavy sigh of relief to see that the lights were on inside. She unbuckled Chelsea, and then the twins, and she told them that they were all going to have to run across the street really fast, but still be careful about the traffic. But then she looked up, and saw that there *was* no traffic. None at all. They were totally alone on Michigan Avenue. She told Chelsea to stick right by her side—*right* by her side, without running off on her own, and that she would scoop the twins up in her arms. Chelsea promised that she would.

Joanna opened up the car door and the rain was coming down so hard that it was painful to stand in it. The wind whipped her clothes against her, and thunder made everything shake around her. She opened the side door, and pulled out the twins, clutching each in her arms. Chelsea ran around the car and joined her, grabbing at Joanna's clothes to steady herself. They all turned to cross the street to La Cantina Grill, double-checking for traffic. None.

But there, in the middle of the street in front of them, between them and the Grill stood a lone figure. His pale face stood in stark contrast to the long, black coat that he wore, and his blonde hair whipped around in the wind. The rain was coming down so hard that Joanna couldn't make out any more details—but there was something menacing, something... *wrong*... about the man.

"We goin', Mommy?" Chelsea asked, wondering why they were still standing there. Joanna didn't move one way or the other.

Maybe we should just get back into the car, she thought to herself.

"Good evening, Joanna," the man said, starting to walk toward them. It was amazing how clearly she could hear his voice over the cacophony of the storm. "I've so wanted to meet you..."

Instinctively, she began to run. She didn't even try to fumble with her keys and go to the car—she just knew that she needed to run. She ran so fast that Chelsea could barely keep up with her. But when she glanced back to see the man, he was still gaining on them, even though he only seemed to be loping along.

She knew that there was a church just up ahead—maybe they could jump inside there. She just prayed that there would be someone there that could help them. But the rain was coming down so hard that she could barely see the sidewalk in front of her. And yet, strangely, she could still see the man behind her perfectly well. And she could hear his voice clearly.

"Joanna—please stop and let's just talk for a while," he said, and his voice sounded so warm and comforting. But something about him still gave her the creeps, and she didn't slow down one bit. And that's when Chelsea's hand slipped out of hers.

She stopped and turned around, yelling Chelsea's name. But she was gone. All Joanna saw was rain and the strange, pale man... and all she heard was rain and the thunder. Chelsea was gone.

"Let me help you," said the man, catching up with her. "Let me help you find Chelsea..."

"Where's my daughter?" she screamed, hot tears streaming down her face and mingling with the rain. "What did you do to her?"

"Let me take you to her..." he crooned, reaching his long, pale hand out toward Joanna's face. He smiled at her, and his teeth flashed. She could see his fangs, and his eyes seemed to smolder with a deep, red glow. "Let me take you to her, and you can be together forever."

"Dear Jesus!" she cried—half a prayer, half an exclamation. "What *are* you?"

She turned and ran, finally reaching the church. For some reason, the man slowed down and lagged behind. The doors of the church were closed and locked, but she leaned against them for strength. She set down one of the twins and grabbed her phone, hitting the "call" button until my phone picked up.

"Tom?" she yelled, panic in her voice.

"Joanna!" she heard me respond. Then she heard some scuffling on my end of the phone, followed by three quick gunshots.

"Tom?" Joanna screamed again. "Can you hear me? Please help us!" The man had caught up to her by that point, standing on the sidewalk, at the base of the steps. He motioned to her to come to him, but instead, she started pounding on the door of the church.

"We're at 2nd Presbyterian, Tom, but—" Joanna continued, trying to get me to come help her, but then she stopped. The thunder crashed like an explosion behind her, and she turned to see the pale man floating in the air, riding on the wind. "Dear God, what *is* this thing?!?" she screamed again, and she heard Chelsea's voice screaming nearby, too. With that, my phone went dead, and the pale man suddenly swooped toward her, his mouth wide and his fangs bared. She could hear the sound of his roaring, even over the crashing of the thunder.

*   *   *

Just before he reached her, something big, fast, and gray blurred between them and knocked the pale man sideways so hard that he flipped in the air and crashed—three stories up—into the Loop Learning Center building across the street. Gasping with shock, Joanna looked down to see what it was that had saved her.

There on the sidewalk stood Pieter Durant... with Chelsea held tightly in his arms. He turned toward Joanna, bolted up the steps in one bound, and kicked in the heavy doors as if they were made of cardboard. "Get in!" he yelled, and he scooped up the baby with his free arm as Joanna ducked inside. He slammed the doors behind them, and she heard the wooden door jam make a loud crunching sound as they splintered. No one was going to be opening those doors again anytime soon.

"M-Mr. Durant!" she stammered. "What's going on? Who was that? Why are you here?"

He continued deeper into the church building, carrying the children with him, so Joanna followed him, repeating her questions. He didn't speak until they'd finally made it into the sanctuary.

"Stay here!" he ordered, finally letting go of the children. Chelsea ran to Joanna and hugged her, shivering.

"What's going on?" Joanna shouted again. Durant frowned, and looked for all the world like he was going to turn around and leave, but then stopped, took a deep breath, and faced her.

"You were under attack, that was a vampire, and I am here because I am attempting to think more like a cop and less like a soldier." He stood for a long moment, just looking at her, as if slightly annoyed. "Does any of that actually help you to better understand the situation?"

"A *what*?" she cried. "You're crazy…"

"Yes, undoubtedly," he sighed in reply. "To believe that the flying villain who controls the weather, somehow influences all other vehicles to vacate the streets, and attacks you *with his fangs* is actually a vampire is obviously far more ludicrous than it would be to believe that the man who saved your life is simply insane. I must be mistaken…" Joanna just stood there, looking like a drowned rat.

"Thank you," said Chelsea with a sniffle, looking up at Durant. His face softened for a moment, looking back at her.

"You are profoundly welcome, young lady," he said in return, with the slightest bow.

*   *   *

"So how did you even know where we were, or that we were in trouble?" Joanna asked, nestling into one of the pews in the sanctuary. Somehow, without her noticing, Durant had found some towels for her and the children, and she began to wrap them around everyone.

"As to the latter," he responded, looking around the room as if studying every facet of it. "When I…" he paused, obviously frustrated with himself, "*lost* my quarry at the university, I had to plan another stratagem. That was when I realized that, since he now knew that we were, as your husband would say, 'on' to him, and since he was beginning his final move, there was no longer any reason for our enemy to hold back from killing you and your children—if for no other reason than to hurt his pursuers. I could thus either pick up the hunt for him anew, or I could come to find you."

"And you chose us…" she replied, tears welling in her eyes.

"Yes, well…" he replied, suddenly uncomfortable. "I had no idea that I should be able to accomplish both options with the same choice…" He stiffened, and that made Chelsea start to giggle, though she didn't know why.

"So you hunt… um… vampires?" Joanna asked, trying to break the tension. "For Interpol, I mean?"

"Something like that," he answered, turning away again as if he wanted to leave.

"So how did you even know where we were?" she asked, trying to get him to stay with them a while longer.

"The *wine*…" he said, turning back to her, a slender smile cracking his craggy face. He took a deep breath, and if I had been there, I would have recognized it as a classic Durant sign that he's starting a long explanation, and I would've told her to settle in and listen.

"The 1811 Château Climens which I brought for you was a '*Cuvée de la Comète*'—a comet vintage from the Sauternes region of Bordeaux, like the Château Lafite or the Château d'Yquem, which was bottled in the same year as Flaugergues' Great Comet of 1811. For some reason which scientists still apparently choose not to understand, these comet wines were bizarrely long-lived and excellent vintages, holding their perfect flavor as *Premier Cru Classé* wines far longer than they logically should. They were *so* sublimely perfect that Tsar Aleksandr I—who had expressly forbidden the importation of French wines into Russia, mind you—nonetheless acquired several cases of them for his own stock.

"As a result, Aleksandr discovered that at least a few cases of the Château Climens had… unusual properties, to put it mildly. Perhaps the wine had absorbed Aleksandr's nearly manic paranoia of all those around him—and, indeed, he certainly died under quite mysterious circumstances—but for whatever reason, drinking the wine together somehow made the owner of the bottle able to discern the physical location of his fellow-drinkers at any given time, at least for the next few days afterward."

"You're kidding…" Joanna said, shaking her head.

"Precisely what your husband would say," he replied. "But by my faith, it's all true."

"No," she said. "I mean, you actually *LoJacked* us with a bottle of *wine*?"

"With a two-hundred-year-old, Premier Cru Classé, Cuvée de la Comète," he corrected her, "undoubtedly worth well over £50,000." Hearing that, Joanna decided that she should probably be listening more carefully. "After Aleksandr's death, his brother, Nikolaj, had the rest of the wine taken to a special warehouse located in Moscow, from which I liberated a few bottles when I traveled through there, years ago. Given the circumstances, I thought it best to remain aware of where all of you were."

"So you stole some priceless Russian wine?" she interjected. "How on earth did you get out of the country with it?"

"To be clear," he corrected her again, "I *liberated* some *French* wine *from* Russia. And I 'got out' on the train…" With that, Durant began to walk away again, toward the outer doors.

"Wait!" Joanna shouted, suddenly worried again. "Where are you going?"

"My quarry is still out there," he answered her. "And there shall never be a better time to end this, once and for all."

"Can't we just stay in here?" she asked.

"*You* can—and *should*," he replied. "You are safe, so long as you remain on holy ground and keep your faith. But you cannot remain here forever, and I cannot let him get away from me again." He began to leave, but Chelsea jumped up and ran to him, wrapping her arms around his leg.

"*Peas* don' go!" she cried. Durant stiffened again, frowned, and then reached down to stroke her hair.

"I will come back for you, little one—I promise," he said, with a gentleness that Joanna had never heard in his voice before. He looked up again at Joanna. "In my crusade, over the long years, I have spent so much time hunting, fighting, and hating that which God hates, that I had begun to lose touch with loving those whom God loves. As your husband argued, I had begun to forget the 'why' *behind* the 'what' to which God has called me. Thus, in my zeal to hunt down my enemy, I have too often lost... those for whom I have cared so much." He looked back down at Chelsea and smiled. "I choose not to do so again," he said. With that, he disentangled himself from her little arms, stroked her hair once more, and walked unhesitatingly toward one of the outer doors. He opened it with a cracking sound, and the wind and rain whipped into the room.

"Mr. Durant," Joanna called out to him one last time. "Thank you—for *all* that you're doing. Thank you for wasting your bottle of wine on my children and me."

"Dear lady, 'twas no waste at all," he called back, smiling broadly. "I've still 37 more bottles just like it..." Reaching under his long coat, he drew out a magnificent sword that gleamed in the lights of the sanctuary chandeliers, and launched out into the storm, slamming the door shut behind him with a crunch.

Background
From *Die Legende von der Ghul Addhéma und die Vampyr*[1] *von Szandor* (1736, H. Spurzheim)

Of the many sordid and bloodied histories which paint the Kingdom of Serbia in the color of red, none is more representative of the region's past and character than the history surrounding the Count of Szandor. Little is known about the life of the Count prior to his being granted his title, save that his name may have been Miloš Keshko or Miloš Dimitrijević (or another altogether), and that he rose to a position of wealth and influence in the wake of the Long Turkish War.[2] It is said that following the uprising in Banat in 1594, this person had fled to Siebenbürgen[3] in order to escape the wrath of the Ottoman, but this is uncertain to most historians as he soon became a favorite of the Sultan upon his return. However it was apparently at some point during this escape that he who would eventually become the Count of Szandor encountered a vampyric presence which infected him with its pestilent bite. Whether the victim died at this point and became himself one of the living dead or was simply tainted by the encounter only to become a vampyr at a later date is not known, though evidence of his life would suggest the former rather than the latter...[4]

One can readily see in the rule of Count Szandor over his people the corruption of soul and politic that epitomized the Kingdom of Serbia under the rule of the Turk[5] though not representative of the character of

---

[1] *Prof. Spurzhiem, by thus documenting Eastern European vampirism, may well have been the original source of the transference of the Serbian word, "vampyr," into the German language (and thus, into the greater consciousness of Europe at large)*

[2] *(1591-1606)—also known as the "Austrian-Ottoman War" or the "Fifteen Years' War"*

[3] *Transylvania*

[4] *Timelines differ in the historical accounts of the life of Grof Szandor ("the Count of Szandor"). Tzortzi (1818) states that he had been granted his Grofovija by Sultan Ahmed I himself in 1611, but D'Arnaud (1859) cites his burial in 1646, describing him as still a "jeunes" or "young man" at that time.*

[5] *It is worthy of note that though this volume was published some years later,*

the Serbian people themselves. He was cruel to the men but even more so to the women and children under his dominion, often luring them to his castle, many never to be seen again. It is also said that he would bewitch the women in some way with such ferocity that he would demand of them "heaps of gold" for each of his kisses and that he engendered in them such a prurient lust that they would provide him such. In this way he became a wealthy and important leader amongst the Serbian nobles and a favorite of the court...

However, the Count of Szandor miscalculated his own strength and ultimately ran afoul of the Sultan Osman II when he refused a direct order to assist in the Turkish invasion of Crete.[6] Upon investigating the rule of Szandor the Sultan's agents gave such a damning report that the Sultan immediately ordered his execution. Had this execution been the common method of beheading this would have undoubtedly meant the end of the history of Count Szandor, but the ardent pleading of his servant Atanasija Bogojevci convinced the Sultan's representative to relent and simply have Szandor hanged in the public square in 1646. Bogojevci then cut the body down and supervised the burial in such a way that no religious icons were used and the body was not treated by any means. It is presumed that in this manner Szandor was enabled to rise from his grave at a later time and resume his vampyric predations, albeit no longer with the benefits of his earlier rank and influence...

The nature and origins of the vampyr's relationship with the ghoul Addhéma is uncertain and yet it is clear that in some way Addhéma found herself bound to him, either through his power expressed over women or through some other means, and slavishly she presented him with the riches needed to continue his extravagance of life. Indeed it is even possible that it was Szandor himself who had converted her to this semblance of life in which she found herself.[7] But such was her accursed devotion to him that she scoured the Earth in a constant search for new treasures to sate his hunger for gold and thus earn another night's embrace with him anew.

It is well documented by Severnnus[8] that this Addhéma subsists on the blood of the living and sustains her illusion of beauty and youth solely by means of applying the scalps taken from young women to her

---

Spurzheim is writing during a time of Habsburg occupation of Serbia under Karl Alexander, the Duke of Württemberg, and his writing thus reflects a strong anti-Ottoman bias

[6] *At the beginning of the Cretan War (1645-1669)*

[7] *Though Féval (1856) suggests that she had been a baroness under King Louis II of Hungary (1506-1526), and thus must certainly have become a vampiress long before Count Szandor was infected in the forests of Transylvania*

[8] *Richard Severn, in his* Tractatus de motu ex sepulchris mortuorum *(1699)*

own hideous skull, not unlike the actions known to us of the Indian savages of the Americas. As she gains merely but a single day of beauty for each year that the victim may have lived thereafter[9] the fiend inevitably seeks the youngest, purest, and most innocent of maidens to murder and dismember so as to extend her attractiveness for as long an interval of time as is possible. This is in keeping with the motto of her lover Szandor "смрт у животу, живот у смрт,"[10] as to the vampyr the living exist only as sources of sustenance and entertainment of the vilest form. It is not enough to simply protect one's self from the attack of the vampyr but also those who are of the fairest of countenance and most innocent of disposition as these feed not only the thirsts of the creature but also its horrific lusts. It is the child whom the vampyr wishes most to destroy in all the world.

---

[9] *Spurzheim uses the word "möglich" here, emphasizing the years that a woman or girl* might *have* potentially *had left to her, had she not been killed by Addhéma*

[10] *Spurzheim keeps the traditional Cyrillic script, but when transliterated into Latin script, this Serbian phrase would read, "smrt u životu, život u smrt" ("death in life, life in death")*

Chapter 24
Endgame

Joanna rushed to a window to watch what was going on outside, and the wind picked up all the more behind Durant. Ruthven hovered— *bobbed*, really, as if he were just floating on the surface of a calm lake— in the air in the middle of the intersection of Cullerton Street and Michigan Avenue, and the howling winds whipped his long, black coat around his body. Rain slashed at the pane of glass, and thunder shook the church building, but oddly, Joanna could see both Durant and Ruthven clearly, and could hear their voices as if they were standing right next to her. It was unnerving.

"I'd thought that Chicago would be the one place you'd never return to, old man," the vampire chuckled toward Durant. "Too many memories of all those dead loved ones…"

"All the more reason to destroy you here, Gowrie," Durant growled back to him, his sword pointed upwards toward Ruthven's heart. Joanna watched him surreptitiously pull some kind of crystal out of his little leather bag with his free hand and slip it into his pocket.

"I'd prefer 'Lord Ruthven,' if you please," the vampire corrected, wagging his finger at him. "The Earl of Gowrie was my father…"

"You've more names in your past than I can count," Durant called back, "and *none* of them yours. You are in truth no more 'William Ruthven' than you were 'William Raffey' or 'Billy Rivers,' so we may drop the pretense of your humanity. What was your *original* name, demon—*before* you began to infest this corpse you wear?"

"Ah…" cooed the vampire. "My original name was *angelic*…" He flashed a toothy smile, baring his fangs in the process. "But I shouldn't want to tell you *that* name, now should I? Why give you any more power over me than the Nazarene already has with that bloody cup? Besides, when we first clashed in 1635, weren't you calling yourself 'Van Draeck?' Or what was it that you called yourself when last we fought, a century and a half ago in Dresden? 'Vordenburg,' was it? How many names have *you* collected over the years, Walker in Daylight?"

"It was 'Reynolds' at that time, actually," Durant replied. "But why the thugs and the gang wars and the cat-and-mouse with the police?

Why draw all of this attention to yourself?"

"Oh, but the charade is the *point*, old man..." said the vampire, spinning in the air with a preternatural grace. "I thought that you of all people would understand that. What is eternal life without the games-playing to enjoy it?"

"You would dismiss the secrecy of the Danse merely so that you could *enjoy* yourself?"

The vampire stopped spinning and became very serious, floating down closer toward Durant. "Oh, I have a special dispensation from Simon for this one," he said with a knowing smile, and his eyes glowed a slightly deeper shade of red. "What's hidden here in Chicago is well worth the risk of exposure..."

"And what, pray tell, would that be?"

"Does this remind you of that night, old man?" asked Ruthven, spinning away again and pointing toward the church. "When we fought near the Dresdner Frauenkirche amidst the glorious flames wrought by Richard Wagner's wretched grenades?" As he spun, he pulled a sword from beneath his long coat in one, fluid motion. It sliced through the raindrops, the steel glistening in the streetlights. "And do you remember this blade?"

"*Chi no Yokubō...*" Durant said quietly, gripping his own sword with two hands now. "Yes, I recall it." Joanna thought that, at least for a moment, Durant looked more than just a little concerned.

"Cup or no cup," Ruthven continued, spinning around with the sword in his hand, "if I damage you enough with *this* blade, there is no recovery, is there, old man? That's how I beat you the last time. I almost killed you once and for all—the Scourge of the Covenant, the Walker in Daylight—dead at my hands, your ancient blood painting Dresden red..."

"As I recall," Durant said, moving onto the church steps for a better position, "you were in town to continue your debauching of that actress, Wilhelmine..."

"Gods!" The vampire threw his head back and laughed deeply. "The woman debauched *me!*"

With that, Durant launched himself into the air, slashing at Ruthven with his sword. The vampire parried with a glinting silver blur, and Durant was back onto the street.

"Slow, old man..." he said, pivoting to face Durant again. "I remember you as faster. But then, you always were slower than I. That's why I cut you nearly in half in our last battle..."

"No," Durant corrected. "That was because your demon blade sliced through the saber I was using at the time. It took me nearly a week to recover from that." He jumped back toward Ruthven and slashed at him again, which the vampire again parried.

"And if I were to, say, cut off your *head* with my lovely here," he cooed, "how long would it take for you to recover from that? I dare say that you'd finally meet your maker, wouldn't you?" He swooped down toward Durant, who dodged the slice, spun, and whipped his own sword around so quickly that he actually cut a piece of Ruthven's long coat.

"There should be flames again, for this final fight..." the vampire laughed, soaring up again.

"I should think that you will see flames soon enough, demon," Durant growled coldly.

"After we first met in 1635," Ruthven continued, "I escaped here to the Americas. I never dreamt that you would ever follow me across an *ocean*. So many a mile, just to find me..."

"Actually," Durant corrected him, reaching into his bag for something, "I came over simply to see young Pieter Schuyler appointed as the first mayor of Albany. I was... close to his family. In fact, I only stayed in the colonies for twenty years—I never even knew that you were here." With that, he whipped out his hand and flung another of his dark, iron knives toward the vampire. When Ruthven dodged to the left, Durant was already leaping in that direction, and gashed the vampire's shoulder with his sword. A thick, black ichor oozed from the wound.

"Blast you!" Ruthven cried, spinning backwards into the air. "I spent years hiding from you—"

"With me not even on the continent," Durant chided, affording himself the smallest of smiles.

"Oh, I realized that eventually," Ruthven spat back at him. "I was content to leave you alone in Europe, while I quietly grew my empire through the apotamkin here in America, but no—you had to come back across the pond again and start interfering in my business."

"You refer to using Chief Pontiac in much the same way as you've been using this 'Angel' fellow here in Chicago?"

"A perfectly good plan, foiled by you." Ruthven began swooping back and forth, looking for an opening at which to strike. "I was ultimately forced to dispose of him to cover my tracks. That set me back *decades*, Huntsman!" With a black blur, he darted at Durant again, who spun out of the way in a gray blur. There was the clanging, resounding music of swords clashing amidst the thunder, but their movements were so fast that Joanna couldn't see what was happening until Ruthven again swooped back up and out.

"You hounded me..." he said to Durant, panting with exertion.

"My only regret is that I did not *destroy* you," Durant replied.

Ruthven pulled back higher and bobbed high on the air again. "I was finally forced to flee back to Europe after that water beastie which Rhiannon conjured up for me failed to kill you. Nearly two hundred years of work in America, *wasted* because of you." A cruel smile stretched across his pale, gaunt face. "On the plus side, however, I heard that it did a nasty turn on your family, eh?"

Durant said something in response, but Joanna didn't hear it. Instead, she heard a familiar voice next to her ear whisper, "Hola, mami…" She turned to see the gang member with the green bandana from the parking lot standing right behind her, so close that she could smell the liquor on his breath. Back in the sanctuary, the big latino in the tank-top had Chelsea sitting on his lap, his hand over her mouth—and she looked very, very frightened.

*   *   *

"Let go of my daughter!" Joanna yelled. The man in the bandana just laughed.

"Or what, chica? You gonna call you husband? He gonna come arrest us, eh?" The other thug began to laugh as well, and that's when Joanna noticed the teenager from outside the chocolatier's shop sitting with the twins. The man next to her reached out and gently stroked her on the cheek.

"I'm warning you!" she said, feeling herself beginning to hyperventilate.

"And *I'm* warnin' *you…*" said another voice from across the sanctuary. A tall, slender Puerto Rican dressed in black stepped out of the shadows. Joanna didn't know him, but it was Raphael Camacho—the Angel. "You not gonna do nothin'—*nothin'…*" He flipped out a switchblade and walked toward the family.

Because she didn't know him, Joanna wouldn't have understood all the things that were wrong with this picture. The Angel had been a high-ranking OA, and yet he was obviously in charge of this little band of ID's. He'd been manipulating the gang war from both ends, taking control of the Orquestra Albany thanks to el Buitre's death, and working with Billy—*Ruthven*—and Mojo and these guys to influence the Insane Deuces. The fact that he was wearing neither green nor yellow made its own statement right there. He wasn't just trying to grow the OA's or take over the ID's—he was trying to grab everything for himself, once all the dust settled. I wonder if he would've really been willing to settle for being Ruthven's second-in-command…

"Now, what I goin' do is make an example outta one o' you," said the Angel, twirling his knife in his hand. "But which one, eh? You both so *preciosa…*" The man with the bandana leered at Joanna again, and the big man with Chelsea started giggling.

"S-Stay away from her!" Joanna cried.

"Oh, so *you* wan' it, no?" the Angel said turning toward her. "You don' wanna watch, eh? You wan' su *hija* to watch?" He squatted down on his haunches next to Chelsea, and tears were streaming out of her eyes. But the big man still had his hand across her mouth, so all that Joanna could hear were quiet whimpers. "You wanna watch us play wi' su madre, lil' one? It goin' be a real pretty game to watch…"

The man with the bandana grabbed Joanna by the shoulders and she screamed. He started laughing as she tried to pull away, saying, "We no got to touch esa gordita on the train—but *you*, we gonna play wi' you for a *long* time, mami…" The teenager with the t-shirt got up from the twins and started walking over to her as well.

The Angel stood back up, turning again toward Joanna. "Don' you worry none, jeva," he said to Joanna with a sick-looking smile as he walked toward her. "We not goin' kill you. But you husband, he not goin' want you back after we done w' you, that's for sure." The man with the bandana laughed and held her tighter. "An' we take real good care of su niños after that…"

"No!" Joanna screamed.

The man holding her grabbed her arms and pulled them behind her back, and the Angel stepped forward to her. He reached out his knife to touch her lips with it. "Shh…" he whispered to her.

*   *   *

Okay, I should probably back up here and tell you about Tony.

I was lying there, bleeding, against the base of the Haymarket Riot Monument. The cross of blood that I'd made was holding the revenants back, but only just barely. They were just waiting for me to black out so that they could rush toward me—as Durant had said, it's not the shape of the cross that keeps them at bay, but the conscious faith *behind* it, and I knew that I couldn't stay awake for much longer. I kept purposely jabbing myself in the ribs, so that the pain would keep me conscious, but I knew that it wouldn't last. The rain poured down, and everything became darker and darker.

And that's when I heard Tony's voice, swearing at the top of his lungs. And that glorious stream of obscenity was accompanied by the hissing and wailing of the revenants, and that sweet, familiar sound of their cracking bones.

I looked through the rain, and there was Tony de Tullio, swinging that wonderful staff of Durant's right and left, smashing revenants everywhere. Yellow-green goo was flying all around him, and his face was an absolute mask of rage. Now, I make fun of Tony a lot (and he deserves every bit of it)—I mean, he's about as quick on his feet as a piano, he's got the social skills of Attila the Hun, and he's not always the sharpest crayon in the box. But when it comes down to it, he's also about the toughest guy I know, and he's as strong as a bull moose. And all of that strength, chutzpah, and grumpy frustration with the world that made up Tony de Tullio was focused at that one moment on killing as many of these unholy things as possible. And it was a wonder to behold.

One even had the chance to grab onto his neck and try to bite him, but he reached up with his other hand and *ripped the thing's head off.* I'm not kidding. He just ripped it off, and then threw the head against the head of another revenant, and they both cracked open with a sickening crunching sound. And with every step, he was making his way closer and closer to me.

"T-Tony…" I called out, and then collapsed into a spasm of more coughing.

"Hold yer horses, Tom!" he yelled back. "I'm killin' pug-uglies here!" He continued smashing them until they actually started backing away from him. There were still dozens of them around us, but they weren't as willing to engage him as they were when he first showed up. He trotted—because it's not like Tony can ever really *run*—toward me.

"H-Hey…" I said weakly.

"Hey yerself," he said back, wiping some of the goo off of his windbreaker. "How's things?" The revenants held themselves back, and I couldn't tell whether it was because of the cross or because of Tony and the Matteh ha Shelomoh. Probably both.

"B-Been better…" I said.

"Yep," he replied, and scooped me up with his free arm. I felt like a bag full of broken glass, and it hurt like—well, like more pain than I'd ever felt before in my life. But I was happy to be getting out of there, and I'd never been so happy to see Tony in all of our years of partnering with one another.

"W-Why… you here…?" I asked as he pulled me with him to his car.

"Well," he said, smacking through the skull of another revenant that had built up enough courage to try to attack him again. "I tried to find Joanna an' the kids, like ya asked, but they're out to dinner, I guess." He swung the staff through the torso of another revenant. "I didn't know where they was, an' she wasn't answerin' her phone, so I figgered I'd just catch up with you instead."

"You actually… *c-called*…?" I asked, shocked.

"*That's* the part that sticks out to you?" he chuckled, swinging the staff around us again, just for good measure. We made it to the car, and Tony set me down to open up the back door. The moment he did, the lead revenant pounced on him from behind and sank its ragged teeth into his shoulder. Tony growled in pain, bashed the thing up against the side of the car to knock it off, and then smashed the Matteh ha Shelomoh down onto its head so hard that the staff split the thing in two, down to its gut. "What *are* these things?" he yelled, wincing. "They smell like old hamburger gone bad…"

"Reven—" I started to answer, and then started coughing again. My side burned.

Tony opened the door and shoved me into the car. Then he jumped behind the wheel, and we peeled out of the parking lot, with revenants skittering after us for half a block. I lay there, amidst the candy wrappers, Styrofoam cups, and old newspapers that littered Tony's back seat.

"G-Go to 2nd Pres…" I stammered out.

"Why?" Tony asked, gunning the gas and turning on his siren.

"Joanna…" was all I could respond. And then I blacked out.

*   *   *

I've been told that my grandfather was a carpenter. I never met him myself, since he died when my mom was only a kid, but I hear that he was a great guy. Apparently, he was working on the second story of a house in the middle of winter and slipped on some ice. He fell two stories onto a frozen pile of bricks, and broke himself into a million pieces. But here's the thing—even with half a dozen broken ribs, a pierced lung and several other lacerated organs, a broken arm, a cracked skull, and a shattered leg, he was still able to pull himself to his car, and drive himself to the hospital. He lived for almost a week, they say.

When I was a kid, I never understood how someone could be that strong. In fact, I really didn't understand how until that night that we pulled over to the side of the road, took a roll of duct tape from the back seat of Tony's car, and taped up my ribs so that I could at least try to function. I could go to the hospital later—Joanna and the kids were the main priority. It says something about Tony and his character that he never did once suggest that we go to the hospital first.

We got to the church, and I saw Durant and Ruthven out front, blurring as they threw themselves at one another with swords in their hands. I was shocked to see Ruthven actually *flying*, but I also confess that I was starting to get used to being a little shocked. But when we saw a side door open, we decided to go through there and check on my family first.

Tony helped me out of the car, and together, we walked into the building. We heard voices coming from in the sanctuary—*male* voices, and what sounded like Joanna's voice, crying. We rushed forward as quickly as we could, but I could only move so quickly, and Tony wouldn't leave me.

"No!" I heard Joanna scream.

As we stepped into the sanctuary, I saw a big man holding Chelsea, and another man holding Joanna, with her arms pinned behind her back.

The Angel stepped forward to her touched her lips with his knife. "Shh…" I heard him whisper to her as I drew my gun.

"*Drop* it!" I said, pointing my pistol at the Angel. I leaned against the wall and coughed.

"Let 'em go, an' yer all under arrest!" Tony yelled to the four of them.

The teenager grabbed for a gun under his shirt and started pulling it out. I pivoted, pulled the trigger, and dropped him to the ground—then turned back to aim at the Angel's head. The man with the bandana instinctively stepped back and put his hands up, but the other two didn't move.

"I'm serious here," Tony said. He pointed his gun at the big man with Chelsea. "Hey, I might even jus' shoot *you* fer general principle…" With that, the big man let Chelsea go, and he stood up, backed up, and put his hands behind his neck as well. Chelsea ran to me, crying, and hugged my leg tight. It hurt, but it was worth it. That's when I made eye contact with the Angel.

"Let her go, Raphael," I said to him as seriously as I could.

"You don' got no strength, ese!" he said to me, smiling.

"You're right…" I admitted. "I'm using all… my strength not to… put a bullet in your brain right now… so make your choice… *ese*…"

*   *   *

I leaned against the window and watched the fight outside as Tony handcuffed all three of them. I wanted to help, but it was all that I could do just to stay conscious and cover him. Joanna sat next to me, telling me what had happened up to that point.

I saw that both of them were wounded, and I wasn't as surprised to see Ruthven's black and bloody wounds as I was to see that *Durant* was bleeding, too. The wounds weren't healing on their own like they always did, and he had a particularly nasty-looking gash across his face.

"How long, old man?" Ruthven called out to him. "How long can you keep this up?"

"Until daylight at least," Durant called back, his chest heaving. "And you?"

Ruthven laughed. "I've had about enough of this, I think," he said. "All I need do is transform to mist, and then back, and I should be mostly healed—while you will need to take a good, long drink from that cup of yours. And where *is* it?"

"Far from here and safe from you…" Durant replied. I thought about it, and I wondered what the vampire community could do with the Holy Grail. Would it repel them like a cross does? Or would it destroy them, since it had held the blood of Christ? Or would it be like the *ultimate* source of nourishment for them, keeping them undead but fully charged forever? I wondered if the *vampires* even knew...

Ruthven flung out his arms and leaned his head back with a smile. And he floated there in the air, with nothing happening. He frowned in confusion and tried it again, and Durant caught his breath while he did so.

"Bloody hell..." Ruthven finally barked, shaking his head. "You still have it, don't you? That bloody diamond from the bloody Comte de Saint-Germain..."

"Which both enables and prohibits transformations of state, yes," Durant answered—and Joanna told me about the crystal that she saw him slip into his pocket earlier. "No turning into mist for you this time, monster."

"You know," the vampire said, taking a deep breath to take control of his anger. "I'd heard that you'd actually precipitated the Seven Years' War by keeping the diamond from Elizaveta Petrovna's agent in Vienna. Is that true?"

"His name was Oleksiy Rozumovsky," Durant said, pulling his sword back up and preparing to engage Ruthven again. "And the incident has been greatly exaggerated over time."

"By Elizaveta Petrovna herself, no doubt..." Ruthven said, and he swooped down again to attack. His sword flashed as it came down hard against Durant's, and the sound seemed like the clang of a bell, reverberating throughout the whole church building.

"She forgave me on her deathbed," Durant said, deflecting Ruthven's blade and slashing his own through Ruthven's leg.

"'Hell hath no fury,' eh, Huntsman?" the vampire replied, spinning back and slicing through Durant's forearm as he did.

"A gentleman does not discuss such things," Durant called back, jumping after Ruthven and swinging his sword through the air, just missing the vampire's neck.

"But I'm no gentleman!" Ruthven yelled, slashing across Durant's chest with his full force. I could see Durant's shirt ripping open, and I saw nothing but blood-red beneath it. The vampire cackled and spun back up into the air. Joanna started crying when she saw Durant crumple to the sidewalk and drop his sword. "I shall feast on the blood from your final heartbeats, Huntsman!" Ruthven cried, swooping down toward him, fangs bared.

At the last moment, Durant scooped up his sword and swung it toward the vampire's chest, impaling him in the process. As he stretched, I could see that the red underneath his shirt wasn't from blood, but from a blood-colored leather armor that he was wearing beneath his clothes, molded to the shape of chest muscles. It looked vaguely Roman.

"The red... knight's... armor..." Ruthven said, his voice coming in raspy gasps.

"Nothing can penetrate it, monster," Durant replied, and twisted his sword with a jerk. The vampire screamed in pain and dropped his own sword to the ground with a clatter. "Not even your damnable Muramasa blade..."

Ruthven spat black blood at Durant's face, and he clawed at him with his long, talon-like fingernails, but Durant held him in place.

"Tell me what you search for here in Chicago, fiend!" Durant growled at him.

"Burn in Hell!" Ruthven hissed back.

"I've another destination," Durant replied, quietly. "Someday, I pray..." With that, he ripped the sword from Ruthven's chest, spun, and lopped off his head in one quick, gray-red blur. Thunder cracked like a bombshell, and lightning lit up the sky. But louder still was the shriek that came from the throat of the dying vampire—a horrible sound that I'll remember in my nightmares for as long as I live.

Within seconds, the storm calmed down to a light rainfall, and the wind died down entirely. Durant reached into his bag, pulled out several cloves of garlic, and began stuffing them into the mouth of the dead vampire. He then kicked the head to the side, and pulled out a wooden stake, thrusting it into the open chest. As he worked, I could see the hair on the head turn from blonde to white, and the gaunt skin shrivel and turn yellow. Even the body seemed to shrink under the long coat. Finally, Durant pulled out that little flask from his *got uechan* and poured its contents over both the body and the head, lighting a match and burning them with blue flames in two separate piles. Durant stood to watch to make sure that every bit was burned up, then slid his sword back into his bag and nodded.

"*Keep* burning..." he said, and spat on the ground. He leaned down—obviously in pain—and retrieved the katana that Ruthven had dropped. With a sneer, he swung it with all of his might against the side of the church, and with a flash of light and a shriek of its own, it shattered into dozens of steel shards. I could feel the church shake with its impact.

He took a deep breath, then turned and saw me in the window with Joanna. He smiled, blood staining his white teeth, nodded at me, then disappeared in a blur.

"Where'd he go?" Tony asked.

"Still revenants... out there..." I replied, and I closed my eyes to rest. Joanna cradled my head in her lap, and Tony busied himself with tormenting the gang members that he'd handcuffed together. I watched as he pulled out his cell phone to call it in.

"We got... really lucky today..." I said to Joanna, coughing and tasting blood in my mouth.

"Luck nothing," Joanna corrected me, leaning down to kiss me gently on my forehead. "It's because we *prayed*, stupid…"

Background
From *Myths and Folktales of the Indians of the American Mid-West*
(1979, trans. G.C. Kenton)

from *An Introduction to American Indian Mythology*

Ironically, in examining these Native American legends we often find striking parallels to European folklore as well. Some of this is to be expected, of course, as humanity's pre-scientific cultures consistently dealt with the same issues from continent to continent—hunger, warfare, tribal power, and (perhaps most noteworthy) confusion over the differences between what one expected to discover and what one actually found to be the case in a given situation. If an outcome differed significantly from what one had expected, then surely the gods must be tricksters who take joy in mischievous and capricious deception. In this way, man's own natural anthropomorphism of his gods created similar myth structures in disconnected societies around the world.

But other parallels are not so easily dismissed as simply echoing a common zeitgeist across cultural boundaries. We may rightly posit an actual, physical exchange of cultural storytelling between the Old and New Worlds, given the contact between the peoples since the establishment of the first Norse colonies a thousand years ago.[1] And what of the possible journey of Prince Madoc and his retinue to the New World less than two centuries after?[2] His Welshmen's wars with the Cherokee nation over Georgia are well-documented,[3] as were the continued Welsh influences on the Indians of the North American plains for centuries afterward, both in physical appearance and in linguistic

---

[1] *The colony of Leifsbúðir was founded by Leifr Eiríksson in 1001, though the first recorded contact between the Norse and Native Americans (whom the Norse called "skrælingjar") was not until Þorfinnr Karlsefni's expedition in 1010*

[2] *For more information, see* An Enquiry into the Truth of the Tradition, Concerning the Discovery of America, by Prince Madog ab Owen Gwynedd, about the Year 1170 *(by John Williams, 1791)*

[3] *As attested to in a letter written by Tennessee governor John Sevier on October 9, 1810*

structures. How was explorer Peter Wynne able to converse with the Monacan Indians so easily in 1608 in his native Welsh, if they had not learned the language from those of Madoc's earlier party?[4] No clearer example exists in history of the absorption of one culture so seamlessly into another as that of the medieval Welsh into the native Monacan…

Several similarities exist between Native American myths and Scandinavian sagas, particularly along the Eastern coast of the United States, due to the Norse influence on the area through their Vinland colonies. The Algonquin legends of Gluskap, for instance, include his use of two birds to bring him information about the world much like Odin's trained ravens (Huginn and Muninn), as well as the existence of an evil god of mischief named Loki who even echoes the Norse Loki's murder plot against Balder using a sprig of mistletoe by hatching his own murder plot against Gluskap using a pine root.[5]

In addition, one can readily see the image of a medieval Norse landing in Central America when one examines the Mesoamerican legends of the feathered serpent god[6] whose worship began at the same point in history that the Norse began exploring the New World (c. 1000 AD). Quetzalcoatl, as he was called, was depicted in two seemingly disparate fashions by the Mesoamericans—first, as a dragon or a serpent with wings unfurled who comes to their shores from the East; and second, as a tall, white, bearded man with bright, blue eyes, who teaches the tribes metalworking, new means of farming, and a new monotheistic religion that encouraged peace and disparaged human sacrifices.[7] These two images can easily be seen as a conflation of the images of a Viking longboat coming toward shore, looking for all the world like a dragon to the indigenous inhabitants, and then emptying its tall, bearded, Nordic passengers ashore to share their own recently-acquired Christian faith. After his departure across the waters toward the East again, Quetzalcoatl promised to return, in a clear eschatological parallel to the Christian Messiah, Jesus.[8]

Likewise, the Hopi of northeastern Arizona worshiped a feathered serpent god whom they called Awanyu, with several parallels to the Quetzalcoatl legends. Awanyu is connected to the Hopi Pahána, the

---

4   *See Mullaney's (1995) book,* The Place of the Stage, *for an account of the episode. It is also worthy of note that the Algonquin name for the often red-haired Monacan tribesmen was the "Mandoag"—a name which may retain linguistic echoes of the name of Madog ab Owen Gwynedd*

5   *See Spence's (1914)* The Myths of the North American Indians, *and Leland's (1885)* Algonquin Legends of New England, *for a more in-depth analysis*

6   *Named "Quetzalcohuātl" by the Aztecs, or "Kukulcán" by the Mayans*

7   *Kåre Prytz even notes striking parallels to the virgin birth narrative of Jesus in his* Vestover før Columbus *(1990).*

8   *See Carl Grimberd's excellent* Menneskenes Liv og Historie *(1955-58)*

"Lost White Brother"—a white-skinned, bearded man who came from and later returned to the East, promising to come back to them some day. Again, it is noteworthy that the desert-dwelling Hopi also referred to Pahána as the "One from Across the Water."[9] Why would they perceive Pahána as an ocean traveller, except that his legends are recalling the same Norse voyage that spawned the Quetzalcoatl myths?

Ironically, in the cases of both Pahána and Quetzalcoatl, Spanish conquistadors were routinely mistaken by the natives for the return of these benevolent, white, bearded gods—sadly assisting in their conquest of the Americas...

*   *   *

Red Horn and the Night Monsters

The People had begun a time of great peace, and the fish and the meat was plentiful at that time. So it was that they grew in number and in health, but also lost some of the fire and the strength which had made them great in the earlier times. This made Earthmaker[10] very sad, for he had created them to be a strong and good people. He also knew of the dangers which faced them, and he allowed the giant Night Monsters[11] to come and to bring them terror and destruction, in the hopes that they would remember their heritage, and rise up against them in strength.

At dusk came the Night Monsters, with their red hair cropped short against their skulls. They were giants before the People, standing more than twice the height of the tallest man. They came to the village and took what they wanted. Every night, they would take four or five of the People to satisfy their hunger, and there was nothing that the village of the People of the Big Speech[12] could do to stop them. They prayed to

---

[9]   *As Frank Waters has noted in his* Book of the Hopi *(1977)*

[10]   *"Mą'ųna"—the Hočągara Creator god who breathed life into the clay forms of the First People whom he sculpted. He then created a succession of five beings to protect humanity—"Wakdjąkaga," the mischievous Trickster; "Kecągega," the braggart Turtle; "Wągíšjahorùšika," the red-skinned being whose name means "man who wears human faces on his ears" (see note #14 below); "Wadexuga," the puffed-up Bladder; and finally "Wašjingéga," the wise Hare (who finally succeeded). For more detailed information, read Danker and White's* The Hollow of Echoes *(1975).*

[11]   *The name used for these creatures in the original Siouan is "Wąge-rucge" ("Man-eaters"); Kenton is thus making use of a translational gloss here. The Wąge-rucge were the Native American equivalent to the European ogre or troll.*

[12]   *This is a literal translation of the tribe's name—"Hočągara"—otherwise known as the "Ho-Chunk" or "Winnebago" (though the name "Winnebago" or "Winìpyägohag" actually means "people of the stinky water," and was*

Great-Grandfather in his canoe in the Outer Ocean[13] to save them, but he would not stand against the wishes of the Earthmaker, and so he did nothing.

The People were too afraid of the Night Monsters to fight for themselves, so Red Horn[14] came to their aid, because he did not know of the Earthmaker's plans for the People. That evening, at dusk, Red Horn stood between the village and the Night Monsters and told them that they could not pass. They laughed at him, with his ears and his long red spike of hair, and he laughed back at them and called them "buffalo" because of their size. They charged the village, but Red Horn fought with the strength and cunning of many braves, and they could not pass.

As the dawn approached the leader of the Night Monsters asked him, "Will you stay here at this one village forever?"

"I will be here at the next dusk," Red Horn answered him.

"But will you be here every night when we attack?" the leader asked again. "We will not merely come at the next dusk, but at the next dusk after that, and the next dusk after that. We will come every night, and will you be here to stop us?"

Red Horn considered these words and found them disturbing. He had not intended to be the protector of only one small village, and he knew that he did not want to stay in this one place forever.

"What would it take to make you stop attacking the People?" asked Red Horn.

---

   originally a pejorative description of the Hočągara given to the French by nearby Algonquin tribes).

[13] *The "De Ją" or "Encircling Lake" of Hočągara cosmology, in which the lone land mass of the earth rests*

[14] *"He-šucka," the fourth spirit created by the Earthmaker to protect humanity. He is described as being blood-red in coloring—his hair, skin, nails, etc., all the same red color—and as having earlobes comprised of the living and interactive faces of human beings (see Radin's seminal 1948 work,* Winnebago Hero Cycles: A Study in Aboriginal Literature*). He was thus also sometimes called "Wągíšjahorùšika" (see note #10 above). Alanson Skinner (in* The Journal of American Folklore, *1925) argues that the faces were not on his physical earlobes, but rather simply on special earrings which he wore. Interestingly, it was not uncommon in medieval Europe for people to make earrings out of old Roman coins which bore the image of whatever emperor sat on the throne when the coin was minted (see Parrish's 1933 article in* Journal of the Royal Society of Antiquaries of Ireland *on medieval jewelry). Due to the much greater skill and detail in European metalworking, Native Americans may very well have perceived wearing such coins as being equivalent to wearing genuine, human faces on one's ears. If He-šucka's red hair and human-faced earrings were carryovers or heirlooms from Madog ab Owen Gwynedd's lost Welsh colony, this may lend additional evidence to Kenton's thesis of the Monacan absorption of medieval Europeans.*

"We will attack this place every night forever," said the leader of the Night Monsters, "unless you make a choice on their behalf. If you choose one of the People to freely give to us at the next dusk then we will take that one person as our meal and be satisfied. But you must know that we will be satisfied only with the flesh of either a beloved innocent child or a revered elderly woman. None other will make us leave the People alone forever."

Red Horn knew that they would not be foolish enough to lie to him, and he knew that what they truly fed upon was horror, and he knew that there would be no greater horror for the People than to know that the Son of the Earthmaker had given one of their own to be devoured by the Night Monsters. So the offering truly would make the Night Monsters leave forever and find another hunting ground, but it would also forever destroy the People's faith in Red Horn as their protector.

The Night Monsters departed with the dawn and Red Horn was left to ponder his decision. He could not stay to protect them forever but how could he offer up a child who might someday grow to be a great chief or the mother of a great man? And yet, how could he offer up a wise woman whose wisdom gives light to the whole village?

By mid-day, Red Horn had become thirsty, and so he walked toward the pungent waters to drink as he considered his options. There he saw a doe and her fawn farther down the shore, lapping up the water. Suddenly, a great black bear came out of the forest and roared its challenge to the deer. Red Horn knew that the bear expected the doe to either freeze in fright or to bolt and run, leaving the fawn unprotected and easy prey. But to the surprise of both Red Horn and the bear, the doe actually leapt between the bear and her fawn. As the bear moved toward her, she reared up on her hind legs and kicked at him with her hooves. Every time the bear attempted to move around her, she did the same—she leapt between him and her fawn, reared up, and kicked at him.

She had no chance of actually harming the bear but the altercation had become wearisome to him, and he did not wish to continue it. With one last roar, he turned away from the doe and lumbered down the bank of the waters, away from both Red Horn and the deer. Immediately, the doe and her fawn scampered in the opposite direction, back into the forest.

Red Horn knew what decision must be made to protect the people, so he took one drink from the waters and then returned to the village. All of the People asked him what decision he would make, but he would not tell them. Instead, he asked for introductions to every single one of the people—the old, the young, the warriors, the children, everyone. He learned the name of every one of the People, and to which family each person belonged, and what kind of a person that they were. In this way, he prepared himself for the dusk.

That evening, just as the sun set, the Night Monsters returned, just as they had promised. The leader of the Night Monsters stepped forward, and Red Horn stepped out to meet him, standing between him and the village once again.

"Have you made your decision?" asked the leader of the Night Monsters.

"I have," answered Red Horn. He asked the villagers to come out and stand behind him, and all of them were there. With that, he walked over to one family and squatted next to a beautiful little girl named Quail.[15] "This one," he said, pulling the little girl out from under the arms of her parents. "This Quail will feed your hunger tonight."

The leader of the Night Monsters stepped forward, saliva dripping from his lips. His brother Night Monsters came forward as well to take the little girl. Quail saw the hunger and the cruelty in the eyes of the Night Monsters, and she began to cry. But Red Horn pushed her out toward the giants.

"No!" cried the girl's mother.

"Never!" cried the girl's father. He pushed past Red Horn and clutched the girl up in his arms. "How can you do this?" he asked of Red Horn.

"I cannot stay here to protect you forever," said Red Horn. "Thus, I have made the decision to give them your daughter. Then the village will be safe."

In response, the father drew his knife and faced the Night Monsters. "You will not take my daughter from me tonight!" he cried to them. "Take my flesh instead, if you can!"

The nearest Night Monster lunged for the father and his daughter but the man's knife was swift and it sliced off the giant's hand. The Night Monster howled in pain and another took its place. But when the People saw that one lone man could fight a Night Monster and hurt it, they felt ashamed that they had stood apart from the fight. They were ashamed at how happy they had felt that it had not been their daughter or their grandmother whom Red Horn had chosen to be given to the Night Monsters. The chief of the People picked up his spear and ran into battle at the father's side.

With that, all of the people ran past Red Horn and attacked the Night Monsters. They had not realized how few giants there actually were on the field and how easily their greater numbers could overwhelm them. Within minutes, all of the Night Monsters were either dead or fleeing for their lives back into the hills.

"I made the decision that you had asked me to make," called Red

---

[15]   *"Wanjk žožuč"*

Horn behind them. "It is not my fault that you could not take the morsel home with you!" The leader of the Night Monsters turned to snarl at Red Horn in response. "But you will keep to your promise and you will never return to this place, yes?"

"Yes," replied the leader of the Night Monsters. "You have kept your side of the bargain, and so we will keep ours. But you have earned the eternal enmity of the Night Monsters, Red Horn!"

But that did not scare Red Horn, as the leader of the Night Monsters had intended. He knew that he could defend himself against them, no matter how many they sent to attack him, or when. But what was more, he also knew that the People of the Big Speech could now defend themselves as well, and so even the Earthmaker was happy with Red Horn because he had brought about what the Earthmaker had intended all along.

"The tragedy of life is that evil can too easily defeat good if good is unwilling to fight back," Red Horn told the People that night. "So what good needs is a reason to fight evil. And there is no better reason to fight than to fight for the children whom we love."

Chapter 25
Tatws Rhost

I spent a day and a half in the hospital, until they were sure that I hadn't damaged myself too badly. But I pushed to be able to get out in time to attend Karen Gage's funeral. Though there was a small turnout for it, Joanna held my hand through the whole thing, Tony was there, and so was Bill Saunders. In fact, he actually cried a little. I've kinda liked Bill ever since that day.

I'm still officially on leave now, and that's what's given me a chance to put all of this on paper. I don't know why, but it just seemed to me like somebody should know about it—remember it. Durant's done so many things in his life, and when he finally dies, all of those things will be washed over and forgotten. Oh, history books will remember this date or that place, but they won't remember Durant as being *part* of those things. I'm making it a point to learn as much as I can about history so that I can teach Chelsea and the twins about what he's done to protect them for all these centuries.

I'm also reminding myself to occasionally quote Kipling to them. My children need to hear the wisdom of good poetry, but beyond that, they really need to hear their father quoting it to them. This world needs more poetry—the *good* kind, the kind that rhymes and makes use of the beauty of the English language. Besides, I can't help now but see elements of the Covenant of the Danse in things like Kipling's words, "When ye fight with a Wolf of the Pack, ye must fight him alone and afar, lest others take part in the quarrel, and the Pack be diminished by war." But the poetry that most comes to my mind when I think of Durant is from Kipling's "The Quest"—

> The knight came home from the quest,
> Muddied and sore he came.
> Battered of shield and crest,
> Bannerless, bruised and lame...
> "My shame ye count and know.
> Ye say the quest is vain.
> Ye have not seen my foe.

> Ye have not told his slain.
> Surely he fights again, again;
> But when ye prove his line,
> There shall come to your aid my broken blade
> In this last, lost fight of mine!"

Durant has fought a thousand battles—a *thousand* thousand, probably—and yet, evil is still out there. You could see it all as a long, fruitless waste of time. Or worse yet, you could see it as a cruel curse from God, that he would put this kind of burden on the shoulders of only one man.

But when I think of Durant, I think of a man who has fought again and again to protect this world, and who sees that protection as a sacred trust. You could try to prove to him that his long quest has been a vain one, but the sheer tonnage of horrors that he's prevented over the centuries would always argue loudly and persuasively that you don't know what you're talking about.

I'm not ashamed to say that I sleep better at night, knowing that Durant is out there... and knowing that I can count him as one of my friends.

*   *   *

He came over to our home one last time, to say good-bye before he left town. I should probably end by telling you about that.

"I see that you've got yourself a new coat," I said, pointing to the long overcoat that swirled around him as he walked in the door.

"Hardly," he replied. "This coat is Gieves & Hawkes, of course." *Of course,* I thought to myself, like I should've known that—or even what that *meant*. "Though I have purchased their clothing for two centuries, I have not been able to bring myself to buy a bloody thing from them for the past decade."

I didn't have a clue what he was talking about, but he let me take it from him anyway. "Joanna wanted to thank you in her own way. She's made you dinner," I told him as I hung the coat on a hook in the hallway.

"No, no. I really must—" he replied, starting to decline the offer. But then the savory odor of roasted potatoes, scallions, and bacon wafted in from the kitchen, and Durant frowned—a strange, pained expression crossed his face. I couldn't tell if he was happy, upset, or just plain confused. "Is that... Is that *tatws rhost*?" he asked, obviously shocked.

"We searched the internet for the oldest Welsh recipe that we could find," I said, smiling. "I hope you like potatoes..." He just stood there, at a genuine loss for how to respond.

Chelsea toddled up to him and yanked on his sleeve, catching his attention. "Mommy made dinner," she told him, holding out her little hand toward his. "It's got tay-toes." He smiled down at her and gently took hold of her hand.

"I know that it does, luv," he said. "Tatws rhost has always been my favorite meal. It reminds me of home… and *family*…"

"Does your mommy make it for you, too?" she asked, pulling at his hand as she innocently led him down the hallway toward the kitchen.

"She did indeed," he said—and now it was my turn to be shocked to see tears welling up in his dark-browed eyes. "As did my wife, once upon a time."

Together, they walked into the kitchen, with me behind them. The twins were already in their seats, smearing their faces with whatever it was that Joanna had placed in front of them. When Joanna saw us, she wiped her hands on a towel, stepped away from her cooking, and gave Durant a huge hug.

"Thank you so much!" she told him, giving him a little kiss on the cheek. I think that he actually blushed. "I know that you're forever traveling here and there, all alone, but I want you to know that you've always got a home and a family *here*, Mr. Durant."

It was one of the nicest meals that we ever ate together.

*   *   *

After dinner, we sat outside and enjoyed the cool evening. But this time, we were drinking lemonade instead of the wine. We talked about where he was off to next, and I asked what he thought Ruthven meant when he talked about something hidden here in town. But he didn't have any more of a clue about it than I did.

"I confess that I am impressed, Detective," he said to me, finally. "I did not know that you would have it in you to overcome Rhiannon on your own, much less destroy her. Not many men could burn the body of someone whom they had… cared for…" I could hear in his voice a pain that echoed from centuries ago. I knew all too well the whammy that she could put on your heart, and I could only imagine what damage she could do over *years* of messing with your mind. But still, something he said struck me.

"Burn?"

"Of course," he said with a shrug. But then he stiffened and turned back to me. "You did *burn* her body, did you not?"

"No," I said, with a horrible, sinking feeling in my gut. "I stuck her on an iron fence. She was dead, Durant—she didn't have a pulse."

"She has *never* had a pulse, you idiot…" he growled.

"But it was iron!" I said, finding myself flailing around with my words. "I thought that iron killed her. You threw an iron knife at her!"

"To incapacitate her!" he shouted. "Iron harms her, but it does not destroy her. Only fire can destroy a water witch!"

"You never said anything about fire!"

"I never said anything about iron, either…"

I slumped back into my chair. I'd never heard anything about anyone finding her body. I just figured that Tony and I would have to investigate her death, and that we could probably just cover things up that way, but no one ever reported it. To be honest, I'd kind of just written it off, what with the ongoing gang war, and was happy that it was at least one less thing to worry about. Now, I had to wonder *why* no one had found her body. What had I done…?

"Detective," Durant said finally with a long sigh. I figured that I was in for a huge lecture, at the very least. I also thought—however briefly—that there was at least a decent chance that he'd actually kill me. To my surprise, he said, "I made the same mistake with her myself, centuries ago…" He turned back to me and started to smile. And then he slapped me on the back and started actually laughing. *Laughing…*

Pieter Durant, *laughing*, sitting in my back yard. It's enough to boggle the mind.

At the end of the evening, he said good-night to Chelsea and the twins, and kissed Joanna's hand as he went to the door. She gave him another hug, and he blushed again. I walked him outside.

"It's going to be relatively boring around here without you," I told him.

"Boredom would be… a diverting change of pace…" he said, scratching his chin under his beard. He turned to leave, and then turned back to me one more time. "You did have a particularly good suggestion, you know."

"Which one?" I asked, surprised.

"Whilst we sat in the dark, waiting to find the corpse of František Sydor behind the library," he said. "You spoke of trying to turn one vampire against another, as you often attempt to do with *human* criminals."

"Absolutely," I said. "We do it all the time in interrogation rooms." He nodded.

"Indeed," he said. "Then I think that I shall seek out the *Queen* of the Vampyri…"

Before I could pick my jaw up from the floor, he was gone.

*　　　*　　　*

So that was the first time that I killed a vampire, the first time that I ate tatws rhost (now a family favorite in our home), and the last time that I heard of Pieter Durant. At least *directly*. Oh, now that I knew what to look for, I could see his work around the world. News reports of unsolved, bizarre crime waves suddenly stopping, all on their own. Stories about people who were miraculously saved by someone moving too fast to be seen clearly. Confessions from criminals who swore that the guy who caught them just *couldn't* be human.

The Knight of the Cup of Christ is out there, and he's keeping busy.

He made me promise not to include anything about him or his involvement in any of my reports, beyond referencing a simple "advisory" role on his part as a visiting inspector from Interpol. And technically, I've kept that promise. There's nothing in my official reports about any of the weirdness. I just never promised him that I wouldn't write a book about it all. But come on—wouldn't you agree that the man deserves some credit for his work?

I have little doubt that someday, he'll come back around here and kick my butt for this. But maybe I'll just have Chelsea answer the door, and he'll melt like butter.

No, he'll probably still kick my butt.

<u>For Further Reading</u>

Al-Hazred, Abd (730) *Kitab al-Azif [or "Necronomicon"] ("Concerning the Dead")*

Aldrovandi, Ulisse (1640) *Historia Serpentium et Draconum ("A Natural History of Snakes and Dragons")*

Allacci, Leone (1645) *De Graecorum Hodie Quorundam Opinationibus ("On Certain Modern Opinions Among the Greeks")*

Augustine (429) *De Cura pro Mortuis Gerenda ("Regarding the Care to Be Taken for the Dead")*

Balfour, François-Honore (1702) *Cultes des Goules ("Cults of Ghouls")*

Binder, Christoph (1611) *Ἀιτιολογικον Theologicum, de Causis Pestis, methodo Analytica explicatis ("Theological etiology for the causes of pestilence, analytical method explained")*

Calmet, Dom Antoine Augustin (1746) *Dissertation Sur Les Apparitions Des Anges, Des Demons Et Des Esprits: Et Sur Les Revenans Et Vampires ("Dissertation on Apparitions, Angels, Demons, and Spirits; and [Dissertation on] Revenants, and Vampires")*—2 volumes

Chabrier, Georges (1938) *Les Histoires Traditionnelles de la Bretagne Ancienne ("The Folk Tales of Ancient Brittany")*

Clyburn, Ezekiel (1804) *Recollections of an Illinois Fur Trapper*

Cortázar, Jorge (1963) *Rey Arturo y los Caballeros de la Mesa Redonda ("King Arthur and the Knights of the Round Table")*

Cunningham, Jennifer (1992) *On the Road: A Personal Travelogue of Illinois*

Danker, Kathleen, & White, Felix (1975) *The Hollow of Echoes*

Davanzati, Giuseppe (1744) *Dissertazione Sopra I Vampiri*
    ("Dissertation on the Vampires")

De Castañega, Fray Martín (1529) *Tratado muy sotil y bien fundado de
    las supersticiones y hechieceria y vanos conjuros y abusiones; y
    otros cosas al caso tocantes y de la posibilidad e remedio dellas
    ("Very subtle and well-founded treatise on superstitions and
    witchcrafts and vain conjurations and abuses; and other things
    touching the cases and the possibility of remedying them")*

De Ruhr, Pierre (1952) *Histoire Des Vampires et Des Sciences Occultes
    ("History of Vampires and the Occult Sciences")*

De Schertz, Charles Ferdinand (1706) *Magia Posthuma ("Posthumous
    Magic")*

De Troyes, Chrétien (1181) *Perceval, le Conte du Graal ("Perceval, the
    Tale of the Grail")*

Del Rio, Martín Antonio (1599) *Disquisitionum Magicarum Libri Sex
    ("Investigations into Magic in Six Books")*

Epiphanes (c. 370) *Contra Hæreses ("Against Heresies")*

Flückinger, Johann (1732) *Visum et Repertum ("Seen and Discovered")*

Garmann, Johann Christian Frederick (1670) *De Miraculis Mortuorum
    ("The Miracles of the Dead")*

Gerard, Emily (1888) *The Land Beyond the Forest: Facts, Figures, and
    Fancies from Transylvania*

Gildas (542) *Libro Verborum Dierum Viventium et Mortuorum ("Book
    of the Chronicles of the Living and the Dead")*

Glaser, Johann Friedrich (1732) *Commercii litterarii ad rei medicae et
    scientiae naturalis incrementum institute ("To the Growth of the
    Literary Trade and the Medical and Natural Sciences Institute")*

Grimberd, Carl (1955-58) *Menneskenes Liv og Historie ("The Life and
    History of Man")*

Harenberg, John Christofer (1739) *Philosophicae et Christianae Cogitationes de Vampiris [or "Von Vampyren"] ("Philosophical and Christian Thinking on the Vampire")*

Heenan, David (1991) *The New Corporate Frontier: The Big Move to Small Town, U.S.A.*

Hideyori, Ishida (1698) *Nagareboshi wa Sora no Namida ("The Falling Stars Are Heaven's Tears")*

Hippolytus (c. 220) *Refutatio Omnium Hæresium ("Refutation of All Heresies")*

Janssen, Johannes (1878-1894) *Geschichte des Deutschen Volkes seit dem Ausgang des Mittelalters ("History of the German People at the Close of the Middle Ages")*

Kenton, George Charles (1979) *Myths and Folktales of the Indians of the American Mid-West*

Kircher, Athanasius (1664-1678) *Mundus Subterraneus ("The Underground World")*

Kornmann, Heinrich (1610) *De Miraculis Mortuorum ("The Miracles of the Dead")*

Kramer, Heinrich, and Sprenger, Jakob (1486) *Malleus Maleficarum [or "Der Hexenhammer"] ("The Hammer Against Witches")*

Leland, Charles Godfrey (1885) *Algonquin Legends of New England*

Lessinger, Jack (1986) *Regions of Opportunity*

Malory, Thomas (1485) *Le Morte d'Arthur ("The Death of Arthur")*

Map, Walter (1190) *De Nugis Curialium ("The Courtiers' Trifles")*

Martyr, Justin (c. 150-155) *Apologia I ("First Apology")*

Mullaney, Steven (1995) *The Place of the Stage: License, Play, and Power in Renaissance England*

Newburgh, William of (1196) *Historia Rerum Anglicarum ("History of English Affairs")*

Phillips, Richard (1752) *Posthumously Collected Letters and Journals of General Richard Phillips, Esqe.*

Phlegon (c. 2nd century) *De Mirabilibus ("Of Marvels")*

Prinn, Ludwig (1503) *De Vermis Mysteriis ("Mysteries of the Worm")*

Prytz, Kåre (1990) *Vestover før Columbus ("Westward Before Columbus")*

Radin, Paul (1948) *Winnebago Hero Cycles: A Study in Aboriginal Literature*

Ranft, Michaël (1725) *De Masticatione Mortuorum in Tumulis Liber ("On the Chewing Dead in Their Tombs")*

Rhys-Jones, Gillian (1984) *Chwedlau Hynafol Cymru ("Ancient Legends of Wales")*

Richard, Father François (1657) *Relation de l'Isle de Sant-erini ("Report on the Island of Santorini")*

Rohr, Philip (1679) *Dissertatio Historico-Philosophica de Masticatione Mortuorum ("Historical/Philosophical Dissertation on the Chewing Dead")*

Rufinus, Tyrannius (c. 405) *Homiliæ ("Sermons")*

Schwartz, Howard (1988) *Lilith's Cave: Jewish Tales of the Supernatural*

Severn, Richard (1699) *Tractatus de motu ex sepulchris mortuorum et viventium futuri effectus in ("Treatise on the movement of the dead outside of their tombs; and their subsequent effects upon the living")*

Spence, Lewis (1914) *The Myths of the North American Indians*

Spurzheim, Hans (1736) *Die Legende von der Ghul Addhéma und die Vampyr von Szandor ("The Legend of the Ghoul Addhéma and the Vampire of Szandor")*

Stoker, Bram (1897) *Dracula*

Taxil, Léo (1891) *La Corruption Fin-de-Siècle ("Corruption at the End of the Century")*

Temme, Jodocus Deodatus Hubertus (1840) *Die Volkssagen von Pommern und Rügen ("The Folktales of Pomerania and Rügen")*

Tesla, Armand (1727) *Supranatural și Manifestările sale ("The Supernatural and Its Manifestations")*

Valvasor, Janez Vajkard (1689) *Slava Vojvodine Kranjske ("The Glory of the Duchy of Carniola")*—15 volumes

Van Draeck, Peer (1642) *De Dødes Bog ("The Book of the Dead")*

Van Swieten, Gerard (1768) *Abhandlung des Daseyns der Gespenster ("Discourse on the Existence of Ghosts")*

Verstegen, Richard (1605) *A Restitution of Decayed Intelligence in Antiquities Concerning the Most Noble and Renowned English Nation*

Von Eschenbach, Wolfram (1225) *Parzival*

Von Juntz, Friedrich (1835) *Von Unaussprechlichen Kulten ("On the Unspeakable Cults")*

Vordenburg, Hieronymous Ambrosius (1872) *Die Geschichte der Vampyren ("The History of the Vampires")*

Waters, Frank (1977) *Book of the Hopi*

Weston, Jessie Laidlay (1896) *Knights of King Arthur's Court*

Whitehead, John (1993) *Guardian of the Grail: A New Light on the Arthurian Legend*

Williams, Ifor (1930) *Pedeir Keinc y Mabinogi ("The Four Branches of the Mabinogi")*

Williams, John (1791) *An Enquiry into the Truth of the Tradition, Concerning the Discovery of America, by Prince Madog ab Owen Gwynedd, about the Year, 1170*

COMING SOON:

THE QUEEN OF PENTACLES
(The Danse, Book Two)

"The horror of the werewolf is not truly in his claws and fangs, but in his heart. There is a reason why werewolves are drawn first and foremost to hunt the ones whom they love when in human form. Ultimately, the curse draws them not to gain animalistic urges, so much as to lose their humanity. Do you see the difference?"

"I think so," I said, but the immensity of that was hard to wrap my head around.

"Do not ever mistake a werewolf for an animal, Detective," he said. "They are not animals—they are *monsters*…" He stared off into the night again. "And the tragedy of it is that every last one of them ultimately *wishes* to be such a monster…"

www.ingramcontent.com/pod-product-compliance
Lightning Source LLC
Chambersburg PA
CBHW030651120726
47905CB00001B/156